The Wrong Highlander

By Lynsay Sands

LYNSAY SANDS

The Wrong Highlander

HIGHLAND BRIDES

AVONBOOKS

An Imprint of HarperCollins*Publishers*

Excerpt from *The Trouble With Vampires* copyright © 2019 by Lynsay Sands.

First Avon Books mass market printing: February 2019
First Avon Books hardcover printing: January 2019

Print Edition ISBN: 978-0-06-289067-2
Digital Edition ISBN: 978-0-06-246890-1

FIRST EDITION

19 20 21 22 23 LSC 10 9 8 7 6 5 4 3 2 1

The Wrong
Highlander

Chapter 1

CONRAN HEARD HIS BROTHER RORY APPROACHING BEFORE HE ever spoke. The man had no idea how to move quietly. He stomped through the woods, snapping branches underfoot like it was his task in life to scare away all wildlife. He'd be murder on a hunt, Conran thought. Which was why he and his other brothers never took him with them when they went on one. Not that Rory would be interested in accompanying them anyway. He was the odd man out in the family—a healer rather than a warrior. Although, to be fair, he had been working out in the practice field of late, building up his strength and skills, he admitted to himself as Rory finally stumbled out into the clearing and greeted him with the question, "How did ye do?"

Conran turned from his saddlebag and stepped back to reveal the way it bulged. "I found loads of snapdragon, catnip, willow, feverfew and celandine poppy fer ye. Almost too much for me bag."

"Celandine poppy?" Rory echoed, and shook his head with a smile. "Look at ye. Ye're even learning the right kinds o' weeds I need."

Conran grimaced and turned back to continue trying to close his overfull saddlebag. "Aye, well, I've accompanied ye on enough o' yer calls to heal others that I've picked up a thing or two."

"Aye, ye have," Rory agreed, crossing the clearing to join him. "More than I expected. Ye always seem to ken what I'll need ere I ask fer it when ye accompany me to visit the ill and ailing. Ye're something o' a natural at healing, brother."

Conran shook his head with amusement. "Dougall said the same thing about me and his horses, and Niels said it about his sheep and wool. The truth is, I'm just good at helping out me brothers. It's made me a jack-o'-all-trades."

"Ye're selling yerself short, Conny," Rory said solemnly. "I think the truth is that while each o' us is very good at one thing, ye're good at many."

"Hmm. As I said, a jack-o'-all-trades. Sadly, I'm no' a master of any though." Finally managing to close the saddlebag, he sighed his relief and then glanced to Rory. "So, do ye feel like a stop at the waterfalls to clean up ere returning? I swear I've weeds and bugs up me butt from traipsing through the bushes and brambles."

"Nay." Rory shook his head with apparent regret. "I still need valerian and yarrow, and then I must stop in to see the innkeeper's daughter. She's fit to burst and likely to have her bairn any day now. I want to be sure all is well with her. Ye go ahead though. I ken ye planned to leave fer Drummond ere the nooning meal. I appreciate ye taking the time to help me search out medicinals first."

"Always happy to help," Conran said with a shrug, and then assured him, "I'll have a quick wash in the falls, and then ride back to the keep to drop off the weeds before heading out."

"Thank ye. I appreciate it," Rory assured him as he mounted up.

"Me pleasure, brother." Conran watched him ride off, and then withdrew the sword from his belt and affixed it to his horse, before removing his plaid and shirt. He was looking forward to a nice wash under the falls. Truly, it felt like he had bugs crawling all over his naked skin under the plaid he wore. Conran knew that wasn't the case, and the feeling was just a result of being hot and sweaty in a wool plaid. Wading through the bugs and sending them flying from the bushes and plants he was harvesting hadn't helped though. Aye, a nice cleanup in the falls was going to be a true pleasure. It would make a new man of him.

"WELL, THERE'S HIS HORSE. NOW, WHERE IS HE?" EVINA ASKED, her gaze sliding around the clearing and then to the river and waterfalls, which appeared empty.

"Mayhap he left his steed here while he searches for weeds."

Evina narrowed her eyes in consideration at the suggestion from the man sitting astride the horse on her right. Donnan. He'd been the first at Maclean for fourteen years. There was no one she'd trust more to accompany her on this trip, except perhaps the man on her left, her cousin Gavin.

When she didn't comment, Donnan pointed out, "The lad did say Rory Buchanan was out gathering weeds for his healing work. The area around here is rich with various plants. Mayhap he leaves his horse here as a main base and returns occasionally with his finds."

Evina eyed the bulging saddlebag hanging from the side of the handsome beast across the clearing, and nodded. It seemed a good possibility. Although it did look to her as if he must be nearly finished with his weed-gathering expedition. In fact, unless he had a second bag that he was carrying with him, he should be done. There didn't look to her to be room for even one more leaf, stem or root in the bag.

"Or no'," Gavin murmured quietly.

Raising her eyebrows, Evina glanced to her cousin and then followed his direction to the water when he nodded that way.

At first, she didn't see anything to explain his comment. There was nothing in the river itself. It wasn't until Evina turned her gaze to the waterfall again that she saw what he'd spotted. The cliff the water fell from was a good twenty feet up. The water rained down in a white, frothy torrent that hid the rocks and anything else behind the sheet of water, and that was what she'd seen the first time. Now there appeared to be an elbow poking out of the water and someone moving around under the spray.

"Looks like we've found him," Donnan said with amusement. "Do we wait for him to come out?"

Evina considered the matter briefly, but that didn't really seem an option to her. Rory Buchanan might rush through his cleaning and be out quickly, but he could also piddle about in the falls for a good long time, but either way, every moment they wasted was one more during which her father lay dying.

"Nay. We fetch him out," she said finally. "And we'll no' take nay for an answer."

"Right," Donnan said quietly, and then glanced past her to Gavin.

Following his gaze, Evina saw that the younger man was already dismounting. Once on the ground, her cousin quickly removed his sword and boots. When he reached for the pin of his plaid, Evina turned her head away and stared at the waterfalls instead to give him privacy. She used to change Gavin's nappies and give him baths as a boy, but he wasn't a child anymore. Besides, while she'd often been accused of being less than a lady, even she wouldn't look on a bare-arsed man.

At least, not on purpose, Evina qualified when her gaze landed not on an elbow protruding from the falls now, but on a bare arse. That was all. The Buchanan had obviously turned under the water and bent over, presumably to wash his lower legs or feet, because while she could now see the outline of his legs through a very thin layer of foamy water, his behind was the only thing out of the spray and on display.

And a fine rounded rump it was too, Evina noted before movement drew her attention to Gavin as he headed determinedly toward the water. She looked away, but not before catching a glimpse of his back, legs and behind. Evina had always thought her cousin a well-built young man, and he did have a nice muscular chest and shoulders. He also had fine legs. Despite that though, he couldn't compare with the Buchanan when it came to rumps. Gavin fell short when compared to the only part of the man she could really see. Her cousin's behind was flat in comparison to the one sticking out of the waterfall.

"When ye said we're no' taking nay fer an answer," Donnan said slowly. "Did ye mean . . . ?"

"I meant exactly what it sounds like," Evina assured him. "We'll kidnap the bastard if we have to, but Rory Buchanan has to return with us. I'll no' let Father die for lack o' the right healer."

Donnan nodded, but then pointed out, "It could mean war with the Buchanans."

"Then we'll battle the Buchanans," she said grimly, and turned to peer at him. "Is that a problem?"

Donnan shook his head. "Nay, m'lady. I pledged me fealty to yer father. I'd give me life fer him. I just wanted to be sure ye kenned the consequences o' this action."

"I ken the consequences," Evina assured him solemnly. "And I would give me life for me father too. If it takes a war to save him, then war it shall be."

Donnan was silent for a moment, and then said gently, "Rory Buchanan may no' be able to heal him either. Yer father may be beyond help."

"Mayhap," she agreed. "But I'd also give me life for just a *chance* at saving him. Hopefully, it'll no' come to war though, and the Buchanan will come willingly."

"I'm thinking that does no' seem likely," Donnan said dryly, and nodded toward the waterfall again.

Evina turned her head quickly, her eyes widening as she saw that Gavin had reached the Buchanan and, rather than talking, the two men were now grappling under the waterfall. Even as she noted that, the pair tumbled off the low ledge they'd stood on and into the river itself.

"Huh," Evina muttered, pursing her lips as she watched the pair rolling and bobbing in the water, alternately wrestling, punching and appearing to try to drown each other. "Ye may be right."

"I'm thinking Gavin might need a hand," Donnan said after several minutes had passed with the men continuing to struggle.

"Aye," Evina agreed with concern as she watched the Buchanan force her cousin under the water and hold him there. When Gavin didn't reappear, or roll the other man under, Donnan dismounted, intending to go help.

Quite sure he'd never make it there in time on foot, Evina cursed and put her heels to her mount. The mare responded at once, bursting into a sprint that took her to the water's edge before Donnan had crossed half the distance. Evina rode right into the water, drawing her sword out as she did. Once next to the man holding Gavin under the water's surface, she reined in hard enough to make her mare rear in the water.

The Buchanan turned a startled face up toward her, their eyes met briefly, and then Evina brought her sword down. The hilt of her weapon slammed into the side of his head with force. She watched him wince in pain and then lose consciousness as her mare settled on all four hooves again in the water.

The moment the Buchanan released Gavin, her cousin reared up out of the water, sputtering. Relief pouring through her, Evina sheathed her sword and slid quickly off her mare's back. She landed in the waist-high water next to the men even as Donnan rushed into the river to approach them.

"Help Gavin," she ordered, noting the way the young man was swaying as he stood up. She didn't wait to watch the man obey, but moved to the Buchanan. Grabbing the healer by the shoulder, she turned him in the water. Her face pinched with concern when she noted his pallor, but she quickly shifted her hold to his hand and dragged him toward shore.

The healer was surprisingly heavy. Evina only managed to pull him halfway out of the river before she had to stop, but at least his head and chest were out. Once she'd dragged him as far as she could onto the grassy shore, she dropped to her knees beside him and quickly turned him on his stomach. Evina then placed her hands on his back and pushed hard and fast, once and then again. Water immediately poured from his mouth and nose. When a third such push didn't bring up any more, she turned him over. When she saw that the man wasn't breathing, she didn't hesitate, but pinched his nose, opened his mouth and bent to blow her breath into it.

"Er . . . m'lady?" Donnan said, sounding uncertain as he let a coughing and hacking Gavin drop to his knees next to her. "What are ye doing?"

"Breathing for him," she muttered between breaths. "Me mother did this to me brother when he near drowned as a lad. It revived him," she explained as she pressed on the Buchanan's chest, before bending to cover his mouth with hers again.

"Looks more like yer kissing on him," Donnan said dubiously, and Gavin released a chuckle of amusement that was raspy and sent him into another coughing fit.

Evina ignored both men and bent to press her ear to the unconscious man's chest. Much to her relief she heard his heart beat and the sound of his drawing breath into his lungs on his own. Straightening then, she peered down at him expectantly, but he didn't open his eyes.

"Ye hit him pretty hard, m'lady," Donnan pointed out solemnly. "He may no' wake up for a bit, but he's breathing now on his own at least."

"Aye," she sighed the word, her eyes sliding over the man's face. He was really quite handsome. She hadn't expected that. She'd heard tales of his skill as a healer, but not one of those stories had mentioned that he was a good-looking man. She'd imagined a plain-faced, scrawny, book-ish man like the priests, who were the only learned men she knew of. Instead, he had a pretty face and a strapping body, she noted, her gaze sliding down his wide, naked chest to his tapered waist. The rest of him was still submerged in water so Evina couldn't look farther.

"M'lady?" Donnan said quietly, drawing her reluctant gaze. "Mayhap we'd best get moving. If one o' his brothers come looking for him and finds him like this . . ."

"Aye." Evina stood abruptly, ignoring the way her wet skirts dragged at her. She glanced quickly around the clearing, but once assured they were still alone, turned her attention to Gavin as his coughing fit ended and he spat in the dirt. "Are ye all right, Gav? Can ye ride?"

"Aye," he growled, staggering to his feet.

Evina watched him with concern, but he appeared mostly recovered. At least he wasn't swaying or coughing anymore and there was color in his cheeks. Nodding, she turned back to the water, a grimace claiming her lips when her skirts slapped cold and wet against her legs. Her mare still stood where she'd left her, and Evina waded back into the water to reclaim her reins and lead her back onto land.

"What do ye want us to do with the Buchanan?" Donnan asked as he watched her mount her mare.

Evina settled in the saddle, arranged her skirts the best she could sit-ting astride as she was and then glanced down to the naked, unconscious man on the ground. He really was a pretty man, a pleasure to look on, she thought, but said, "Bind him hand and foot, toss him over his horse's back, and then tie him hand *to* foot to be sure he does no' fall off."

"Do I dress him first?" Donnan asked, not looking pleased at the thought, and Evina supposed pleating a plaid and dressing an unconscious fully grown male in it might be something of a task.

She shook her head. "Nay. Just throw his plaid over him once ye've ensured he'll no' fall off his mount as we ride. And mayhap tie it down somehow so it does no' fall off him either."

Donnan nodded and then glanced to Gavin. "Are ye well enough to fetch his mount?"

"O' course," Gavin said irritably, and headed away muttering, "Took in a bit o' water, is all, but I'm fine now."

They watched him go, and then both Evina and Donnan shared small smiles. Gavin was always a bit touchy at any suggestion that he may not be up to par. He was young yet, but determined to prove he was a man.

"The Buchanan'll no' be pleased at being knocked unconscious," Donnan predicted solemnly as he shifted his attention back to the unconscious man.

"Nay," Evina agreed on a sigh, her eyes wandering toward the still-submerged lower half of the unconscious man's body before she caught herself and drew it back to his face. This hadn't been how she'd hoped this task would go. She'd planned to have an amiable chat with the man, and convince him to come with them. Knocking him out and dragging him home with them had only been a last-resort possibility if he'd refused to accompany them willingly. However, things rarely went according to plan in her experience.

Shaking her head, she glanced warily around the clearing again before her gaze settled on her cousin leading the Buchanan's mount to them.

"Thank ye," Donnan said, taking the horse's reins from Gavin. "Go fetch our beasts while I get him on his horse."

Nodding, the younger man moved quickly away to retrieve their waiting horses.

Evina watched Donnan bind the Buchanan's hands and feet and then frowned when he caught him by his tied hands and drew him into a sitting position.

"Can ye manage on yer own? Or do ye need me to help ye with . . ." Evina's question died in her throat. Donnan already had the man over his shoulders and was carrying him the few feet to the Buchanan's mount. She watched silently as he slung him over the beast and quickly attached a rope between his bound hands and his feet under the animal's belly so that he wouldn't slide off during the ride.

Evina supposed she shouldn't be surprised at how easily Donnan had managed the task. It was why she'd brought him along on this journey. The man was huge and strong, his neck as big around as her thigh, his upper arms bulging with muscle and his shoulders almost twice the width of most men's. He probably could have carried the three of them if necessary, Evina thought as she watched him arrange the Buchanan's plaid over his back and fasten it around his neck and knees to keep it in place.

"That should do," Donnan announced as he stepped back from his handiwork.

"Aye," Evina agreed as Gavin reached them, already astride his mount and leading Donnan's. She waited as the first mounted, but once he was settled and had the reins of the Buchanan's horse in hand, she turned her own mount to lead them out of the clearing. Her thoughts were already on the ride home and the quickest way there. It was usually a two-day ride, but she intended to make it in a little more than one. There would be no stopping to eat or make camp at night. They would eat in the saddle and ride nonstop, as they had on the way out. Her father's life depended on it. If he still lived.

That last thought made Evina press her lips tight together and spur her horse into a run before they'd even left the clearing. Her father couldn't die. He just couldn't. He and Gavin were all the family she had in this world.

CONRAN GROANED AS PAIN DRAGGED HIM BACK TOWARD CON-sciousness. It wasn't one pain, but a whole battery of pains, and they were assaulting him from nearly everywhere. His arms, his legs, his ankles and wrists, his stomach and his damned head were all throbbing, pounding or aching at the moment and he didn't understand why. He also didn't understand what he was seeing when he was finally able to open his eyes. Everything was just a fuzzy blur at first, but even when his vision cleared he couldn't quite grasp what he was staring at.

Something dark brown was filling most of his vision, although there was a strip of something blue on one side. Unable to figure out what the brown was, Conran turned his head slightly to peer at the blue instead, hoping that might be more comprehensible. But beyond the blue he could see the tail end of the horse he was apparently on, and beyond that, what appeared to be an upside-down rider following.

Although the rider wasn't the one who was upside down, he was, Conran realized suddenly as he stared at the large man and the scenery disappearing behind him. He was hanging upside down on a horse, his stomach across the saddle, with his legs hanging down one side and his shoulders and arms the other.

That explained his aching stomach, Conran supposed as he bounced on the beast's back, his stomach slamming into the pommel and top of the saddle. His aching head could be blamed on the blow he now recalled taking back at the river, and his ankles and wrists hurt because they were both presently bound, and tightly too. There also appeared to be a rope attached to his bound hands that disappeared under the belly of the beast he lay on.

Conran wasn't positive what that rope was attached to at first, but when he tried to draw his hands toward himself, a tug on his ankles gave him the answer. His wrists and ankles were trussed up and tied together under the horse. If he slipped, his weight would drag him down so that he hung under the animal like a boar tied to a spear to be carted home after a hunt. Did that happen, he was likely to be kicked in the head. Brilliant.

Turning his face, Conran peered at the blue cloth next to his head. Someone rode with him. Presumably to keep him from slipping, he supposed. He could feel pressure on one butt cheek, as if someone were pressing down to keep him from shifting and slipping under the animal.

The naked man who'd attacked him while he was cleaning up at the waterfall? he wondered, but then took a look at the cloth next to him again. Not a plaid, and not braies either. The blue cloth draped, looking more like a skirt to him. It was pulled tight because the rider was astride, but it was a skirt he was sure. Conran let his eyes follow the cloth down to where it ended just above a strip of dark brown that might have been the bottom hem of braies worn under the skirt, and then there were a bare couple of inches of pale calf showing above the top of brown leather riding boots.

Conran hung there for a moment, simply staring at the bit of skin, and then tried to lift and turn his head to look at the rider presently touching his bottom so familiarly, but the movement made the pounding in his head increase in severity enough that he quickly gave up the effort. After waiting a moment for the pain to ease back to a dull throb again, Conran called out instead. Or at least he tried. Even he couldn't hear the weak sound of his breathless voice over the drumming of the horses' hooves. Aside from the fact that his position made it impossible to take in enough air to propel anything of volume, his mouth and throat were dry as old bone.

Unable to get the rider's attention, Conran tried to make himself relax, but his position was damned uncomfortable, and growing more so by the moment. He had to get the attention of the person he rode with. After a moment of debating the situation, he finally simply turned his head and bit into the patch of naked skin above the leather boot.

It immediately became obvious that it had been the wrong move. Rather than slowing to a halt at the realization that he was awake, the rider clenched the hand on his bottom in a startled response, driving sharp nails into his ass. The unknown female must also have yanked on the reins in surprise with her other hand too. At least, that was his guess when the animal suddenly reared up with a distressed whinny.

Cursing, Conran closed his eyes and tried to brace himself as his world turned on its end.

"Cousin!"

Groaning, Evina rolled onto her back, and opened her eyes, unsurprised to find Gavin next to her, concern on his face.

"Are ye all right?" he asked, looking her over.

"Fine," she sighed as he helped her sit up. Glancing around she spotted the Buchanan on the ground a few feet away, next to his now-calm horse. Donnan was kneeling beside him.

"Is he okay?" Evina asked anxiously. Ignoring the aches and pains assailing her, she struggled to her feet with help from Gavin, and moved to lean over Donnan so that she could get a look at the Buchanan's face. Seeing his closed eyes, and pale face, she sighed with disappointment. "He's unconscious again."

"Again?" Donnan glanced back at her with surprise.

Evina nodded. "He woke up briefly just moments ago."

"Are ye sure?" Donnan asked.

"Aye," she said with a grimace. "The bastard bit me leg."

"He *bit* you?" Gavin asked with a laugh of disbelief.

Evina nodded again. "It startled me into yanking on the blasted reins, which is why his steed reared."

"He's unconscious, but breathing fine and seems good other than another bump on his head," Donnan announced, straightening. "Must have got it when he hit the ground."

Evina relaxed a little. They'd both come off the horse when it reared. She'd tumbled backward, and he'd slid down the horse's back right behind her. He'd still been trussed up, ankles and wrists, with a rope attached between them. She supposed they were lucky he'd only suffered a blow to the head and hadn't been trampled or dragged about by his mount.

"We're only an hour from Maclean," Donnan said quietly. "It might be better to get him there before he wakes again."

"Aye," Evina agreed, absently rubbing her elbow. She'd landed on it hard when she fell off the horse. It was tender, probably badly bruised, as was her hip, but she hadn't broken anything, and she was conscious, so, all told, she'd fared better than the Buchanan.

"Gavin can take him on his horse for the rest of the ride," Donnan said as he picked up the man and straightened.

Evina didn't argue. This wasn't the first time the Buchanan had slid off his saddle. It had happened shortly after they'd left the clearing. He'd slid down, headfirst toward the ground, and then hung under the horse's belly, faceup with the rope attached between his bound ankles and wrists across the saddle. Well, he would have been faceup if he'd been conscious. He hadn't, however, so his head had just fallen back, his long hair dragging on the ground.

They'd stopped at once, of course, to re-situate him across the saddle, and then had decided someone should ride with him to be sure it didn't happen again. Evina had taken the duty because she was the lightest, and they'd hoped it wouldn't slow his horse down too much to have her ride with him. But they were close to home now; Gavin's horse could handle the two of them and still move fast for this last bit of the journey. The beast had originally been Donnan's until her father had gifted his first with the steed he now rode. The animal was used to carrying the bigger man, and Gavin and the Buchanan together probably didn't weigh that much more than Donnan did on his own, he was that large.

"Mount up, Gavin, and I'll lay him over the saddle in front o' ye," Donnan ordered as he carried the Buchanan past her.

"Are we going to untie and retie him around me horse?" Gavin asked, leading the way to his mount.

"Nay. We're close enough I think we can do without the bother. Just keep a hand on his back to keep him from slipping off for the rest of the journey," Donnan instructed.

Gavin mumbled something of an agreement as he mounted his horse, then leaned over and reached out to help place the Buchanan across his horse's back in front of him. The two men quickly ran into trouble, however, thanks to the rope between the man's bound wrists and ankles.

"Just a minute," Evina said, pulling out her dirk and hurrying forward when she saw the problem. While the two men held him aloft, she quickly cut the rope between his hands and ankles, and then stepped back and out of the way, aware that her cheeks were now a fiery red. She couldn't help it. The way they'd been holding the man, his jewels had been dangling to the side of her face, and while she'd tried not to look, it had been impossible not to take a couple of quick glances.

Shaking her head in an effort to remove what she'd seen from her mind, Evina left the men to arrange the Buchanan to their pleasure and moved away to remount her mare.

"Lead the way, m'lady," Donnan rumbled once they were all back in the saddle.

She didn't have to be told twice. Turning her mare, Evina spurred her into a fast jog she hoped Gavin's steed could keep up with. She was eager to get home and see that her father was all right. Or, at least, that he still lived. If he'd died while she'd been out fetching the Buchanan back to help him—

Evina pushed that thought determinedly away, but spent the remaining hour of the journey praying that Rory Buchanan was as good as the stories claimed and could save her father's life.

Chapter 2

"Oh, thank the good Lord ye're back, m'lady. I was starting to fear ye'd be too late."

Evina turned from dismounting to see her maid, Tildy, rushing down the stairs toward her. The woman was wringing her hands, lines of worry creasing her old face.

"He's still alive though?" Evina asked sharply, moving to meet her at the base of the stairs.

"Aye," the maid said at once, squeezing her hands reassuringly when Evina took them. "But barely, and I'm no' sure for how much longer if something is no' done. He's burning up, he is."

"Something will be done," Evina assured her, and turned to where Donnan was removing the still-unconscious Buchanan from Gavin's mount. She heard Tildy gasp beside her as his naked front was revealed, and then Donnan tossed the man over his shoulder and turned toward her.

"Yer father's room?" he asked as he approached.

"Aye." Evina turned at once to lead the way.

"Is that the Buchanan brother what's a healer?" Tildy asked, huffing up the stairs on her heels.

"Aye," Evina murmured.

"He's bigger than I expected," she muttered, and then asked, "What happened to him? Why is he unconscious? And naked and tied up?"

"There was a—" grimacing, Evina sorted briefly through words in her mind and chose "—an incident."

"What kind o' an incident?" Tildy asked grimly, her voice a little stronger.

"It does no' matter, Tildy," she growled as she pushed her way into the keep and started across the great hall. "The important part is he is here."

"But unconscious," Tildy pointed out. "How can he help yer father if he's unconscious?"

"We'll wake him up," she assured her.

"How?" Tildy asked at once.

The question made Evina change direction. They'd arrived during the evening meal and the tables were full of Maclean people eating and drinking. Evina grabbed one of the nearest pitchers of ale distributed so generously among the tables, and then hurried to follow Donnan as he carried the Buchanan above stairs.

"M'lady?" Tildy rushed to keep up with her. "What—?"

"All will be well, Tildy," Evina interrupted firmly. Sparing the maid a glance, she frowned and added, "Ye look exhausted. Ye've no' rested at all since we left, have ye?"

"Have *you*?" Tildy countered, eyebrows arched, and when Evina looked away toward the top of the stairs and let the subject drop, she added, "I thought no'. Ye must ha'e ridden day and night to get there and back so quickly."

Evina didn't deny it, but merely grunted with irritation as they reached the landing. She moved around Donnan then and led the way to her father's door.

It was midsummer, the days hot enough that even the castle became uncomfortably warm at times, but her father's room was positively stifling when they entered. It also smelled of rot and, for a minute, she feared her father had passed, but a moan from the depths of the furs piled on the bed told her otherwise and Evina released a relieved breath as she rushed to his side. Frowning at his flushed face, she set the pitcher of ale on the table next to the bed and reached out to touch his cheek. Concern claimed her as she felt the heat radiating from his skin before her fingers even touched him.

"He's boiling. Why is it so hot in here?" she asked with dismay.

"He kept complaining he was cold, and asked us to build up the fire," Tildy said quietly.

Evina eyed the roaring blaze in the fireplace with concern, and then turned to watch Donnan carry the Buchanan into the room.

"Set him here," she instructed, gesturing to the chair she'd had moved next to the bed when her father had first fallen ill. Donnan did so at once. He then took the time to cut away the rope binding the unconscious man's hands and ankles before stepping back.

Evina stared. The Buchanan was slumped in the chair, his chin on his naked chest, his legs spread and his family jewels dangling between like—

"Good Lord!"

Blinking, Evina glanced around in time to see Tildy drag a fur off the bed. The woman then rushed forward to lay it over the Buchanan's lap, covering the more important parts. Standing back then, she shook her head and turned to arch an eyebrow at Evina.

"What kind of incident sees a man naked and unconscious?" she asked, tight-lipped.

Evina automatically opened her mouth to answer. It was habit more than anything. Tildy had been her nursemaid as a child. She'd been answering to her since she was born, but before she could explain, the woman added, "And why is he wearing his plaid as a cape rather than in the proper fashion? He looks ridiculous."

"We tied the plaid around his neck and his knees, originally," Evina muttered, moving forward to untie the upper portion. It had come undone from his knees when he'd fallen from the horse the second time. "'Twas to keep it on him while we were traveling. He was lying across his horse's back on his belly at the time."

"Because he was unconscious," Tildy suggested.

"Aye. 'Tis hard to dress an unconscious man in a plaid." Evina got the material untied and then glanced around at Donnan. She didn't have to say anything; he was already moving forward. He lifted the man just enough so that she could tug the cloth out from under him, but not enough to dislodge the fur. Once he set the Buchanan back down, she draped the thick material over him on top of the fur, tucking it around him like a blanket.

"And how is it he came to be unconscious?" Tildy asked as Evina finished her task and stepped back.

She hesitated briefly, but finally admitted, "I hit him in the head with me sword hilt."

"You—!"

"He was drowning Gavin," Evina explained defensively. "I had to do something."

"So, ye knocked him senseless? And then what? Ye did no' kidnap him, did ye?" Tildy asked with alarm.

"Nay!" Evina snapped, and then frowned guiltily as she admitted, "Well, aye, mayhap a little."

"Mayhap ye kidnapped him a little?" Tildy asked with disbelief. "There's no such thing as kidnapping someone a little, lass. Either ye kidnapped him, or ye did no'."

When Evina didn't respond, but simply frowned at the unconscious man, Tildy asked, "Did he agree to come, or no'?"

"Nay," she grumbled unhappily, and then quickly added, "But he did no' disagree either."

"Oh, Evina," Tildy said on a sigh. "I raised ye better than this, lass. Ye can no' run about kidnapping naked men and bringing them home, no matter how handsome and strapping and well-hung they are."

"Tildy!" Evina turned on her with a scowl. "What he looks like and how he hangs had nothing to do with it. I brought him home to tend Father."

"Well, a bloody lot of good he's going to be at tending yer father, unconscious as he is," Tildy pointed out with disgust.

Muttering under her breath, Evina grabbed up the pitcher of ale she'd set on the bedside table and turned to pour it over his head. This was why she'd stopped to grab the ale to begin with; she'd hoped it would help revive him . . . and it appeared to be working, she noted as the man came to sputtering, cursing life.

CONRAN WAS DREAMING HE WAS FROLICKING WITH A RED-headed beauty with blue eyes when liquid splashed over his head, tearing him from his dream girl's embrace. He wasn't happy about that and came to roaring life, cursing and bellowing as he lunged to his feet, only to fall silent and still as he found himself staring at the very same redheaded beauty he'd just left.

Well, not quite the same, Conran realized as he looked her over. She had the same face with full, luscious lips that gave him ideas, and bright blue pools for eyes. But instead of long, flowing, dark red hair and a lovely gossamer gown that revealed her round, burgeoning breasts and the curve of her hips, this one had her hair tugged back tight in a bun and wore a filthy, plain, ill-fitting dark blue gown that seemed to emphasize the shadowed hollows of exhaustion under her eyes.

Movement drew his attention to the pitcher she was even now setting on a bedside table and Conran scowled and ran his hands quickly over his face to wipe away the liquid dripping down it. Ale. He could smell and taste it. Not bad ale either, he acknowledged as he licked it off his lips. But a damned rude way to wake him.

"Where am I?" The question popped out as he scowled over the group standing around him—a poor copy of his dream woman, an old female servant and two soldiers, he noted—but paid them little attention, instead scanning the room quickly. It was a bedchamber, but not one he recognized.

"Maclean," the younger woman said. "Ye're a guest of the Macleans."

"Guest?" His voice was dubious. The last thing Conran remembered was a naked man attacking him while he was bathing. Well, no, he realized, his eyes narrowing on the redheaded woman again. He also recalled her, riding up on a horse while he grappled with his attacker in the river. She'd slammed a damned sword hilt into his head, he remembered, his eyes narrowing on her. "Ye knocked me senseless."

"Ye were drowning our Gavin," she responded abruptly, but didn't even bother to look at him as she said it. Instead, the lass turned to peer worriedly toward the bed.

Conran followed her gaze, but all he saw was a mountain of furs piled on it. Mouth tightening with irritation at her lack of attention, he growled, "If yer Gavin is the fellow who molested me while I was bathing, he deserved it."

She finally deigned to give him her attention then, but Conran barely noticed. A muttered curse had made his head swivel toward the two soldiers in the room. His eyes narrowed on the smaller one this time. He looked somewhat familiar, but with his hair dry and clothes on, it took Conran a minute to recognize him as his attacker. Once he did though, he growled, "You."

The man shifted uncomfortably. "I was asked to fetch ye out o' the water. Me apologies, m'lord, if ye mistook me intentions and thought ye were under attack."

"I was bathing, alone, naked and without me weapon when another naked man suddenly appeared and grabbed me," he pointed out with disgust. "O' course I thought meself under attack. Any man would."

"Really?" the girl asked, and Conran watched the larger soldier glance her way and nod. He didn't bother to look, but heard the frown in her voice as she asked, "Well, why did ye no' tell me that?"

"The situation was somewhat urgent," the larger man reminded her in a deep rumble of a voice. "We needed to hurry and could no' wait for him to finish his ablutions."

"Right. Urgent," the girl muttered, and turned to peer at the bed once more.

Conran followed her gaze, wondering what she found so fascinating about the damned furs.

"Also," the man continued, "I was rather hoping Gavin would talk fast enough to reassure him all was well ere the Buchanan resorted to violence."

"No one talks that fast," Conran assured him dryly. "And I would no' have heard him anyway over the rush of the waterfall." When the man tipped his head in acknowledgment, Conran glanced back to the girl and asked shortly, "So? Why have I been kidnapped?"

"Ye've no' been kidnapped," she said quickly, turning back with something like alarm. Managing a somewhat strained smile, she added, "Truly, m'lord, we mean ye no harm at all. We are no' enemies. In fact, we are admirers of yer skills in the healing arts."

Conran snorted, and then growled, "I was knocked senseless, trussed up, tossed over a horse and unwillingly transported away from Buchanan to Maclean. Lass, that is kidnapping."

"She is a lady no' a lass," the large man said sharply. "Ye'll afford our lady the proper respect she is due and address her as Lady Evina."

Conran raised a doubtful eyebrow at the words. The lass looked far and away from a lady at the moment. More like a dirty street urchin in that filthy blue dress. He narrowed his eyes as he recalled the blue draped over the leg he'd bitten. Then what she'd said moments ago finally sank through his head.

"Healing arts?" he asked sharply.

"Aye, the tales of yer skill have spread far and wide, Lord Buchanan, and we are in desperate need of those skills. Me father, Fearghas Maclean, is very ill. Please, just come take a look."

Conran shook his head, realizing it was Rory they wanted. Obviously, they'd grabbed the wrong brother, he thought, but hesitated to say as much for fear it would see his brother treated as roughly as he had been.

While he stood, uncertain of what he should do or say in this situation, the lass grabbed his hand and drew him toward the bed. Her voice was desperate as she begged, "Please, just look at him. There must be something ye can do."

"Nay." Conran tugged his hand from hers. He was not the healer.

"Aye."

Conran scowled. "Ye kidnapped me. Why would I help ye in return for such rough treatment?"

Several expressions flitted across her face—dismay, anger, desperation—and then Lady Evina took a deep breath and let it out slowly. Raising her shoulders, she said quietly, "Please, m'lord. I apologize if Gavin's approaching ye in the waterfall frightened ye. That was no' our intention."

Conran scowled at the comment, disliking the suggestion that he'd been afraid.

"In fact, we ne'er intended for any o' the unfortunate events that followed to occur," she continued. "The truth is that we rode to Buchanan to approach ye to beg yer assistance in saving the life o' me dear father. However, it all went terribly wrong when ye attacked Gavin."

Great, now he was the bad guy, attacking a man who just wished to gain his attention, Conran thought, and almost shook his head in wonder at how skillfully she'd turned the tables.

"And once ye were unconscious, we could hardly leave ye there, naked and vulnerable. Anything might have happened to ye should the wrong sort have found ye like that."

That was clever, Conran acknowledged. Not only was he now the bad guy, but she had also been saving him by kidnapping him.

"But I felt I could no' leave me father alone fer too long fer fear he would die before I could return," she continued. "It meant we could no' stay to guard ye until ye woke. So, instead, we brought ye back with us to keep ye safe . . . hoping that once ye woke and we could speak with ye that ye'd agree to help." Bowing her head, she added, "I would be pleased to offer ye anything ye desire that 'tis within me power to give ye, if ye would only try to help me father. He means everything to me. I cannot lose him."

Well, hell, Conran thought with irritation. She was a clever wench. Not only had she swallowed her pride and made a pretty plea, she'd managed to twist everything so that her kidnapping him seemed almost a kindness. More than that though, she'd revealed her very real caring and concern for her father. If he refused to at least look at the man now, he'd feel a complete ass.

Sighing, Conran ran a hand through his long hair, and then frowned as he felt something. Plucking it free, he lowered his hand and peered at the small prickly branch he'd pulled from his hair.

"Please?"

Conran shifted his gaze to Lady Evina. Her eyes were shiny now, though whether with tears or anger, he couldn't tell. He was leaning toward tears though, and supposed the least he could do was look at the man. He could decide what to do from there.

"Fine," he muttered now. "Take me to him."

"Perhaps ye could dress first," the old woman suggested in arid tones.

Eyebrows rising, Conran followed her glance down to see that his plaid and a fur were lying on the floor on top of and in front of his feet, but otherwise he was completely naked.

"They fell off when ye woke and leapt up," Evina said, her gaze never dropping below his face. The way she said it suggested that he'd been wearing the plaid at least, but he recalled being naked on the horse. The damn thing must have been draped over him and slid off when he stood.

Shaking his head, Conran bent to snatch up the plaid and moved to the other side of the bed where there was room to kneel and pleat the item of clothing on the floor. His movements were economical, but not rushed. Conran was not embarrassed by nudity, his or anyone else's. He'd skinny-dipped with his brothers two or three times a week for the first twenty-odd years of his life and still did on occasion. Between that and helping Rory with his work with the ill and injured, which necessitated dealing with people in all states of dress and undress, he saw no shame in the human body.

Conran did find it interesting that Lady Evina hadn't seemed embarrassed by his nudity either though. Most ladies would have blushed and stammered and probably even turned their back while they spoke to him, if not leave the room altogether until he'd clothed himself. But she'd stood there, just inches away, as if he were fully garbed. Her gaze had never dropped below his face though, Conran thought, running the past few minutes through his mind as he worked. Interesting. Maybe. He wasn't sure. He couldn't figure the woman out. Just when he thought he knew what to expect, she surprised him . . . which fascinated him.

Conran was just finishing the last pleat when a white shirt appeared before his face. Pausing, he sat back on his heels and glanced to the man holding it out to him. It was the one who had attacked him under the falls, the smaller of the two soldiers. Although that description was misleading. The man wasn't small by any means. In fact, he was about his size, but next to the mountain of a man that was the other soldier, this one looked wee.

"Yer shirt," the soldier said quietly. "I tucked it in me saddlebag and brought it back fer ye."

"Thank ye," Conran said grudgingly as he took the shirt. He tugged it on quickly, and then donned the plaid, and turned to the people waiting patiently on the other side of the bed. Raising his eyebrows, he said, "So . . . if ye'll take me to yer father, I'll see if there is aught I can do."

He expected Evina to lead him out of the room. Instead, she walked to the bed, and peered down at the top of the pile of furs stacked there. "Da? Rory Buchanan is here. If anyone can save ye, 'tis him. Are ye awake, Da?"

Conran moved closer to the bed, his eyes widening when he spotted the shriveled old face just visible above the mountain of furs. Taking in the flushed cheeks and glazed eyes when the man opened them, he began to frown and leaned down to press the back of his hand to Fearghas Maclean's forehead.

"Dear God, he's burning up," he said with dismay, and tugged his hand away. The man was hot enough to cook a meal on without need of a fire.

Frowning, Conran straightened, thinking the fellow did need his brother's skills, and immediately. But if he was now at Maclean, it would take at least two days, more likely three, to ride to Buchanan and bring him back. If his brother would even come, Conran thought. Rory was very worried about the innkeeper's daughter. The lass was a wee thing, and her husband was a big bull of a man. Rory was afraid the birth of their bairn could kill the lass. He wasn't likely to be willing to leave her until the birth was done and over. That left taking the Maclean to him, but the state he was in, Fearghas wasn't likely to survive the journey.

Conran frowned over the predicament and then uttered a soft but fervent curse. He'd have to do what he could for the Maclean himself, and try to get his fever down. If they managed that, they might be able to transport him to Buchanan for Rory to tend him. Fortunately for them, after helping Rory out so many times, he did know how to bring down a fever. He promptly began to tear away the furs on the bed and toss them to the floor.

"What are ye doing?" Evina asked with alarm, trying to stop him.

"He has a fever," Conran pointed out, ignoring her attempts and continuing to remove the furs. Dear God, where the hell had they got all of them?

"Yes, but he was complaining that he was cold," she protested, grabbing up the furs he'd just removed.

"Because he has a fever," he muttered. But when she started to return the furs even as he removed them, Conran paused and straightened to glare at her, his mouth opening and then closing again as he *really* looked at her. The woman was pale as death, with great smudges under her eyes that could only be exhaustion. She needed sleep and wasn't likely to seek it until she was sure her father was all right . . . unless she was made to.

"Do ye want me help or no'?" he said finally.

Her eyes widened incredulously. "Aye, o' course, but—"

"Then get out," Conran interrupted grimly.

"What?" she gasped with amazement.

"I want that damned fire put out, the window shutters opened, a cold bath brought up and ye gone," he added firmly before continuing. "And do no' return. If ye do, I will leave."

"But . . ." The lost look on her face as she peered down at her father was almost his undoing and Conran nearly rescinded the words, but then he noted the way her hands were trembling, and he held firm. The lass was beyond exhausted. She'd probably been doing without sleep to tend her father before riding out for Buchanan, but he was quite sure she hadn't slept at all over the last two or three days as she'd traveled to fetch him back. If the woman didn't soon rest, she'd collapse and fall ill herself.

"Yer filthy, ye reek and ye're swaying on yer feet," Conran snapped harshly, suspecting gentle wouldn't work with this woman. "Ye're no' fit to be in a sickroom. Take yerself out o' it, find a bath and then yer bed, and do no' return until I say so."

"You—I—" she stammered, shock and anger coloring her cheeks, and Conran began to suspect he may have overdone it a bit.

Mouth tightening, he used the only weapon he had—her concern for her father. Lifting his chin, he growled, "Well? Are ye leaving, or am I?"

"Evina," the older woman said gently, touching her arm.

Mouth tightening bitterly, Lady Evina gave a stiff nod and turned to stride from the room, slamming the door behind her.

"See that she has something to eat and then sleeps," Conran ordered the old woman. "And tell her I'll leave if she does no' do both. I've no desire to be tending her as well as her father."

Nodding, the maid rushed to the door to chase after her lady.

"And do no' forget to order a cold bath fer yer laird," Conran barked as the old woman slid into the hall.

The moment the door closed behind her, he turned to the two soldiers still in the room and repeated, "Open the window shutters and put out that damned fire. We have to get him cooled down or his brains will boil."

The two men moved at once to obey, and Conran went back to removing the furs, his mind already on what he'd seen Rory do when he had a patient with a fever that he needed to bring down.

"The arrogant ass," Evina growled, stomping down the stairs, aware that Tildy was on her heels. She'd glanced over her shoulder when she'd heard the bedroom door open and close behind her and had spotted the woman rushing after her. "Ordering me from the room. He is me father. I should be there."

"Aye, lass, but mayhap this is for the best," Tildy said a touch breathlessly as she followed her down to the busy great hall.

"How is it for the best that me father is being deprived o' his daughter's presence? He is ailing and needs me," she said plaintively.

"He needs the Buchanan more just now," Tildy said solemnly.

Evina grunted in response as they started across the great hall. The tables were still full of people enjoying their repast.

"And ye could do with food and a rest," Tildy continued as they started walking along the trestle tables. "Why do ye no' sit down? I'll order the bath and ask Cook to prepare ye a meal. Ye can eat and then retire and rest a bit."

"I'm no' hungry. Or tired fer that matter," Evina growled, which wasn't completely true. While she wasn't hungry, she was a touch tired. Much less tired than she'd been when they'd finally arrived here, but her blood was up and a lot of her exhaustion had been chased away by her anger.

"Well, the Buchanan said ye were to do both or he'd leave," Tildy reminded her firmly.

Evina turned on her with dismay. "Surely he did no' mean that?"

The maid nodded solemnly. "I think he did. He said he has no desire to look after ye as well as yer father do ye make yerself ill, and I was to see ye ate and rested or he would leave."

"He acts as if he thinks he can order me about!" Evina snapped furiously.

"He can," Tildy said firmly. "Unless ye're willing to risk his leaving and no' tending yer father?"

Hands clenching at her sides, Evina growled under her breath, and turned to walk to the high table.

"That's me good lass," Tildy said with obvious relief. "Ye just relax a bit. I'll go order the bath fer yer father, and have food sent out to ye."

Evina dropped onto the bench at the high table with a disgusted mutter. She disliked being told what to do at the best of times, but being ordered about by the Buchanan just rubbed her nerves raw. No one had mentioned in the many tales about him that he was a dictatorial bastard. It was always about how wondrously skilled Rory Buchanan was, and how he was a miracle worker, snatching the ill and ailing back from the jaws of death, and returning them to health. He'd practically been painted a saint by those she'd spoken to, but Rory Buchanan was no damned saint. He was rude, mean, uncaring and thought so highly of himself he believed he had the right to order her around. To blackmail her into doing as he said.

"M'lady."

Evina glanced up to blink in surprise at the maid waiting for her to sit up so she could set down food and drink. It was only then that Evina realized she'd rested her elbows on the table to prop up her chin with her hands. Sighing, she sat back and smiled wearily as the woman set a trencher of beef and roasted vegetables, as well as a cider, before her.

"Do no' fret, m'lady," the maid said encouragingly. "The laird'll get well now the Buchanan is here. He'll be up and about in no time. Ye'll see."

"Aye," Evina said, forcing a smile. "I'm sure he will."

Beaming, the maid nodded and hurried away, leaving her to her meal.

Evina watched her go, and then glanced around the tables, noting the way the people of Maclean were casting glances both her way and toward the stairs leading up to the bedrooms where their laird lay in his sickbed. No one approached her though, and she was grateful for it. She wouldn't be good company just now anyway, Evina thought, her nose twitching as the scent of the food that had been set before her reached it. The beef smelled good. Delicious. Especially after more than two days with naught but oatcakes and apples eaten on horseback.

Sitting up a little straighter, Evina retrieved her *sgian-dubh*, pulled the trencher closer and began to eat.

Chapter 3

CONRAN LEANED FORWARD TO CHECK HIS PATIENT'S FOREHEAD again, and was rather proud to note that the fever, while still present, was much reduced. The Maclean was only a little warmer than he should be. The man's color was also better, his cheeks pink, but not as flushed as they'd been when he'd first seen Fearghas. Both were good signs and Conran hoped they meant that he'd got all the infected flesh when he'd cleaned the wound he'd found while bathing the old man in the cold bath he'd sent for.

He'd had Donnan and Gavin remain to help him bathe the man. It was as they'd stripped away his nightshirt that Conran had spotted the large, angry wound on the old laird's behind. It had been impossible to tell what had caused the infected, inflamed and oozing scabbed wound. Conran had asked about it, but neither soldier had seemed to know when or how their laird had suffered the injury.

Leaving the matter for the time being, Conran had concentrated on just submerging the Maclean in the cold water and keeping him there. Of course, the moment the water had closed around his overheated body, the man had begun to thrash and cry out as he tried to escape the cold.

Weak as Fearghas had appeared in his sickbed, it had taken the three of them to keep him in the water. But the effort had been worth it. The man had cooled relatively quickly, and then Conran had had the soldiers help get him out, dry him off and lay him on his stomach on the bed. Donnan and Gavin had then helped further by holding the old man still while Conran had cleaned the wound he'd noticed on his arse. Fortunately, he'd accompanied Rory on enough healing jaunts to know the unknown wound was probably the source of the man's fever, and that the infection needed to be cleaned out to bring it down permanently.

In the end, Conran had to cut out a large section of the man's arse to get it all. He'd then packed the wound as he'd seen Rory do with other patients, and bandaged it before covering the old man and letting him rest. That had been hours ago and Conran had been watching the man alone for most of that time. He'd released Donnan and Gavin to go have their sup and get some sleep after catching them yawning a time or two. He'd realized then that while he'd been unconscious and rested during the ride here from Buchanan, the two men had ridden straight through both ways and were no doubt as exhausted as their lady.

Now it was close to dawn. At least that was Conran's guess by a glance at the gray sky outside the open window shutters, and he found himself now yawning as weariness crept up on him. He was also hungry, Conran acknowledged with a frown, and glanced toward the door, wondering if there would be anyone up or around who could at least lead him to food, if not bring him some.

He slid his gaze back to Fearghas Maclean and leaned forward to feel his forehead again. Finding it little different than the last time he'd checked, Conran shifted impatiently and then stood and moved to the door. The old maid had offered to fetch him food before retiring, but he hadn't been hungry then. He was now.

Opening the bedchamber door, Conran started out into the hall and then paused as he noticed the woman on a pallet lying across the doorway. Lady Evina. She was sleeping as he'd insisted, but not in her room. Instead, she'd chosen a spot as close to her father as she could manage without entering his bedchamber.

Mouth softening, Conran peered at her silently for a moment, noting how small she really was. Considering the force she'd used in slamming her sword hilt into his head, he would have expected there to be more to her than the whip-thin figure he could see where this gown lovingly hugged her. But she was truly a petite little thing, he noted as he gave her the once-over.

Conran could see a resemblance to her father. Evina had her father's eyes and hair color. He'd noted the red threads of hair sprinkled among the gray on the father's head as he'd tended him. She also had his strong chin though, he saw now. But she must have got her slightly tipped nose from her mother. Fearghas had a much larger, hawkish nose. And her face was a soft oval with high cheekbones, while the Maclean's was long and lean and presently scruffy with several days' beard growth.

She was a beauty though, Conran acknowledged, letting his eyes slide again over her face and hair. She'd obviously taken a bath. Her face and her hands were clean. The pale, yellow gown she wore was as well, and the hair she'd had scraped tight back into a bun earlier presently fell in soft waves around her face, much as the hair of the woman in his dreams had.

Feeling his body responding to the memory of that rather lusty dream, Conran grimaced and quickly turned his gaze away from her to peer across the landing and over the rail at the great hall below. Much to his surprise, the room was a hive of activity with half the people up and moving quietly around, while the others were just stirring.

Apparently, it wasn't as early as he'd thought. The gray light he'd spied through the open shutters must be a result of a coming rain rather than the hour. On the bright side, that meant Cook should be up and about, and there would be something for him to eat.

Conran's gaze dropped to the woman again and he briefly debated what to do. He didn't wish to wake Evina, but didn't want to leave her lying there on her hard little pallet either.

Turning, Conran peered back into the laird's bedroom, considering the large bed the man was in. There was more than enough room for Evina to sleep there without it disturbing her father's rest, he decided, and it would certainly be more comfortable than sleeping on the hard floor.

Decision made, he bent to scoop her carefully and gently into his arms. Much to Conran's surprise, he managed the task without waking her. Letting out a little breath of relief, he held Evina close to his chest and straightened with her, then turned to walk to the bed.

All went well until he walked around to lay her next to her father. Conran was perhaps halfway up that side of the bed when he tripped over what felt like a discarded fur on the floor. Caught by surprise, he stumbled forward several steps, his arms tightening around his burden as he tried to keep his balance.

Despite Conran's best efforts, he couldn't save himself. The only thing he could do was throw himself toward the bed at the last moment, with the hope to at least give himself and the lass a softer landing than the floor would offer.

IT WAS SOMETHING PULLING TIGHT AROUND HER LEGS AND shoulders that drew Evina from sleep. Blinking her eyes open, she was just in time to note the Buchanan's face above hers, and his expression of alarm as they tumbled forward. She had no idea how she'd gotten into his arms, but didn't care in that moment. She simply threw her own arms around his shoulders and cried out as they fell toward the floor.

Evina was sure they were in for a hard landing, one she would take the brunt of, so was quite surprised when instead of the hard, wood floor slamming into her back and side, she landed on something softer. It gave under her weight, but then the Buchanan came down on top of her, his body pushing her deeper into the softness she'd landed on.

"Are ye all right?"

Evina opened eyes she hadn't realized she'd closed at that question and blinked in confusion at the Buchanan. While he'd pulled back slightly, the man was still resting on top of her, his face so close she could count the stubby hairs growing around his mouth. They outlined his full lips, and Evina was sufficiently distracted by those lips that she merely stared. They looked incredibly soft in comparison to the prickly stubble. But then Evina knew his lips were soft. She'd felt them when she'd blown air into his mouth after pulling him out of the water.

Absorbed by his lips and her thoughts, Evina didn't at first realize his mouth was lowering toward hers until it brushed gently across her own. She tightened up in surprise then, and shifted her hands from where they still grasped his shoulders. She moved them to his chest instead.

Evina did so with the intention of pushing him away, but her hands never pushed. Much to her surprise, they merely curled into the cloth of his plaid as the caress of his mouth on hers brought a bewildering rush of sensation and feelings clamoring up inside her.

He tasted of cider, Evina noted when his tongue pushed between her lips to explore her mouth. It was the last near-sensible thought she had. In fact, had she the ability to describe it, Evina would have said that at that point her brain disengaged altogether, overwhelmed by the excitement and desire that suddenly exploded to life inside her. She wasn't aware that her hands had begun tugging desperately at his plaid, or that little mewls of need and pleasure were sounding in her throat as she began to kiss him back, her mouth emulating his.

Evina felt one hand close over her breast through her gown and gasped into his mouth at the fire that went whipping through her body. She arched her back, instinctively pressing eagerly up into the caress. Conran responded to the silent invitation by finding her pebbling nipple and pinching it lightly through the cloth of her gown. When she cried out into his mouth in response, he ran his thumb over the hard bud again and again in what might have been meant as a soothing caress, but merely made her squirm and shudder under him.

The Buchanan groaned as her actions made their lower bodies rub together, and then ground down into her, his kiss becoming more demanding. Evina responded in kind, kissing him eagerly back, her hips pushing up in return. She wasn't at first aware that his free hand had snaked under her skirt and was gliding up her outer leg; it wasn't until it slid around and his palm pressed between her thighs that she became aware of it.

Evina broke their kiss on a gasp, and then glanced sharply toward the door as a knock sounded. She heard the Buchanan utter a soft oath, and then his weight was off of her. She turned to see that he was leaping to his feet next to the bed just as he grabbed her hand and pulled her up with him. Evina was on her feet so swiftly she was nearly dizzy, and then she whirled to stare wide-eyed at Tildy as the maid bustled into the room.

"Oh," the woman said, coming up short to peer at them with surprise, and then her eyes began to narrow and her body to stiffen.

"I was going to head below in search of food, and found Lady Maclean asleep on the floor outside the chamber door," the Buchanan explained calmly. "I thought to bring her in and let her sleep in here where she might be more comfortable. I even managed to pick her up without waking her. However, then I tripped over a fur and tumbled onto the bed with her once I got her inside." He offered a self-deprecating grimace and shrugged. "I fear I am not always the most coordinated member of me family."

"Oh." Tildy relaxed, a faint smile claiming her lips. "Well, that would explain m'lady's flustered and disheveled appearance," she commented with amusement, and then closed the door to move farther into the room. "No harm done though. Ye got lucky landing on the bed and no' the floor."

"Er . . . aye," the Buchanan said with a crooked smile.

"Shall I fetch ye food? Or would ye be wanting a break from the room and the chance to go below to eat at table?" Tildy asked as she stopped at the bed to peer down at Evina's father. Glancing up to the Buchanan, she added, "'Tis why I came. I thought ye must be hungry by now."

"I think I could do with a break," the Buchanan murmured, moving toward the door. "Thank ye."

Evina stood where she was, feeling bereft as she watched him go. Her body was still aching from his attention and craved more of it.

"Oh!"

Tearing her gaze away from the now-closed bedchamber door, Evina glanced to Tildy with alarm. "What is it?"

"Oh," Tildy repeated, more calmly, and pressed a hand to her chest as she shook her head. "Nothing. 'Tis just that for a moment I thought yer father's eyes were open and he was awake. But it must have been a trick o' the shadows in here. He's sound asleep still."

Evina glanced down at her father. His eyes were closed, his face in repose. Bending over him, she pressed a hand to his cheek, relieved to feel how much cooler he was. Good Lord, Rory Buchanan *was* a miracle worker. He'd only arrived the night before and her father was already improving, she thought, and then smiled when he moaned and turned his face into her caress. "Da?"

His eyes blinked open slowly and settled on her face. "Daughter?"

Evina winced at the rasp to his voice, but nodded. "Aye."

"I'll fetch him some mead to wet his whistle," Tildy murmured, hurrying for the door.

"How are ye feeling?" Evina asked, settling on the edge of the bed and watching him with a combination of worry and relief. He was awake. He was not fully recovered yet and was still ailing, but she never thought she'd see him even this well again.

"Better than I did yesterday," he growled, lifting one hand weakly before letting it drop back to the bed.

Evina took his hand in hers and squeezed gently.

Her father shifted restlessly, and then scowled and asked, "Who was the man trying to drown me in me bath?"

Evina frowned, a combination of concern and confusion rising within her at the question, and then understanding pushed the expression away, and answered, "Rory Buchanan. He was no' trying to drown ye. He was trying to cool ye off."

"The water was ice cold," he complained.

"Aye. Donnan told me the Buchanan said 'twas necessary to get yer temperature down," she said soothingly. "And it worked. Ye're much better today."

Her father grunted at the claim, and then asked, "How did he get here?"

"Who?" Evina stalled.

"The Buchanan," he growled impatiently. "Who do ye think?"

"Oh, aye," she muttered, and forced a smile as she admitted, "Well, I took Donnan and Gavin with me and fetched him."

"And he came willingly?" the Maclean asked, eyes narrowing as if he knew something about the way the man had got here.

Evina hesitated, several responses coming to mind, including the truth, but in the end, she simply said, "He is willing to help ye, Father,

and we are lucky he is. Tildy and I had tried all that we could think of
and nothing was working to get yer fever down. Yet he's achieved that
in one night."

"Hmm," he muttered, and shifted restlessly before asking, "And
where is he now?"

"Below, breaking his fast," she answered at once.

"By himself?"

She blinked at the question, surprised by it. "Well, aye. He's taking a
break and I am sitting with ye while he eats."

"Hmm," he grunted, and then narrowed his eyes and asked, "What is
he like?"

Evina sat back slightly, startled by the question. "He seems very . . .
competent," she finished finally because, really, she hadn't spent much
time with the man. At least, not while he was conscious. What she had
seen of him conscious, aside from that he was an amazing kisser, which
she would never tell her father, was that he was apparently well-hung.
That was something else she would never tell her father.

"And?" her father prodded.

"And what?" she asked uncertainly.

"Surely there is more to the man than his being competent," he said
with exasperation.

"Aye, well . . . he's bossy," Evina added, irritation beginning to prick
at her as she recalled his ordering her from her own father's room as if he
had a right to. She almost told her father that the man had bit her too, and
tried to drown Gavin, but that would mean explaining how he'd come to
be there, so she kept the information to herself. It didn't stop her from
thinking about it and getting irritated herself though.

"Hmm."

The sound drew her gaze to her father to see that he was eyeing her
closely.

"Well," he said finally, "even so, he should no' be left to eat on his own.
He's a guest here. Ye should go keep him company. Tildy can sit with me,"
he added before she could protest, and as if the sound of her name had
conjured her up, the bedchamber door opened and Tildy bustled back in
with the drink she'd gone to fetch.

"Go on," her father said, tugging his hand free of hers. "Keep the lad company, else he might feel unwelcome and leave ere he finishes healing me."

Evina peered from her father to the maid and back, but then sighed and stood. Her father had taught her that hospitality was important here in the inhospitable north of Scotland. Besides, if he was willing to put up with Tildy's company to get her to leave, he was serious about this. Her father usually avoided the maid like the plague.

"I'll come sit with ye again later," Evina murmured, heading for the door.

"While ye're down there, ask the Buchanan if the laird can have something to eat now he's awake," Tildy suggested. "I should have done it meself, but did no' think o' it until just now."

"Aye," Evina murmured, and stepped out of the room. She pulled the door quietly closed and then walked to the top of the stairs. With one hand on the rail, she looked down over the busy great hall until she spotted Rory Buchanan seated alone at the high table. One of the maids must have directed him there, she supposed.

Evina stared at him silently, her mind battling with itself. While part of her wanted to go below, throw herself at him and get him to give her some more of those kisses she'd enjoyed so much, the rest of her was horrified that she'd let him kiss her at all. She didn't even like the man, for heaven's sake. He'd tried to drown Gavin, and then he'd bit her, and yes, perhaps there were good explanations for those two things— well, at least the drowning-Gavin part, Evina supposed. She couldn't think of a good excuse for his biting her. But none of that mattered anyway, because there was no good excuse for his throwing her out of her own father's room last night. Or for the insulting way he'd done so. In her own home! And when she was so obviously worried sick about the man.

Nay. She didn't want to go anywhere near Rory Buchanan again. Unfortunately, her father had just ordered her to. She watched Donnan approach the man and knew that he was doing so only because the Buchanan was all alone. He was taking up her hostess duties in her absence, she acknowledged with shame, and started down the stairs.

"HOW'S HE DOING?"

Conran glanced to the large man who had just settled on the bench beside him.

Donnan. The Maclean's first. A huge bull of a man who he was coming to realize was as wise as he was big. A rare combination. Men of this soldier's size generally didn't have smarts to go along with their brawn. But this man had said and done a couple things while they'd worked at cooling down Fearghas last night that had made Conran think he might be an exception to that rule.

"Better," he said finally, realizing the soldier was still awaiting an answer. "He is no' out o' the woods yet, but his fever has gone down quite a bit."

"Good," Donnan said, relaxing slightly and glancing around before gesturing at a passing servant. The woman smiled and nodded as she flew by and Donnan returned his gaze to Conran. "How's yer head?"

"Oh." Conran raised a hand to feel the knot on the side of his forehead where Evina had slammed her sword hilt into him, and then to the one on the back of his head where he'd apparently hit it on falling off his horse. They both felt a little smaller than they'd been when he'd woken up here last evening. The aching, thankfully, had ended shortly after waking.

"Fine," Conran said finally. "I'm a fast healer."

Donnan nodded, and then suddenly said, "Lady Evina would no' have hit ye but she was worried about ye drowning Gavin."

"He's important to her, is he?" Conran asked, trying to sound uncaring, but aware that he was suffering a touch of a jealousy he really had no right to. He barely knew the woman.

"Everyone here at Maclean is important to Lady Evina," Donnan said solemnly.

"O' course," Conran murmured, relaxing, until the man continued.

"Although Gavin is mayhap a little more important than most. At least, she tends to favor him."

"Does she?" he asked grimly.

"Aye. But then there's good reason."

"I'm sure there is," Conran said dryly.

"He is her first cousin and she did raise him after his parents died," Donnan added.

Conran glanced at him with a start. "How could she have raised him? He's older than her, is he no'? He looks older."

Donnan grinned and shook his head. "Gavin's a big boy for his age, carries himself well, and his facial hair came in early, but the lad's only sixteen."

"Good God!" Conran said with true amazement. He would have guessed the boy was at least twenty-five. "How old was he when his parents died?"

"Two," Donnan answered.

"And Lady Evina was . . . ?"

"Ten."

The answer came from over Conran's left shoulder and in a woman's voice. He turned his head slowly, unsurprised to find Evina standing behind him.

Nodding a silent greeting, he let his gaze rove over her. There was still a hint of hectic color in her cheeks. From their tumble on the bed? He wanted to think so. Certainly, that was why her hair was mussed and her gown wrinkled. She looked like she'd just tumbled from bed, or been tumbled on one, Conran thought with an inner smile, and only wished they hadn't been interrupted. Although he supposed he should be grateful they had. Evina was a lady, the daughter of the laird here. She wasn't to be trifled with.

"I was ten when Gavin came to us," Evina added quietly now.

Realizing he'd been sitting there ogling her, Conran forced a polite smile to his face and commented, "That's young to take up mothering the lad."

Evina relaxed a little and shrugged. "Me own mother had died just weeks before. There was no one else to do it."

Conran felt his eyebrows raise at this news, but did the math. She was ten when Gavin came at the age of two. He was sixteen now, so Evina was twenty-four . . . and still unmarried. Why?

"Ah, here we are."

Conran glanced around at Donnan's words to see that the servant the man had gestured to earlier was pausing before them with a large platter in hand. It held pastries, cheese and fruit, he noted as a second woman appeared with two mugs and a pitcher of what appeared to be cider.

"Thank ye, lassies, but ye'd best fetch another mug for Lady Evina," Donnan said with a smile as the two women finished setting down their burdens and straightened.

"No mug," Evina said, moving to settle on the bench next to Conran. "I'll have mead instead, please, Sally."

"Aye, m'lady." The woman who had brought the cider bobbed a curtsy and the two women rushed off.

"Tell me, Lady Maclean, why are ye no' married?" Conran asked once the servants had moved away.

Evina had raised up off the bench to reach for a pastry on the tray when he'd asked that. She froze briefly at the question, he noted with interest, and then took a pastry and settled back in her seat before answering, "I have. I'm actually Lady MacPherson."

Conran blinked at the simple words, shock rolling through him. She was married. Dear God and he'd kissed her. She'd kissed him back too.

"The Buchanan says yer father is improved," Donnan commented into the silence that had fallen.

"Aye. His fever is down," Evina said easily as if she hadn't just sent Conran's world into chaos. Then she added, "And he's awake. In fact, I was to ask if he could have something to eat?"

Conran stared at her silently, his mind in an uproar. Not one of his thoughts was about her father though. His mind was full of her scent, and the feel and taste of her. Her excited gasps and mewls of sound were still ringing in his ears. He could still taste her on his tongue . . . and she was *married*.

"Broth perhaps, m'lord?" she asked, curiosity on her face now as she watched him.

Forcing his mind to her question, Conran sucked in a deep breath and turned toward the platter to grab a couple of pastries.

"Broth would be fine," he growled, standing up with the pastries he'd taken. "I'd appreciate yer asking yer cook to send it up. I need to go check on him now he's awake."

Conran didn't wait for a response, but headed for the stairs at a quick clip, his mind roaring. *She is married!*

He shouldn't care, Conran told himself firmly. He hardly knew her. She'd knocked him senseless, kidnapped him, dragged him here trussed up and naked . . . and she kissed like an angel. Or a whore, he supposed. There had been no holding back, no tentativeness to her. She'd opened for him like a flower, spreading her legs and writhing in his arms like a well-trained lightskirt . . . because she was well-skilled, he realized. She was married after all, and apparently free with her favors.

Christ! Where was her husband? Was she as free and easy with every man who visited Maclean? Perhaps he shouldn't complain. Perhaps he should just take her up on what she offered and bed the woman, scratch the itch that had been raised in him.

It wasn't the first time a married woman had offered herself to him. Conran had never accepted before. He believed in the sanctity of marriage. But he was tempted this time. Evina was a tasty little bundle and full of passion. He wanted to drink up that passion and bury himself in her eager body.

Just thinking about it had him hard as he mounted the stairs to her father's room. Conran wanted to strip her gown away and see those full soft breasts he'd touched through the cloth. He wanted to caress and suckle them, and he wanted to bury his face between her thighs and sip of her essence. He wanted her strong legs wrapped around his hips as he thrust into her, and then he wanted to flip her over and take her from behind, pulling her hair as he drove into her. Christ! He wanted her every way it was possible to take a woman.

An image came to mind of her on her knees taking him into her mouth, and Conran stopped at the top of the stairs, battling the urge to turn around, rush down, grab Evina by the hand and lead her someplace where they could do all those things. But then he gave his head a shake and forced himself to continue forward. She was a married woman, with a husband who wouldn't take kindly to his wife indulging in such things with another man. At least Conran wouldn't take kindly to her sleeping with someone else if she were his wife. Where the hell was her husband?

Away performing his service for the king, he supposed. Or perhaps off with some lover somewhere. Maybe there was a reason Evina had been so free with him. Mayhap her marriage was miserable and her husband neglected her.

Conran shook his head slightly. It didn't matter. She was married. He would do better to stay away from her while here. His conscience couldn't bear his trysting with a married woman when there were so many unmarried and available women out there willing to satisfy his needs. From now on, he would keep his distance from Lady Evina MacPherson, he told himself firmly . . . and just hoped that was something he could manage.

Chapter 4

"WHAT'S GOING ON BETWEEN YE AND ME DAUGHTER?"

Conran was reaching out to retrieve more bandages from the trunk he'd pulled over beside the bed when the Maclean asked that. The question startled him sufficiently that he dropped the wrappings on the floor. Cursing, he bent to pick them up and eyed the bits of dirt and pieces of rushes clinging to the formerly clean cloth. Conran tossed the soiled material aside with disgust and grabbed a clean one.

"Well?" Fearghas Maclean asked, sounding testy.

"What do ye mean?" Conran asked carefully. Nothing was going on between him and Evina. At least, nothing had gone on between them in the four days since he'd learned she was married. He'd been avoiding her like the plague since then. Fortunately, she appeared to be doing the same, making it easier for him to steer clear of the temptation she offered with her very presence.

"I ne'er see the two o' ye together," the Maclean growled, sounding annoyed. "She sits with me while ye eat, and leaves the minute ye return. 'Tis like ye're avoiding each other. Are ye still mad at her for kidnapping ye and dragging ye here?"

Conran sat back to peer toward the man's face, but since Fearghas was lying on his stomach in the bed with his head down, he couldn't see his expression. Narrowing his eyes, Conran asked, "Ye ken about that?"

"I was awake when they first brought ye up here," he admitted. "I heard everything. Well," he added, his voice wry, "most o' it anyway. I was a bit out o' me head at the time. The fever was doing me in. But I got enough to understand ye did no' come here willingly."

Conran remained silent for a moment and concentrated on packing the wound, but finally said, "I am no' angry about that. I do no' believe she intended to kidnap me." Well, certainly she hadn't intended to kidnap him, he thought. He wasn't Rory. But he didn't even think she'd planned to kidnap Rory. "'Twas just an unfortunate turn o' events that ended with me being knocked out, and carted here without their gaining my agreement first."

"Hmm," Fearghas muttered, and then asked, "So why are the two o' ye avoiding each other?"

"Where is her husband?" Conran asked instead of answering the question.

"Her what?" The Maclean reared up on the bed, pushing his chest up with his arms and turning to gape over his shoulder at him with amazement.

"Her husband," Conran said, his eyes narrowing suspiciously. "I asked why she was no' married and she said she was."

"Oh. Aye."

Conran caught the grief that flashed across the laird's face, but then the Maclean allowed himself to drop back to lay flat again with a sigh. A moment passed before he answered his question though.

"Her husband's dead."

The words were blunt and spoken in an empty voice that told Conran how much the loss had affected Fearghas Maclean. Conran stared at the back of the man's head, his thoughts in a mass of confusion. Part of him wanted to shout, "Yes!" at the news that Evina was widowed and so had not been messing about behind some poor husband's back when they'd kissed on this bed. The other part though was noting that Evina's husband had obviously been well-loved by his father-in-law, and he suspected that meant probably by Evina too. Was she still in mourning? How long ago had the husband died?

"He drowned some years back," Fearghas added sadly as if he'd asked the question aloud. "Long enough ago I forget some days that she was ever married. And then other days I can think of little else but what happened that day. 'Twas a terrible tragedy."

Conran returned to packing the man's wound, but his mind was filled with Evina. She wasn't married. She was widowed. Dear God, this changed everything. Being widowed was much better than just being unwed. It meant she was no innocent. She was a woman experienced in the bedchamber, and free to indulge in affairs if she wished. So long as they didn't flaunt the affair too much, no one would think twice about their having one. He could stop avoiding her and start wooing her instead.

A heavy sigh drew his attention back to his patient and Conran considered him briefly. The Maclean had obviously been brought low by thinking about Evina's husband's death. Which made him feel like a bit of an ass for being so grateful that she was widowed. Hoping to distract him, he asked, "Are ye going to tell me how ye came by yer wound?"

"What wound?" The Maclean glanced over his shoulder with befuddlement.

"The one I am presently tending to, m'laird. On yer left arse cheek," he said dryly as he packed the last bit of bandage into the large hole in the man's derriere.

Snorting, the Maclean turned his head away. "'Twas no wound. The only thing on me arse was a boil that's come and gone as it pleased for years."

"For years?" Conran asked with disbelief. "Why did ye ne'er tend to it?"

"Well, I could no' even see it being on me arse as it was, could I? How could I tend it?"

"Ye could have had Tildy lance it or—"

"Oh, hell, no!" Fearghas Maclean roared, interrupting him. "That lass has been trying to get a look at me arse for better than a decade. Since before me dear wife passed even. The hell if I was giving her an excuse to see and fondle me jiggly parts," he said with affront, and then added, "Besides, 'twas a bit o' bother when 'twas tender, but otherwise no' a problem."

"No' a problem," Conran muttered to himself with disgust, and then snapped, "It damned near killed ye, m'laird."

"What?" The Maclean glanced around with amazement and then shook his head. "Leave off. The fevers are what near killed me, no' a bloody boil."

"The boil was the reason fer the fevers," Conran growled impatiently. "Yer left butt cheek was so full o' infection and rot when I got here I had to cut half of it away. That infection is what caused the fevers. Ye're lucky it did no' kill ye."

"Ye jest!" he said, raising himself up to peer around with dismay. "All o' this from a blasted boil?"

"Aye," Conran said shortly.

"Well, hell," Fearghas Maclean muttered, and flopped back on the bed again. Heaving a sigh, he said, "'Tis good ye cut it out, then."

Shaking his head with exasperation, Conran continued his work, but then said, "I'm thinking I should send a message to Buchanan to let them ken where I am and that I'm well. They'll be worrying about me."

"Aye." A frown sounded in the Maclean's voice. "Well, we can no' have yer family fretting. Ye write a message and I'll have one o' the men carry it to Buchanan fer ye right quick."

Conran relaxed a little. He hadn't been treated like a prisoner, but the way he'd arrived had made him wonder if they would refuse to allow him to send a message to Buchanan. He hadn't really thought they would, but there had always been the chance. However, the Maclean was willing to send a messenger for him, so all was well.

He really should have thought to do so sooner than this though, Conran acknowledged. His brothers must be worried sick about him, he thought with a frown, and wondered if now was not the time that he should admit to the Maclean that he was actually Conran Buchanan, the fourth son, and not the sixth son and healer, Rory.

Considering how to broach the subject, he finished with the wound and then stood and moved to his saddlebag on the bedside table. Conran had intended to make another tonic for the man. One he'd made several times under Rory's instruction. His brother said it was to build a patient's blood and help them sleep, both of which could only aid in Maclean's healing, he assured himself. It wasn't that he'd planned to have the man sleep the afternoon away so that he'd be free to seduce his daughter.

Truly. However, when Conran got to the table and picked up the saddle-bag, it was empty.

"What the hell," he muttered, opening the bag and peering into its yawning depths.

"Oh, aye, I forgot to tell ye," Fearghas said behind him. "Tildy sent maids up to change me bed linens while ye were breaking yer fast this morn, and one o' them knocked yer bag over. Yer weeds all got mixed together and in the rushes, so she swept them up and put them in the fire so the dogs would no' eat anything that might make them sick."

"What dogs?" Conran asked with surprise. He hadn't seen one since arriving.

"*My* dogs," the Maclean said as if that should be obvious.

"I've seen no dogs since I got here," Conran explained his ignorance.

"They've been kept out in the bailey since I fell ill. But they usually sleep in here." Frowning slightly, he added, "They're probably following Evina around while I'm unavailable. Well, when she does no' come up here," he added.

Conran nodded and set the empty bag on the table, then began to rub the bridge of his nose between his thumb and forefinger as he pondered what to do about having lost all of Rory's weeds. Obviously, he needed to replace them, and quickly. The Maclean was on the mend and would survive without them, but Rory would need them. His brother was probably fretting up a storm over his disappearing without delivering them to Buchanan as he promised he would. That would have been the first telltale sign that all was not well and he had not left willingly.

"No' to worry though," the Maclean said now. "I've arranged to fix the problem."

Conran let his hand drop from his face and turned in question to the man. "How?"

Fearghas opened his mouth, and then paused and smiled as a tap sounded at the door. "I'll wager there's the answer now."

Curious, Conran turned toward the door as it opened, his eyebrows rising when Evina entered with a tray in hand and Gavin on her heels.

"THANK YE," EVINA MURMURED TO GAVIN AS HE OPENED THE door and held it for her. She took several steps into the room and then slowed when she noted that Conran was still with her father. Usually he was out and below at table by now, leaving the way clear for her to take her noon meal with her father. It was what he'd done the last four days since their encounter in this room. She'd just assumed he'd continue the practice, and when she'd noticed he wasn't at table yet as she'd carried the tray across the great hall, she had assumed he was simply in the garderobe or something. She'd been wrong.

Raising her chin, Evina continued forward and forced a smile to her lips. Keeping her tone light, she said, "They're serving the noon repast below, so I brought up lunch for Father." Focusing her gaze on her father only, she added, "We can eat together while Lord Buchanan goes below to take a break and enjoy his meal. As usual."

Evina winced as the last words slipped out. Even to her they sounded a bit snippy, almost accusatory, as if she were commenting on the fact that he was still there and she didn't like it.

"That's sweet, me dear, but there's going to be a change in routine today," Laird Maclean announced, sounding suspiciously cheerful, she thought, and wished she could see his expression. That was the one thing most annoying about his constantly lying on his stomach to avoid pressure on his bottom. She could never see his expressions when they talked, and they'd talked a lot the last few days. Mostly about the Buchanan. Her father was constantly asking her questions about the man, or telling her things about him. She had begun to suspect the man was up to something. She still did.

"What change in routine are we having?" Evina asked warily, stopping next to the bed with the tray.

"Our healer needs more weeds," her father announced. "Ye need to show him where to get them."

"What?" she asked with alarm. "But he had a whole saddlebag full of weeds. He—"

"I fear they were lost this morn when one of the lassies knocked it over while changing me bed linens," her father said, raising himself up so he could turn to look at her. "Unfortunately, they got mixed in with the rushes and had to be disposed of."

"But . . ." Evina turned a blank expression to him. "I was here when they changed the linens. I do no' recall—"

"I only noticed after ye left the room," he said easily. "I had the maid clean it up when she returned with me emptied and clean bedpan. Ye'd left by then," he added with a shrug, letting his head drop again. "Regardless, he ca no' heal without his medicinals, so ye'll have to take him out and help him hunt up more."

Evina frowned, and shifted on her feet. Avoiding looking at the Buchanan, she finally said, "Fine. I'm sure Gavin can take him out to—"

"Nonsense," her father interrupted at once. "The lad does no' ken the first thing about weeds and where to find them. Besides, I have another job for him."

"But . . ." She cast around desperately for an excuse, and then held up the tray. "What about the nooning meal? I was going to eat with ye and ye should no' be left alone—"

"Tildy can sit with me," he interrupted again.

"Tildy?" Evina said with amazement. Her father generally avoided any situation where he might have to be alone with the woman for more than a couple minutes. The maid had been mooning after him for years and her father acted like her affection might be infectious, avoiding her like she was a leper, and yet this was the second time he'd willingly arranged for her company.

"Aye. Tildy," the Maclean said firmly. "That way, ye can go without worrying." Apparently, thinking the situation was decided then, he lifted his head and turned to look at her cousin. "Gavin, go down and ask Cook to pack a lunch for yer cousin and the Buchanan. They can take it with them and eat as they hunt for medicinals."

"Aye, Uncle." Gavin headed out of the room at once, casting Evina an apologetic look as he went. He seemed to know she was not pleased with this turn of events.

"Rory, lad, why do ye no' go ask Donnan to speak to the stable master to arrange for yer and Evina's horses to be saddled," her father suggested now. "I'd have a word with me daughter."

"O' course." The Buchanan grabbed his empty saddlebag and turned to leave the room.

Evina frowned after him. The man had been smiling. She hadn't seen him smile in . . . well, she didn't think she'd actually seen him smile once since encountering him in the clearing five days ago. At least, his expression whenever he'd seen her the last four days had been hard and closed . . . ever since that kiss here in this room when she'd acted such a tart, she thought on a sigh.

"Evina."

Blinking her thoughts away, she glanced to her father uncertainly.

"Come. Set the tray down on the bedside table," he instructed solemnly.

Mouth tightening, Evina did as he ordered. She eased the tray onto the table, carefully pushing the few items on it across its surface with the tray itself until they all fit on it.

"Now, sit for a minute," he said when she'd finished the task.

Again, she did as he asked, but Evina eyed him warily. He was definitely up to something. She just had no idea what.

"I want ye to be on yer best behavior this afternoon," he said quietly.

Evina stiffened. "What do ye mean? I'm always on me best behavior," she muttered, wondering if he knew about the kiss.

"Are ye wearing braies under yer gown?"

That question caught her by surprise. "Aye. Why?"

"Because ladies do no' wear braies, ride astride or carry swords," he said grimly. "Take them off."

"What?" she asked with amazement.

"Ye heard me. Take them off. Right now," her father said firmly, and when she just stared at him, he raised himself up slightly and turned to scowl at her. "I'm closing me eyes and counting. The braies had best be on me bed by the time I reach ten and open them again." The Maclean then actually closed his eyes and began to count.

Evina stared at him blankly until he reached three, but then jumped up and quickly yanked her skirts up to reach her braies and tug them down and off.

"There," she snapped, letting her skirts drop and tossing the braies across the bed as he reached eight.

Her father opened his eyes and smiled when he shifted so that he could look around and see the braies on the end of the bed. "Good. Now the sword."

"The sword?" Evina asked, and started to shake her head. "I—"

"Ladies do no' carry swords around on their person," he said firmly. "Remove it and set it on the braies. Ye can have it back when ye return."

"A fat lot of good 'twill do me then," she snapped at once. "If ye're going to make me ride outside the bailey with him, that's when I'm most likely to need me sword. We could be attacked by bandits, or—"

"I'm sure Rory can protect ye against anything that might crop up," he said, unconcerned.

"Rory is a healer, no' a warrior," she said with disdain.

"And ye're a lady, no' a young lad," he snapped back, and then said slowly and firmly, "Ladies do no' carry swords. They are sweet, and gentle. They smile, and coo, plea prettily and compliment a man. *They do no' hit him in the head with the hilt of their sword and drag his naked arse back to my castle!*"

"He told ye," Evina whispered with dismay.

"Sword," he growled, pointing toward the braies on the bed.

Biting her lip, Evina removed her sword and set it carefully on the bed.

"He did no' tell me," her father said now. "I was awake and heard everything when ye arrived back and were arguing here in me chamber."

"Oh," she breathed, and then sucked in a mouthful of air and said defensively, "Ye were very sick at the time. Deathly so. I was just trying to get him back here to save ye."

"For what?" the Maclean asked dryly. "So I'd be healthy when his brothers came to kill us all for kidnapping one of their own?"

Evina's eyes widened incredulously. "I'm sure he will no' send for his brothers. He seems perfectly content helping ye. I have no' had to hold me sword to his throat to get him to do it or anything as I feared on the ride back. He—"

"O' course he's acting content," her father snapped. "He is alone in a strange castle, surrounded by strangers, all of whom are armed while he is no'. Did ye expect him to refuse to tend me, or tell ye he would complain to his brothers about his treatment? Only a fool would do that. Ye might kill him and bury him here so no one ever kenned what happened to him."

"I ne'er would!" Evina gasped with amazement.

"I ken that," her father said wearily. "But he does no'. The Buchanan does no' ken ye, lass. He kens none o' us. What do ye think he's been thinking while being kept here?"

"I . . ." Evina shook her head helplessly. She hadn't really thought much on how he might be feeling. They weren't keeping him prisoner with guards on him or anything. She'd assumed he understood that he was a guest, not a prisoner. Not that he wouldn't have been a prisoner had he refused to help her father. The truth was, she would have made him help her father at sword point had he refused at first. But he hadn't; he'd set to work on the man the moment he saw how ill he was.

"The Buchanans are becoming a very powerful family, lass," her father said solemnly. "The boys have been marrying into, and becoming lairds over, keeps with their own armies. If ye go up against one, ye'll find yerself dealing with all o' them, and all o' their soldiers. That would be the Buchanans, the Drummonds, the Carmichaels and the MacDonnells combined. And their friends the Sinclairs would no doubt join in any battle they took on as well. All those armies at once would crush Maclean . . . and Rory's asked to send a message to his family," her father told her unhappily before admitting, "I fear what he's going to say, but can hardly refuse to let him send a message else he *would* be a prisoner."

Evina's eyes had widened further and further with every word out of her father's mouth, until she was now gaping at him with horror. She truly hadn't considered the fact that the brothers had married into their own keeps complete with armies, or that they'd doubtless combine forces with the Buchanan army in any battle they took up.

"Where is his sword?" her father asked now.

"What?" She blinked at him in confusion, her mind still picturing a massive army under half a dozen flags, marching on Maclean.

"I presume Buchanan had a sword with him when ye found him?" her father said grimly.

"Oh, aye. I think so." Evina added that last bit because she wasn't at all sure. "If so, Donnan probably has it."

He nodded. "Then have Donnan fetch it and ye return it to the Buchanan ere ye leave the bailey."

Evina nodded, but then shifted restlessly and asked, "What if he rides off for home the minute he has his horse and sword back?"

"He will no'," her father said with certainty, which just rather confused her. He was suggesting the man thought himself a prisoner and would call up the Buchanans—all of the Buchanans under each family name—against them in retaliation. Why wouldn't the man then flee at the first opportunity to do just that?

"But if he thinks he's a prisoner here—" she began to argue the point.

"Ye're going to assure him he's no' a prisoner," her father interrupted firmly. "Say something soothing when ye give him the sword. Tell him that ye just forgot to give it to him ere this."

Evina smiled wryly at the suggestion. That was the truth after all.

"And then thank him prettily for taking such good care o' me. Tell him ye appreciate it dearly."

Also the truth, she thought.

"And try to give him a compliment or two. And smile," he added, looking her over with a testy frown. "And let yer hair down, lass. Go on, take it out o' that bun thing ye're always putting it up in."

"Why do I have to take it down?" Evina asked with bewilderment as she reached up to unpin her hair.

"Because ye're much prettier with it down. More womanly."

Evina paused with half the pins out to gape at him. "What does that matter?"

"Ye catch more flies with honey than vinegar, lass. We want the lad to like ye."

"What? Why?" she asked with disbelief.

"So he does no' call up the Buchanans and the Carmichaels, and the Drummonds and—"

"Yes, yes," she interrupted impatiently, going back to removing pins. If Rory was going to complain about being brought here and demand his family seek vengeance, her wearing her hair down rather than up wouldn't make a lick of difference, Evina was sure. But she also didn't think it was good to upset her father just now. He was still recovering from being deathly ill, and she was actually beginning to worry about his faculties. Rory had said did they not get the fever down his brains would boil . . . or had he said something about them turning to pudding? She wasn't sure; she'd heard it secondhand from Gavin after they came below that first night and she had been exhausted at the time. Perhaps he'd said both, but, whatever the case, she was beginning to think some damage had been done by the high fevers.

Evina's father never troubled himself with the goings-on at Maclean. He generally left that to her while he rode off to hunt or fish or visit with friends. But now he was involving himself. It was something she had been hoping for, for some time now. Unfortunately, he wasn't making any sense. He said Rory felt like a prisoner and might seek vengeance, but didn't worry about his leaving once he had his horse and sword. And he seemed to think that if she was just a little friendlier to the man, Rory would give up any idea of seeking vengeance on them. But her father knew she was no good at toadying to others. Just telling her to be nice to him guaranteed she'd inadvertently insult him the next timethey met.

Truly, she was growing very concerned about her father.

"Much better."

Evina grimaced at that compliment as she finished loosening her hair and quickly finger-brushed it away from her face.

"Ye're as lovely as yer mother was when I met her."

Evina frowned at the sadness in his voice, and then glanced toward the door as a knock sounded. As before, the person didn't wait for a welcome, but opened the door and they both watched Gavin enter, a sack in one hand and a rolled-up fur in the other.

"Cook put together a nice repast, and I grabbed a fur from by the fire below for them to eat their meal on," the lad announced, moving toward the bed.

"Good thinking, lad. Give them to Evina so she can go. The horses are probably saddled by now, and the Buchanan waiting."

Evina accepted the sack and rolled-up fur, and then frowned and glanced to her father.

"Go on," he said encouragingly, and when she turned to leave the room, he added, "And remember what I said, make him like ye."

"Make him like me," Evina muttered as she closed the door.

"Make who like ye, m'lady?"

Evina glanced around sharply at the question, and grimaced when she saw Tildy approaching up the hall.

"The Buchanan," she said wearily, heading for the stairs. "Father's sending me out to look for medicinals with Rory and wants me to be nice and make him like me so he will no' call up his brothers' armies to punish us for bringing him here."

"Oh, he would no' do that, I'm sure," Tildy said at once, falling into step beside her. "As fer making him like ye, that should no' be hard. I think he likes ye well enough already."

"The Buchanan?" she asked with amazement, and when Tildy nodded, Evina shook her head. "He's always cold and stern around me."

"Well, that's a man for ye, hiding their feelings and such. But he's always looking at ye when he thinks ye are no' looking back," she informed her lightly. "And that's a sure sign o' liking."

"Really?" Evina asked with interest as they reached the bottom of the stairs and headed for the great hall doors.

"Aye, but then ye do the same when ye think he is no' looking too," Tildy announced.

Evina flushed with embarrassment, but didn't comment. What could she say? She did look at the Buchanan when he was looking elsewhere. She couldn't help it. He was very handsome, and she kept remembering his kissing and touching her and . . . well, then she'd peer at him. Probably with a stupid longing-type look as she wished he'd kiss her again. There was no way she could explain that. It was beyond Evina how she could lust after a man she didn't even know, let alone like.

"If ye're going to be out hunting up weeds with the Buchanan, who's sitting with yer da?"

"Ye are," Evina said wryly.

"Really?" Tildy practically squealed, and Evina smiled with amusement. The woman was obviously pleased at the thought that he'd actually requested her presence again. Although Evina suspected her father hadn't really intended for the woman to sit with him. She didn't think he would have sent for Tildy once she was gone. But now he didn't have to. She'd done it for him.

"Aye, that's what he said," Evina assured her. "I took a meal up for the two of us and he said nay, he'd have it with you, as I was to go look for medicinals with the Buchanan."

"Oh, goodness," she said breathlessly, her cheeks flushing. "I'd best get up there, then."

"Aye," Evina agreed easily.

"Have a nice time looking for weeds," Tildy said excitedly, and turned to rush away.

Evina smiled with amusement at the thought of her father's consternation when Tildy showed up ready to eat with him. Her smile faded though when she reached the keep doors and she stared from it to her full hands. She was just shifting the fur and sack to free one hand when the door opened and Donnan started in.

"Oh, m'lady." He stopped just in time to avoid trampling her, and then glanced down to the items in her hands and reached to take them. "Let me get those fer ye, m'lady."

"Thank ye, Donnan, but first," she said, stepping back and out of reach. "Did the Buchanan have a sword with him when we came upon him in the clearing?"

Donnan's eyebrows rose in surprise at the question. "Aye. 'Twas strapped to his horse."

Evina relaxed a little. "Where is it now?"

"In yer father's room," he answered.

Evina sighed with exasperation. "Well, if he wants me to give it to him, then why did Father no' just give it to me instead o' telling me to ask ye for it?"

"I do no' think he kens 'tis there," Donnan said with a shrug. "I put it on the mantel in there the night we arrived with the Buchanan." Stepping inside, he let the door close and said, "I'll go fetch it at once."

"Thank ye," Evina murmured, moving to the side to get out of the way of anyone coming or going.

Donnan swept past her and hurried for the stairs. The man was fast on his feet. It seemed to her he hardly disappeared from the top of the stairs than he was coming back down them.

"I'll carry it," he offered as he approached and eyed the items she already held. "In fact, why do ye no' give me the fur too?"

Evina handed it over without protest. She'd only refused the first time because she'd needed him to fetch the sword, but the sack of food she held was quite heavy. If she were to judge it by weight, she'd have said the cook had packed enough food for a small army. Leaving the sword and fur to Donnan, Evina turned and opened the door for him, smiling when he slipped through with a chagrinned, "Thank ye."

"To the stables?" he asked as they started down the stairs to the bailey.

"Aye. Ye had the horses saddled?" she asked as they started that way.

Donnan nodded. "The Buchanan said yer father ordered it so the two o' ye could fetch more medicinals. I spoke to the stable master, and then left the Buchanan with him while I returned to the keep to speak with yer father."

"To be sure he truly did order it?" she guessed, unsurprised that he would check. He'd probably instructed the stable master and the men at the gates not to let Rory leave until he'd verified that he was allowed to.

"Aye," Donnan admitted, and then asked, "Ye're going beyond the castle walls?"

Evina could tell he obviously had qualms about the plan. She had a few of her own, but said, "Aye. Father insists I'm to take the Buchanan out to replace his weeds."

"Hmm," Donnan murmured.

"What's that mean?" Evina asked at once. She recognized his "hmm" as the sound he made when he thought he knew something others might not.

"Yer father has been asking me a lot of questions since his fever dropped," Donnan said quietly.

"About?" she asked warily.

"About ye . . . and the Buchanan," he responded.

"What kind of questions?" Evina asked, her feet slowing as she waited for the answer.

"Whether ye speak to each other or anything else when no' in the room with him," he admitted.

Evina frowned over that, but asked, "What did ye say?"

"That ye're ne'er in each other's company out o' his room that I ken of. That one is always with him and the other away. Ye do no' spend any time together apart from in passing when ye trade places at his side."

Evina nodded. What he said was true. She and the Buchanan didn't spend any time together outside the room, apart from in passing as one entered and one left. At least, they hadn't since that first morning when they'd fallen on the bed and he'd kissed her. But she had no idea why her father would ask such a question.

"Here we are."

Evina raised her head to see that they had nearly reached the Buchanan and the stable master. The two men stood outside the stables with her mare and his horse already saddled and waiting.

"Let me take that, m'lady," the stable master said, rushing forward to take the sack of food from her.

"Thank ye," Evina murmured, watching with interest as the Buchanan moved forward and took the fur, not the sword, from Donnan. Wondering if he hadn't recognized it, she took the sword from her father's first and thanked him for his assistance. As Donnan nodded and moved away, she turned to watch the Buchanan finish securing the first two items to his saddle. She'd expected at least one of them to go on her horse, but didn't mind if he wished to carry everything with him.

Of course, if he was planning to ride off now that he had his horse and sword, the food would certainly come in handy. Although he didn't yet have his sword, she recalled, and held it out when he'd finished securing the first two items and turned back to her.

"Ye forgot this."

The Buchanan eyed the sword briefly, but merely arched an eyebrow at her in question.

Shifting her feet uncomfortably, she explained, "It's been on the mantel in me father's room since ye arrived."

"I did see it there," he admitted.

"Aye, well, ye forgot it when ye came out here, so Donnan fetched it down for me to give to ye," she said lightly.

The Buchanan arched his other eyebrow at that. "Will I need it?"

Several answers came to mind. *Ye will if ye plan on riding off back home*, or *That depends on what yer plans are*, but she settled on simply saying, "One can ne'er be too careful when leaving the safety o' the castle."

Nodding solemnly, he took the sword and slid it through the belt around his waist. Raising his head then, he asked, "Then why are ye without yers today?"

"Good question. Ask me father," Evina muttered as she swung away to walk to her mount. Reaching her mare, Evina grabbed the pommel and started to raise a foot to the stirrup to mount, and then froze.

"Is something amiss, m'lady? Do ye need a leg up?" the stable master asked, hurrying to her side with surprise on his face. She hadn't needed a leg up since she was a child. Evina hated asking for help, so had learned quickly to manage things on her own.

"Nay, a sidesaddle," Evina said finally on a sigh, lowering her foot from the stirrup. There was no way she could ride astride without braies on.

"A sidesaddle?" the stable master echoed with bewilderment. "I do no' think we have one."

"Surely me mother rode sidesaddle when she was alive?" she asked with a frown.

"Oh, aye!" The man brightened. "I'll go fetch it."

"I gather ye usually ride astride," the Buchanan commented as the stable master rushed off.

Evina turned to peer at him, unsurprised to see that he was already mounted. He would have done so when she moved to mount her mare. "Aye."

"Why sidesaddle today, then?" he asked with curiosity.

"Because Father insisted," she admitted.

"Why?" he asked with surprise.

Evina shook her head, and then asked, "Do ye think 'tis possible he suffered some damage to his head from the fevers? Gavin said ye did say he could did the fever get too high."

The Buchanan's eyebrows rose at the question, but he considered it briefly, and then nodded. "'Tis possible, but I have no' seen any sign o' it."

"Ye do no' ken him though, and might no' notice right away," she pointed out.

"True," he agreed with a faint smile.

"Here we are. 'Tis a little dusty, but—Oh, hell!"

Evina glanced to the side just in time to see the stirrup strap the stable master had in one hand snap. The man managed to hold on to the saddle for a moment with his other hand, but then it slid to the ground.

"It has no' been used in years. I guess the leather is in bad shape," the stable master muttered, bending to pick up the damaged saddle.

"Ne'er mind. Lady Evina can ride with me," the Buchanan announced.

"Oh, nay, I—" Evina's protest died on a gasp as his arm suddenly snaked around her waist from behind and she was lifted up onto the saddle before him.

"Hold on," the Buchanan ordered, and immediately turned his mount and urged it toward the bridge out of Maclean . . . at speed. So far, this trip wasn't going at all to plan, Evina thought with dismay as they charged out of the bailey.

Chapter 5

"THAT SHOULD BE GOOD ENOUGH, AND THIS SEEMS A NICE spot. Why do we no' stop and eat now?"

Evina straightened slowly from the horehound she'd been gathering. She rubbed her lower back as she glanced from the bulging saddlebag the Buchanan was carrying to the clearing they were standing on the edge of.

"Aye," she said on a weary sigh, more than ready to rest if not eat. After the exciting start of his dragging her up on his horse and charging out of the bailey, their trip had calmed down considerably. The minute they were away from the keep, he'd slowed his horse and asked where he should go. He'd followed her directions, and before long they'd both been off the horse, gathering the weeds and wild herbs he needed for healing.

Some of the plants they'd gathered were ones they had in the garden at Maclean. Evina had told him as much and offered for him to take what he liked from there, but he'd said, "Why pilfer the gardens when they are growing wild out here? The ones in the garden might be needed later," he'd pointed out, "and the ones in the wild would just wither away unused."

Evina had shrugged and gathered what he wanted. Now his saddlebag was full to bursting again and she was exhausted. It felt like they'd been walking the woods and fields for a full day gathering herbs and weeds, although they had probably only been at it for a little over two hours.

"Tired?" the Buchanan asked sympathetically as he slung his saddlebag over his horse's back.

"Aye," Evina said simply as he gathered his horse's reins and moved toward her. She could play at swords for hours in the practice field with the men, but harvesting plants was backbreaking work her body was unused to, using different muscles than fighting did. Not having had the nooning meal yet probably didn't help either, she supposed.

"The middle o' the clearing looks a likely spot for our meal," he suggested after pausing beside her to glance around.

Evina nodded silently, uncaring where they sat so long as they sat.

"Here." The word was her only warning, and not really much of one, Evina decided as he suddenly clasped her by the waist and tossed her up onto his horse. Grabbing the pommel to keep from sliding off, she peered at him wide-eyed, and he grinned. "Ye're done in. Just rest on me mount and I'll walk ye out to the middle o' the clearing."

Evina forced herself to relax, and settled more comfortably in the saddle as he led the horse. It was a much longer distance than she'd initially thought, and she was grateful for his kindness by the time they reached the desired spot.

"Here we are," he said cheerfully, lifting her off the horse moments later.

"Thank ye," Evina murmured, turning to unhitch the sack of food from the saddle as he grabbed the fur and quickly unrolled it on the ground. She swung back just in time to see him remove his sword from his waist and lay it on the fur. They then both dropped to sit on it, and Evina glanced around as she set the bag down in front of her. Seated as they were, she couldn't see over the tall grasses unless she craned her head, she noted, and smiled faintly as it stirred old memories.

"What's brought on that smile?" the Buchanan asked with interest.

Evina shrugged, and turned her attention to opening the sack of food. "This spot reminds me o' me brother, Daniel. He used to like to play in places like this—high grass we could creep through and hide from each other in, then leap out and scare each other. 'Twas usually war games," she explained.

"Ye have a brother?" the Buchanan asked with surprise. "Yer father's ne'er mentioned him."

"He would no'. Daniel died when I was eight," she said softly. "I do no' think Father ever truly got over it."

"I'm sorry," he murmured, and then asked, "How did he die?"

Evina shrugged and began pulling out the food Cook had packed: a roasted pork leg, bread, cheese, boiled eggs, cold boiled potatoes, custard, cherries, a skin of wine and two mugs. Closing the bag once it was empty, she set it aside and finally said, "I'm no' sure. I was little. He got sick. Healers were brought in. Mother prayed until her knees were bleeding from kneeling, but . . ." She shrugged again. "We lost him."

"So yer brother died when ye were eight, yer mother when ye were ten . . ." He hesitated and then said, "And ye raised Gavin from two on."

"Aye." Evina smiled faintly at the thought of her cousin. He'd been such an adorable little boy. All rosy cheeks and childish laughter. He'd brought sunshine and happiness back to Maclean after weeks of dark misery and mourning. If nothing else, she would always love him for that. Sighing, she watched the Buchanan use a *sgian-dubh* to carve hunks of meat off the pork leg, and asked, "What about you? Father mentioned ye have brothers?"

"Aye. Six of them now," he announced, and passed her a hunk of meat on the end of his knife.

"Now?" she asked quietly as she tugged the bit of meat off the *sgian-dubh*.

"There used to be eight of us boys," he explained quietly. "But Ewan, the younger twin of our eldest brother, Aulay, died some years back. In battle."

"I'm sorry," Evina murmured.

The Buchanan nodded, but said, "We have a sister too. Saidh."

He stopped talking to take a bite of meat, and they both fell silent for a bit to concentrate on eating. While Evina hadn't been much interested in food when he'd first suggested stopping, she found herself starved now that they were sitting and the food was laid out. They made a good effort at putting away everything Cook had packed for them, and had turned their attention to the custard and cherries when the Buchanan asked, "So why did yer father no' wish ye to wear braies and ride astride today?"

Evina took a moment to readjust her mind from the food to conversation. She spent another minute trying to think of an excuse that sounded likely, and then just settled for the truth. It was always easier to go with the truth. No lies to have to remember.

"He thinks 'twill make ye like me more if I'm more ladylike and agreeable," she admitted, and wasn't terribly surprised when he stiffened, his eyes widening and then narrowing suspiciously.

"Why would he want that?"

"Because he's worried about the message ye want to send to yer family," she admitted. "He's hoping if ye like us ye'll be less likely to complain to yer brothers about being kidnapped and will no' have them lay siege to Maclean to claim recompense," she said dryly.

The shout of laughter that burst from him startled her slightly, but Evina smiled faintly as she watched him. He had a nice laugh, and his face was positively gorgeous lit up with humor as it presently was.

"But I was no' kidnapped," he said once his laughter faded, and then reminded her of her own words when he added, "Ye merely took me because ye felt it unsafe to leave a handsome bastard like meself naked and unconscious in the clearing on me own."

"I ne'er said handsome," she protested at once, flushing.

"So ye do no' find me handsome?" he asked with a wounded expression.

"Well, aye, but—" Evina began with confusion, then cut herself off and scowled at him for tricking her into admitting as much when a grin replaced his feigned upset.

"But?" the Buchanan queried with a crooked smile.

"But ye're bossy and cranky as old boots too," she ended, her eyes narrowed.

"Are old boots cranky?" he asked with obvious amusement.

Evina scowled at him and reached for a cherry, but he grabbed the hollowed-out bread loaf Cook had set them in and pulled them out of her reach. Grinning at her consternation, he plucked one up by the stem and held it out toward her.

"Nah-ah," he said when she reached for it. "Open yer mouth."

Evina narrowed her eyes on him, but then her gaze slid to the cherry. It looked ever so succulent and sweet dangling there, the color a red so dark it was almost black. After a hesitation, she leaned forward and opened her mouth. When he lowered the cherry between her lips, she closed them and tugged, leaving him with the stem.

The Buchanan watched her with a smile and then popped a cherry into his own mouth and said quietly, "The message I want to send home is no' to complain about the manner in which I came to be here."

"Nay?" Evina asked, her suspicion plain.

"Nay," he assured her. "While that was unfortunate, once here at Maclean I am the one who agreed to stay. No one made me, and I'm no' a prisoner, so I've naught to complain about," he assured her. "I wish only to let them ken where I am and that I'm well."

"Oh," Evina murmured, frowning as she considered how worried they must be. He'd just disappeared as far as they knew.

"So ye need no' be especially nice or try to make me like ye," he said with amusement.

"Good," Evina said with relief, relaxing back on the fur.

"Would it have been such a trial to try to be nice to me?" he asked with curiosity.

"Aye," Evina assured him, and then realizing how that sounded explained, "I'm no' very good at that sort of thing. If I'm told to be nice to someone, I tend to do the opposite by accident."

"By accident?" he asked with interest, and when she nodded, he raised his eyebrows. "How does that work?"

"I do no' ken," Evina admitted on a sigh. "I just get tense and tongue-tied, and usually end up insulting the person somehow."

"So, if yer father told ye to be unkind to someone, would the opposite be true? Would ye then find it hard no' to be nice to them?" he queried with amusement.

Evina smiled faintly at the question, and shrugged. "I do no' ken. He's ne'er asked me to be unkind to anyone."

"Hmm." He was silent for a minute and then asked, "How kind were ye supposed to be to me?"

Evina eyed the innocent expression he was giving her dubiously, and assured him, "No' *that* kind. I'm his daughter, no' the local lightskirt. If that's what he'd wanted he'd have sent Betsy to yer room."

"I do no' have a room," he reminded her. "I've been sleeping on a pallet in yer father's room to stay close by in case he needs me."

"Oh, aye." Evina frowned slightly, and then assured him, "I'll see to arranging a room for ye when we get back. Father's well enough I should no' think ye need stay in his room at night anymore."

"Thank ye," he murmured, and then grinned and added, "But do no' feel ye need send Betsy to me. Me tastes run more to prickly beauties with red hair, than blond amazons with large . . . lungs," he finished delicately.

Evina blushed at the compliment and then blinked and speared him with a look. "How did ye ken Betsy was a blond amazon?"

Conran shrugged and grinned. "She already offered herself to me."

"She did no'!" Evina said with amazement.

"Aye, she did," he said. "The first night I went below for sup. She offered to be dessert."

"She did no'!" Evina gasped out again.

"She did," he assured her. "But as I said, I've found I prefer red-haired beauties, so I refused her kind offer."

Evina stared at him uncertainly, unsure how she was supposed to respond to that. She had red hair, but didn't consider herself a beauty, and he'd been so stilted and cold around her since that kiss in her father's room . . . She wasn't sure why he was suddenly so relaxed and easygoing with her.

"I thought ye were married."

He spoke the words so softly Evina almost missed them. She tilted her head with confusion. "I was. I told ye that."

"Aye. But I did no' realize ye were also widowed," he explained solemnly. "I thought ye were married still. And that ye kissed me despite having a husband."

"I would no' do that!" she cried with dismay, sitting up straight. "Besides, I did no' kiss ye, ye kissed me," she added quickly, feeling her face heat up with a combination of embarrassment and something else as she recalled the kiss in question.

"Aye, I did. But ye kissed back," he responded, and Evina blinked as his breath brushed over her cheeks and lips. How had he moved closer without her noticing? He was just inches away now. Close enough to—

Evina stiffened in surprise when his hand suddenly slid around her neck, his fingers driving up through the hair at the back of her head to cup her scalp. That's all. He just cupped her head and met her gaze. He continued. "But now that I ken ye're widowed and would no' be being unfaithful, I'd really like to kiss ye again."

"Please." Evina had no idea where the word came from. Her brain didn't send it out. It was like her body had a mind of its own. Or at least her lips did, since they whispered the word. It didn't matter though. She'd said it, and that was that. The hand at the back of her head pulled, his face came closer and huzzah! His lips were on hers, and it was as wonderful as the last time.

With pleasure and need rushing through her, Evina opened to him, drinking in the taste of cherries as his tongue slid in. Passion infused her and her body responded as if it had been sleeping for years and was being brought back to life, softening and pressing into him.

At first, the Buchanan merely kissed her, his lips and tongue dancing with hers, his head slanting one way and then the other, until she was moaning and pressing even closer, her arms creeping around his shoulders.

Evina wasn't sure afterward if he lifted her into his lap, or she crawled there herself; she just knew she was desperate to be closer to him and suddenly was. Straddling him on the furs, she ran her hands into his hair, and kissed him desperately, and then gasped into his mouth when he clasped her bottom through the cloth of her gown and shifted her closer, until his hardness was pressing where it could do the most good.

Holding her tightly there with one hand, the Buchanan suddenly let his other drift up to cover one breast. Evina moaned with pleasure in response, and arched eagerly into the caress even as his hand urged her tighter against his hardness.

"Aye," the Buchanan growled as he tore his mouth away, and then he pressed kisses across her cheek to her neck, and Evina gasped and tilted her head. She felt him tugging at the neckline of her gown, and the next thing she knew the cloth suddenly fell off her shoulder, leaving one breast bare. Some part of her mind was shocked, but then his cool hand closed over the warm flesh of one breast and Evina couldn't stop her moan of pleasure.

The Buchanan nipped at her neck in response, and then urged her back slightly. Evina glanced down then, and bit her lip as she saw the darker skin of his suntanned hand on the lily-white skin of the breast he'd bared. Her gaze shifted when he then tugged the top of her gown lower to reveal the second breast, and she instinctively arched, her lower body rubbing against his as he claimed that breast with his other hand too.

"Beautiful," he growled, squeezing and massaging her flesh until her nipples tightened to two hard points. He then bent his head and claimed one of those points, drawing it into his mouth and teasing it with his tongue until she was writhing in his lap.

"M'lord, please," she gasped, her nails digging into the tops of his shoulders. Evina had no idea what she was begging for until one of his hands dropped away and down, only to slide up under her skirts. She was vaguely aware of it drifting up her thigh, but there was so much going on she wasn't really sure of what he was doing until his fingers glided across the damp flesh at her core.

Evina cried out in shock and froze, until his fingers began to circle and move back and forth over an area that had never been touched before. She began to shake and shudder then, her body responding despite her shock, and then her hips began to move, her body chasing his teasing caress and the mounting excitement building in her.

She was vaguely aware of crying out, and murmuring insensible nonsense, but mostly she was clutching his shoulders, and striving toward something she didn't understand. And then he nipped lightly at the nipple he'd been laving, and something pushed up into her, breaking some tiny thread of need and making her scream and shudder and clench around his hand as her body began to convulse. That's when he removed his hand, clasped her hips to shift her slightly and brought her down so that something much larger than his fingers pushed up into her, splitting her in half.

Evina's pleasure ended on a startled shriek of pain, and her eyes opened in shock as she realized what had just happened. He was inside of her. He'd taken her maiden's veil. How had it happened? How could it have been so easy and fast? All he'd done was kiss and touch her. She still had her gown on, for heaven's sake. And he wore his plaid. It shouldn't be this easy.

She was awash with so much shock and confusion that it took Evina a moment to realize that she wasn't the only one who had stilled. The Buchanan too had frozen and, after a moment, pulled back slightly, leaning his upper body away from hers. Aware that he was looking at her, Evina forced her eyes open, and met his gaze.

"But ye were married," he said with amazement.

Evina merely stared at him, incapable of explaining anything just then. She'd just lost her innocence. She was still perched on his cock, for God's sake. And all that pleasure she'd chased and so briefly enjoyed was completely gone now, replaced with confusion, fear and regret. Not to mention a sharp pain between her legs that was most unpleasant.

"Ye're shaking," he muttered, suddenly with concern. "Do no' cry. 'Tis all right."

Evina blinked, realizing only then that yes, indeed, tears were leaking from her eyes. And she *was* trembling. Good Lord, she never cried, and this was certainly no time to act like a ninny, she told herself grimly. So, she'd lost her innocence? She hadn't been saving it for anyone anyway, Evina reminded herself. She'd already been married and widowed, and her father had promised she could remain unwed and run Maclean until her dying days and then leave it to Gavin. That was the plan.

This was fine, Evina assured herself. She'd experienced the bedding, learned that she wasn't missing a thing and could now live out the rest of her days knowing she hadn't lost out on much by not marrying. Their priest had always said the marriage bed was a trial the woman had to suffer to pay for Eve's misdeeds. Now she knew it to be true. While she'd experienced a very brief pleasure, it certainly was not worth the pain she was now suffering. Good Lord, had he used his manhood, or was it his sword he'd shoved up inside her?

"Perhaps . . ." the Buchanan began uncertainly, and then paused and shifted slightly to peer past her.

"What is it?" Evina asked, glancing over her shoulder. Sitting on top of him as she was, Evina was high enough to see over the grass, but she didn't see anything alarming.

"I thought I saw—" He broke off with a curse just as pain punched through her back.

Suddenly gasping for breath, Evina turned back to him with alarm, and then followed his horrified gaze down to her chest. Much to her bewilderment there was a bloody arrow tip sticking out of her breast, she saw, and then the Buchanan was tumbling them both sideways to the ground.

Evina landed on her side with a grunt, and took a minute to catch her breath, but she didn't seem to be able to. Frowning, she opened her eyes to look at Rory, but he was gone. Confused, she glanced around and spotted his feet. They were moving, and there was another pair of feet there, she noted, and then heard the clang of metal against metal and followed the sound up to see that he was in a sword fight with someone.

He wasn't half-bad, Evina decided after watching him for a minute. Impressive even, she thought as another man came into view and she realized he was fighting two at once. Not just a healer after all, she acknowledged, and then found her eyes closing.

Evina blinked them open what she thought was a mere moment later, but it must have been longer than that, because the two men Buchanan had been fighting were now lying unmoving on the ground near her, and the Buchanan was fighting a different man. And there were two other men battling right beside them, she saw. One of them was—

"Gavin!" Evina cried with alarm as the man her cousin was battling caught him in the arm with his sword tip. She'd meant to scream, but didn't have the air to manage it. Her voice was barely conversation level. Still, it was enough to make the men stop fighting briefly and glance her way. Evina stared at Gavin's startled and pain-filled face and shook her head. He couldn't be there. This had to be a dream, she decided as her eyes closed again.

The next time her eyes opened, the world was rushing past to the sound of drumming hooves, and the Buchanan was holding her tight to his chest, saying, "Hold on, Evi. We're almost there."

She wanted to ask almost where? Evina also wanted to ask if it had really been Gavin she'd seen, and if he was all right, but her eyes closed again before she could get the words out.

Chapter 6

"*H*ow is she?"

Conran glanced up from a sleeping Evina at that question, and watched as Fearghas Maclean hobbled into the room. While the man was up on his feet, walking obviously pained him. But then, half his derriere was missing and just starting to heal. He would be hobbling for a while, Conran thought absently, and then realized the man was waiting anxiously for an answer.

He shifted his grim gaze back to Evina. Conran had helped Rory clean similar wounds before. Still, he'd wished the other man was here for this one. He'd been very worried he might make a mistake and do her more damage than good. However, everyone had been looking to him to handle it, and that certainly hadn't been the moment to admit that he was not the great healer Rory Buchanan. He'd done the best he could, but it had been slow, grueling work.

"I removed the arrow, and cleaned and closed the wound," he said on a weary sigh, and then shook his head with wonder as he added, "I do no' ken why, mayhap 'twas the position of the arrow, but she did no' lose as much blood as I would have expected. I think she'll be all right."

"Thank God," Fearghas murmured as he reached the bed and dropped to perch his uninjured butt cheek on the side of it. Brushing a strand of hair away from his daughter's face, he muttered, "I should have let her take her sword."

"She ne'er would have got to use her sword, and 'twould no' have prevented her taking the arrow. That was our first warning there was anything amiss," Conran told him quietly.

"Aye, o' course," he said unhappily.

"How is Gavin?" Conran asked, sitting back in his chair.

"His arm is sore, but he'll be fine. I sent him to find his bed," the Maclean murmured. "Tildy cleaned and sewed his wound while ye were busy with Evina. The maid is good with wounds," he added. "But perhaps ye could take a look when he wakes up to make sure all is well though."

Conran smiled wryly, thinking the woman had probably handled more of such wounds than him, but he could hardly say so, and merely nodded. "O' course."

"Thank ye," Fearghas said quietly. "And thank ye for today."

"Today?" Conran asked, unsure what he meant. He'd already thanked him for tending Evina's wound.

"For what ye did in the glen," the Maclean explained. "Gavin said ye were very good with a sword, and took out two of the men yerself almost ere he could get there to help ye."

"Oh, aye," Conran murmured, and then frowned and asked, "What was Gavin doing there?" He'd been more than a little surprised when the man had appeared out of nowhere to help him with the bandits that had beset them.

The Maclean just shook his head, and caressed Evina's cheek. "He and Evina are all I have o' true value in this world and I nearly lost them today."

They were both silent for a minute and then Fearghas glanced to him and suggested, "Why do ye no' go have something to eat and then find yer bed too? Ye've missed a lot o' sleep o' late tending to me. I'll look after her. Ye need yer rest."

Conran hesitated. He'd rather stay and watch over Evina, but he *was* tired . . . and food would not go amiss. Still—

"Evina's marriage to the MacPherson?" he said abruptly, and then paused, unsure how to proceed. He wanted to know how she could possibly have been married and never bedded. How she had retained her maiden's veil. But he could hardly ask outright without revealing how he'd discovered she'd still had her maiden's veil, and that he'd taken it in the clearing before they were attacked.

"What about it?" Fearghas asked. "I told ye she was married and he died."

"Aye." Conran frowned.

"MacPherson," the Maclean murmured now, and shook his head. "She's carried the name since she was wed at ten, but that's something I forget too. I still think of her as Maclean like me," he admitted, his lips twisting. "She'll always be Evina Maclean to me."

Conran glanced to him sharply and asked with disbelief, "Ten? She was married at ten years old?"

"'Twas in name only," Fearghas said, waving away his outrage.

Conran raised his eyebrows.

"Me son had died two years earlier," he explained. "It left Evina as me only heir, which meant her husband would rule Maclean when I died. She'd been betrothed to the MacPherson's second oldest boy, Collin, since birth. So, when he reached the age where he would be sent away for training, I wanted him to take that training here at Maclean. I was hoping 'twould allow him to get to ken the people, and how Maclean works," he explained. "So that our people would have his loyalty once he took over."

"Smart," Conran murmured when the man paused briefly.

"I thought so at the time, but that fine idea gained me nothing and cost me much in the end," the Maclean said wearily, and scrubbed one hand over his wrinkled face. "Anyway, the MacPherson was fine with that, but he was ailing and did no' expect to see the end of the year. He wanted the wedding to take place while he was still alive to see it, so part of the deal for Collin to come to Maclean was that the two should marry first. At MacPherson."

"But if Evina was only ten . . ." Conran frowned and pointed out, "The legal age for a lass to marry is twelve."

"Aye." Fearghas nodded. "We had to get special permission from the king and the church. 'Twas allowed with the proviso that the wedding was no' to be consummated until she turned twelve."

"But the MacPherson lad did no' live that long," Conran guessed. He hadn't been mistaken. He'd definitely taken Evina's innocence. Dear

God. And he hadn't done it gently. Had he known, he would have gone more slowly, prepared her better and—What was he thinking? Had he known she was an innocent, he would have let her be. Good God! He'd taken her innocence!

"How did ye ken the MacPherson boy died ere consummating the marriage?" the Maclean asked, one eyebrow arched.

Conran stiffened and then shook his head helplessly. He had no answer he was willing to give and didn't have the wit at that moment to come up with a lie.

Fortunately, the Maclean didn't press him. Instead, he said, "Aye. He drowned just days after the wedding. On the journey back to Maclean, in fact. He ne'er even saw the home I hoped he'd rule."

"So, he died on the ride home after they were married . . . when she was ten?" Conran asked with a frown.

"Aye," the Maclean murmured.

"But . . . did Evina's mother no' die when she was ten too?" he asked, and then answered himself. "Aye, I was told Evina was ten when Gavin came here just weeks after her mother died."

"Aye, me dear wife died trying to save the MacPherson lad," the Maclean said solemnly, and then explained, "We left MacPherson the day after the ceremony and celebrations. All was well the first day and night of travel, but on the second night we made camp by a fast-moving river. 'Twas known to be dangerous, but no one intended to bathe there so we felt 'twould be safe enough. Unfortunately, the boy slipped and fell in while trying to gather water. The current caught him and dragged him under. Mairi, me wife, rushed in to try to save him before we could stop her, and Lachlan, me first at the time, went in after them both, and they all went under. We found their bodies upriver the next day. 'Twas a terrible tragedy."

Conran shook his head and breathed out a sigh. It *had* been a tragedy. The Maclean had lost his wife, and Evina had lost both her mother and husband at the same time. Although he suspected the loss of the husband would not have been as crushing. She probably hadn't even met him ere the wedding and had only known him a day or two.

"I'm surprised the marriage was no' dissolved," he commented after a moment of silence had passed. "'Twas no' consummated after all."

Fearghas grimaced and nodded. "Aye. The MacPhersons were understandably upset at the loss o' their son, and blamed us for it. They petitioned to have the marriage annulled and the coin they'd given as a wedding gift returned, but the king refused. He said both sides lost a loved one in the incident, and while the marriage had no' been consummated 'twas no' from lack of intent, but through tragedy. The marriage would stand, and the gifts remain with the widow."

"So, Evina is a widow who was ne'er truly married," Conran murmured quietly, and shook his head. He'd never imagined that scenario when he'd been told she was a widow. All he'd been thinking was . . . Well, his thoughts had mostly been about what it freed him to do. And he'd done what he wanted the first chance he'd got, seducing her in a field, and taking her innocence with a complete lack of finesse and not a degree of tenderness. God's teeth, he'd kissed his way under her skirts, caressed her just until she'd found her first taste of pleasure, and then had thrust into her like a bull goring the first idiot stupid enough to get into his paddock.

Conran now suspected Evina hadn't even realized what was happening until it was done. He could still hear her scream of pain and shock, and recall the stunned look on her face when he'd pulled back to peer at her.

"Is something amiss, lad?" Fearghas asked suddenly. "Ye're looking a little green around the gills."

"I . . . Nay," Conran muttered, and stood abruptly. "I need to think. I mean sleep," he corrected himself quickly as he headed for the door. "Call me if she wakes, or needs me."

He didn't wait for the old man's response, but slid from the room and then just stopped and stood there in the hall, unsure where to go. He didn't have a room here. Evina was going to arrange one when they got back, but . . . There was nowhere he could go and think.

"Ye'll be wanting a room."

Conran glanced around at that comment to see Tildy bustling toward him.

"Aye. Please," he murmured.

"The laird asked me to prepare one fer ye while ye were out collecting weeds," the maid said, moving past him. "Follow me."

Turning, he fell into step behind her as she led him past the chamber next to Evina's room. As they passed the closed door, she murmured, "That's Gavin's room if ye're wanting to check on him later."

Conran glanced at it, but didn't slow. He would check the lad later, but just to see that his wound had been properly cleaned and he couldn't see any sign of infection. Although he wasn't sure he'd be able to tell until infection set in. Rory might have, but he didn't have enough experience.

"This will be yer room."

Conran turned his attention forward again to see Tildy pausing at the next door. He followed her inside and glanced around with curiosity. There was a large bed, a small table by the window with a pitcher and ewer on it and a presently empty fireplace.

"Donnan brought yer sword and saddlebag in here while ye were tending to Lady Evina, and the laird ordered some shirts and plaids to be provided for ye. He said to apologize fer no' thinking o' it ere this," Tildy said solemnly. "I've already ordered food to be brought up fer ye and a bath. Betsy will help ye in the bath, if ye like?"

"Nay," Conran said at once. "I can manage the bath on me own. Thank ye."

The woman beamed at him, obviously pleased at his refusal of Betsy's help. In fact, if he were the suspicious sort, he would have said it had been a test to see if he'd dally with the castle lightskirt.

"Oh, that must be yer bath," Tildy said as a tap sounded at the door behind her. Turning, she opened it and stepped aside to allow servants to carry in a large tub and pail after pail of water. The last servant to enter was Betsy, and Tildy stepped in front of her. "He said he'd no' be needing yer help."

"Oh, nay," Betsy protested, trying to skirt around the woman, her gaze locking on Conran when Tildy blocked her again. "Please, m'laird, I'd be happy to bathe a handsome, strapping man like yerself, and I'm ever so good at it. I'd clean ye real well, especially those parts others neglect."

Conran merely shook his head and turned his back to watch the servants pouring water into the tub. He didn't like to be rude, but he'd already had to refuse Betsy once and knew she could be hard to put off. She was the persistent sort.

"Come on now, Bets," Tildy said firmly. "Out with ye. He's no' wanting yer help."

"But he's so handsome," Betsy complained as Tildy ushered her out of the room. "And he's young too. He's the kind o' man 'tis a pleasure to . . ."

Tildy closed the door on the rest of the woman's words and moved back to stand beside him to oversee the filling of the bath. She then ushered everyone out, assuring him, "I'll have Cook wait a bit on sending up yer meal, so it does no' cool while ye bathe."

"Thank ye," Conran said, and unpinned his plaid the moment the door closed. He was shrugging out of his shirt even as the heavy cloth slid to the floor. A glance down then made him pause. If there had been any question of Evina's innocence, the dried blood on his cock answered that question. He had definitely breached her maiden's veil.

"Damn," he muttered, and stepped over the side of the tub to sink into the water and wash away the proof.

It seemed things weren't as simple as he'd thought they were when he'd discovered Evina was a widow. Not simple at all.

PAIN WAS THE FIRST THING EVINA WAS AWARE OF, A BONE-DEEP throbbing in her upper chest that she knew at once would not pass quickly. Biting back a groan, she opened her eyes to see what was causing it and blinked in surprise as she found herself staring at the light blue drapes around her bed. She was in her room, Evina realized, and was surprised by that for some reason. The last thing she recalled . . . Oh, yes, the Buchanan telling her to hang on, they'd be there soon. Here, she presumed, and glanced down at her chest. The arrow was no longer there. At least, the furs covering her were lying flat on top of her chest.

"Evi!"

She glanced to the side at that startled gasp, and blinked when she saw the Buchanan sitting up from a slumped position in a chair next to the bed. His expression was relieved, she noted as he shifted to the edge of his chair and leaned forward.

"I'm sorry, so sorry," he said with a sincerity and regret that made her eyebrows raise.

"For what?" she asked with confusion, her voice raspy and dry. Her throat hurt too with the effort, but she added, "Ye did no' shoot the arrow."

"Nay, no' for that," he said on a sigh. "For what happened ere that."

"Oh," Evina said weakly, flushing as she recalled what he was referring to. The very brief experience that had started as all passion and pleasure and very quickly ended in pain and regret.

"I thought ye an experienced widow who would enjoy a dalliance," he explained apologetically. "I had no idea ye yet retained yer innocence."

She stared at him blankly. He'd thought she'd enjoy a dalliance? What did that mean? The answer seemed obvious enough. His only interest had been in bedding her a time or two while here, and then he'd planned to ride off back to Buchanan, or somewhere else to dally with some other widow or such. She was just another Betsy to him . . . to be bedded and left behind.

Evina supposed she shouldn't be surprised. They hardly knew each other, and her behavior had hardly demanded respectful treatment. She never should have let him even kiss her, let alone touch and suckle her breast, and she should have slapped him silly the minute she felt his hand under her skirts. Instead, she'd moaned and pleaded and egged him on, eager to experience what he was offering.

Well, Evina thought grimly, she'd had her experience, and a terrible disappointment it had been too. Not that she hadn't found pleasure, but it had been so fleeting it was hardly worth the pain that had followed, or the self-disgust and regret she felt now.

"Evi?"

She peered down at his hand as he clasped hers and then tugged her hand free. She had no interest in listening to his false apologies. He wasn't sorry for what he'd done, so much as for the fact that she hadn't been the experienced woman he'd thought her. He was just scared she would demand something of him, marriage perhaps, to satisfy her honor. But Evina had no interest in marrying him . . . or anyone else for that matter. She just wanted him to go away so she could forget this whole, awful experience.

"Evina?" he said now with concern.

"'Tis fine," she murmured huskily, unable to even look at him. "'Twas a lesson learned. I am fine. Just tired. I'd like to sleep now."

A surprised silence followed, but Evina didn't look at him. She just wanted him to go. Unfortunately, he didn't appear to be of the same mind.

"I'm afraid we have to talk about this," he said quietly. "I took yer innocence."

Evina shifted impatiently. "I'm aware o' that, m'lord. I was there. But 'tis fine. I was no' planning to marry again anyway, and I certainly would no' now that I ken how unpleasant the marriage bed would be."

The abrupt way he jerked upright drew her gaze around and she noted his expression. He couldn't have looked more pained had she actually slapped him. Her words had obviously hurt his pride. Apparently, he'd thought the experience would be pleasurable for her. She couldn't imagine why. Everyone knew only the man found pleasure in the bedding.

"Evina," he began with a frown, and then paused and glanced toward the door as it opened.

"Oh, Lord Buchanan, ye *are* in here," Tildy said with surprise. "The laird said ye probably would be, but I felt sure ye'd be in yer room. When I didn't find ye there though, I—"

"Is there something ye wanted, Tildy?" Evina interrupted quietly, hoping the maid would take the Buchanan away and save her from any more of this humiliating conversation. She just wanted to forget the whole thing. Why wouldn't he just go away and let her? she wondered, and then became aware of the stunned silence in the room, and focused on the maid to see her gaping at her, a combination of joy and surprise on her face. The moment their gazes met though, the woman rushed forward.

"Oh, m'lady! Ye're awake! Thank the saints!"

"Aye, she is," the Buchanan said on a sigh as the old servant reached the bed, and bent to hug Evina. "She just woke up, in fact. And could probably use something to drink. Do ye think ye could fetch her some mead?"

"Aye," Tildy said, straightening and whirling back toward the door, only to stop after a couple of steps and spin back. "Oh! The laird sent me to fetch ye, Lord Buchanan. He wishes to see ye."

"Fine," he said grimly.

When the maid remained where she was, waiting, he glanced back and scowled. "Ye've passed along the message. Ye can go and fetch that mead now."

Tildy hesitated and then asked, "But what should I tell the laird? He wanted me to bring ye back."

"Tell him I'm speaking to his daughter and will join him in a moment."

"Very well," Tildy said on a sigh. Turning to the door, she added, "But I would no' take long if I were you. Yer brothers do no' seem the patient sorts."

"Me brothers?" Conran said sharply, standing up.

Tildy stopped in the door and swung back. "Aye. They arrived just ere dawn, and have been arguing with the laird ever since. Now they've asked to see ye." Turning back to the door, she added, "But I'll tell them—"

"I'm coming!" Conran interrupted, quickly moving around the bed.

"That ye're coming," Tildy finished with satisfaction as she held the door open for him to leave the room. Once he'd disappeared down the hall, she turned back to smile at Evina. "I'll be right back with that mead."

"Nay, wait!" Evina called as the maid started to close the door. When the old woman paused and swung back, one eyebrow raised, she waved her over. Tildy hesitated, and then stepped back inside and closed the door.

"What is it, m'lady?" Tildy asked kindly as she approached the bed. "Are ye hungry too? O' course ye are. I'll fetch ye some food too. Or mayhap broth. Would ye like me to find some pillows to prop behind ye so ye can sit up?"

"Nay. Thank ye though." Evina managed a grateful smile, and then said, "Ye mentioned the Buchanans are here and have been arguing with Da since arriving?"

"Aye," Tildy said dryly. "And they're a loud bunch. Woke me from a sound sleep before the sun was even up. I've been running ever since."

"What are they arguing about?" Evina asked the moment the maid fell silent.

Tildy made a face. "I could no' hear. I tried, but yer father posted Gavin in the hall to keep anyone from getting too close."

"Gavin?" Evina said softly as she recalled thinking she'd seen him in the clearing.

"Aye, the poor lad. And him still healing from that wound he took to the arm while fighting off those bandits with the Buchanan. I told him he should really go rest and let his arm heal. I said I'd stand guard in the hall in his stead, but he was having none of that," she said with disgruntlement.

"He *was* there in the clearing," Evina murmured with a frown.

"Aye. 'Tis lucky he came across the two o' ye when he did and could help the Buchanan fight off those bandits."

"Why was he out there?" Evina asked, recalling her father saying he had a task for him. As she recalled, that task was why Gavin couldn't go in her stead to show the Buchanan where to find the weeds he needed.

"Oh. Well, I do no' ken," she admitted. "Young Gavin was hurrying out o' yer da's room as I arrived to sit with him that day."

Evina lowered her head unhappily, her mind awash with confusion.

"I did hear yer da say, 'Do no' lose them and report what ye see back to me,' as Gavin came out the door though," Tildy admitted. "And then the lad rushed below and out of the keep."

Evina jerked her head back up at this news. "Do no' lose who?"

"I do no' ken," Tildy admitted with a shrug.

Evina frowned, suspecting she did know and that it was she and Rory he'd sent Gavin to watch. What was her father up to? He was the one who had sent her out with the man. Why then send Gavin to watch them? Shaking her head, she muttered, "And now the Buchanans are here?"

"Aye, and are they no' a strapping bunch o' lads," Tildy said with awe. "'Tis like standing in a forest o' tall trees to be in the same room with 'em."

"Hmm, I did no' think Rory had sent his letter yet," Evina muttered. "Apparently, he had though, and he did complain after all to his brothers about how he came to be here."

"Oh, nay, Lord Buchanan has no' sent a letter yet. I ken yer father assured him he'd send a courier with it, but the poor lad ne'er got the chance to write it. He's been sitting watch over ye since the attack. He ne'er got around to writing a message to be sent."

Evina's eyes widened at this news. "Then why are the Buchanans here?"

"I think yer da sent fer them," Tildy admitted.

"What?" she asked with amazement. "Why?"

"I do no' ken, but after I finished tending Gavin's wound, yer father sent me away so he could talk to him. He spent an hour in his room, and then came out and sent for his seal. A courier left ere the sup with the message he wrote, and now the Buchanans are here, so I'm assuming he sent fer them."

"He sent for them last night and they are here already?" she asked with surprise, thinking the messenger should not even have arrived at Buchanan yet. Mayhap they'd somehow got wind that Rory was here, and had already been on the way when they encountered the messenger. Or mayhap they came and missed the messenger entirely.

"Nay. He sent a messenger out four nights ago," Tildy corrected her gently. "Ye've slept through four nights and three days, lass."

"I did?" she asked with dismay.

"Aye," the maid said solemnly. "I was beginning to fear ye'd ne'er wake, so was most pleased to see yer eyes open when I came in."

Evina smiled at her faintly, but the expression was quickly replaced with a frown as she considered what her father could be up to. If he'd sent her and Rory out to pick weeds and sent Gavin to watch them . . . Had he been hoping to catch them at something they shouldn't have been doing? If so, then Gavin had no doubt had an earful to tell him, she thought with alarm. And then her father had sent for the Buchanans to . . .

"Oh, dear God," Evina breathed, and pushed aside the furs covering her.

"What are ye doing, lass? Ye were sore injured! Ye should no' be trying to get up," Tildy cried, bending as if to prevent her rising, but stopping short of actually touching her.

"I have to," Evina got out through gritted teeth as she tried to sit up and pain raced through her chest. Trying to ignore it, she gasped, "Help me. We have to stop Da."

"Stop him from what?" Tildy asked with concern, taking her arm to help her up.

Evina didn't answer; she couldn't speak at the moment. She was too busy trying not to pass out as she struggled to her feet. Dear God, her chest hurt. Even breathing caused a burning pain. Breathing hard now as she was felt like she was being repeatedly punched. It was enough to make her want to just collapse back on the bed and hopefully lose consciousness. Unfortunately, that wasn't an option. If her father was up to what she thought he was, she had to stop him.

Chapter 7

 CONRAN PUSHED THE DOOR TO LAIRD MACLEAN'S ROOM OPEN and then stopped abruptly on the threshold as he stared at the four men in the room. His oldest brother, Aulay, and his two younger brothers, Rory and Alick, were all there, as well as Evina's father. He scowled briefly at the old man who was standing next to the mantel rather than lying abed as he should be, but then Conran pushed the door closed and turned his attention to Aulay. "What are ye doing here? How did ye even ken where I was? I ne'er got the chance to write ye and tell ye I was here."

"I wrote them," Fearghas Maclean said solemnly.

"Aye," Aulay growled. "A messenger arrived from Maclean just after the sup the night before last."

"Oh." Conran relaxed somewhat and then smiled crookedly. "Ye must have been worried sick ere the message arrived to let ye ken I was okay."

"Actually, we had no idea ye were missing," Aulay said wryly.

"What?" Conran blinked at this news and then shifted his gaze to Rory and frowned. "But ye must have realized something was amiss when I did no' drop off the medicinals as I promised."

Rory grimaced. "I'm afraid I was held up at the inn, dealing with the innkeeper's daughter for several days. Her labor was long and hard as I feared, but she survived. I only arrived home the day before the message arrived at Buchanan, and when I realized ye had no' dropped off the medicinals, I just assumed ye'd forgotten and set off, taking them with ye."

"Aye," Alick said with amusement. "He was fair froth with ye until we got the message and learned what really happened."

Conran scowled at this news, offended that his brother would imagine he'd forget something like that. But rather than address it, he turned to the Maclean. "Why did ye write them?"

"He wrote to apologize," Aulay answered for the old man. "In his message, he explained he was sorry that his daughter had kidnapped *Rory* and dragged him back here to Maclean, and explained that it was all in a desperate bid to save his life." His eldest brother arched an eyebrow, his lips pursed. "Ye can imagine our surprise since Rory was sitting right in front o' me while I read the message."

"Ah." Conran grimaced and glanced from his brother to Laird Maclean, and back. Both men were looking at him as if he'd piddled on the floor. "Aye. Well," he muttered, "there was a bit o' a mix-up there."

"Nay? Do tell," Aulay said dryly.

Conran scowled at his sarcasm, and said firmly, "First o' all, Evina did no' kidnap me." Turning to Fearghas then, he glared at him grimly for throwing his daughter under the horse that way, and barked, "What were ye thinking telling them something like that?"

Before the man could respond, Aulay asked with interest, "So, she did no' drag ye here to Maclean, unconscious, over the back o' a horse?"

"And naked?" Alick added with a grin, obviously amused at the thought of it.

Conran scowled at his youngest brother. "How I got here is no' important."

"Is it no'?" Aulay asked mildly.

"Nay, it is no'," Conran assured him, and then admitted, "There was a bit o' confusion at the start, but once here, I stayed o' me own free will."

"Confusion like their thinking ye were me?" Rory asked, arching an eyebrow.

"Aye," he admitted with a grimace. "They meant to take ye, but got me instead."

"And ye said naught because . . . ?" Fearghas Maclean asked, finally speaking up.

"Well, I hardly wanted me brother kidnapped too, did I?" Conran snapped irritably. To his thinking, the Maclean had nothing to complain about. He'd saved his life, hadn't he? Which was something his daughter, or Tildy, could have easily done if he'd revealed the sore on his bottom to them. That was the only reason they hadn't been able to deal with the situation. They'd been fighting blind; not knowing about the wound, they'd thought him down with some exotic ailment.

"I thought ye were no' kidnapped?" Aulay pointed out.

Conran glanced to him sharply, and then cursed, and shook his head. "All right, I was brought here, unconscious. But I was no' really kidnapped. They could hardly just leave me there in the woods naked and unconscious, could they?" he pointed out, using Evina's own argument, and then assured him, "And as I said, I chose to stay once here."

"Why?" Aulay asked at once.

"Aye, why?" the Maclean asked with interest.

"Because ye were so ill," Conran answered abruptly, and turned to his brother to explain. "His fever was extremely high. I kenned the man would no' last long enough for Rory to be fetched back, and I thought I kenned what he'd do, so I did it. And it worked," he pointed out, turning back to the Maclean. "Look at ye! Yer fever's gone and yer even up hobbling around." Conran paused to frown now, and added with concern, "Which ye really should no' be doing, m'laird. Ye may tear yer stitches, or start yerself bleeding again."

"Stitches?" Rory asked, drawing his gaze. "He told us he merely had a fever. That ye managed to bring it down, and he's well now."

"He had a fever because he had a boil on his arse that was so infected I had to cut away near half his behind to get it all," Conran told him grimly.

Rory's eyebrows rose, but he considered the Maclean, who was now looking both embarrassed and annoyed. Finally, he said, "Well, ye must have done a fine job. He's up and about and no longer feverish."

Conran shrugged. "I did me best, but ye still may want to take a look yerself now ye're here."

"Later," Aulay said impatiently. "We've other matters to deal with now."

"What other matters?" Conran asked warily.

"Well, the Maclean wrote to offer his daughter's hand in marriage for her 'desperate attempt to save his life' by kidnapping Rory," Aulay informed him dryly.

Conran stiffened, and then said, "But yer already married, Aulay."

"He did no' offer *me* her hand," Aulay said with exasperation. "He was offering to give ye her hand. He only wrote to me, because I am the eldest brother, and head o' the clan."

"And the one most likely to lay siege to Maclean to get ye back," Rory added dryly, and then frowned and added, "Or who the Maclean thought was me . . . Actually, he offered *me* her hand in marriage. The letter said Rory Buchanan."

"What?" Conran growled.

"Aye," Alick said with a grin. "And he promised to make Rory his heir. He'd become laird here when the Maclean passes."

"Aye, it did say Rory Buchanan," Aulay agreed, his eyebrows rising. "Now is no' this a pickle?"

"It's no' a pickle," Conran snapped. "Rory can no' marry her."

"Why?" Aulay asked with interest.

Conran merely scowled at the question, his feelings in an uproar. He'd been more than eager to bed Evina, but hadn't ever contemplated marrying her. He hadn't considered that an option. He was a fourth son, with a small inheritance, and some coin of his own he'd made helping out his brothers with their various endeavors, but had no castle to put a wife in. He was hardly in a position to offer marriage to someone like the Maclean's daughter. Most men like the Maclean would want a man with better prospects for his daughter.

"O' course," Alick said, drawing him from his thoughts. "He made that offer ere he learned ye'd tumbled his daughter and—Ouch!" he complained, grabbing the back of his head when Aulay smacked him.

"Shut it," Aulay growled, and then lowered his voice to say, "Ye do no' ken who may be listening outside the door. The whole Maclean clan does no' need to ken Conran ruined their laird's daughter. Are ye trying to shame the lass or get Conran strung up?"

"Sorry," Alick muttered, rubbing his head. "I was no' thinking."

"Ye rarely do," Aulay said grimly, and then turned to Conran and said quietly, "Alick is right though. When we got here, the man was understandably froth. He did no' even allow me to introduce Rory and Alick before announcing that the situation had changed: Rory had tumbled the lass in the field ere they were attacked by bandits. The marriage was no longer an offer, but a demand. Rory would now have to marry the lass to save her honor."

"That's when yer brother introduced me to these two lads here." Fearghas gestured to Alick and Rory. "As ye can imagine, I was a bit dismayed to learn ye were no' the man I thought ye were."

Aulay nodded and then raised his eyebrows in question. "So? Is the Maclean's daughter ruined?"

Conran stood frozen for a moment, completely stunned. He hadn't imagined anyone knew about what had happened in the clearing . . . except perhaps the bandits. But then he recalled Gavin appearing suddenly in the clearing. The arrow had already hit Evina, and the bandits had rushed from the woods to attack him when the lad had suddenly appeared. At the time, he'd considered it a lucky happenstance that Evina's cousin had been passing when needed. But now he wondered what the lad had been doing there. Had he been sent to watch them? Had he seen the whole thing? His kissing and caressing Evina, and then taking her innocence?

Conran noted the Maclean's satisfied expression and felt his stomach drop as he realized he'd been completely wrong about his eligibility when it came to Evina. The Maclean didn't think him not good enough to be a son-in-law. It looked to him as if the man wanted him for the position. So much so, in fact, that Fearghas Maclean had set him up. At least, he'd apparently wanted him for a son-in-law when he'd thought him Rory, Conran thought. Fearghas obviously got rid of the weeds as an excuse to get him and Evina away from the keep and alone in the hopes that something might happen between them . . . and then Gavin had been sent to be a witness.

But had Evina been a party to the plot? Conran wondered, and considered the possibility that he hadn't been the seducer at all. After a moment though, he shook his head. Nay. He was the one who had initiated things. He was the one to kiss her first, and then to caress and so on. And he'd pulled her down on top of his cock, taking her innocence. Mostly, Evina had just held on and responded, and her responses had shown her inexperience. In fact, if he hadn't been so desperate to plant his cock in her, he would have realized she wasn't the knowledgeable widow he'd thought she was before breaching her innocence, he acknowledged.

Besides, there was no mistaking Evina's shock when it happened. She'd looked almost traumatized. And then there were her comments just now in her room. Much to his chagrin, she hadn't at all enjoyed the experience. At least, not enough to make up for the pain that had followed. She'd certainly made it clear she had no desire to repeat it.

Nay, Evina hadn't been the seducer. She wasn't skilled enough for that. But she had, at least, been bait. And he'd taken that bait. Now, it looked like her father was offering her in marriage . . . to Rory of all people, he thought grimly, and then glanced toward the bedchamber door when it burst open.

A brief stillness fell over the room when Evina staggered in. She had a plaid wrapped around her shoulders that didn't completely hide the fact that she was dressed only in a tunic, and she was leaning heavily on Tildy.

"Daughter!" the Maclean cried, pushing away from the mantel and hobbling as quickly as he could toward her. "Ye're awake!" The old man hugged her briefly with obvious relief, and then pulled back to frown at her. "Ye were sorely wounded, lass. Ye should be abed. What are ye doing up?"

"What are *ye* doing, Da?" she countered breathlessly. "Why was Gavin in the clearing? Why are the Buchanans here? What have ye *done*?"

"Now, lass," the Maclean said soothingly, taking her free arm and helping Tildy to get the girl to one of the chairs at the table by the fire. "I'm just looking after yer future."

"Me future?" she gasped with amazement. "Maclean is me future."

"Aye, but what o' a family?" her father asked with a frown. "A husband and bairns?"

"Ye said I did no' have to marry," Evina reminded him grimly. "Ye said I'd always have a home here. I'm to run Maclean, and then Gavin will take over from me when I retire or die."

"Aye, I did say that," he agreed, but then added with regret, "But that was before."

"Before what?" she asked sharply.

"Before I nearly went to meet me maker," the Maclean growled, and then took a deep breath, shook his head and said, "Lass, I was sure I was going to die, and I was preparing meself. I was thinking on how I'd see yer mother again, and how happy I'd be to see her . . . and how very angry she'd be with me for no' ensuring ye married again, and had babies."

"She would no' be upset," Evina assured him quickly. "She'd ken I do no' want to marry."

"Aye, but what o' bairns o' yer own?" her father asked. "And do no' lie and say ye have no interest in babies. I saw ye with Gavin. Ye were a fine little mother, fer all ye were only ten. I ken ye must want children."

"I've thought on it," Evina admitted, and then scowled in Conran's direction and added, "But to get bairns ye have to bother with that bedding business and I've no interest at all in that. 'Tis painful and unpleasant and just awful," she finished unhappily.

Fearghas blinked at those words and then turned to scowl at Conran. "What the devil did ye do to the lass?"

"Nothing," he said abruptly, and then grimaced. "Well, o' course I did something, but . . ." Pausing, he took a deep breath to calm himself and then said carefully, "Thinking her an experienced widow, I was perhaps a little bit eager, and showed less care and finesse than I could have."

"Hmm," the Maclean grunted, and then turned to Evina and patted her shoulder, muttering, "I suppose getting shot with an arrow at the end did no' help."

Evina snorted at the suggestion and snapped, "The arrow hurt less than the breaching."

"Oh, now," Conran protested, sure she was exaggerating.

"Ye do no' think so?" Evina asked archly. "Which would ye rather have driven into ye? An arrow this big?" She placed her thumb and forefinger about an inch apart to signify the widest part of the arrow tip. "Or something this big?" Now she held her hands in a circle, thumbs to thumbs, and forefingers to forefingers.

A startled laugh slipped from Conran. When the others turned on him, he bit it back and said, "While I appreciate the compliment, m'lady. No man's equipment is *that* big around."

"Yers was," she assured him. "The size of a battering ram. At least it felt like it was."

Conran grinned at the suggestion. "Talk like that could make a man fall in love with ye, lass."

Evina scowled and turned to her father. "I am no' marrying him. I do no' even *like* him."

"Ye seemed to like him well enough when the two o' ye were rolling around on top o' me in me deathbed," Fearghas snapped.

"'Twas no' yer deathbed," she snapped right back, and then her eyes widened in horror. "Ye were awake?"

"A dead man would have been hard-pressed no' to wake up had the two o' ye fallen on top of him and commenced to moaning and rolling about as ye did on me," the Maclean roared, and then took a deep breath and said more calmly, "Ye've ne'er, ever shown such an interest in any other man, no' once through the years, lass. So I thought, well, ye obviously liked him and should marry him. I just had to sit back and wait fer the two o' ye to come to that conclusion yerselves. But ye two idiots were avoiding each other. Ye barely even looked at each other unless ye thought the other was looking away . . ." Grimacing, he admitted, "It fell to me to see to it meself."

Evina narrowed her eyes and growled, "So ye sent us out alone in hopes we'd misbehave, and put Gavin on us to catch us in the act?"

"Which ye did," her father pointed out, and added triumphantly, "Which just proves ye *do* like him!"

"I don't!" she snapped. "And I will no' marry him. I'd rather have me arms and legs cut off than do that."

"Would ye rather marry our other brother here?" Aulay asked suddenly, and gestured to Rory.

"Aulay!" Conran growled.

"'Tis who her father offered her to," Aulay said with a shrug.

"What?" Evina asked, glancing from brother to brother with bewilderment.

"It seems ye kidnapped the wrong man," the Maclean explained quietly. "That is Rory Buchanan. Ye brought *Conran* Buchanan home. But thinking Conran was Rory, 'twas Rory I offered marriage to in me message."

"What?" she repeated, her voice growing weaker. Worse yet, her eyes now sought out Conran, appearing bewildered and wounded.

The combination was enough to move Conran to say, "O' course she'll no' marry Rory. She can no'. No' when she could be carrying me child."

The way Evina glanced down sharply to her stomach and covered it protectively with one bemused hand just underlined her innocence for him. He hadn't got the chance to spill his seed, but she didn't appear to know that and truly believed she might be carrying his child.

"Oh, well, if she's carrying his child, then I suppose I'd best no' marry her," Rory said with a shrug, and then said to the Maclean, "Ye'll have to make the offer to Conran instead. 'Tis his bairn."

"Damned right," Conran said, nodding grimly. If anyone was marrying her, he was. He wasn't letting someone else raise his son . . . that she couldn't possibly be carrying, he realized with a frown as confusion welled up within him.

"Over me dead body," Evina snarled.

"Gentlemen," Fearghas said into the silence that followed. "Tildy here will show ye to yer rooms. I think perhaps I need to have a word alone with me daughter."

When Aulay nodded and speared Conran with a look, he sighed and fell into line with his brothers as they all followed Tildy out of the room. He told himself it was for the best. He didn't think he wanted to marry Evina, but every time she said she didn't want to marry him, he wanted to change her mind. And the thought of someone else marrying her just made him want to break something. It was better for him to get away from her and think this through alone, where he could make a decision that wasn't based on hurt pride, or whatever she was stirring in him.

"I'm afraid two o' ye will have to share a room," Tildy said quietly as she led them along the hall. "We've only two o' the three guest rooms left. These last two rooms here," she added as they passed Conran's room and continued on toward the two doors beyond it.

Conran considered just going to his room, but knew Aulay wanted to speak to him and would just hunt him down, so followed his brothers, and murmured, "Thank ye, Tildy. We'll sort out who gets which room," when she opened the first of the two doors for them and turned back in question.

The old woman stared hard at him for a moment, but then stepped away from the door. "Very well," she said grimly, and then turned her gaze to Aulay, her expression softening. "Would ye like me to have refreshments brought up? And perhaps some food?"

"Aye, thank ye," Aulay answered. "'Twas a long journey and we rode through the night to get here. Some food, drink and then a rest would be welcome."

Nodding, the maid turned and hurried away to the stairs.

They were silent as they watched her go, and then Aulay said, "Rory, ye and Alick can have this room. I'll take the next."

Nodding, both men wandered into the room to check it out.

"Come," Aulay said, putting a hand on Conran's shoulder to urge him to continue forward. Stopping at the last door, he opened it, but then paused to glance back up the hall and pursed his lips briefly. As he finally entered the room, he commented, "Yer inheritance will come in handy when ye marry the lass, brother. It'll allow ye to build on more guest rooms up here. Three just will no' do with the size o' our family when we come to visit. And if ye have bairns ye'll no' even have the three."

"If we marry," Conran muttered, following him into the room.

"If?" Aulay asked as he stopped at the foot of the bed and glanced around.

"Well, the Maclean offered her to Rory, no' me," he pointed out, and then muttered, "Besides, a lifetime seems a hefty price for a couple minutes in the clearing."

"A couple minutes is all it takes," Aulay said dryly, and then turned to eye him. "And ye ken the Maclean will make the offer to ye now he kens what is what and Rory has stepped back from the offer." When Conran didn't comment, he added, "It sounded to me like ye were intent on marrying her when ye pointed out she could be bearing yer bairn right now. Was I wrong?"

Conran shifted uncomfortably, knowing that was true.

"Although," Aulay continued, "I will confess I thought at first that ye were no' pleased with the idea." He raised his eyebrows in question. "So, which is it? Do ye plan to marry her, or do ye no'? I'll support ye either way," he added solemnly.

"Ye will?" Conran asked with surprise. He'd felt sure his brother would force him to marry Evina. He had ruined her after all.

"Aye, o' course I will. We're family," he said solemnly. "So? Yay or nay?"

Conran turned away and considered the question, but he didn't really see a choice. While he hadn't spilled his seed, he *had* ruined Evina. He'd carried away the proof of her innocence on his cock, and it was now gone. He couldn't just walk away and pretend it hadn't happened. On the other hand, she didn't want to marry him . . . Which had the obtuse effect of making him want to marry her and prove that the bedding could be a pleasure, and that he could make her happy as a husband. Conran was quite sure he could make her happy. He also suspected he could be happy with her.

It wasn't just her uninhibited passion that made him think that. Conran had been watching Evina since arriving here. Not just in passing either. He'd often watched from the window in her father's room as she'd moved around the bailey, handling castle affairs and practicing in the bailey with the men. Evina walked with a confident stride he'd only ever seen with his sister, Saidh. She handled her sword like she'd been born with it in hand. She handled the men with the same natural skill, and he could tell they respected her. They obeyed her orders at once and without complaint.

But there was more. Their outing to collect medicinals had been rather revealing. He'd deliberately put the gathering of the plants before the meal to see how she was when she was hungry and tired and Evina hadn't complained once. She also hadn't got snappy or cranky either. She'd merely got a bit quieter, her humor getting drier. Conran had enjoyed her wry sense of humor and honesty that day. Evina had flat-out admitted she was supposed to be nice to him, and that she was bad at that kind of thing. She'd admitted her faults with a complete lack of self-consciousness. As if it was just the way it was, and he could take it or leave it as he wished. Conran found he wished to take it.

"I guess I'd best marry her," he said finally.

"Good, good." Aulay slapped him on the back and then urged him toward the door. "I really did no' want to have to beat the shite out o' ye."

Conran stopped in the hall and turned sharply on him. "I thought ye said ye'd support me either way?"

"Aye," he agreed. "And I would have. As yer brother I'll support ye in anything ye do. And that would have included beating the shite out o' ye until ye saw yer duty in this situation," Aulay assured him.

"Ye could try," Conran said grimly, and turned to head for his own room.

"Brother?"

"What?" He turned back with a scowl.

"The first time is always tricky," Aulay commented, "but it sounds like 'twas particularly difficult for Evina."

"Aye," Conran said on a sigh. "Thinking her experienced, I acted more quickly than I would have had I realized otherwise."

Aulay nodded. "I suggest ye do some wooing then, and show her that there is pleasure to be found in the marriage bed."

When Conran arched his eyebrows at the suggestion, Aulay shrugged.

"This is a good deal for you. Ye'd have a home and people o' yer own," he pointed out. Smiling faintly, he then added, "Besides, I like Evina. I think she'd be good for ye."

"Ye like her?" he asked with surprise. "Ye hardly ken her."

"I ken her actions and she's shown spunk," Aulay said with a shrug, and then asked, "Did ye ken she is usually the one who trains the men at practice and gives them their orders?"

"Aye," Conran admitted. "I did ken that."

"And she took two men and came to fetch ye herself for her father," Aulay pointed out. "She did no' send someone else to do her dirty work. And I gather she knocked ye out to save her cousin?" When Conran nodded, he smiled. "She reminds me o' Saidh, and I'm thinking ye could use a Saidh in yer life. With Evina for wife, ye'd ne'er need worry about the running of the castle when ye have to rush off to help one o' our brothers as ye're wont to do. She can handle matters in yer stead."

Conran blinked in surprise as he realized he was right.

"However," Aulay said now, "Evina does no' have brothers to make her do the right thing here. And I suspect her father will no' be able to force her. He might order it, but I would no' put it past the lass to run away rather than marry ye."

Conran stiffened at the suggestion.

"I'm thinking wooing and bedding her well and often are the only way ye'll be getting her before a priest. Understand?"

"Aye," Conran said, and he did. He had to erase her memory of the first time with several good memories. It didn't really sound a hardship. The first time may have been disappointing, but the situation had been unusual. The next time he'd find his pleasure, but not until he'd ensured she found hers several times first. It was a challenge, but now that he was thinking of it, one Conran was rather looking forward to. He could still feel her body closing warm and tight around him as he'd plunged into her. It had felt damned good. So much so that it had taken him a moment to recognize what the brief resistance he'd met had been. Evina's scream of pain had helped him identify it, and then the whole situation had gone downhill fast, but the warm, wet glove of her body encasing his cock was something he would not mind experiencing again.

"By me guess ye have perhaps two weeks to do it," Aulay commented, reclaiming his attention.

"Two weeks?" he asked with surprise.

"I should think 'twill take that long for Saidh and Greer, and all of our brothers and their mates, to get here for the wedding," he explained.

"Edith and Murine will need to find wet nurses. Their bairns are far too young for travel."

"Aye," Conran murmured thoughtfully, and then pointed out, "It's going to be hard to woo Evina while she's stuck in bed though. She was badly wounded and should no' be up and around."

"I guess ye'll have to entertain her in bed, then," Aulay said with amusement. "I'd suggest strip chess."

Conran blinked. "Strip chess?"

"Aye, me Jetta particularly likes that one. Every time ye take one o' her chess pieces, ye get a piece of clothing too, and 'tis the same for her with yer pieces."

Conran's eyebrows flew up at the explanation. It was hard to imagine Aulay's sweet wife, Jetta, playing such a game.

"Come to see me if ye need any other ideas. I have many o' them," Aulay said with a grin. Murmuring, "Good luck, brother," he closed his door.

Sighing, Conran turned away. He started out, headed for his room, but changed his mind halfway there.

Chapter 8

EVINA REMAINED SILENT AFTER THE BEDCHAMBER DOOR closed behind the Buchanans. She didn't know what to say. Her mind was awhirl with several different worries and fears.

"A baby running the halls again would be nice."

Evina glanced up at her father's words and bit her lip. "Could I really be with child?"

"Ye ken that better than I? Did he breach ye?"

"Aye," Evina sighed the word.

"Then aye, 'tis a very real possibility," he said solemnly, and then pointed out, "Ye can no' let the child grow up a bastard, lass. No' when the father is here and willing to marry ye."

Evina closed her eyes briefly, and then opened them and blurted, "But he does no' *want* to marry me, Da. I was no better than Betsy for him."

"He said that?" her father asked aghast.

"Aye," she said, and then grimaced and admitted, "No' the Betsy part. I sorted that out on me own, but he apologized and said he was sorry. He'd thought me an experienced widow who would be happy for a *dalliance*."

"Hmm," her father murmured. "Well, I'm no' surprised. He *is* a fourth son with little in the way o' prospects. He probably assumed his suit would ne'er even be considered. That I would be like most lairds and demand a first son with a castle, lands and wealth of his own for ye."

"Why?" she asked with surprise. "I am yer only heir and we could only live at one castle at a time. If we had two, one would always have to be left unattended."

"Exactly me thinking," he said wryly. "But for some, a lot is ne'er enough. They must have more."

Grimacing, Evina lowered her head and peered at her stomach again, wondering if Conran's seed had taken root. And if she could bear to have a husband.

"Ye'll have to marry him, lass," her father repeated solemnly. "Why do ye no' give him a chance and see if ye might no' like him? He seems a nice lad to me."

"A nice lad?" she asked with disbelief. "He lied about who he was."

"Did he lie, or did ye just assume he was Rory, and he did no' correct ye?" the Maclean asked gently.

Evina's mouth tightened. "He lied by omission, then."

"He also saved me life," her father pointed out. "And when he found out I'd told his brothers ye'd kidnapped him, he defended ye, assuring them he was here willingly."

"Did he?" she asked with surprise.

"Aye. In truth, daughter, he's been very understanding about everything, even the manner in which ye brought him home. I would no' have been nearly as good about it meself had some strange woman knocked me out, and dragged me across the country, naked, tied up and hanging over the back o' me horse. It's part o' the reason I think he'd make ye a good husband. He's obviously coolheaded and patient, and a lass as trying as ye needs a man like that."

When Evina narrowed her eyes and scowled at him, he shrugged. "'Tis the truth. I fear I have no' been a good father since we lost yer mother. I let ye do as ye like, and now ye're far too used to having yer own way."

When Evina glowered at him, refusing to even speak to the suggestion, her father shrugged. "Well, if there's a possibility ye're with child, ye'll have to be wed and quickly. That means ye either marry Conran Buchanan, or I accept the MacMurray's latest offer and ye arrange a marriage contract with him."

"Nay!" Evina gasped with dismay. Their neighbor, MacMurray, had been making offers for her hand in marriage for years now. But he was a pretentious little prick with a nervous laugh and a tendency to be cruel to his servants. Evina knew darned right well he'd be just as cruel to her if he ever got her to agree to marriage and had her under his thumb. Her father knew it too, which is why he'd always refused the offers. She couldn't believe he'd even consider the partnering now. That told her just how serious he was about her having to marry now that she might be with child.

Good Lord! All of this because of a few minutes in a field that she'd regretted from the second it happened.

"Well, then, I suggest ye seriously consider wedding Conran Buchanan," her father said quietly. "Else I'll have to look elsewhere, and MacMurray would accept ye at once."

Evina frowned and lowered her head, her thoughts whirling as she considered everything. Her father was right. Conran had been rather good about her kidnapping him. He'd told her at their picnic that he had no intention of complaining about it to his brothers. And he hadn't. Her father had. Besides, she could hardly fault him for thinking her an experienced widow. She was the one who had told him she'd been married.

And then, if she considered his perspective, he'd been set up. Really, they both had. Her father had arranged an excuse to send them off on their own, and then sent Gavin to bear witness to force the man to marry her. By all rights, Conran should be stomping about, shouting and screaming about being set up so. Instead, he was willing to marry her.

"I'd rather ye marry the Buchanan, lass," her father said now. "I think ye could be happy with him, but if it does no' work as I think 'twill and ye're no' happy . . ."

"We could always kill him," she suggested.

Her father bent a dry look on her, and shook his head. "'Tis a good thing I ken ye well, and ken that was a joke."

Evina merely grimaced. It had been a joke . . . mostly.

"Nay, if it does no' work, ye may no' have to live with him."

Evina jerked her head back with surprise. "What?"

"Well, if he proves unkind or unbearable, we can always send him out to live in the hunting lodge on the edge o' Maclean land."

"But he thinks he would be yer heir and run Maclean when ye die," she pointed out.

"I made that offer to Rory Buchanan, no' Conran, and we have no' written up the contracts yet. Changes can be made," he said with a shrug. "I'll put off writing up the marriage contract for a couple weeks while ye get to ken him."

"A couple weeks?" Evina asked dubiously, wondering how he would put off the Buchanans for that long.

"Aulay Buchanan said 'twould probably take that long for his sister and brothers and their mates to get here," he explained. "They want to hold the wedding until they can all attend."

"Oh," Evina said, relaxing a bit. She didn't have to decide anything right away. She had two weeks to sort out her future. That was something at least.

"I'll go fetch Donnan to carry ye back to yer room," he murmured, moving toward the door.

Evina almost told him not to bother and assured him she could manage on her own, but then thought better of it. Getting here with Tildy's help had been a struggle. Her father was still recovering and couldn't help her himself, and as much as she hated to admit it, she wouldn't make it back on her own.

"Oh! Buchanan."

Evina glanced around at her father's startled words to see Conran Buchanan framed in the doorway.

Conran nodded solemnly and said, "It occurred to me that Evina might need help getting back to her room when ye're done talking, so I thought I'd wait out here."

"Oh, aye." Her father glanced back at her in question, and Evina sighed, but then nodded. She was supposed to get to know him and she only had two weeks to do it. She may as well start now.

Turning back to the door, her father opened it wider. "Come on in, then. We are done talking and she is no doubt tired."

Conran nodded, entered the room and crossed to where she sat.

Evina started to get up, but paused and gasped as pain assailed her again. She then released another gasp as Conran scooped her up in his arms, plaid and all.

"Ye should no' be walking, lass," he said quietly, cradling her against his chest and turning toward the door. "Ye've been sore wounded and need to heal. Ye could be pulling yer stitches out running about like this."

"I did no' exactly run here," Evina pointed out, keeping herself as stiff in his arms as she could.

"Nay, ye did no'," Conran conceded, nodding to her father as he walked past him.

Evina didn't respond and they fell silent as he carried her down the hall to her room. But once there, she stiffened even further in his arms and glanced around with a frown. "Me door is open."

"Aye, I opened it ere I came to stand outside yer father's room. I thought 'twould be easier than trying to open it with me arms full, or making ye open it and possibly pull yer stitches," he explained.

"Oh," she murmured, thinking that wasn't just considerate, it showed forethought. Relaxing a little against his chest, she peered at him with curiosity. "How long were ye standing outside the door?"

"No' long," he said with a shrug that shifted her slightly against his chest as he crossed the room.

Evina stared up at him silently and then offered a quiet, "Thank ye."

"Me pleasure," he responded solemnly as he paused to set her down on her bed.

Conran straightened then and hesitated, uncertainty crossing his face. "Yer wound should be checked."

Evina stiffened, alarm racing through her. She knew he was the one who had tended her wounds up to now, and then there was the fact that he'd seen her breasts bared before. Still, she felt a great deal of discomfort at the thought of his baring her chest now that she was awake, and not an excited mass in his arms.

"But no' by me," Conran added.

Evina let her breath out on a sigh of relief, and then suggested, "Tildy can look at it."

Much to her surprise, he shook his head. "I'd rather me brother did it."

"Yer brother Rory . . . the healer," she added grimly, some of her resentment showing. The man had taken her innocence without even telling her his true name.

Sighing, Conran settled on the edge of the bed and peered at her solemnly. "I ne'er meant to lie to ye. One minute I was cleaning up under the falls after having helped Rory collect medicinals, and the next I was struggling with a stranger, and then knocked out by a beautiful lass with red hair."

That explained the weeds in his saddlebag that had made her think he was Rory Buchanan, Evina thought unhappily, barely giving notice to his compliment. He'd called her that before, a red-haired beauty, but . . . Well, she just assumed it was one of those flowery compliments men were always throwing around to gain something. She had no idea what he hoped to gain. As far as everyone was concerned, she had to marry him. There was no wooing needed.

"And then I woke up here," he continued. "At first, I did no' tell ye who I was because . . . well, frankly I did no' want Rory suffering the same treatment I had. But then when I saw how sick yer father was, I kenned the situation was desperate, and aye, Rory was needed. But I also kenned there was no way to get him here in time. So, I did what I could."

"And let us continue to think ye were Rory," she said quietly.

Conran nodded apologetically.

"Even as ye were kissing and touching me," Evina added, anger beginning to writhe in her stomach. Dear God, she hadn't even known the proper name of the man she'd let take her innocence. At least Betsy knew who she was servicing.

"That was no' well done o' me," Conran admitted quietly. "But, in truth, I was no' thinking o' me name at the time. In fact, after first letting ye all think I was Rory, I did no' think much on it again. Ye all called me 'Buchanan,' or 'm'lord,' most o' the time. Even yer da mostly called me 'lad.' In truth, I do no' recall any o' ye actually addressing me as Rory."

"I thought o' ye as Rory though," she said quietly. "I thought ye were Rory, and ye were Rory in me head. And now ye're . . ."

"Conran," he said quietly.

"Conran," Evina echoed, testing the name and not at all sure she liked it. She was used to thinking of him as Rory. Conran felt strange in her mind.

They were both silent for a minute and then he shifted, looking uncomfortable, and said, "Should I fetch Rory to tend to ye?"

"Nay," she said quietly. "I think I'll let Tildy tend me from now on."

Concern crossed his face. "Rory is really very good at healing, Evina. And yer wound is a serious one. Ye'd do better to let him tend it or at least check that I did everything right."

Evina lowered her gaze, her mind arguing with itself. She really wasn't comfortable with the idea of baring her chest for Conran's brother and would rather Tildy tend it. On the other hand, Rory Buchanan was quickly gaining the reputation as the best healer in Scotland and he might have a tonic that could ease the difficulty she was having breathing, not to mention her pain. She was still debating the issue when a knock sounded at her door.

Conran stood at once and moved to answer it.

Evina stiffened as she watched him, half suspecting it would be Rory at the door, calling to check on her. But instead, it was Tildy, she saw. The woman was carrying a tray of both food and drink, and she definitely wasn't pleased to see Conran there. In fact, judging by the blistering look she gave him as she moved past him, Evina would say the maid wasn't pleased with Conran at all. But then the maid had heard the conversation in her father's room. She knew he'd let them think he was Rory when he was Conran, and that he'd tumbled her in the field.

"I thought ye'd be ready fer that broth and some mead now," Tildy said, her expression easing as she approached the bed. "Ye have no' eaten since the attack, and need yer strength fer healing."

"Aye. Thank ye, Tildy," Evina murmured as the woman set the tray on her bedside table.

"Shall I feed ye?" Tildy asked, casting her an uncertain glance.

Evina smiled faintly at the woman's expression. The maid knew how much she hated to admit she needed help of any kind. This was no exception, and she opened her mouth to refuse the offer, but Conran did it for her.

"I'll help her, Tildy. Thank ye," he said firmly.

The maid turned another scalding look on him. "I asked m'lady, no' you, sirrah."

Evina's eyes widened incredulously at the insult in her addressing him as sirrah. Afraid Conran would get angry and dress her down for it, she said quickly, "'Tis fine, Tildy. Ye've enough on yer plate what with the Buchanans here and such. There's no need to stay here with me."

"Are ye sure?" Tildy asked, turning to her with concern.

"Aye. Go on about yer business and leave the tray here. I'll be fine," she assured her solemnly.

"Hmm." Tildy shifted her hard gaze to Conran, but then nodded grimly and turned to bustle out of the room.

"I'm starting to think Tildy no longer likes me," Conran said dryly, moving to inspect the broth and mead.

"She was me nursemaid until I was married, and then became m'lady's maid. She's always looked out fer me," Evina said quietly.

"And is no' pleased that I no' only let ye continue to believe that I was me brother Rory, after I was conscious, but took yer innocence," he suggested.

Evina felt her face flush with embarrassment, and scowled at him for causing it. "I'd appreciate it if ye could see yer way clear to no' mentioning that again."

"Very well," he said quietly, lifting the mug of mead and settling on the bedside with it. "If ye agree that we forget about it and start fresh."

"Start fresh?" Evina asked, eyeing the mead greedily. She was very thirsty. Unsurprising, she supposed, since she'd slept for so long without food and drink.

"Aye," he said solemnly, and then held out his free hand and said, "Good day, Lady Evina. My name is Conran Buchanan. 'Tis a pleasure to make yer acquaintance."

Evina hesitated, but then placed her hand reluctantly in his and whispered, "Good day."

Smiling, he squeezed her fingers, and then released her hand to hold up the mead. "May I help ye sit up and prop some pillows behind yer back so ye can drink?"

"Aye," she breathed, relieved that he wasn't going to insist on holding the mug to her mouth and treating her like a child or invalid.

Nodding, Conran set the mead back and stood to help her sit up. He then rearranged her pillow and rolled up a fur to put behind her back so that she had support to sit. "How is that?"

"Good," Evina said a little breathlessly, and then as an afterthought, added, "Thank ye."

"Can ye hold the mug yerself?" he asked, picking it up.

"Aye," she answered, and then nearly dropped it when he placed it in her hand. Closing his fingers over hers, Conran prevented the spill and then urged her to drink without comment.

Grateful that he didn't make a big deal of it, Evina watched him place the mead on the table and pick up the broth instead, but then asked, "Did ye and Gavin manage to capture all the bandits?"

"Nay," he said, turning to her with the broth. "We killed three, injured and captured one who died here later, but one got away."

"Oh," Evina murmured as he spooned up some broth and held it out to her. She opened her mouth to accept the offering and then closed her eyes as she swallowed the light broth. It was beef broth, and bursting with flavor, the best thing she'd ever tasted . . . which told her just how hungry she was. She'd never been very keen about beef, preferring chicken and pork.

"Actually, I suspect the one who got away would ha'e killed Gavin had ye no' called out when ye did," Conran announced as he scooped up more broth, and held it out. "The bandit had already wounded Gavin's sword arm, and was swinging his sword back, preparing to gut yer cousin, when ye startled us all by calling Gavin's name."

"Oh," Evina murmured with a frown, and then accepted the broth. She hadn't really noticed that the man was swinging his sword back in preparation of a killing blow. Just that he'd wounded her cousin.

"After that," Conran continued as he collected more broth with the spoon, "Gavin seemed to regather himself more quickly than the bandit and managed to get his sword back up before the man could strike the killing blow. The fellow just turned and fled then," he told her solemnly. "Donnan has sent men out to the woods every day to hunt for the one that got away, but so far there has been no sight of him. Or any other bandits, for that matter," he murmured, concentrating on his task.

"Was Gavin badly hurt?" she asked between spoonfuls.

"Nay. He got lucky. 'Twas a mild wound at best," he assured her solemnly. "He's back to practicing in the yard with the other men."

"Already?" Evina asked with surprise.

Conran nodded. "Donnan is taking it easy on him, but aye."

"Oh, good," she murmured, but shook her head when he held out more broth. "I am full."

Conran glanced down at what remained of the broth, and then smiled slightly as he set the full spoon back in. "Ye did well. There is little left. 'Tis a good sign, I think."

Evina watched him set the broth back on the side table, but shook her head when he tapped the mead and raised an eyebrow in question.

"No' right now, thank ye," she murmured.

Nodding, he left the mead and stood to pace the room. "I am sorry."

Now that she'd had something to eat and drink, Evina found herself weary, and her eyes had been drifting closed when he spoke. Now they popped open. "What for?"

"For . . . everything," Conran said wryly after a hesitation.

Evina was silent for a minute as she watched him pace. As promised, he hadn't mentioned the events in the field, but that was still included in his apology, she knew, and felt sure he deserved whatever guilt he was suffering that had brought out yet another apology. But then she recalled her father's words about how he'd been good about being kidnapped and such, and she sighed and said, "I should apologize too."

When he stopped pacing to peer at her with surprise, she pointed out, "I kidnapped ye and brought ye here in the first place."

"'Twas no' a kidnapping," he reminded her with a crooked smile.

Evina smiled despite herself and shook her head. "Aye, it was. Or 'twould have been if ye'd been conscious and refused to come to help me father. I was that desperate to see him healed."

Understanding softened his expression, and he shrugged. "But I was no' conscious. And ye could no' just leave me there, naked, defenseless and unconscious by the river. So . . . ye were saving me too. Thank ye for that, by the way."

"I'm the one who knocked ye unconscious," Evina reminded him with amusement, and when he merely shrugged, she added, "And then there is me father."

"Hmm. Aye. He was a difficult patient," Conran commented. "The man is testy, and impatient with being ill now that he's feeling a little better, but I would hardly blame ye for that."

"I meant for his trapping us the way he has," she said with exasperation.

Conran was silent for a moment as he continued to pace, and then he peered at her solemnly. "Did ye ken what he was up to when we rode out?"

"Nay," Evina assured him quietly. "I only realized what he'd done after Tildy came to fetch ye and said yer brothers were here, and then told me that Da was the only one to send out a message." Meeting his gaze, she added, "I would no' have been a party to it had I realized what he was up to ere we rode out that day."

"Because ye do no' wish to marry me?" he asked solemnly.

"Because I did no' wish to marry any man," she corrected, and he moved back to the bed to peer down at her face with interest.

"Why?"

Evina shrugged uncomfortably. "I was married already. I did no' like it."

"Evi, ye were married for three days at ten years old and in name only," he pointed out with exasperation. "What was there to dislike?"

Evina lowered her gaze to the coverings he'd pulled up over her, and began to pluck at the fur on the top one. "Me husband told me on the first day of the journey back that as his wife I had to do anything he told me to," she said quietly. "After which he produced a worm he'd been saving in his pocket, and ordered me to eat it."

"The little bugger," Conran said with wonder. "What did ye do?"

"Punched him in the face," she admitted.

Conran grinned. "Good for you."

"No' so good," Evina assured him. "I was punished for it. Me da gave me a good whipping," she added. "And I was told that aye, technically a wife had to do as her husband said. But I could refuse to eat worms and, by rights, he could no' punish me for it until I was twelve and the wedding was consummated."

"Hmm." He frowned.

"Collin, me husband," she explained, unsure he knew his name, "he apparently did no' ken about his no' being able to punish me until the marriage was consummated. On the second day of the journey, he hit me when I refused to eat a wormy apple."

"What was his fascination with worms?" Conran asked with disgust.

Evina shrugged with bewilderment. It was beyond her. She'd never seen the attraction herself, but said, "'Twas no' just worms. He drowned because he was trying to catch a fish to make me eat raw."

"Yer father said he was fetching water," Conran said with surprise.

Evina shook her head. "That's what Father tells people, but in fact, Colin was standing on a log, dipping a bucket in to try to catch a fish."

Conran grunted with disgust. "It sounds like yer husband was a spoiled brat."

"Aye," she muttered.

"But he was a lad, Evina," he added quietly. "I am no'."

"Me uncle was no' a lad," Evina said solemnly.

Conran stilled, and asked with confusion, "Yer uncle?"

"Gavin's father, Garrick MacLeod," she explained quietly. "He beat me aunt Glenna to death for displeasing him somehow."

Conran sat back with dismay. "That is how Gavin came to be here?"

"And Donnan," Evina murmured. "He was Garrick's first. He'd pledged his fealty to both me uncle Garrick on accepting the position, and to me aunt Glenna when she married me uncle. But Donnan had to choose between them in the end."

"And he chose yer aunt," Conran murmured.

Evina shrugged. "Donnan's own father had been free with his fists when drinking. There is nothing he hates more than a man who enacts violence against women and children. After years of suspecting me uncle's doings, he saw him at it with the last beating and that was the final straw. He decided his loyalty was to me aunt. He bundled them up, me aunt Glenna and Gavin both, and brought them here to Maclean in hopes me father could keep them safe from me uncle. Me aunt did no' live more than an hour after arriving here, just long enough to tell me father what had happened and to beg him to look out for Gavin and ne'er let his father get him back."

Evina sighed. "Tildy said me aunt had wounds inside that could no' be healed. Bleeding inside. But truly, there were enough wounds on the outside to kill her anyway. To this day I have ne'er seen anyone so battered and bruised as Aunt Glenna. Both her arms were broken, one o' her legs and several ribs. Traveling here must have been agony fer her," she said quietly. "Donnan said he wanted to let her heal before leaving, but she knew she would no' survive, and was determined to get Gavin away from his father."

"Surely yer uncle was punished?" Conran said with a frown. "Correcting a wife is allowed, but beating her to death is no'."

"Nay," Evina said on a sigh, and then grimaced and admitted, "Well, God punished him."

"God?" he asked dubiously.

Evina nodded. "Father was preparing to petition the king for justice in me aunt's murder when uncle Garrick's brother, Tearlach, arrived at Maclean. It seems Garrick, on realizing Donnan had taken me aunt and Gavin away, rode out after them, determined to bring them back. He was still drunk, however, took a tumble from his horse and broke his neck."

"Ah." Conran nodded. "So why was the brother there? Why did he no' just send a messenger?"

"He wanted our silence," she said grimly. "He had inherited the title and castle, and had no interest in Gavin, but wanted to ensure our silence on the matter. He didn't want the MacLeod name tainted by his brother's actions. In exchange for our silence, he offered a king's ransom in jewels and coin. He called it a thyftbote."

"A theft fine," Conran said grimly.

Evina shrugged. "Murder is looked on as a theft of life."

"And yer father accepted?" Conran asked, sounding outraged.

"No' at first," she said solemnly. "But then, as he explained it to me later, he realized that Garrick was dead, and me aunt was dead, but Gavin yet lived. His name too would be sullied. He'd grow up the son of a murderer, and at least this way he'd have an inheritance. Father kept the thyftbote for him and plans to give it to him when he is eighteen."

Conran was silent for a moment. He was impressed that she'd told him this. It was another example of her honesty. Many would have kept such dark family secrets just that, a secret. As if the fact that it happened somehow reflected on them. She had told it simply and without concern for how he would take it. But what he was seeing was that her aunt's story, while a tragic one, was made more so because it had happened when Evina was ten. That was a very impressionable age, and with it following on the heels of an immature boy for a husband who tried to make her eat worms and hit her when she refused, it must have just seemed like men, or at least husbands, were the devil.

"Evina," he said finally, "I'm sorry about what happened to yer aunt, but I can promise ye I would ne'er beat ye."

Conran knew that hadn't soothed her when she asked, "But what if ye want me to do something I do no' want to do?"

Conran sat back again and peered at her solemnly. "I ken ye're afraid o' ending up like yer aunt, but—"

"Aye, I am," Evina interrupted him to agree. "But I also do no' want to be beaten for disobeying, or refusing to do something I do no' want to do," she said grimly. "And I will."

When Conran raised his eyebrows, she nodded solemnly. "'Tis the truth, I'm no' very good at doing what I'm told if I do no' agree with it," she admitted quietly. "Father puts up with me 'rebellious nonsense' as he puts it. But who's to say *ye* would? And if we married, 'twould be yer right to beat me," she pointed out.

"I've ne'er beaten a woman in me life, Evi," Conran told her firmly. "No' even me sister, Saidh, and if anyone deserved a beating 'twas her. Yet even when wrestling and play-battling, me and all me brothers were always careful no' to hurt her. I think I can safely promise no' to ever beat ye."

Evina nodded, but was thinking he'd hardly admit he would beat her night and day. She'd never marry him then.

"I suppose it's difficult for ye to trust that what I say is true," he murmured after a moment, surveying her expression. When she didn't respond, he suggested, "We could put it in the marriage contract."

"That ye're no' allowed to beat me?" she asked uncertainly.

"Aye, and that if I do . . ." He paused, apparently unable to come up with a suitable punishment. Evina had one though.

"If ye do, then ye have to live in the hunting lodge on the edge o' Maclean and leave me to live here alone in peace," she suggested quietly.

Conran raised his eyebrows at the suggestion, but nodded. "Very well. We'll put that in the marriage contract, then."

"Okay," Evina agreed, relaxing a little. She wondered though if he really would. If so, she might just be willing to marry him. Certainly, his agreeing to do so made her happier and more relaxed about this getting-to-know-him business.

Chapter 9

"So, YER FATHER WAS MORE INVOLVED IN THE RUNNING OF Maclean ere yer mother's death," Conran commented as he surveyed the chessboard.

"Aye," Evina murmured. "Da did no' care about much for a while after Mother died. Truth be told, neither did I," she admitted wryly. "We both moped about like a couple o' jugglers who'd lost their balls. It, o' course, affected everyone at Maclean. They were all grieving their mistress as well. Mother was well-loved by our people."

Conran grunted in understanding.

"But then Gavin arrived," Evina said with a smile.

"And?" Conran prompted, glancing up with interest when she fell silent. He'd spent the last five days since Evina woke in her company, trying to win her over. They'd played chess, Nine Men's Morris and various other games, chatting lightly as they did. But this was the first time she'd opened up about her past again and what had shaped her. It was the first sign she was relaxing around him and beginning to trust him.

While Conran was very aware that his time was running out to convince her that marriage had more to offer than their rather disappointing experience in the clearing, he'd refused to rush things. He was glad he had. Once she'd started talking, even just about day-to-day things and such, he'd found Evina was intelligent and had a good sense of humor. He was actually coming to like her, and see their upcoming marriage as more than a duty, or even a challenge. Conran was beginning to think they might suit each other rather well.

"Well, at first 'twas a bit o' a trial," she admitted with amusement. "I had little experience o' raising a bairn, and he was only two to me ten. But Tildy was there to help and I got the hang o' it. Things improved. Besides, 'tis hard to mope about when there is a child gadding around," Evina said with a faint smile. "Gavin was always laughing and rushing this way or that. He brought life back to Maclean. Even Da found some interest in what was going on again and started to come around."

Conran smiled. "Aye, children can be a blessing that way. Me nieces can drive me sister mad, but they have her and her husband wrapped around their little fingers. The rest o' us too. There's nothing I would no' do for the little buggers," he admitted wryly.

"Ye'd welcome a child, then?" Evina asked.

"Oh, aye, I'd like a passel o' them," he said at once, his attention split between the game and the conversation . . . until he became aware of the silence his answer brought on. Glancing up quickly, he noted her expression and recalled that she might not welcome making those children . . . yet. He hadn't shown her the pleasure that could be found in the making.

"Evi," Conran said quietly. "I ken yer first experience was no' a wholly pleasing one, but the first time is often difficult fer the lass, and I fear I did no' go as slowly and with as much care as I would have had I kenned ye were so inexperienced. I promise ye though, the next time will no' be like that."

Evina flushed and waved his words away as she lowered her face to stare at the chessboard. She obviously didn't want to discuss this, and it wasn't the first time she'd pushed the subject away. It had been skirted several times over the past couple of days. Anytime anything was said that came anywhere even close to the subject of sex, or the marriage bed, she shied away from it like a horse from an abusive owner bearing a crop. It made him feel horrible. She wasn't a weak woman. To react like this, she must have experienced a great deal of pain with the breaching. He needed to get her past that.

"Evi," Conran said quietly, and when she reluctantly raised her gaze to him, he said, "I'd like to prove that to ye."

She blinked at the words, and then her eyes widened as she realized what he was saying, and she started to shake her head.

"I promise I'll stop the minute ye ask me to, but ye liked it when I kissed ye, did ye no'?"

Evina paused, uncertainty entering her expression.

"What if I just kiss ye, then, to start?" he suggested solemnly.

"Just kissing?" she asked, eyes narrowed warily.

Conran could tell that she was tempted. That was a relief. At least he knew she'd enjoyed his kisses. He'd thought so, but after the mess he'd made of the breaching, he hadn't even been sure about that.

"Just kissing. I promise," he assured her. "I'll no' even touch ye with me hands except to hold ye."

EVINA CONSIDERED CONRAN SOLEMNLY, TEMPTED BY THE SUG-gestion. She hadn't been allowed from her sickbed yet, so she'd sat up and he'd stacked furs and bolsters behind her to support her, and they'd set the board on her lap. Conran had then settled on the side of the bed, one foot on the floor next to the bed, and the other curled under the up-per leg of the first as he faced her. It left her unable to escape his gaze in any way except to drop her eyes to the chessboard on her lap as she considered his suggestion. She had enjoyed his kisses. But that's what had led to the other stuff that had led to the pain, she reminded herself. Her mind immediately argued that he was promising kissing only, and that might be nice.

Biting her lip, Evina struggled with herself briefly, and then gave one very small nod. It was all that was needed. His breath leaving him on a relieved sigh, Conran leaned across the chessboard, and pressed his lips gently to hers.

Evina remained still at first, just enjoying the featherlight brush of his lips over hers, but then his mouth pressed more firmly, and his tongue slid out. Closing her eyes, she opened her mouth to him and sighed as he filled her. It was as nice as she recalled, his tongue exploring and stir-ring a fire in her belly that had her moaning and easing forward, trying to get closer.

She was vaguely aware of the chessboard and pieces sliding from her lap and toppling off the bed to the floor as her arms crept around his shoulders, but Evina paid it little attention. Conran had all of that. Or his lips did, and the things he was doing with them as his mouth slanted over hers, first one way and then the other.

When his mouth broke from hers, Evina opened her eyes and stiffened slightly, but he was pressing kisses across her cheek. She gasped in surprise and shifted as his lips reached her ear and sent new swirls of excitement spinning through her. Conran's mouth moved down her neck next, and he kissed, nibbled and scraped the sensitive skin lightly with his teeth.

Evina moaned and let her head fall back, her hands moving to cup his head now as he made his way down to the top of her tunic. She shuddered when he ran his tongue lightly along it, aware that she was panting, and beginning to shift her legs restlessly, and then his mouth lifted again. She opened her eyes and lifted her head, expecting and even eager to have him kiss her lips again, but instead his mouth came down on her uninjured breast, finding the nipple and beginning to suckle it through the quickly dampening cloth of her tunic.

"Oh!" Evina gasped, her hands clenching in his hair.

Conran lifted his head at once to glance up. Voice soft, he murmured soothingly, "'Tis all right, I'll no' touch ye. Kissing only."

"Aye, kissing," she breathed, and then bit her lip as he urged the loose neckline of her tunic off one shoulder with his mouth. When it dropped away to reveal the breast he'd been kissing through the gown, Conran claimed her nipple again, this time without the damp cloth in the way.

"Oh, God," Evina cried, arching into the caress, and then shaking her head at the unbearable pleasure that coursed through her as he took most of her breast into his mouth and let it slowly slide out, his teeth lightly scraping the tender nipple as it escaped. He didn't claim it again though, but instead laved the underside of her breast and then began to kiss his way down her stomach.

Panting with mounting excitement, Evina glanced down with confusion to see that the other shoulder of her tunic had somehow slipped off her shoulder. The tunic now lay around her waist, leaving her bare from her midriff up. Even as she noticed that, Conran lifted his head and kissed her lips again. This time his mouth was demanding and the kiss almost violent with need. Evina responded in kind, her arms tightening around his shoulders as he tugged away the pillows and furs propping her up and urged her to lie back.

The moment Evina was lying flat, he tore his mouth from hers and made another pass down her body, stopping to lavish her breast with attention, before continuing down her stomach. Conran's kissing and nibbling stopped where the tunic and furs started, but then he tugged the furs aside.

Evina stiffened and lifted her head then, but he returned to kissing her lower stomach, and then ran his tongue along the top of where the tunic had gathered, and she gasped and jerked beneath him as her muscles jumped in response. When he went lower though and pressed his mouth against the loose material gathered between her legs, she stiffened, and opened her eyes, struggling with an urge to scramble away from him until he blew his breath on her, warming the material he was dampening, and the eager flesh beneath.

Swallowing, Evina caught her hands in the linen on either side of her and waited, breathlessly, and then gasped in surprise when his mouth dropped lower to press kisses to her knees below the hem of the tunic. When he began to trail kisses up one thigh, pushing the tunic ahead as he went, Evina cried out, and shifted her legs as she began to tremble. By the time Conran's mouth reached her core, she was strung as taut as a bow and tugging viciously at the linen. But when his mouth settled there and he began to kiss her most intimately, she cried out and rose halfway up on the bed, her hands reaching for his head.

Conran didn't try to stop her, but he didn't halt what he was doing either. Ignoring the fingers that caught in his hair and tugged, he pressed deeper, his mouth sliding between her folds to lash her sensitive flesh with his tongue.

Evina cried out and dropped back to lie flat on the bed again. Eyes wide open, she stared blindly up at the bed drapes overhead, her body shimmying under his attention as he kissed and licked and teased, whipping her into a frenzy of desperate need. Evina was hardly aware of what she was doing when she raised her knees, planted her feet flat on the bed on either side of him and pressed down, lifting her hips up into this new pleasure. Her body was responding of its own accord, seeking the tongue that was rasping across her aching flesh, and the lips nibbling and sucking eagerly. But when his tongue slid out, pressing into her there as it would if he were kissing her mouth, Evina screamed and bucked as her body convulsed with the pleasure she'd experienced so briefly before.

This time it was not brief, and there was no pain to follow. Conran continued to lash, suckle and nip, driving her over the edge again and again, until she lost her mind a little. Literally. By the time he stopped, she was a shuddering, mindless mass in the bed, aware of little else but the way her body was pulsing in the aftermath.

When Evina regained awareness, it was to find herself curled up against his chest in the bed, Conran still fully dressed, and her with her tunic tangled around her waist leaving everything else bare but for the bandage on her one breast, held in place by a strip of linen that ran along the tops of her breasts and around behind her and back and another along the bottom of her breasts. She was lying on her uninjured side, with her leg thrown over both of his, and his arms were around her as he rubbed her back soothingly, careful to avoid putting any pressure on her bandaged wound.

At first, Evina just lay there in his arms, unsure what to do or say. What she'd just experienced had been . . . well, it had been stunning, amazing, mind-shattering. But now she was more than a little embarrassed and un-sure how to proceed. The man had just . . . and she had . . .

Good Lord, that brief bit of pleasure she'd experienced in the clear-ing had been nothing next to this. It had been like a peck on the cheek compared to a proper, full-mouth kiss with caressing hands and grinding bodies. She had never imagined the marriage bed could be as wonderful as that, and wondered what other pleasures there were to enjoy there.

"I should let ye rest."

Evina stilled at those soft words, unsure how to respond. Before she figured it out, he had eased her from his arms and was sliding out from beneath her to stand up.

"I'll visit ye again later, after ye've rested," Conran murmured, already heading for the door.

Evina watched him go silently, her wide eyes on the way his plaid was tented in front. It seemed she hadn't been the only one excited by that, just the only one who had found her release.

Conran didn't encounter anyone in the hall on his way from Evina's room to his own, and was grateful for it. Feasting on her body had been a delight. Her gasps and moans, and mewls of excitement and pleasure, had stirred a matching excitement and desire in him. The way she'd writhed and shuddered under his ministrations had been almost maddening, and his body had urged him to pin her down and sink himself into the moist depths he'd been tasting, but he'd managed to ignore those urgings and keep his promise. Only just. Now he was as hard as a sword under his plaid, his cock aching with the need to find its own release. Something he intended on seeing to as soon as he reached his room. Or at least that had been the plan, he acknowledged as he entered his room to find Aulay there, lounging on his bed with his hands intertwined behind his head.

"Ah! There ye are," Aulay said, sitting up and slipping his feet to the floor as Conran paused in his open doorway. "I suspected ye'd be along soon enough when I heard Evina cry out. The girl has a fine set of lungs on her, and ye were obviously showing her the benefits o' the marriage bed as I suggested. Those screams did no' sound pained or angry."

Conran closed his eyes on a sigh. It appeared he wouldn't be tending his aching cock any time soon.

"Although, from the looks o' ye, ye did no' show her how the mating itself could be pleasurable, but stuck to pleasuring her alone."

Conran's eyes popped open and he noted without surprise that his brother was eyeing him below the waist with a combination of amusement and sympathy.

"No' got that far yet, eh?" he asked.

"Nay," Conran growled, moving forward again and pushing the door closed behind him. "What did ye want, Aulay?"

"Just to warn ye that Saidh and Greer arrived while ye were about yer business with Evina," he said solemnly. "I expected them to be the last to arrive, but Geordie rode out to pass on the news o' yer nuptials and they left at once to ride here with him, so ye may no' have the two weeks as I first thought."

"What?" Conran asked with alarm.

Aulay shrugged apologetically and stood up. "I'm sure Dougall and Niels and their wives'll no' be far behind, so ye may want to speed up yer efforts with Evina while ye can."

"Damn," Conran breathed as his oldest brother left the room. He'd thought he still had a week and a couple days to manage the situation. It seemed likely though that if Saidh and Greer had already managed to get here, he only had a couple of days left, at best. He seriously needed to move matters along with Evina.

He'd take the next step after sup this evening, Conran thought grimly. From kissing to touching. But first he needed to tend to himself or he'd be hard-pressed not to move it along faster than he planned.

"LADY MacDONNELL SEEMS AN INTERESTING WOMAN. LAIRD Conran's sister, Saidh, married Greer MacDonell," Tildy explained when Evina looked confused, and then continued, "She seems a lot like you. No' dainty and fussy like a lot o' the ladies o' the nobility. She carries a sword as ye do, and I'm quite sure I spotted the bottom o' braies peeking out from under her skirts as she sat down. She asked to come see ye, and I said I'd check to see if ye were awake. So . . ." Tildy paused, and raised her eyebrows. "Are ye up to meeting yer soon-to-be sister-in-law?"

Evina opened her mouth, closed it again and then sighed and started to sit up.

"Let me help ye, lass." Tildy rushed forward at once, but Evina waved her away.

"I can manage, Tildy. Thank ye," she murmured, shifting the pillows and furs back into place behind her back to lean against. Her wound wasn't as painful as it had been at first and her breathing was much improved. She was actually feeling well enough that she was beginning to chafe at being stuck in her bed all the day long, and was thinking she may go below stairs the next day. Or mayhap tonight for the sup. If they had company, she should really make an effort to be a proper hostess.

"Ye're looking better," Tildy commented out of the blue, and when Evina glanced at the maid with surprise, she said, "Ye've got some color in yer cheeks and seem more . . . I do no' ken . . . relaxed?" she suggested.

Evina felt her cheeks heat up at the words, knowing exactly what had brought about the color and her relaxed state. Conran's "kisses." Dear God, the man was . . . well, one hell of a kisser. Her body was still giving off little intermittent pulses of something that wasn't quite pleasure now, but like an aftershock, and her limbs were all shaky and quivering still. Yet it had to be a quarter hour since Conran had left.

"I'll bring up some mead, and mayhap some pastries fer the two o' ye if Cook has any, shall I?" Tildy suggested as she watched Evina rearrange her furs to cover the tunic she'd redonned just before Tildy had arrived.

"Aye, I suppose," Evina murmured, frowning as she felt an unusual nervousness beginning to creep over her. She had no idea why she was suddenly nervous. Evina had never before been a shy lass when it came to meeting people. But then this was Conran's sister, who might actually become her sister-in-law if things continued as they were going. Conran's "kisses" had gone a long way toward convincing her that perhaps the marriage bed was not the trial and chore she'd thought it must be after her experience in the field. She wasn't completely convinced, but truly, she was leaning that way.

"I'll go tell her ye're awake and happy to see her," Tildy announced once Evina was situated.

"Thank ye." Evina managed a smile, and watched the woman leave, then sat and watched the door anxiously. She didn't have long to wait. Conran's sister must have been waiting in the hall, for it seemed that Tildy had barely closed the door behind her before it opened again and a beautiful, dark-haired woman swaggered in. That was the only way to describe it. Saidh Buchanan MacDonnell did not take mincing, little, ladylike steps as most noble females did. She strutted into the room, hips swaying, and the sword strapped to her waist swaying with them.

"Ye must be Conran's Evina!" was her greeting, and it was accompanied by a wide grin. "I'm here to give ye all the dirt on him, so ye can blackmail him as needs be."

Evina's eyes widened at the words, and she reached up weakly to pat the other woman's back when she stopped at the bedside and bent to hug her.

"Welcome to the family, sister."

"Oh." Evina forced a smile and nodded as the woman straightened. This didn't seem to be the time to tell her that she hadn't totally made up her mind to marry Conran. Not that she'd probably tell her anyway. She wouldn't tell anyone if she decided not to marry him. She'd pack her few belongings in a bag, saddle her horse and leave. Evina had no idea where she'd go, but she wasn't going to marry if she wasn't ready and if she wasn't sure the man would not abuse her. She'd cut her hair, bind her breasts, dress as a man and work as a mercenary if she had to. She could handle a sword as well as every man here at Maclean.

Well, if she was pregnant that could be a problem, but she'd worry about that later. At the moment, she just had to get through this visit.

"I ken ye're no' sure about marrying Conran, and are no' convinced o' the pleasures o' the marriage bed, but I promise, while the first time is painful, after that 'tis much better."

Evina stiffened, her eyes shooting to Saidh's face with shock.

"Ye can no' keep a secret in a castle, Evi," she said gently, and then asked, "Is it okay if I call ye Evi?"

"Aye," she muttered, wondering if she'd heard Conran refer to her as Evi. He was the only one who called her that.

"Good." Beaming, she dropped to sit in the chair next to the bed, and added, "I also understand ye've some fears about the husband's right to beat ye and such, and I want to assure ye, Conran would ne'er beat a woman. None o' me brothers ever would. And I can say that with complete certainty, because if they were o' the temperament to beat women, I'd ha'e been beaten long ago, several times over."

"Conran said the same thing," Evina told her with amusement.

"Well, then, ye ken 'tis true," Saidh assured her. "I promise, no matter how hard I punched or kicked them, and how badly I hurt them, no' one o' me brothers has retaliated in kind and hurt me back."

Evina's eyebrows rose incredulously. "Ye punched and kicked them?"

"I've done worse than that," Saidh assured her. "Someone had to keep those big idiots in line."

Evina just stared at her, thinking she believed she might like Saidh a good deal.

"And I'd do it again if I ever heard one o' them had hurt their wife or any other woman," she assured her. "I promise. If Conran ever missteps, ye tell me, and I shall take care o' him fer ye."

"Or help *me* take care o' him," Evina said quietly because, really, she wasn't the sort to stand by and take abuse without fighting back.

Saidh grinned. "I think I'm going to like ye, Evi."

Evina smiled, the first true smile she'd given her since the woman had arrived in her room. She glanced to the sword at her waist, noting that, like hers, it was a true sword made to suit her size, and asked, "Are ye really wearing braies under yer gown?"

"Aye," Saidh admitted, looking slightly surprised at the question.

"Tildy mentioned she thought she saw braies peeking out as ye got up from the table," Evina explained, and then admitted, "I wear them too. 'Tis much easier to ride astride with them on."

"Oh, aye," Saidh agreed enthusiastically. "And riding astride is much better than riding sidesaddle."

"I agree," Evina assured her. "Besides, 'tis hard to engage in battle practice in the yard in a skirt. I usually—"

"Tie it up around yer waist to keep it out o' yer way?" Saidh suggested, and then grinned when Evina nodded. Shaking her head, she breathed, "Oh, Evi . . . we are going to be grand friends."

Evina beamed back and nodded. "Aye, I believe we will."

They were still grinning at each other when a knock sounded at the door.

"Come in," Evina called as they both glanced toward the door. She wasn't terribly surprised when Conran entered, followed by two servants, one with a tray of food in hand, and one carrying a pitcher and two mugs. He'd had dinner with her each night since the attack, and this was the routine.

"Sister." Conran didn't appear surprised to see Saidh there, and smiled at her as he held the door for the maids. "They are serving the sup below and yer husband is fretting ye'll miss it."

Saidh rolled her eyes and then turned to Evina and advised, "Be prepared, once ye're with child, ye're husband will become a fretting Fiona. At least me Greer is. All he does is natter at me to eat more, sleep more, ride less and stay out o' the practice yard. 'Tis most annoying."

Evina blinked, her hand moving unconsciously to her stomach.

Fortunately, Conran quickly drew Saidh's attention, saying, "Fretting Fiona? I can no' wait to call him that." And then he blinked and asked with dismay, "Ye're no' with child again, are ye?"

"Shut it," Saidh said with a scowl as she got to her feet. Moving past him toward the door, she announced, "I like Evi. Ye'd best be good to her, else I'll come to Maclean and kick yer arse."

Conran just shook his head with irritation and muttered, "Go eat yer sup."

"I mean it," Saidh assured him as she sailed out the door with the maids following.

He grimaced, but merely waited until the door had closed behind them and then turned to offer Evina an apologetic smile. "I'm sorry. I tried to prevent her coming up, but she was determined."

"'Tis fine. I like her," Evina said honestly.

"I suspected ye would," he said wryly, moving to the table by the fire where the maids had set the trays. Conran stopped at the tray with the pitcher and mugs on it and poured the golden liquid into both mugs. Setting the pitcher back, he then turned to carry the mugs toward the bed, but Evi shook her head and pushed her furs aside. "Why do we no' sit at the table tonight?"

Conran paused, uncertainty crossing his face. "Are ye certain?"

"Aye," she assured him as she wrapped the plaid Tildy had set on her bedside table around herself. "I am growing heartily sick o' being stuck in this bed. I think I'd like to sit at table, if only up here."

"Wait. Let me help ye, then," he said, hurrying to return the mugs to the tray and then moving back to the bed just in time to take Evina's arm as she got to her feet. "Take it slow," Conran cautioned. "And tell me if ye need to stop to rest."

Evina snorted. "The table is across the room, m'lord, no' across the bailey. I think I can manage it."

"Ye're recovering from a nasty wound, Evi," he said solemnly. "Ye're no' as strong as ye like to think ye are just now."

Evina didn't respond. Mostly because after the few steps they'd covered, she already didn't have the air to speak, and her legs were beginning to tremble, she realized. Good Lord, she was weak as a kitten, Evina thought with dismay.

"Are ye all right?" Conran asked with concern.

Pressing her lips firmly together, Evina nodded. She would make it to the table, or kill herself trying. Obviously, lying about for so long had weakened her. It was her chest that had been hurt, not her legs.

Much to Evina's relief, she did make it to the table, though she was leaning heavily on Conran's supporting arm by the time they got there. Still, she'd made it. That was something anyway, she told herself as he pulled out a chair and settled her in it.

"Hungry?" Conran asked as he took the second chair.

Evina nodded, still too shaky and breathless to speak yet. Much to her relief, Conran didn't fuss about her weakened state, but simply went about shifting one of the trenchers on the tray in front of her, and the other in front of himself, and started to eat. It took a couple of minutes for Evina to feel recovered enough that she attempted to eat. Her hand was still trembling a bit, but she managed to get a bite of cheese to her mouth without dropping it, so considered that a victory. After chewing and swallowing, she asked, "What was it like growing up with so many brothers and a sister?"

Conran seemed surprised by the question, and paused to think before answering. "Noisy."

"Noisy?" she asked with amusement.

"Aye. Noisy, chaotic, fun . . . sometimes annoying as hell, but mostly wonderful," he admitted with a smile, and explained, "None of us ever lacked for someone to play with, and we always had each other to depend on."

Evina felt a touch of envy at his words. She and her brother had been little more than a year apart in age. She'd loved him dearly, and they'd been very close. Both of them had trailed their father around on his daily tasks when he was home, and Daniel had never let the fact that she was a girl interfere with play. Much to their mother's distress, they'd run about the bailey playing at war, fighting with wooden swords and wrestling in the dirt and grass like a pair of "savages" as she'd described it. But then he'd died, and she'd been alone. Evina supposed her mother could have tried to rein her in then, but Lady Maclean hadn't had the heart to, at least not for the first year after his death. Her mother had known how much Daniel's death was paining Evina. She'd let her continue to trail her father around during the day. But when the negotiations began regarding bringing Evina's betrothed to Maclean for his training, and the subject of holding the wedding early came up, her mother had been almost in a panic.

It had taken a year for the men to hammer out an agreement and get permission from the king and the church for the wedding. Her mother had spent that time trying to turn Evina into a proper lady. Mairi Maclean had been kind and understanding, but firm, and Evina had learned a new respect for her mother. Where before she'd seen her as the weaker of her parents, she'd learned how smart and hardworking she actually was. The two of them had become quite close over that year, and her mother had succeeded in her task of making her more ladylike, at least on the surface. But then she too had died and Evina had felt lost.

She wondered now if having more than just her brother as a sibling wouldn't have helped with the death of both Daniel and her mother. She was sure it wouldn't have made those losses any less painful, but it might have made it easier for her to carry on. She would have had some support at least.

It mattered little, Evina supposed as she took a sip of honey mead. She hadn't had siblings to cushion the loss. Swallowing the sweet beverage, she set the drink back on the table, and said, "Tell me about yer brothers and sister."

Conran considered the request briefly, and then said, "Well, Aulay is the eldest. He runs Buchanan and our people."

Evina nodded, and asked, "His scar? Was he injured as a child?"

"Nay. As an adult. In battle some years back," he said quietly, and then added, "We lost our brother Ewan in the same battle. He was Aulay's twin, born just minutes after him."

"That must have been hard for him," Evina murmured.

"Aye," Conran agreed solemnly, and then cleared his throat and continued, "And then there is the second oldest of us, Dougall. He's much like Aulay in temperament, stern and no' much o' a talker. But he has a way with horses, and bred and raised them ere meeting his wife, Murine. He still does despite being laird of Carmichael now."

"I've heard of his horses. They are supposed to be the best in Scotland."

"Aye, they're fine beasts," Conran assured her, and then continued. "Niels is the next oldest. His interest was in sheep and wool ere he met and married Edith Drummond."

"And does he still raise sheep and make wool despite marriage to Edith?" Evina asked before sliding a bit of chicken into her mouth.

"Only for the people of Drummond," Conran said with a smile. "He moved his sheep there and has fresh plaids made for every member of Drummond twice a year."

Swallowing the food in her mouth, Evina said with approval, "That's kind of him."

"Aye. Especially considering the coin he could get selling the wool elsewhere," Conran said seriously.

Smiling faintly, Evina asked, "And who is the next oldest?"

"Me," Conran admitted wryly. "And before ye ask, I've no special skills. I do no' have a way with horses or sheep or any other beastie."

"But ye're a fine hand at healing," Evina pointed out. He was the one who had healed her father and tended her own wound, and had done a fine job at both.

"Nay. Rory is the healer. I just picked up a thing or two from helping him. Just as I learned a bit about horses from helping Dougall, and about sheep from helping Niels." He shrugged. "I ken a bit about many subjects."

"Which would make ye a good laird," Evina murmured thoughtfully. For a laird who had wide and varied skills and knowledge was surely better than one who knew only how to run a keep.

"Mayhap," Conran said with a shrug, and then asked, "Would ye like more? Are ye still hungry?"

Evina glanced down at her trencher, surprised to find it was empty. The short walk to the table had apparently done her appetite good at least. Hopefully it was the first step in rebuilding her strength too, she thought as she shook her head, and murmured, "No, thank ye."

Nodding, Conran took her trencher and set it back on the tray with his own. He then picked up the tray and headed for the door to set it out in the hall for one of the maids to get without disturbing them, and asked, "Would ye like to play a game at the table? Or return to yer bed now?"

Evina hesitated. She was feeling a little tired now that she'd eaten, but wasn't eager to return to her bed, so in the end said, "Here is fine," as he returned to the table.

Conran merely nodded and settled in his seat, but then glanced around and suggested, "Or we could sit on the fur in front of the fireplace. We could even have a small fire if ye like. There is a chill in the air tonight. I think a storm is coming down from the north."

"That might be nice," Evina said, glancing toward the fireplace. She'd noticed it was a touch chilly, but had assumed it was just her, something to do with her still recovering from her injury.

Conran was up at once and moving to start a small fire, and it was indeed small, a couple of logs and a few leaves to start it. While he was busy with that, Evina stood and moved the few feet to the fur, relieved when she managed to get there without becoming more than a little breathy.

"Here."

She glanced to him with surprise when he was suddenly beside her, offering his hand to aid her in lowering herself to the fur.

"Thank ye," Evina breathed as she arranged the plaid she'd wrapped around her shoulders cape-style so that it covered her properly.

"What would ye like to play tonight?" Conran asked, still standing.

"Whatever ye wish," she decided, not really caring one way or another.

"We did no' finish our chess game. Shall we try it again?" he asked.

Evina felt her cheeks heat up and closed her eyes briefly as she recalled why exactly they hadn't finished the game, and what he'd done to her. She'd been nervous about meeting him again after his leaving earlier, concerned that she would be embarrassed by what they'd done and her responses when he returned. But with Saidh there, she hadn't even thought about it, until now.

"If ye like," she said in a strangled voice.

"Evi?"

She could hear the concern in his voice, but didn't lift her head or open her eyes. "Aye?"

"Lass."

Evina gave a start when she felt his hand brush her cheek and jerked her head up, her eyes blinking wide.

"Are ye upset?" Conran asked with concern.

"Nay."

"Ye're embarrassed," he realized, and then shook his head. "Ye've no reason to be embarrassed with me."

"I'm no'," she lied.

"Nay?" Conran asked, a smile curving his beautiful mouth, and then he ran a finger lightly over her lips and asked, "Did ye enjoy our kissing this afternoon?"

Now her face was on fire, but Evina raised her chin and said honestly, "Aye."

"I did too," he admitted. "Would ye like me to do it again?"

She stilled at the offer, shocked to feel her body respond to just the suggestion. Her breasts tightened, the nipples hardening, and she felt a liquid heat pool low in her belly as if he was already kissing her. Swallowing, she raised her chin a little higher and nodded. "Aye."

"I'd like that too," Conran said, his voice becoming raspy. "May I touch ye too this time?"

Evina blinked. Touching? She'd enjoyed his touch and caresses in both her father's room and the field. It was just the breaching she hadn't liked, so she nodded again, her body beginning to tingle at the thought of what he might do to her.

"Thank ye." Conran leaned forward as he murmured the words, his breath brushing her lips, and Evina was just letting her eyes droop closed in anticipation of his kissing her when she felt his hand at her breast. Giving a start, she pushed her eyes open again even as his lips covered hers.

Sighing, Evina leaned into him, her mouth opening before he even requested entrance. Conran accepted the invitation, his tongue sweeping into her mouth as he palmed, squeezed and then caressed her breast.

Evina wasn't really aware of either of them moving or his urging her back to lie on the furs; she was just suddenly there, her arms wrapped around his neck as he leaned over her, kissing and caressing her. This time it was his fingers that traveled her body rather than his mouth, and in some ways, Evi enjoyed this more, because it meant he never stopped kissing her. She didn't protest when she felt him tugging her tunic open to free her breast to his touch, Instead, Evina sighed into his mouth and arched her back, lifting her breast upward in an invitation he accepted at once. She moaned as his rough hand covered her breast and he began to toy with the erect nipple.

Her eyes opened when Conran broke their kiss to lean up though, and Evina watched through droopy eyes as he peered down at her. His face was a mixture of shadow and the dancing light from the fire, and she caught her breath at how beautiful he was even as Conran murmured, "Beautiful," in a raspy voice.

The word made her glance down at herself to see that his body was casting her in shadow from the dim light creeping through her open shutters, while the fire was painting her with the same dancing light on his face.

He shifted slightly then, moving lower to claim her eager nipple with his lips, and she let her head fall back to the floor and moaned as he laved and suckled at it. When his hand moved down to her leg, she stiffened, but he immediately released her nipple to murmur reassuringly, "Just touching."

Evina bit her lip, but then forced herself to relax, and he rewarded her with another kiss, this one demanding all of her attention as he thrust his tongue between her lips and reignited her briefly dampened passions. When his hand began to move up her outer leg, she simply enjoyed it, secure in the promise that it would be just touching.

She had enjoyed his touching her in the field, but that had been nothing next to his touching now. His hand moved up her outer leg, around to her behind and squeezed briefly, before continuing up her back and then around to slide across her stomach, pushing her tunic before it as he'd done while "kissing" her earlier. Evina sighed and moaned by turn as his hand moved over her, and then cried out into his mouth when it slid back down, not stopping until it was between her legs.

Conran caught the sound and deepened his kisses as he began to caress her there, his fingers dancing across her damp flesh with a deft skill that soon had her raising her knees and shifting her hips into the touch. When his finger slid into her, she stiffened, and waited for the pain, but there was none. Still, she remained frozen for a moment, just experiencing his touch as his finger remained in her and he continued to caress the center of her excitement with his thumb, and then she couldn't bear it anymore and began to shift her hips again, pushing back as he stoked her fire.

When her pleasure overtook her, Evina cried out into Conran's mouth, but as before he didn't stop. He continued to caress her, driving her back to the pinnacle again until she was crying out once more, her body shuddering with another release, and then another, and yet another, until she was sobbing her pleasure and clinging to him as if he were the only safe haven in a storm-tossed sea.

Chapter 10

"A BATH?" TILDY ASKED WITH SURPRISE. "YE DO NO' NEED A bath."

"I bathe once a week every week, Tildy, and wish to have one now. Just order a bath for me, please."

"But ye've done naught but lay abed since ye were injured. Ye're no' dirty."

Evina scowled at her. "Me hair feels dirty and limp and I should like to clean it."

"Aye, well, 'tis a bit limp and sad-looking," Tildy admitted, and then heaved a sigh. "Fine. I'll order ye a bath . . . but only if Rory Buchanan says 'tis all right."

Evina glowered at the servant's back as she bustled out of the room. She was used to having her orders obeyed at once, not questioned and considered subordinate to someone else's opinions. Besides, Rory Buchanan had not even seen her wound. Evina had refused Conran's repeated efforts to get her to let his brother check the injury, instead having Tildy tend to cleaning it and changing the bandages. Now she suspected she'd have to allow him to see it to get Tildy to agree to her taking a bath. Unless he decided she shouldn't either. In which case, Evina suspected she could shout the order until she was blue in the face and would not get her bath. And she desperately wanted one.

Tildy was wrong. She hadn't merely been lying about. She'd been writhing and moaning and sweating up a storm here in her room as Conran showed her some of the pleasure that could be had in a marriage bed. Last night especially, between the fire and the way he heated her blood, Evina had been soaking wet when Conran had finally gathered her in his arms, laid her in her bed and covered her up before slipping from the room.

He'd done it without saying a word, and she'd been too wrung out from what he'd done to her for her to protest or say anything to him. Now she was feeling a bit unsure of herself. His leave-taking had been rather abrupt to her mind. In fact, it had seemed as if he couldn't wait to get away from her quickly enough, and she was worrying over the reason why. Had she displeased him? Responded too eagerly to him? Should she have refused to let him kiss and touch her? Was he disgusted by her eager behavior?

The kissing and touching business had been his idea, but perhaps it had been a test to see if she would allow it again and she had failed the test. Evina didn't want to wait until later in the morning when he usually came to see her. She wanted to see him earlier than that. She planned to try to go below to break her fast, and she wanted to be clean, and as pretty as she could be, when she did. Purely for her pride's sake, Evina assured herself. What other reason could there be?

"WHERE DO YE THINK YE'RE GOING?"

Conran stopped walking abruptly, and blinked at his little brother when Rory suddenly stopped following Tildy and whirled to ask him that question. Frowning, he glanced ahead to where Tildy had reached the door to Evina's bedchamber and was entering. "With you," he answered.

"Nay."

"Nay?" he echoed, jerking his gaze back to his brother with surprise.

"Nay," Rory repeated firmly, glancing over his shoulder briefly at the sound of another door opening farther up the hall. When it proved to just be Aulay leaving his room, Rory turned back to add, "Ye'll wait below."

"The hell I will," Conran said at once. "She is me betrothed."

"Aye, which is why ye've no business being in there," Rory said firmly. "Evina has repeatedly refused to allow me to check her wound. She's obviously no' comfortable with the idea, and yer presence will no' help. Go wait below."

Conran opened his mouth to refuse, and then grunted in surprise when Aulay caught his arm as he drew even with them, and turned him around.

"Come along, brother," Aulay said, tugging him down the hall. "Let Rory do what he does best."

"But she—" he began.

"Will be fine," Aulay interrupted. "Rory is good at this. Let him tend her."

Conran scowled, but didn't bother arguing further. Aulay had a good hold on him and wasn't letting go. He would wait below whether he liked it or not. Sometimes it was damned annoying having brothers, he thought with disgust.

"Well, someone does no' look happy this morn," Saidh said with amusement as Aulay led a still-scowling Conran to the table moments later.

"He wanted to accompany Rory to check Evina's wound," Aulay said calmly as he settled at the trestle tables and drew Conran down beside him.

"Oh, no, that would no' have gone well at all," Saidh said at once.

"Why?" Conran asked with surprise.

"Because ye're her betrothed," his sister said simply, as if that should explain everything.

It didn't for him, however, and Conran scowled again. "And that is why I should be there."

"Nay. That is why ye should no' be there," Jetta assured him, drawing his gaze to Aulay's petite wife. She and his brother, Geordie, had arrived with Saidh and Greer the day before. Geordie and a retinue of soldiers had escorted Jetta to MacDonnell, and then continued on with them from there.

"But why?" Conran asked with exasperation.

"Because the wound is on her chest," Saidh said with a shrug.

"Which is why I should be there," he growled with exasperation. Rory shouldn't be looking at Evina's breast without him there.

"Conran," Jetta said gently. "When Rory looks at a wound, all he sees is a wound, no matter where on the body it is. Howbeit, ye will look on it as Evina's wounded body. If ye see what I mean?"

"Nay," he said at once, "I do no' see what ye mean."

"She means ye'll see Evina's wounded breast while Rory will see a wound that just happens to be on Evina's chest," Saidh said shortly.

When he continued to peer at them uncomprehending, Jetta frowned and added, "Ye look at her like a man. Rory looks at her like a healer, and having the two of ye there would make her uncomfortable."

"But why?" he repeated, really not getting what they were trying to tell him.

"Oh, for heaven's sake, Con," Saidh snapped. "Having ye leering at her breast while Rory is trying to check her wound would make her uncomfortable."

"I would no' leer," he protested indignantly.

The expressions on the faces of his family members suggested no one believed that. Deciding it was a waste of time to try to argue the point, Conran scowled and simply grabbed a pastry and bit into it, trying not to imagine Rory even now unwrapping the bandages from Evina's chest and revealing her breasts, or at least her injured breast. Her other one was not covered by the bandages and would be bare from the moment Evina lowered her tunic, which she'd have to do for Rory to remove the bandages. He was up there right now, looking at her breasts, touching the injured one, checking for—

"Ye did a fine job, brother. I'm impressed."

Conran glanced up sharply at those words, and blinked at the sight of Rory claiming the empty space between him and Geordie on the bench. There was no hiding his surprise as he asked, "Ye're done already?"

"Aye, well, Tildy got there ahead o' me and helped Evina remove the wrappings and arrange a plaid around her so that I would only see the injury itself. I took a look, and 'tis healing nicely. No sign o' infection, and yer stitching was better than me own. As fine as Mother's when she was sewing. I think the scarring will be minimal. I told her she could have a bath, just to try no' to get the injury itself wet, and then I gave Tildy a salve to put on it ere she replaces her bandages after her bath." He shrugged. "It only took a couple minutes."

"Oh." Conran glanced toward the stairs.

"Tildy came below with me to fetch the servants with the bath," Rory said solemnly. "She'll no' want to see ye while she's bathing."

"Right," Conran murmured, but couldn't help thinking he could offer to wash her back and squeeze in another lesson on the benefits of the marriage bed if he went up. He'd barely had the thought when Tildy hurried through the great hall, headed for the stairs. A passel of servants followed her, carting a big tub and pails of water, some of them steaming.

"Tildy must have ordered the water to be heated before she came to ask me to check Evina's wound," Rory said as they watched the parade of people head up the stairs.

"Aye. She'd been looking for ye for quite a while ere ye came below," Conran told him, and then arched his eyebrows. "Ye slept rather late this morn."

"Aye, well, there was a pretty blond lass who wanted me to take a look at something for her last night and I was quite late getting to bed," Rory said with a shrug.

"Was her name Betsy?" Conran asked.

Rory stiffened in surprise. "How did ye ken?"

"Just a lucky guess," Conran said with amusement, his gaze slipping past him to the stairs to watch for the servants' return. It didn't take long before the parade of servants were making their way back down the stairs. Which meant her bath was ready, and Evina was no doubt even now stripping and stepping into a steaming tub of water. It made him wonder if she was the sort to take long baths, or fast ones, and how long it would be before he could go above stairs.

"Remember, ye're no' supposed to get yer wound wet."

"I'll be careful," Evina assured Tildy as she stepped over the edge of the tub and eased down to sit in it. A small sigh slid from her lips as the warm water closed over her and she briefly shut her eyes as her body relaxed. She'd been tense ever since Tildy had arrived to inform her that Rory Buchanan was on his way to check her wound. But it hadn't been nearly as bad as she'd expected. Tildy had helped. Before Rory arrived, she'd quickly removed the linen covering her injured breast, and then wrapped a plaid around Evina's shoulders that she'd held together so that just the injured side of her back and the top of her wounded breast remained visible. Rory had come in, talked softly, asking if this or that hurt as he'd inspected and prodded her injury, and then had nodded, proclaimed her well enough to bathe, gave them a couple instructions and a salve and then left the room. It had been that easy, and hadn't taken more than a couple minutes. It made Evina feel a little foolish about refusing to let the man look at it until now.

"Here. Hold this over yer wounded breast and I'll wash yer hair first."

Evina blinked open eyes she'd just closed and stared at the small strip of linen the woman was holding out.

"'Tis in case some water drips down yer face to yer chest," the maid explained. "The healer suggested it."

Nodding, she accepted the small bit of cloth and placed it over her breast, holding it there with one hand.

"Try to lean yer head back so I can dampen yer hair."

Evina grasped the edge of the tub with her free hand and eased forward in the water until her bent knees were squished against one end of the tub. Once she'd given herself as much room as she could, she then leaned back, holding tightly with her one hand to keep from falling onto her back in the water and submerging her upper body and the wound along with it.

"Good," Tildy said with approval. "Tell me if ye start to tire and need a break."

Evina merely nodded and closed her eyes as Tildy picked up a pail and tipped the water over her hair. The maid worked quickly but carefully, managing to wet and soap the long tresses without getting water or suds anywhere near her chest or even her shoulders. But as quick as the woman was, the muscles in Evina's arm were soon trembling with strain by the time she was ready to move on to the rinsing. She wouldn't have said anything, and would have tried to last for the rinsing too. However, Tildy noticed and insisted on a break before she moved on to rinsing. Evina accepted the decision silently. She hated to admit weakness, but there was no way to hide it when it was visible as it presently was, so she eased up into a sitting position with relief.

"Here, I'd best . . ." Tildy didn't bother to finish the phrase; she simply wrapped a fresh linen around Evina's soapy hair and head, explaining, "'Twill keep anything from dripping down yer chest and back now ye're sitting up."

"Thank ye," Evina murmured, removing the still-dry strip of linen from her wound.

"Do ye want me to help ye with the rest o' yer bath?" Tildy asked with concern.

"Nay. I'll manage, and I'll keep the wound dry," Evina added before Tildy could give her the warning again.

The maid nodded, relaxing a little. "Well, then, I'll strip the linens from yer bed and remake it while ye do that."

"Thank ye," Evina murmured again, and then turned her attention to soaping and cleaning herself as the woman bustled about the room, making up the bed with fresh linens and tidying up here and there. She finished before Tildy, but merely waited patiently until the woman completed the things she wished to do and returned to the tub.

"Shall I rinse yer hair now?"

"Aye, please." Evina slid forward in the tub again and then eased back and tipped her head back to be rinsed.

"Here."

She glanced down with a start as something light was laid over her injured breast. Spotting the scrap of linen she'd held there during the washing, Evina pressed one hand gently on the edge of it to keep it in place and then tightened the fingers of her other hand over the rim of the tub and closed her eyes.

Tildy was thorough but quick. It was just moments before she was wringing out Evina's hair, and wrapping another dry linen around it.

"Oh, damn," Tildy muttered suddenly as she helped Evina sit up in the water with the linen around her head.

"What is it?" Turning, she raised an eyebrow in question as she noted the old woman's vexed expression.

"Well, I've used both the linens I brought up," Tildy pointed out. "Now I've naught fer ye to dry with."

Evina's gaze slid to the sopping linen Tildy had wrapped around her soapy hair to keep her from getting her injury wet. It now lay a soapy wet mess in the rushes.

"There are bed linens in the chest," Evina pointed out.

Tildy clucked with irritation. "Nay. I'll no waste a good bed linen on this. I'll fetch another linen for ye to dry with. Will no' take a moment. Ye just relax there for a bit. Yer arm was shaking again by the time I finished rinsing anyway. Ye can no doubt use a break ere ye try to get up."

Evina didn't get a chance to agree, disagree or comment. Tildy talked all the way to and through the door, closing it on the last word.

Shaking her head with amusement, she leaned back against the cold metal, only to wince as it pressed against the entry wound in her back. It was only then it occurred to her to worry about whether that had got wet while her hair was rinsed. Evina didn't think so, but supposed she'd find out soon enough when Tildy rewrapped her.

A soft shuffling sound caught her ear then, and she frowned, wondering if they had mice. She'd have to tell Tildy to put down some black hellebore with barley meal. Evina hated mice. She wasn't afraid of much, but seeing one of those little creatures scampering across the floor was enough to make her squeal and leap about like an idiot. It was most embarrassing. Aye. She'd talk to Tildy about the hellebore when she returned, Evina thought, and then stilled in surprise when something pressed down on her head, pushing her down in the tub.

Her eyes popped open at once, and Evina opened her mouth on a startled cry that was silenced when soapy liquid poured into her mouth as she was forced under the water's surface.

"HAVE YE HEARD ANY NEWS FROM DOUGALL OR NIELS? WHEN do ye expect them to arrive?"

Conran heard Geordie ask the question, and was truly interested in the answer. It might give him an idea as to how long he had to convince Evina that the joining itself wasn't the nightmare she'd been led to believe by their first experience together. However, he spotted Tildy coming out of Evina's room then, and all of his attention focused on her.

It must mean Evina was done with her bath, he thought as he watched the maid walk along the landing toward the stairs. Although the water and tub still had to be removed, Conran supposed. Tildy was probably coming down to fetch the servants back up to do just that, and then he could—

His thoughts died and he scowled when Tildy suddenly stopped half-way down the stairs and whirled back the way she'd come. The woman was shaking her head with apparent exasperation as she trudged back up the stairs. She seemed quite annoyed about something. His guess would be that she'd forgot something.

"Did ye hear that, Conny?"

"Hmm?" Conran muttered, aware of Aulay's voice asking a question, but not really paying it any attention as he watched Tildy return to Evina's door and open it. He completely missed whatever Aulay said next, because he was focused on Tildy. He'd seen the way the maid had seemed to blanch once she opened the door. By the time she began to shriek in horror and disappeared into the room, Conran was already on his feet and racing for the stairs.

He heard the cries of confusion and concern behind him as he ran, but Conran didn't slow to explain. He didn't know what the hell was happening himself, just that something was very wrong.

As fast as Conran moved, he knew his brothers were directly behind him. Because at least one of them crashed into his back when he stumbled to a halt just inside the room at the sight of Tildy trying to pull Evina's naked and wet body from the tub. That wasn't what brought him to a halt, however; it was the fact that Evina's eyes were closed and she was as pale as death, her skin and lips bearing a slightly blue tinge that made his balls shrivel.

"Help me!"

That screech from Tildy did the trick, and Conran charged forward to scoop Evina out of the warm water.

"Set her on the bed," Rory ordered, appearing beside him.

Conran obeyed automatically, carrying her still form to the bed and setting her there on her back.

"On her stomach! Turn her over, and let her head and upper chest hang off the bed."

Conran glanced around at that barked order to peer uncertainly at the Maclean. The man hadn't been at table, so must have come from his room, drawn by the scream as well.

"Do it!" the man barked, hobbling toward the bed.

Conran glanced to Rory, but did as the man said.

"Pound her back," the Maclean growled, stopping beside him as Conran finished turning Evina onto her stomach on the edge of the bed so that her upper body hung off, her head dangling toward the floor.

"M'laird," Rory began soothingly, and Conran glanced to him, awaiting his instruction. Rory was the healer. He would know what to do.

However, before Rory could finish whatever he'd intended to say, Donnan was suddenly there beside Conran, pushing on Evina's back once, and then twice, and finally a third time, before he quickly turned her over and bent to kiss her.

"What the hell!" Conran roared, and reached for the man, but the Maclean caught his arm to stop him.

"He's breathing for her," he growled.

Conran turned his gaze back to Donnan and then shifted to the side to get a better look and saw the man wasn't kissing her, so much as blowing air into her mouth while pinching her nose. His attention shifted to her chest and he saw it expand slightly with each breath, and then a choking sound drew his eyes back toward her face as Donnan straightened and Evina began sputtering and coughing.

"Damn," Rory breathed. "I ne'er would have thought to do that."

"Me wife did it to our son when he was a boy and fell into the loch, taking in water. She was desperate. She pushed on his back to get the water out that she could, and then she breathed into him until he could breathe for himself," Fearghas said quietly. "It worked. Even she was surprised that it did."

"Evina did the same for ye after she got ye out o' the river when she knocked ye out. 'Tis how I kenned to do it. I'd ne'er seen it ere that," Donnan announced, getting to his feet and backing away to make room as Tildy rushed forward with a plaid in hand.

"She did?" Conran asked with surprise.

"Aye. Donnan thought she was molesting ye," Gavin announced, drawing Conran's gaze around to see that the room was full of people. His brothers, his sister, their mates, Donnan, Gavin, Fearghas, Tildy and even Betsy were all there, he noted, and then turned back to the bed as Tildy helped Evina sit up and wrapped the plaid around her to cover her up.

"Me wound got wet," Evina mumbled, sounding apologetic of all things.

"What happened?" Conran asked, moving closer to the bed, and just barely restraining himself from picking her up and holding her. Color had flooded her face, just emphasizing in his mind how pale she'd been when he'd first entered.

When Evina shook her head with bewilderment, Tildy said, "I was going below to fetch another linen for her to dry with. But halfway down the stairs I thought I should take the dirty tunic and bed linens down with me fer laundering to save a trip later, so turned back."

"Aye?" Conran said impatiently. He'd seen her leave and turn back. He wanted to know what had happened to Evina.

"When I came back in, there was a man bent over the tub, holding m'lady under the bathwater," Tildy said with a shudder that spoke of how much that sight had affected her.

"What man?" Fearghas snapped. "Where'd he go?"

Tildy turned to her laird and shook her head with bewilderment. "I do no' ken. He just . . . disappeared," she said almost plaintively.

"What?" Conran asked with disbelief.

Tildy nodded firmly. "Truly, he did. I screamed, and he did no' even glance around. He just let m'lady go and ran toward the fireplace. I rushed forward to grab m'lady and try to pull her out of the tub, and then looked for him, but he was gone. Just gone. Like a ghost."

"Did ye see who it was?" Fearghas asked grimly.

Tildy shook her head unhappily. "All I saw was his back."

A curse from the Maclean drew Conran's gaze just before the man barked, "Everyone out but me daughter and her betrothed."

Conran stared at the man with surprise. He had to admit that while the Maclean had seemed thin and frail-looking from illness since his arrival, he appeared powerful and strong in that moment. Conran wasn't at all surprised when everyone began to shuffle out the door.

"Aulay," he said quietly, and when his eldest brother stopped and turned a questioning face his way, Conran asked, "Would ye and the boys wait in the hall, please? Ye may yet all be needed, and Rory definitely will."

Aulay nodded, and then ushered everyone out.

Conran settled on the edge of the bed next to Evina then and wrapped his arm around her to draw her against his chest. She was trembling and shivering, so he rubbed her arm soothingly as he glanced to her father and spoke his guess aloud. "A secret passage?"

"Aye," the Maclean growled, and hobbled over to the fireplace. Reaching up, he grasped the torch holder on the left of the fireplace and turned it on the wall until it was upside down. As he stepped back, a portion of the wall slid silently open. "From what Tildy said happened, this is the only way he could have escaped."

Nodding, Conran eased Evina away, and stood to cross the room and join Fearghas at the entrance to the passage in the walls of the castle. Squinting into the darkness, he asked, "Who else kens this is here?"

"Evina, Gavin and meself," he answered promptly.

"Who else?" Conran asked.

"No one," the Maclean responded, and his expression said it all. It hadn't been him, and Evina was the victim. That left Gavin.

"'Twas no' Gavin."

Conran turned toward the bed at that raspy growl from Evina. She was sitting up straight now. Her shivering and trembling had stopped. It looked as if anger had chased them right out of her, because there was no mistaking she was angry.

"How can ye even think it, Da?" she asked now, her voice painfully hoarse and getting worse each time she spoke. "Gavin would ne'er hurt me."

"I would no' believe it o' him either, lass," her father said wearily. "But there simply is no one else who kens about the passages in the walls, and how to open them."

"Obviously, there is," Evina countered. "Because it could no' have been Gavin." When her father's expression didn't change, she added, "Tildy said me attacker disappeared by the fireplace. But Gavin was here with the rest o' ye when I woke up."

"He could have slipped into the adjoining bedchamber through the entrance there, and joined everyone in here," her father pointed out solemnly.

"Aye, mayhap he could have. But he'd no' do that to me," Evina argued with frustration.

Cursing, Conran turned and moved to the door.

"What are ye doing?" Fearghas barked before he could open it.

"I need a torch to search the passage," he said quietly.

The Maclean frowned and then said, "We'll need help searching it. It splits into two different paths and neither o' them should be searched alone." He paused briefly, a battle warring on his face, and then the Maclean sighed and said, "Aulay and Rory seem trustworthy."

"Everyone in me family is trustworthy," Conran assured him. "Even Greer. But I can do with Aulay and Rory."

When the Maclean nodded, he opened the door and then stopped as his gaze slid over the group in the hall. While he'd asked his brothers to wait upstairs, he'd expected the others to go below. None of them had. In fact, their numbers seemed to have grown with servants and soldiers filling their ranks.

Smiling apologetically, Conran said, "Aulay and Rory, I need ye in the room. Geordie, I need ye to stay up here and make sure no one leaves or enters through this door, please."

"I can help search the secret passages," Saidh said at once, stepping forward.

Conran glanced at her with surprise. "How did ye—?"

"Oh, please, brother," she said with disgust. "Have ye yet been in a castle that does no' have them? I think it must be a royal decree: *'When building a castle, loyal subjects will be sure to install a secret passage.'*"

"We men can search the passage while Saidh and Jetta sit with Evina," was Greer's counteroffer.

Saidh turned a scowl of irritation on her husband. "Rory is the healer. He should sit with Evina. I want to help search the tunnels."

"No' in yer condition," Greer growled.

"Why must ye act like being with child is the same as being crippled?" Saidh asked with frustration.

"Because I love ye," Greer snapped.

"I think ye should take this argument below stairs. Or mayhap to yer room," Conran added dryly as he noted the way Greer's declaration had made his sister soften and sway toward him. Turning to his brothers then, he added, "The Maclean requested Aulay and Rory and 'tis his castle. So, if the two o' ye are willing?"

Nodding, Aulay bent to press a kiss to Jetta's forehead and murmured something in her ear. He then followed Rory to stand next to him.

"Jetta, if I carry Evina to yer room, would ye be good enough to sit with her until we are done?" Conran asked now.

"O' course," she said at once, straightening as if she'd been knighted.

"And Greer and I will guard them," Saidh put in sweetly.

Conran smiled wryly at Greer's annoyed expression, but merely nodded and said, "I'll bring her out."

He didn't wait for a response, but hurried back into the bedchamber, aware that Aulay and Rory were following.

"How many kenned about the passage ere this?" Aulay asked once he'd closed the bedroom door behind them.

Conran glanced over as his brothers walked to the open entrance to the passage and peered into the darkness. "Three."

"Three," Fearghas agreed.

Evina said, "We do no' ken."

Aulay turned back to raise his eyebrows.

"Evina and Gavin are the only ones I told about it, and I was the only one still alive who kenned about it ere that," Fearghas growled.

"But since 'twas neither Da nor Gavin who attacked me, someone else obviously kens about it that we're no' aware of," Evina put in determinedly.

Conran noted the frown beginning to pull at Aulay's face, and then a thought struck him and he turned away from the bed, and strode back to the door to the hall. He paused briefly after opening it, startled to find that not only was everyone still there in the hall, but the group had grown again with more soldiers and servants and even Cook having joined the ranks. It spoke well of Evina that they were all so obviously concerned about their lady, Conran thought as he searched the group for Tildy. Spotting the woman pacing at the back of the group, with worry on her face, he slipped into the hall and maneuvered his way through the crowd to approach her.

"Oh, Lord Buchanan." She met his gaze anxiously as he stopped before her. "Is m'lady all right?"

"Aye," Conran assured her. "She is fine. I just wanted to ask ye, did ye recognize the man trying to drown yer lady?"

"Nay," she said at once.

"So, he was no one ye ken?" he asked with relief.

Tildy shook her head, and then frowned and added, "Well . . . he maybe did look a bit familiar. But I did no' get a good look. His back was to me."

"How was he familiar, then?" Conran asked, and when she frowned, he suggested, "Describe him to me."

"Well, he was big, but no' big like Donnan, big like Gavin," she explained, and then added, "And he had long dark hair like Gavin, and . . ." She shook her head. "I really did no' get a good look at him."

"Could it have been Gavin?" Conran asked quietly.

"Oy!" Gavin said with shock, moving through the crowd to stand next to them, but Conran ignored him, his attention on Tildy. The maid had flinched away from the suggestion as if he'd struck her in the face.

"Oh, nay!" she cried with dismay. "He'd ne'er hurt m'lady. Why, she's like a mother and sister all rolled into one to him."

"Aye, she is," Gavin said grimly. "I'd sooner die than hurt Evina. She and me uncle are me only family. They took me in as a boy and raised me. How could ye think I'd hurt her?"

"Because you, the Maclean and Evina are the only ones who kenned about the passage," Conran said unapologetically.

Gavin frowned, but before he could respond, Tildy said stoutly, "Well, someone else must ken about them, then, because I am positive 'twas no' Gavin."

Conran turned back to scowl at her. "Ye can't be positive. Ye just said he was the same size and had the same hair as Gavin and ye didn't see his face."

"Aye, but the man's hair was greasy and matted and his clothes filthy and ratty," Tildy argued, and shook her head. "'Twas no' Gavin."

Conran didn't argue the point further. Gavin didn't have matted hair, and his plaid and shirt were clean. The attacker hadn't been Gavin.

"Ye didn't truly believe I'd hurt Evina, did ye, Uncle Fearghas?" Gavin asked now, and Conran swung around to see that not only the Maclean, but Aulay and Rory too, had followed him out into the hall.

"I'm sorry, lad," the Maclean said now with true regret. "I should have known it couldn't be you. But as far as I ken, you, me and Evina are all that kenned about the passages. I couldn't think who else it could be. I still can't. No one else should ken about them."

Gavin relaxed a bit, but assured him, "I told no one about them."

The Maclean grimaced, but nodded and glanced to Conran to say, "We can sort out how the bastard kenned about the passages after we catch him."

"Aye. We'd best go find him, then," Conran said grimly, and grabbed the lit torch in the holder on the wall next to him.

Nodding, the Maclean turned to head back into Evina's room. Rory and Aulay followed, but Aulay grabbed the torch from the other side of the door as he did.

Conran was halfway across the room to the passage entrance when he spotted Evina. She'd wrapped the plaid around herself like a toga, and was out of bed, dragging a gown out of the chest at the foot of her bed. The stubborn woman was still healing from a chest wound, and had nearly been drowned, but he had no doubt she'd intended to dress herself and join them in the hall to defend her cousin.

Conran didn't know whether to shake her for putting someone else's well-being ahead of her own, or kiss her for being a woman who was strong and loyal and didn't hesitate to protect the people she loved. He suspected it was a quandary he'd experience often in the years ahead.

Shaking his head, Conran started toward her, and then paused and peered down at the torch he held.

"I'll hold it for ye," Rory said quietly, taking the torch from him.

"Thank ye," he murmured, and then hurried to Evina and scooped her up.

Caught by surprise, she squawked in alarm and dropped the gown she'd just pulled out of the chest. She also formed a fist and pulled her hand back, ready to plow him one, but stopped when she saw it was him.

"Oh," she said on a sigh, and then scowled at him. "What happened? Ye did no' accuse Gavin of trying to drown me and have him shackled up in the dungeon, did ye?"

"Nay. I asked Tildy what she saw," he explained as he turned to carry her to the door.

"And?" she asked abruptly.

"And ye were right. 'Twas no' Gavin," he admitted. "Jetta is going to sit with ye, and Saidh and Greer are going to guard ye while we search the passage."

"Who is Jetta?" Evina asked with bewilderment as Rory opened the door for them. The question made Conran realize she hadn't yet been introduced to his sister-in-law, or probably even told she was here.

"I am Jetta," Aulay's wife announced, moving to the front of the group waiting in the hall and smiling at her.

"Evina, this is Aulay's wife, Jetta," he introduced her. "She arrived yesterday with Saidh and Greer and me brother, Geordie."

"Oh." Evina managed a smile and nodded at the woman, offering a polite, "'Tis a pleasure to meet ye."

Before Jetta could respond, Greer stepped up and said, "I'll take her. I ken ye want to get to yer search."

Conran almost refused the offer and carried Evina down the hall himself, but aware that Aulay, Rory and Fearghas were waiting, he reluctantly handed her over, muttering, "We'll be quick as we can."

Nodding, Greer started off down the hall with Saidh and Jetta following and Tildy close on their heels.

"Do ye want me to help Greer guard Evina? Or stay here and guard the door with Geordie?" Alick asked, drawing his attention away from the small group.

"Go with Greer, please, Alick," Conran said without hesitation. With so many people here, Geordie didn't need any extra help watching the door. Mostly his job would be to keep anyone from entering the room and seeing where the passage entrance was.

"Will do," Alick said, and hurried after the small group. Conran offered Geordie a nod then, and reentered the bedchamber.

Closing the door, he took the torch Rory was holding for him and led the way across the room. Pausing at the open entrance, Conran stepped just inside and held his torch up to look around. It was extremely narrow and the darkness seemed to devour the light. He couldn't see far at all before the light was crowded out. "Where does the passage go?"

"It leads along the wall on this side of the castle all the way to the tower, and then it splits," the Maclean growled, managing to stay on his heels despite his hobbling. "One path turns sharply with the wall and becomes stairs leading down to a passage on the ground floor that exits by the apple grove behind the kitchens. The other leads to stairs that curve with the tower and lead down to a tunnel under it that travels away from the castle to a—Damn!"

Conran glanced around in surprise to see that the Maclean had moved away from him and was now hobbling back across the room.

When Aulay raised his eyebrows in question, Conran merely shook his head and followed the old man. He wasn't terribly surprised to find the hall still full of servants and soldiers milling about when the Maclean opened the door, so stopped behind him to block any view into the room. They all knew about the passage now, he was sure, but they didn't need to know where it was in the room.

"Donnan," Fearghas Maclean barked, and the soldier moved to the front of the crowd at once. "Take twenty men and go search the valley two miles west o' the loch. Nay, take thirty men. Collect anyone ye find there and bring him back," the Maclean added grimly.

The man nodded and rushed toward the stairs at once, tagging several soldiers he passed on the way and taking them with him.

"Gavin!" the Maclean snapped when the lad started to follow. "Donnan can find someone to replace ye. I need ye to take the same number o' men and go around behind the kitchens." He paused briefly and then added, "Ye ken where."

Gavin nodded, and followed the same path Donnan had, calling out to several of the remaining soldiers to accompany him. Despite that, the hallway was still crowded with people. It looked to Conran like more servants and soldiers had made their way above stairs each time they'd opened the door.

"Let's go," the Maclean said grimly, turning back to him.

Nodding, Conran stepped aside to let him enter and then closed the door on the curious eyes trying to see into the room and turned to lead the man back to the passage entrance.

"Right," Conran said as he plunged into the dark passage, thrusting his torch out ahead. "Aulay and Rory can take the path that leads behind the castle when we get to the split, and ye and I can take the path away from the castle," he suggested, and then recalled that the man was still recovering from an injured arse and said, "Or mayhap ye and Rory should take the path around behind the castle if 'tis shorter."

"I can manage the path away from the castle," the Maclean assured him, his voice harsh. "The bastard tried to kill me daughter. I'm no' letting him get away with that."

"Nay," Conran agreed grimly.

It was Rory who asked, "What if he's already out of the passages and tunnel?"

"If he took the passage around behind the castle he'll stand out like a sore thumb among me people and be captured at once," the Maclean said firmly. "But if he took the tunnel that leads out beyond the wall, the men will beat him. 'Tis a very long tunnel and the men will be on horseback. Even if he ran flat-out the whole way, they'd beat him there."

Conran didn't comment, he merely nodded, counting on it being visible in the torchlight. But he was silently hoping the man was still in the passages somewhere. He'd like to get his hands on the bastard himself.

Chapter 11

"*R*ORY OBVIOUSLY DID NO' TROUBLE HIMSELF TO SEE TO BANdaging yer wound ere hying off with the other men, did he?" Saidh asked with annoyance.

Evina merely shook her head as Greer set her down on the bed in the chamber Aulay and Jetta were using.

"Oh, dear, ye're bleeding," Jetta said, moving to her side at once.

Evina glanced down. The plaid had slipped at some point, revealing the top of her breast and the wound there. Blood was sliding from it and disappearing under the plaid.

"Damn," she muttered in an irritated whisper. The wound hadn't bled since the second day, but it seemed its getting wet, or perhaps her struggles against the man who had tried to drown her, had opened it up again.

She wasn't the only one cursing. As Tildy hurried to her side, she had some fine choice words to say about the men running off without tending her wound first.

"I'll have to get me medicinals, the salve Lord Rory gave me and some linens from yer room and bind ye up again," Tildy said with annoyance as she examined the wound.

"Here we go again," Alick muttered.

"Here we go what?" Tildy asked with confusion.

"They'll no' let ye go back to me room any more than they did me, Tildy," Evina reminded her.

Evina scowled at the young man, still annoyed that they hadn't let her go back to her room to fetch clothes. They had nearly been to this room when she'd recalled the gown she'd dropped when Conran had picked her up so abruptly and startled her. She'd immediately asked Greer to set her down so that she could return to her room to collect the gown and a tunic, but everyone had protested the suggestion. Not wanting to have to sit about in mixed company with only the plaid wrapped around her for covering, Evina had argued strenuously. But when Saidh had offered to loan her a tunic and gown, she'd finally relented. She'd rather have her own clothes, but Greer and Alick simply weren't going to allow her to return alone to her room. Borrowed clothes would have to do.

"I have some wrappings and medicinals," Jetta announced now, hurrying to a chest against the wall. "I always bring them with me when we travel. Just in case," she added, not needing to say more. Accidents happened, and it was always good to have such things on long journeys.

"Perhaps we should step out in the hall while the women tend Evina's wound, Alick," Greer suggested.

"Do ye think we should?" Alick asked. "Conran wanted us to watch her. What if there is a passage entrance in here and her attacker uses it to get to the women?"

"I'm sure that with the women here . . ." Greer began, and then paused and frowned as his gaze moved to his wife and settled on her still-flat stomach.

Saidh's eyes narrowed angrily on her husband, and she opened her mouth, but before she could spit out whatever she would have said, Jetta blurted, "'Tis fine. I'll grab one of Aulay's plaids and Saidh and I can hold it up to give Evina privacy while Tildy tends her wound. Ye can stay."

Saidh snapped her mouth closed, but continued to glower at Greer.

Biting her lip, Evina glanced at the pair silently. She could quite easily imagine this same argument cropping up between her and Conran if they married. Did she really want that?

"WHY ARE YE STOPPING?"

Conran didn't respond right away to Laird Maclean's hissed question. He stayed still, never taking his gaze off the shifting darkness in front of them as he listened, but finally whispered, "I thought I heard a scuffing sound from ahead."

They were both silent for a moment, and then the Maclean sighed and muttered, "'Twas probably me shuffling along behind ye. Sound carries oddly in here. A noise from behind can seem like it came from in front, and another from in front can sound as if it came from behind."

Conran wasn't convinced and waited another moment. But when he didn't hear anything else, he started forward again. After another couple of minutes though, he asked, "I thought ye said there were stairs leading down just beyond where the passages separated?"

"Nay, I said they were *a bit beyond* where the passages separated," the Maclean corrected.

"Well, what do ye consider a bit?" he asked with irritation. It seemed to him that they'd gone quite a distance since parting ways with Aulay and Rory.

"They should be just ahead. Here, let me lead the way so ye do no' come upon them unexpectedly and take a tumble. They're steep, the edges on the stairs deadly sharp. Ye do no' want to tangle with them."

Conran stopped and turned sideways in the narrow passage. Pressing his back tight to the wall, he held his torch high and waited for the older man to slide past. It was a tight fit, but the Maclean managed it. Although the wince that crossed his face, and his sudden inhalation halfway through the maneuver, suggested to Conran that the old man might have rubbed his injured behind up against the opposite wall in passing. Fearghas didn't complain about it. However, Conran noted that he was hobbling a little more than he had before as he led the way to the stairs.

"It's narrow and turns," the Maclean warned, pausing suddenly. When he put one hand out to the side to brace himself, Conran suspected they'd reached the stairs and held his torch up a little higher. Over the man's shoulder, he could see the steps hewn into the stone, and that they disappeared around a curve. They were entering the wall of the tower now, the stairs following the curve around the outside as they descended.

Conran waited, watching until the man was three or four steps down. He started to follow then, but a noise behind him made him hesitate.

Turning, he held the torch up and started back the way they'd come, his eyes narrowing as he searched the shadows. He didn't see anything, but something had made that noise.

"Oy! What's happening? The light is dimming. Buchanan?" the Maclean shouted, sounding distressed.

"I'm here," Conran reassured him, spinning back the way he'd come. He started forward, but a slight sound, almost like an exhalation, made him stop once more. Before he could turn again to look around, he was punched in the upper back.

Caught by surprise, Conran stumbled forward three steps. It was only three, because on the third when his foot came down, the ground suddenly wasn't there. It was the first stair tread leading down, but by the time he realized that, it was too late. He'd lost his balance and was falling.

Conran shouted as he went. He heard the Maclean's responding shout of alarm, and then he was crashing and rolling down the stairs, pain exploding in his head, his shoulder, his leg. He was vaguely aware of something catching at his plaid at one point, but it barely slowed him. A tearing sound rent the air as he continued careening down the sharp, hard steps. By the time Conran came to a halt at the bottom of what he'd begun to think was an endless stairwell, he was hurting everywhere. But he hadn't been knocked unconscious. That was something.

"Buchanan!" That shout was followed by the sound of the Maclean hobbling quickly down the stairs after him and he wondered a little dazedly how he hadn't knocked the man down in the narrow space, and sent him tumbling too.

"Are ye all right, lad?" The Maclean's voice sounded closer this time and Conran wanted to tell him he was all right, but was busy trying not to scream in pain. Dear God, he hurt everywhere, but his back hurt the worst.

Something brushed up against Conran's foot, but he couldn't see what in the darkness, so was relieved when the Maclean spoke. "That's you, is it? Damn, lad, ye took a hell of a tumble." His voice was at the same level as Conran now, and he guessed that the man had dropped to his knees beside him. "I should have warned ye the stairs were uneven and like to trip ye up if ye were no' careful."

"I didn't trip. I was pushed," Conran hissed through his gritted teeth.

"Pushed?" Fearghas gasped with a new alarm.

"Aye, well, punched in the back, really," he said grimly. "Either way, I didn't fall, and the bastard is here somewhere."

"Damn, he could be creeping up on us as we speak," the Maclean growled. "It's bloody dark in here without the torch. I can no' see a thing, whether we're alone, how badly ye're hurt, nothing."

Conran had no idea where the torch was. He'd dropped it as he fell, and it had apparently gone out. He didn't bother to say that though; he was busy listening for any sound of someone approaching.

"Can ye stand?"

Conran gave up listening and slowly began to sit up. Everything hurt. His head, his chest, his back, his shoulder, his hip, his knee . . . but he managed to sit upright. Now he just had to stand. Grimacing, he braced one hand on the ground and one on the wall and started to push himself to his feet. His legs were oddly weak and shaky, however. Probably from the shock of the fall, he thought grimly.

"Here." The Maclean felt around until he found the hand Conran had braced against the wall and drew it up over his shoulder. "I'll help ye up, son. Just put yer weight on me."

Conran shifted slowly, bracing his other hand on the wall now to help take his weight as he half pushed himself upward, and was half pulled to his feet.

"Damn," Conran breathed once he was upright. He was standing, but felt like hell and thought he must have taken a good crack to the head.

"Ye're none too steady on yer feet, son," Fearghas said with concern. "Mayhap I should go get some help."

"Nay!" Conran grabbed his arm to stop him as the man started to shift away in the dark. "If whoever punched me is still here, they could attack ye. It's better to stick together. I'm fine. I can make it. Just give me a minute to catch me breath."

The Maclean held his tongue, but Conran could practically feel his concern reaching out to him through the darkness. Fortunately, after taking a few deep breaths, he felt a good deal steadier.

"Let's go," he said, shuffling in the direction he thought the stairs must be. A little relieved breath slipped from him when the toe of his boot bumped up against the first step.

"Take it slow and easy," Fearghas warned, following so closely behind him Conran was sure he could feel the heat from the old man's body at his back.

"Aye," was all Conran said. Slow and easy was all he could manage at the moment anyway. At least, at first, but after several steps some of the aches began to recede and he started to feel a little better and began to move more quickly. Dear God, the stairs felt as endless going up as they had coming down, and Conran was just about to ask how much farther the Maclean thought they had to go when he heard his name called. Pausing, he peered up, and noted the weak light creeping around the curving staircase, pushing into the darkness ahead of them.

"Aulay?" he asked, quite sure that was who had called his name.

"Aye," came the reply. "We heard shouts. Are ye all right?"

"I've been better," he muttered, starting to move again, but warned, "He's up there somewhere. The bastard punched me in the back and sent me tumbling down the stairs. We're coming up now."

"Is anything broken?" Rory asked. "Do ye need help?"

"Nay," Conran sighed the word, and then said it louder, before adding, "I lost me torch, is all, so we're moving slowly. We'll be there . . ." He paused in surprise as he took the next step and realized how close to the top they'd been when the lit torch and a lone figure came into view.

"Rory?" he asked, squinting at the figure as he continued up the steps.

"Aye. Aulay's checking the passage for yer attacker," Rory explained his absence.

Nodding, Conran took the last few steps up to the landing in silence, relieved to get off the deadly stairs.

"Ye're rubbing yer head. Did ye hit it?" Rory asked, holding the torch toward him briefly as the Maclean moved up beside them.

"Aye, and 'tis pounding a bit," Conran admitted in a mutter.

"Are ye all right?" Aulay asked, coming out of the shadows.

"I'll survive," Conran said with a shrug that made him wince. Damn, the bastard had hit him hard. His shoulder was killing him.

Aulay was silent for a minute, and then pointed out, "For someone to push ye, they had to have got around behind ye."

"Aye," Conran murmured, peering into the darkness of the passage.

"He must have slipped into one of the bedrooms until we passed and then come out behind us," Fearghas said grimly.

"We should have stationed someone in each of the rooms before we entered the passage," Conran said grimly. "But I thought from Tildy's description that he was an outsider and would just flee."

"What about her description made ye think he was an outsider?" Rory asked with interest.

Rather than answer, he asked, "Have ye seen anyone at Maclean wearing ratty clothes or who were so unkempt their hair was matted?"

"Nay," Rory admitted, appearing surprised. "Everyone I've seen seems to make an effort to look clean and presentable."

"Aye, me wife always insisted on it," Fearghas growled. "She said filth spreads disease and she'd no' have the servants and soldiers bringing in lice and fleas and illness." He sighed, and then admitted, "After she died, I probably would have let well enough alone and allowed the servants and soldiers to carry on as they wished, but Evina was her mother's daughter. She insisted things continue as they had before."

"So, the attacker has to be an outsider," Aulay murmured.

Fearghas ran a hand through his wiry hair in agitation. "I just can no' see how an outsider found out about the passage."

"Ye say ye only told Evina and Gavin?" Aulay asked.

"Aye."

Conran frowned. "Then one of them must have told someone else."

The Maclean scowled at him for the suggestion. "Nay. Neither of them would tell anyone."

"Perhaps when they were children," Rory suggested gently.

"Neither of them kenned as children," Fearghas countered. "I did no' tell Evina until she was sixteen. Gavin either. I only told him just months ago on his birthday. Neither of them would reveal the secret to another. I'd stake me life on it," he said with certainty.

When no one had any other suggestions as to how an outsider could know, Conran shifted wearily and said, "We'll need to station men in each room with an entrance to the passage so that he can't use them to avoid us as we search the passages again."

"Or I could just lock off the entrances from each room," the Maclean suggested.

Conran glanced at him sharply. "They lock from the inside?"

"Well, aye. Ye have to be able to secure them for just such a situation as this," he pointed out.

"O' course," Conran agreed with a wry smile, but then his expression grew serious and he said, "Ye shouldn't go alone in case he's in one of the rooms right now."

"He probably is," Aulay said now. "He pushed ye from up here, and neither Rory nor I encountered him on our return along the path around the castle. He must have slipped into one of the rooms after pushing ye."

"Aye, and he can slip out again as we enter the rooms to lock the entrances, unless someone is here," Conran pointed out. "Will ye and Rory—?"

"We'll guard the passage until ye get each of the entrances locked," Aulay assured him.

"Thank ye," Conran murmured. "Then I'll accompany Laird Maclean. We'll try to be quick."

When the two men merely nodded, Conran turned to head up the passage.

"Con?"

Pausing, he glanced back in question, noting his eldest brother's serious expression in the light from the torch. "Aye?"

"Ye need to start with the Maclean's room, and move this way. The passage starts there."

"Aye, he's right," Fearghas murmured behind him.

Conran didn't bother mentioning that he'd thought of that himself; he merely asked the Maclean, "Ye can open it from this side, can ye no'?"

"Aye. Follow me." The old man squeezed past him and led the way to the end of the passage. It took them away from the light cast by Aulay's torch. Conran was about to suggest his brother move farther down this way, but Aulay did it of his own accord.

"Stand there." Fearghas took Conran's arm to shift him so that his body blocked what he was doing from his brothers. The old man then turned a rock that looked just like all the others, and stepped back as a section of wall slid outward.

"We'll search the laird's room before we lock the entrance from inside," Conran told his brothers as he started to follow his soon-to-be father-in-law into the room. "We'll open it again and give ye the all clear before we lock it and move on to Evina's room."

He heard Aulay's grunt of acknowledgment as he stepped into the chamber.

The bright light after so long in the dark was blinding. Conran paused just inside the room, blinking rapidly in an effort to regain his sight more quickly.

"Damn, we were in there so long I forgot 'tis early morning yet," the Maclean growled, rubbing his eyes irritably.

Conran glanced to the open shutters. Dazzling sunlight was pouring through them and filling the room, highlighting the fact that it was empty, and didn't have much in the way of hiding spaces. Just two places that he could see—under the bed, or in one of the chests against the wall.

"I'll check the chests," Fearghas growled when Conran moved to the bed and dropped to his knees.

Conran merely nodded, and looked under the bed. He was getting back up almost as soon as he got down. The only thing under it was a half-gnawed bone. He supposed it must have been left behind by one of the dogs the Maclean had mentioned. Joining the man at his chests, Conran opened one and began pulling out shirts and plaids.

"Surely that's no' necessary," the Maclean said with surprise.

"We once had someone we were hunting evade us by hiding under the clothes in a chest," Conran said grimly.

"Oh." Fearghas eyed him with interest. "Did ye catch them?"

"Aye. Eventually," he muttered, and dropped the clothes back in. Conran closed that chest, and moved to the second one even as the Maclean started dragging bed linens out of the one he'd been searching.

"Empty," the Maclean announced a moment later.

"Mine too," Conran said, letting the lid of the chest he'd been rifling through slam shut.

Nodding, Fearghas moved back to the passage entrance, opened it and stuck his head out to tell Aulay and Rory the room was clear, and they were locking the entrance and moving on to the next room.

Geordie was standing guard outside the door to Evina's room as requested. But there were so many people around him it was hard to tell at first.

"Get on with ye," the Maclean growled as he led Conran through the group. "Surely ye've all got work to do. Get to it. Me daughter's fine and there's nothing more to see here."

The crowd dispersed quickly, everyone heading for the stairs, and Geordie nodded in greeting. He also raised an eyebrow at the fact that they'd come from behind the crowd rather than out of Evina's room, but Conran didn't explain. He merely nodded at his brother in response and followed Fearghas Maclean into Evina's room. Aulay stood in the open entrance to the passage when they entered.

Conran acknowledged him with a glance and then peered around the room. Everything looked just as it had when last he saw it. As with the Maclean's room, there were just the chests, and under the bed to check. They made quick work of it.

"Rory and I'll move down the passage to the next entrance," Aulay said once they'd finished. He then slid away from the entrance as the Maclean started to close and lock it. That done, they moved on to the next room, nodding at Geordie again in passing.

After a quick search of Gavin's room, where Saidh and Greer were staying, they were moving on to Conran's own room. He didn't even have a chest though, so it was a quick check under the bed and they were done.

Conran had entered each room with his hand on his sword, ready to draw it if needed, but as they approached the room Rory and Alick had been given, he unsheathed it altogether to hold it at the ready.

"Aye, I'm getting a little tense meself," the Maclean said quietly.

"Trouble?" Geordie asked, approaching.

"The bastard has to be in one of these last two rooms," Fearghas explained solemnly.

"This room," Conran corrected him, and then pointed out, "Aulay and Jetta are staying in the last room, and Greer, Saidh, Jetta and Tildy took Evina there while we searched the passages. There is no way he would go there. That leaves only this room for him to hide in."

"Well, hell," the Maclean muttered, and reached for his own sword even as Geordie did.

"Ready?" Conran asked once they all had weapons in hand.

"Aye," Geordie said quietly.

"Open it," the Maclean growled.

Nodding, Conran tightened his grip on his sword and thrust the door open with his free hand. The three of them then lunged through together, swords raised and eyes wild as they searched the . . . empty room.

Feeling a little foolish, Conran lowered his sword and grimaced at the other two men.

"No chests," the Maclean pointed out. "Yer brothers only brought bags with them."

Conran merely nodded and moved to look under the bed. He did it from several feet away though, just to be safe. But it was a wasted effort. This room too was empty. Getting back to his feet, he glanced to the other two men and shook his head.

"Well, hell," Fearghas muttered, and slid his sword back into its sheath. Frowning, he glanced toward the fireplace, and then toward Geordie. Seeing that Conran's brother had walked back to stand in the doorway and peer out into the hall at something, the Maclean quickly walked over to the fireplace and turned the torch holder next to it.

Aulay appeared at once when a section of wall slid silently inward. He opened his mouth to speak, but when the Maclean put a finger to his lips in a motion to be quiet, and then waved him in, he merely raised his eyebrows and led Rory to the center of the room. His brothers were then good enough to keep their backs to Evina's father, allowing him to lock down the passage without witnesses.

"I gather ye did no find the man?" Aulay said once the Maclean had closed and locked the passage and moved to join them.

Conran saw Geordie glance over his shoulder with surprise at Aulay's question, but merely shook his head. "And Greer, Alick and the women are in the last room so the attacker can't be there."

"Where the devil did the bastard go?" Fearghas asked with frustration. "He could no' have slid past us on the steps, 'tis too narrow. He should have been in the passage or the rooms. Unless . . ." He turned to Geordie. "No one came out into the hall?"

Conran nodded in appreciation when Geordie stepped back into the room and closed the door before speaking. The Maclean was so upset he'd started talking about the passage with the door wide open. Not that it mattered, he supposed. Everyone probably understood there were passages in the keep now.

"No' that I saw," Geordie answered, and then pointed out, "But there were a lot of people in the hall, and someone could have slipped out of one of the rooms and joined the others without me noticing."

"Ye'd have noticed," Conran said with certainty. "Filthy and with matted hair, he'd have stood out among the others."

"Aye," the Maclean muttered, and glanced to Aulay and Rory. "And ye're sure he didn't get past the two o' you?"

Both men shook their heads, but Rory added, "There is no way he could have slid past us in the passage we took. There simply wasn't room," Rory said with certainty. "Ye're sure he wasn't in any of the bedchambers?"

"Positive," Conran assured him.

"Did ye check the chests in each room thoroughly?" Aulay asked, his gaze narrowing.

"Aye," Conran assured him. "We took out clothes and linens or whatever was in them."

"So, he isn't in the passages, or the rooms," Aulay murmured, and then frowned. "He didn't just disappear into thin air. We've missed something."

"Aye," Conran agreed. "But what?"

Aulay shook his head, obviously not coming up with anything either. "Conran."

"Hmm." He glanced to Rory absently, his mind on Tildy's description of the man who had tried to drown Evina. While everyone at Maclean was well-kempt, it occurred to him that he *had* seen someone with matted hair and filthy ratty clothes since coming to Maclean, but—

"Ye're bleeding."

"What?" Conran asked with surprise, his attention captured. Raising his eyebrows, he glanced down at himself, but didn't see any blood.

"Yer head," Aulay growled as Rory crossed the room to get a better look at him.

"Oh." Conran shrugged that concern away. He'd noted that as he'd searched the laird's room. He'd felt something drip down his cheek as he'd bent to look under the bed, and had wiped it away with the back of a hand. There had been blood on his hand afterward, but it hadn't seemed a lot, so he hadn't worried overmuch about it.

"Ye've a nasty knot and gash," Rory announced, clasping his chin and the back of his head to tilt him this way and that as he squinted at his scalp.

"'Twill go nicely with the other two bumps I got ere arriving here," Conran said dryly, tugging his head free of his brother's hold. "'Tis fine. There did no' appear to be much blood when I wiped it away."

"How are ye feeling?" Rory asked, frowning at the wound on his head. "Any dizziness? Is yer vision all right? Nausea? Confusion? Headache?"

"Me head hurts a bit," he admitted. "And aye, I'm a might confused, but only about how a bandit could find out about the Maclean passages."

"A bandit?" Fearghas asked aghast.

"Aye," Conran said solemnly. "The bandit who injured Gavin and then escaped is the only person I've met since coming to Maclean who matches Tildy's description."

When the Maclean looked nonplussed at the words, and then frowned and shook his head, he added, "All of the bandits were a mangy crew, but the one who got away fit Tildy's description perfectly. He was a match for Gavin, the same basic size and shape, and had long, matted and greasy hair as well as dark ratty clothes," he explained, and then sucked in a sharp breath as Rory poked at the wound on his head. He scowled at his brother and then turned back to see that the Maclean was staring at him as if he'd gone daft.

"The bandit may have fit the description, lad," Feaghas said dryly. "But I somehow don't think a mangy bandit could find out about our passages."

Conran nodded. That had been his thought too, but . . . "It's possible he paid a servant to tell him about any points of entry to the keep."

"Aye, but as I told ye," Fearghas said as if weary of repeating himself, "only Evina, Gavin and meself ken about the passages."

"That ye ken of," Conran said softly, and added, "'Tis hard to keep secrets in a castle with so many eyes and ears, m'laird. A servant could have been listening at the door when ye told Gavin, or even when ye told Evina years ago. Or one of yer people may have stumbled on the entrance in that clearing ye told Donnan to take men and search. That is where the passage leading down comes out, isn't it?"

"Aye," the Maclean admitted reluctantly.

"Well, one of yer people may have found the entrance entirely by accident and followed it up to the passages in the walls, and then told someone about it, who told another and—Ow! Damn, Rory! Leave off!" he growled as his brother's prodding sent sharp pain through his head.

"There is what looks like a splinter o' stone in the gash," Rory said grimly. "I'm going to have to get it out, or 'twill infect."

"It very well could be the bandit who escaped," Aulay said mildly as Rory moved over to his medicinal bag and began to gather items. "However, the question is where he is now." Raising an eyebrow, he asked Conran, "Is it possible he pushed ye down the stairs and got into the room Jetta and I are using ere Greer got there with Evina and the other women?"

Conran considered the possibility. The room was the last along the passage. He'd passed Evina to Greer, and then gone back through the room and along the passage. It was dark and slightly uneven while the hall was flat and well-lit, he was sure he'd moved much more slowly than Greer and the women would have traversed the hall the same distance. It didn't seem likely that the attacker had pushed him down the stairs and then managed to get into that bedchamber and hide before Greer got there with the women. Well, at least, not unless—

"If Greer and the women were delayed for some reason in reaching the room, then perhaps he could have managed to punch me and flee back to the room ere they entered," he admitted, and then glanced to Geordie in question. "Did they go straight to the room?"

"They started to," Geordie said quietly. "But then Lady Evina asked to go back to her chamber. She was no' comfortable in just the plaid, and wanted to go back for a gown. Greer said nay, her father had wanted everyone out. She insisted that didn't include her, and they all started arguing about whether she was capable o' fetching a gown on her own, or—Where are ye going?" Geordie broke off his explanation to ask as Conran spun on his heel and headed for the door.

"Next time, Geordie, just say, 'Nay, they didn't go straight there,'" Aulay suggested dryly as he started to follow Conran.

"Wait a damn minute, Conran. I need to tend yer head wound ere ye—" Rory's words died as Conran opened the chamber door and they heard a muffled shriek and a crash from the next room.

"Nay!" Evina said with disbelief to Saidh's words, her attention immediately reclaimed from watching Greer and Alick carry a chest across the room to set by the fireplace. Jetta and Saidh had held up a plaid to give her privacy while Tildy had tended her wound and then helped her dress in the borrowed clothes. But once that was done, Tildy had gone below to fetch beverages for everyone, and Jetta, Saidh and Evina had all taken up positions on the bed, sitting cross-legged in a triangle. It was Jetta who suggested the men make use of her chests and sit on them. The men were now moving them across the room to sit by the empty fireplace. She supposed it was an effort on their part to give them some privacy to talk.

"Aye," Saidh assured her with amusement, drawing her back to the conversation.

"Ye had three bairns at once?" Evina asked with dismay. She'd never met anyone who'd had more than one child at a time. She'd heard tales of such things, but—

"Aye, three girls," Saidh said with a grin. "They're two and a half now, thank goodness."

"Why thank goodness?" Evina asked with curiosity.

"Because I don't think I could have handled a fourth child while the first three were still in nappies or teething. But the lassies are done with both. Well, for the most part anyway. There may be one or two teeth still to come, but that should be done by the time I have this one," she said, placing a hand on her stomach.

"What if ye have triplets again?" Evina asked, eyeing her stomach with wonder.

Saidh shrugged. "Then I hope they are boys to balance things out."

"Ye would no' mind having three again?" she asked with surprise, her gaze sliding back to the men as they set down the first chest and returned for the second one at the foot of the bed.

"Whether I mind or no' won't make any difference to the number that shows up," Saidh said with amusement. "So why fret over it? I just hope however many there are, they are healthy."

"Healthy is good," Evina agreed, glancing down to her own stomach and wishing the same for the baby she might be carrying.

"Triplets run in the family," Saidh announced, and then amended, "Well, twins do."

"Do they?" Evina asked with concern.

"Aye. Aulay and Ewan were twins," Saidh told her. She glanced down at Evina's stomach and teased, "So, perhaps you'll have two or three bairns at once yerself when ye start having them."

"Accck!" Evina shrieked, and then peered sharply toward the fireplace as Alick lost his grip while lowering the chest and it dropped with a heavy thud. Shaking her head with amusement when Alick made a face, she looked back to Saidh and said, "Do no' even jest about something like—"

Evina broke off mid-sentence, turning wide eyes toward the door this time as it suddenly crashed open and Conran, his brothers and her father all charged in, swords at the ready.

Chapter 12

"*W*HERE IS HE?"

Evina's eyes widened at that growl from Conran, and when his gaze landed on her, she pointed to Greer and Alick by the chests. They were the only "hes" in the room. Apparently though, they weren't the "hes" in question. At least, that was the conclusion she came to when everyone suddenly began to move. Aulay and Geordie strode to the chests, drawing her attention when they opened them and began pulling out the dresses inside. She gaped at them briefly, and then shifted her attention back to Conran just in time to see him fall out of sight. Frowning, she shifted closer to the edge of the bed and peered over to see that he'd dropped to look under the bed.

"What is happening?" she asked as he straightened again.

Rather than answer, Conran glanced to his brothers, one eyebrow raised.

"Nothing," Aulay said, dropping the gowns back into the chest he'd been searching even as Geordie closed the lid of the second one.

"So, he did get away," her father said, sounding disappointed.

Evina frowned as she realized that they'd come here looking for her attacker. Obviously, they hadn't found him in the passages, and she assumed they'd searched the other rooms before this one, so he'd got away. The thought made her reach subconsciously for the dirk she normally wore at her waist, but of course it wasn't there.

"YER HEAD'S STILL BLEEDING," RORY SAID INTO THE SILENCE that had fallen over the room, and Evina saw that he had moved to

Conran's side to examine the bleeding wound on the side of his head. Frowning, the healer headed for the door, muttering, "I'd best go get me medicinals."

Evina eyed the wound with concern. It looked much worse than the blow she'd given him with her sword, or even from his falling off his horse. Before she could ask if he'd lost consciousness from the injury, Conran said, "We should move everyone from this room to Evina's chamber so Laird Maclean can do what needs doing here."

"Aye," her father agreed. "Better to get it done now ere some distraction or other occurs and it gets overlooked."

Evina didn't have to ask what needed doing. She suspected her father would want to lock down the entrances to the hidden passage so that her attacker couldn't return through them and harm anyone else. In fact, he'd probably done that with the other rooms ere reaching this one. At least, she thought the one in her room must be locked off, since the suggestion was they move there and not—

Her thoughts scattered on a grunt of surprise when Conran suddenly scooped her up off the bed. Evina instinctively grabbed for his shoulders, her fingers digging into the hard muscle to hold on as he straightened with her. She noticed the wince that crossed his face when she did, and then became aware of the dampness under the fingers of the hand on his left shoulder and lifted her hand to see warm, sticky blood covering her fingers.

"Ye're bleeding," Evina said with dismay.

"Aye," Conran growled, and explained, "Someone pushed me down in the passage. I hit me head."

"I'm no' speaking about yer head. Yer shoulder is bleeding too," she said, shifting in his arms in an attempt to get a better look at where the bleeding was coming from. Evina managed to glimpse the top of his upper back, but the plaid he wore was dark blue with dark red and dark green running through it and his long hair covered a good portion. Still, she did manage to see a large spreading darkness on his back.

"It's sore," he admitted. "I must have scraped it in the fall as well. 'Twill be fine."

"Rory should look at it," Evina said with concern as she moved her hand over his back and noted the cloth was sopping wet with blood.

"*Rory* would look at his head if me brother would stay still long enough for me to do so."

Evina glanced around at that exasperated comment to see Rory ahead of them in the hall, his medicinal bag under his arm, a pitcher of liquid in one hand and bandages and linens in his other. It reminded her of his announcement that he'd get his medicinals and take care of Conran's head wound.

"Nay, no' his head. His back is bleeding something fierce," Evina said, not hiding her concern.

"Good Lord! She's right," Alick said, hurrying up behind them to get a closer look at the back of Conran's plaid.

"'Tis fine," Conran growled, moving around Rory to continue up the hall.

"'Tis no' fine," Evina countered in a growl of her own. "Ye're injured and need tending. Put me down. I can walk."

"We're almost there," he argued, rather than do as she asked. When she scowled at him, Conran added, "And I like holding ye."

Evina blinked, her anger softening at the claim. The words didn't ease her concern, however, and she glanced over his shoulder, relieved to see that Rory was following closely on their heels. His attention was on Conran's back as he walked and the grim expression on his face told her Conran wasn't "fine." But she held her tongue until he had her in her chamber and was setting her down on the bed.

"Ye need to sit down," she said solemnly, popping back to her feet and grabbing his hand to drag him toward the fireplace.

"Lass," Conran began wearily as she led him to the table and chairs by the fire.

"Please," Evina insisted, pulling out the nearest chair for him. "Just sit and let yer brother tend ye."

Conran scowled, but sat down. However, he also caught the other chair around one leg with his foot and drew it closer. He then used her handhold on him to urge her into it as he added, "Only if ye distract me while he does."

Evina merely nodded and remained in the seat, her fingers entangled in his.

"Well, I'm glad ye're finally willing to sit still long enough for me to look after ye," Rory said dryly. "But I can't do it through yer plaid and shirt."

Conran reached up to remove the pin of his plaid. Once it dropped to lie in his lap, he quickly tugged the shirt he wore under it up and off.

Evina remained seated facing him as he did this, her eyes the only thing that moved. They slid over the wide expanse of chest now bare before her with interest. She'd seen the man completely naked when she'd first kidnapped him, but hadn't taken the time to study him. In fact, while he'd done the most intimate things to her, she'd never been this close to him without his shirt and plaid on while he was conscious. It was a sight to see, she decided. Enough to make her want to reach out and run her hands over all that muscled flesh.

"Ye weren't punched, ye were stabbed in the back."

Evina glanced sharply to Rory at that announcement and saw that he was frowning as he pressed clean linens to Conran's back.

"How bad is it?" Aulay asked, appearing suddenly next to Rory, and Evina glanced around to see that everyone but her father had followed them to her room and were now moving to crowd around Rory to get a look at Conran's back. Even as she noted that, her father entered the room. His first words proved he'd heard Rory's announcement as he approached.

"The bastard! Trying to drown me daughter, and then stabbing her betrothed? Who the devil is he and what is he after?"

"I wouldn't mind finding that out myself," Conran said grimly. "That and how the hell he got away?"

"He must have got past ye on the stairs after pushing ye down them," Aulay said quietly.

"Ye were pushed down the stairs?" Evina asked with dismay. All he'd said was he'd been pushed and taken a tumble; he hadn't mentioned that the tumble was down the stairs in the passage. He was lucky he hadn't broken his neck.

"I'm fine." Patting her hand reassuringly, he turned to her father and added, "'Tis lucky I didn't take ye down them with me . . . which I've been wondering about. Ye were in front of me on the stairs—how is it I *didn't* knock ye down them?"

"Hmm?" Her father glanced to him with surprise, and then said, "Oh. Well, there are three shallow crevices spaced out in the inner wall between the top and bottom of the stairs. They're just deep enough for a body to press into them to allow others to slip by. I was close to the first one when I heard ye falling behind me, and I pressed meself into it. I tried to catch ye as ye rolled by. I grabbed at ye, caught yer plaid, but . . ." He shook his head. "Yer plaid ripped, a strip tore free and ye kept going."

"That's how he got away," Conran said into the silence that fell. "He must have pressed himself into one of the crevices while ye were helping me up down at the bottom. Without the torch to light the way, we must have walked right past him in the dark."

"Damn," her father growled with apparent surprise. "It ne'er occurred to me that he might ken about the crevices. But then, he should no' have known about the passage either and he did."

"Ye sent Donnan down to the clearing," Evina pointed out. "If my attacker slipped past ye and continues down to the exit in the clearing . . ."

"Hopefully Donnan and the men will catch him," the Maclean finished, and then he glanced toward the hidden entrance and narrowed his eyes. "Or he may be on his way back up, or simply hiding in the tunnel if he saw the area was flooded with men."

"All the entrances to the bedchambers are locked now," Conran pointed out. "If we position someone at the entrance behind the castle so he can't leave, ye and I could ride down to the other entrance and enter that way. We could trap him and—"

"*Ye* aren't doing anything o' the kind," Rory said firmly. "Ye've lost a good deal of blood with this injury, and I still have to remove the stone from yer head wound. I'm amazed ye're yet sitting upright, but quite sure ye won't be for long. Someone else will have to accompany Laird Maclean."

"I'll accompany ye, m'laird," Aulay offered quietly, and when her father hesitated, he added with understanding, "Ye can even blindfold me for the ride out and until we get inside the actual tunnel if 'twould make ye feel better."

Evina's eyebrows rose at the offer. But then being a laird with his own castle that probably had its own secret tunnels, Aulay would understand that they were secret for a reason. Still, she wasn't surprised when her father sighed and shook his head. "Yer brother will soon be me son by marriage. It makes ye family. I guess I can trust ye with the secret. There's no need for a blindfold."

Aulay merely nodded his head solemnly in acknowledgment of the trust the man was showing him.

"Ye'll need to pad yer saddle, Laird Maclean," Rory announced, tossing aside the cloth he'd been pressing against Conran's back to stop the bleeding, and picking up an already threaded needle. "Take a length of cloth, roll it up and shape it in a circle, and then set it between ye and the saddle so that it's around the wound on yer arse and keeps it from hitting the saddle as ye ride."

"Me arse is fine," her father muttered, turning to head for the door.

Rory shrugged and turned to begin stitching up Conran's back. "Ye're the one who will suffer if ye do no' listen to me."

Her father muttered something uncomplimentary about healers being as bad as women, but Evina noticed that rather than heading for the stairs when he left her room, he turned toward his room. Hopefully to fetch a plaid to roll up as Rory had suggested, she thought, and then glanced to Conran when he suddenly squeezed her hand almost painfully.

"Sorry," he muttered, through tightly ground teeth. There was no mistaking the expression on his face as anything but pain. Rory was sewing now. A lousy thing to have to suffer through, Evina knew, and rubbed Conran's hand gently to distract him.

There was silence in the room for a minute, and then Saidh suddenly released a soft chuckle.

"What's so funny, sister?" Conran asked grimly.

"I was just realizing that no' one of us so far has managed a wedding where the bride, or groom, or both, weren't healing from wounds, bruises or poisoning."

"Hmm," Rory murmured dryly. "Ye *have* all shown a distressing tendency to pursue rather adventurous courtships so far."

"Ye make it sound like we each looked around for the most troublesome partner and chose them for that reason," Saidh said with a scowl.

"Well, ye didn't pack up and leave when arrows started flying and people started getting stabbed as any sensible person would do, did ye?" he pointed out.

Saidh opened her mouth, looking ready to scald him with a tongue lashing, but then snapped her mouth shut and shook her head before saying, "I hope finding the partner ye marry goes much more smoothly than everyone else's has so far, Rory. But if it doesn't, I hope I'm there to remind ye o' yer words on this day."

Rory paused briefly, concern flickering across his face, but then went back to sewing up Conran's back without responding.

Saidh's words had made Evina curious, however, and she decided she'd have to ask her what they were talking about later. It sounded like there might be an interesting story or two in there somewhere, she thought, and then glanced to the door as Tildy hurried into the room carrying a full tray.

"I passed the laird and Aulay Buchanan on the way up and they said ye were all up in m'lady's room now, so I brought the food and drink here. But some o' ye may want to go below. Laird and Lady Carmichael just arrived and Cook has the women serving the nooning meal a little early for them after their journey."

"Murine and Dougall are here?" Saidh asked with excitement.

"Aye," Tildy said heavily as she reached the table and set down the tray she carried. Shaking her head, she muttered, "I'm no' sure where I'll put them to sleep though. Every room is taken now."

"Move Conran in here and give them his room," Greer suggested. "That way we'll only have to guard one room."

"And I'll only have to visit one room to tend them both," Rory added, apparently liking the idea.

"And Conran can protect Evina if someone gets past the guard at the door," Saidh put in.

Eyes wide, Evina glanced from person to person as they listed the reasons Conran should stay in her room with her, and then looked to

Tildy, expecting her to refuse the idea. After all, she and Conran weren't married yet and might never be. Evina still hadn't made up her mind about that. But much to her amazement, the woman considered the suggestion and then nodded. "Aye. If we're lucky Laird and Lady Drummond will arrive this afternoon and the priest can marry them at dinner. If no', Lord Conran can sleep on a pallet on the floor, and I could always sleep in here as well to act as chaperone. Aye. A good idea," she said with satisfaction, and bustled out of the room, apparently to arrange for Conran's room to be prepared for his brother and sister-in-law.

"I suppose we should go down for the nooning meal and greet Murine and Dougall," Saidh said once the maid had left. Smiling at Evina, she promised, "But we'll bring Murine up to meet ye after we eat, won't we, Jetta?"

"Aye." The petite woman smiled widely. "I think the two of ye will like each other."

"Oh," Evina said weakly, and then watched the two women bustle out of the room with Greer following.

"I suppose we can't go eat?" Alick asked, looking uncertainly at Geordie. "We have to guard the door once Rory is done, right?"

"Go ahead," Geordie said easily. "I'll guard the door until ye're done and then go down and eat once ye've finished and come up."

"Thanks. I'm hungry," Alick announced, and hurried from the room as if afraid Geordie might change his mind and retract the offer.

Evina glanced around with bemusement, amazed at how quickly the room had emptied. It had been crowded with people just moments ago, but now there was just Geordie, Rory, herself and Conran.

"Whoa!"

Evina glanced sharply to Rory at that sharp cry, her eyes widening when she saw him grabbing Conran by the arms as he started to topple sideways in the chair. Geordie immediately moved to his side to help hold their brother upright, and Evina shifted her gaze to Conran's face, only she couldn't see it. His head was bowed, his hair hanging down and hiding his features from her. Even as she noted that, Rory stepped to the side and caught him under the chin to lift his face, revealing that his eyes were closed and his face slack. He'd lost consciousness.

"Is he all right?" Evina asked with concern.

"Aye." Rory let Conran's head lower again and returned to his position behind his back to continue his work. "He lost a lot of blood. I'm surprised he lasted as long as he did. He just needs rest and some food to build his strength back up and he should be fine . . . so long as infection doesn't set in," he added.

Evina nodded and retrieved her hand from Conran's to lean back in her chair with a sigh. Scents from the food on the tray Tildy had brought up were wafting around them. It smelled delicious, but she wasn't really hungry. Instead, she was suddenly weary. A lot had seemed to happen this morning, and she was still recovering from her own wound.

"Geordie, help Evina to bed. She's still recovering and should be resting," Rory instructed without seeming to even glance her way.

"I can manage on me own," she said quickly when Geordie started to release the hold he had on Conran. Smiling at the man, she added, "And Rory needs ye to help with Conran."

When Geordie hesitated, she patted his arm and stood to shuffle to the bed, not leaving him a choice. Evina managed the short walk, but was glad to reach the bed when she did. She was still ridiculously weak. Sitting as she had been, she'd felt fine, but the moment she exerted the least little effort, her strength slid out of her like water out of a tipped bucket. Although she hadn't seemed to have that problem when she'd urged Conran across the room to the table. She supposed worry and adrenaline had given her strength then.

Sighing, Evina lifted the linens and furs and climbed into bed without removing Saidh's gown. She hated to do it, but she wasn't taking it off with Conran and his brothers there. As it was, Evina half expected that she'd be so uncomfortable in the gown that she'd have trouble falling to sleep. She thought she'd lie awake until the two brothers left and she could remove it, but she'd barely slid into her bed, curled up on her side and closed her eyes and she was drifting off to sleep.

CONRAN WOKE UP ABRUPTLY. HE WASN'T SURE AT FIRST WHAT had drawn him from sleep, until something moved against his groin, drawing his attention. Glancing down with confusion, he stared at the furs stacked on top of him and noted that they looked somewhat lumpy. Reaching for the linens and furs, he started to lift them as one and froze as he realized the lump was Evina. She was completely buried under the coverings, even her face hidden where her cheek rested against his chest. The woman was curled around him like a cat, her arm across his chest, and one leg thrown over his hips. She was completely dressed, he saw, but the gown she wore had risen and was tangled around her hips. And while he was in his shirt, which when standing reached past his groin, it too had risen and was presently tangled around his hips as well, leaving his family jewels exposed.

Sighing sleepily, Evina shifted again, her leg sliding across his groin once more, and Conran eased the linen and furs back into place and just laid there. Unmoving. Hardly breathing, as he debated what to do.

He didn't want to disturb her, but now that he was awake, Conran was becoming aware of several different needs. He was hungry. He was also thirsty, but more importantly, he had a serious need to relieve himself just at that moment. On top of that, the way she kept rubbing up against him was stirring other needs as well.

When Evina murmured sleepily and shifted restlessly against under the coverings, Conran almost groaned, and then couldn't take it anymore and carefully eased out from under her and the coverings both. He was immediately sorry when the movement sent sharp pain through his shoulder, but didn't stop until he was out and standing next to the bed.

Conran peered down at the stack of furs then, wondering how Evina could breathe under there. His next thought was to wonder how he had ended up in bed with her. The last thing he recalled was Rory working on the wound on his back at the table by the fire. He had a vague recollection of a discussion about his moving to her room to make way for Dougall and Murine, but thought the suggestion had been for him to sleep on a pallet on the floor. How had he ended up in the bed rather than on a pallet?

Shaking his head over that, Conran turned away from the bed and headed for the door. He needed to use the garderobe quite urgently. Any other questions could be dealt with after that.

Conran found Geordie and Alick outside the door when he opened it. Geordie was sleeping on a pallet across the doorsill, Alick on another in front of him. It made it impossible to get out without stepping on one of them, which he supposed was the point. No one could get in past them either. He was considering retreating into the room to see if there was a chamber pot anywhere when Geordie's eyes suddenly popped open. Spotting him, his brother immediately sat up.

"Ye're awake," Geordie said softly as he got to his feet.

"Aye," Conran murmured, slipping into the hall and pulling the door closed as Alick rolled over and started to rise as well.

"Ye must be hungry," Geordie commented. "Ye slept through both the nooning and the sup."

"Aye," Conran admitted, but he was already moving past his brothers toward the end of the hall where the garderobe was. "I'll be right back."

Leaving them by the door, he hurried away to tend to his needs.

Geordie stood alone outside the door to the bedchamber by the time he returned, and when Conran raised his eyebrows, he explained, "Alick went below to search out some food and drink fer ye."

Conran grunted at that, and asked, "What happened when Aulay and the Maclean searched the passages again? Did they find the bastard who tried to drown Evina?"

Geordie shook his head. "There was no' a trace of him in the passage or the clearing."

"Damn," Conran breathed with a frown, and then muttered, "Where the hell did he go?"

"The best we could come up with is that he slipped out before the men got to the clearing, or that he managed to hide himself until they gave up and left the area," Geordie said, and then added, "But Laird Maclean and Aulay went down and locked the outer entrance from inside when they got back. He'll no' get back in the keep that way."

"Well, that's something anyway," Conran murmured, and then asked, "Did he have any idea who it might be?"

"They all seem to be going with the idea that 'twas the bandit who got away after attacking ye and Evina outside the bailey," Geordie said with a shrug.

"Aye, but why?" Conran asked grimly. "Bandits generally stick to attacking travelers or people caught outside the gates. They don't take the risk of following their victims in the castle. And if they did get in the castle, you'd think they'd steal something and sneak back out, no' try to drown the lady of the house and leave empty-handed."

"That's true," Geordie agreed, a frown now curving his lips too. "'Tis odd behavior at best."

"Aye," Conran murmured. They were both silent for a moment, considering that, and then Conran asked, "How did I end up in Evina's bed? I thought I was to take a pallet in her room?"

"Ye were awake for that part, were ye?" Geordie asked with amusement, and then explained, "There was no pallet there when Rory finished working on you. No one thought to bring one up. The bed was big, and Evina wasn't taking up more than a quarter of the one side, so we just put yer shirt back on ye and tucked ye in on the other side."

Conran arched an eyebrow. "Does Laird Maclean ken?"

"Aye," Geordie assured him. "He was pleased to ken ye're in there in case of another attack."

A footfall caught his ear then and Conran glanced toward the stairs to see Alick just stepping onto the landing carrying a tray of food and drink. It looked to be enough for two, he noted.

As they watched him approach, Geordie murmured, "Aulay said to tell ye that Dougall and Murine arrived today in case ye hadn't heard that. He also said to tell ye that he expects Niels and Edith to arrive tomorrow, so he hopes ye've completed that project ye were working on."

Conran glanced to him sharply, opened his mouth, closed it again and sighed. He knew exactly what project Aulay was referring to—bedding Evina so she knew it wasn't the painful ordeal her first time had been. Unfortunately, he hadn't got that far.

"He also said to tell ye if ye haven't, then to get to it. He does no' wish to see ye left at the altar by a runaway bride," Geordie added.

Conran cursed under his breath, and turned to take the tray from Alick as he reached them.

"I got enough food for Evina too, and I got her mead and, you, ale," Alick announced as he gave up the tray.

"Thank ye," Conran said with sincerity, and turned to the door as Geordie opened it for him.

"Good luck, brother," Geordie said as he pulled the door closed behind him.

Conran took several steps into the room with the food and then stopped, his gaze sliding from the bed to the table by the fire. There was already a tray on the table, he noted, and vaguely recalled Tildy bringing it in while Rory was working on him. It didn't look like it had been touched and he supposed that meant that Evina hadn't eaten anything either since his injury. Actually, he realized, while he'd broken his fast, she'd not even done that ere she was attacked. It was probably why she was still sleeping, he thought, and headed for the bed.

Conran set the tray on the bedside table and then eased to sit on the bed next to the pile of furs and considered the mound of coverings briefly before starting to remove them. Once down to just the linen, he paused. Evina was visible now. The linen started just below her chin and draped over her body, outlining her curves. Conran swallowed, and then grimaced as he was recalled to one of the other needs he'd become aware of when he woke. Thirst. Turning, he grabbed the nearest mug off the tray and raised it to his mouth. It was the ale, so he gulped a good amount of it down, and released a little sigh as he set the mug back.

He turned to peer at Evina again. She was quite lovely in sleep, Conran noted. Her stubborn little chin was more relaxed, and there was no sign of anger, impatience or fear shadowing her features. Although a lot of that had eased from her expression this last week since he'd started his wooing anyway. It hadn't completely left her though. There had still been a hint of wariness about her and the occasional troubled look that had made him suspect she hadn't quite resigned herself to marrying him.

Although, in truth, Conran didn't want her resigned to the fact that she had to marry him. The more he got to know her, the more he found he actually wanted to marry Evina, and the more he wanted her to want to marry him. She fired his blood. The few lessons he'd managed regarding the bedding had left him aching and wanting, and he was eager to progress to the actual joining. He knew without a doubt that it would be good this time and that their marriage bed could be a place of pleasure.

But it was more than that. Conran actually liked the woman. He'd enjoyed the talks they'd had while playing games here in her room as she healed, and he'd come to admire her. She was smart, and brave, with a quirky sense of humor that he appreciated, and Conran had quickly concluded that they would deal well together once he got her past the fear of the marriage bed that their first time had created. It had quickly become clear to him that Evina threw herself into everything she did with passion and pleasure. That was part of the reason their first time in the clearing had been such a debacle. She'd been uninhibited, and responded eagerly to him, and he'd assumed that was a result of her experience rather than her nature and gone too quickly. But that passion and eagerness would serve them well in the marriage bed once he proved to her that the pain she'd experienced was just the breaching, a one-time thing. He felt sure her resistance and wariness regarding their marrying would fall away once he showed her that the joining could be as pleasurable as the other lessons he'd taught her.

Conran glanced to the mead Alick had put on the tray and back to Evina, debating whether to wake her with kisses and caresses and seduce her, or to just wake her to eat and drink, and then try to seduce her. The latter option was probably what he should do, he thought, but it would give her a chance to raise her guards again and she looked so soft and open in sleep . . .

EVINA SIGHED SLEEPILY AND TURNED ONTO HER BACK, HER BODY stretching under the caressing hand moving along her side and down her hip. At first, she thought she was still asleep and dreaming, but then that hand moved back up her body to tug her gown and tunic off one shoulder and down her arm, baring her uninjured breast. When a hand then closed over what had been revealed, the last of sleep's grip slipped away and Evina opened her eyes on a small gasp, her body instinctively arching upward into the caress.

"Ye're so damned beautiful."

She blinked at those softly whispered words and focused on Conran. He was seated next to her on the bed, clad in only his shirt, she noted, and it seemed the most natural thing in the world that he should be. At least her body seemed to think so as it hummed under his attention.

"Are ye thirsty?" he asked softly.

Evina met his gaze, but hesitated to answer. His fingers had found and begun to pluck at her hardening nipple and it was causing complete chaos in her body. Partially a result of the excitement he was stirring, and partly in anticipation of the wild pleasure she knew could follow if this continued. Unfortunately, now that he'd mentioned it, Evina realized she was absolutely parched and, after a moment, she reluctantly nodded.

As she'd feared, Conran immediately stopped his caressing. His hand slid away and then under her shoulder to ease her upright as he quickly rearranged both pillows on the bed so that she could lean against them. He then turned away to reach toward a tray on the bedside table.

Evina glanced down at herself. The lacings of her gown were undone and it, and her tunic, were still hanging off one shoulder, leaving her breast bare. She considered covering it up, but then decided that was rather like closing the stable door after the horse was out and turned her attention to the tray instead. She noted the drinks, but also the food, and felt her stomach stir with interest. But then Conran picked up one of the drinks and offered it to her.

Evina accepted it with a whispered, "Thank ye," and lifted it to her mouth to drink, her eyes widening when he tugged his shirt up and off over his head. She watched him toss it aside, and then turned her gaze to his naked chest as she drank thirstily. But she nearly choked on her drink in surprise when Conran then suddenly bent his head and claimed the nipple he'd been caressing, his mouth closing over it and drawing on it gently.

Swallowing quickly, Evina watched, mesmerized, as he let it slide free of his lips so that he could lick, nip and suck it back in again. But then he let it slide free once more and straightened to tap the bottom of her mug, silently urging her to drink again. Evina automatically took another swallow of the sweet mead, and then watched as he took the drink and set it back on the tray.

"How is yer wound?" Conran asked as he turned back. His tone was casual, as if they weren't sitting there, him naked, and her with one breast out.

"Fine," she said, and then cleared her throat when the word came out a husky whisper.

"Sore?" he asked.

Evina shook her head and he smiled, and then kissed her. It was a sweet, questing kiss at first, his mouth drifting over hers before settling and pressing more firmly as he eased her gown and tunic off her other shoulder. Both of her arms were down at that point, and the material slid down both arms and off her hands too when she lifted them. It left the material to gather around her waist, leaving her bare from there up. She didn't get to fret over that long before Conran distracted her by sliding his tongue out to rub along the seam between her lips. Evina forgot all about her clothing and opened her mouth to him.

The tone of the kiss immediately altered, becoming more demanding as Conran slanted his mouth over hers and thrust with his tongue. Evina sighed into his mouth and returned that demand as her hands found and smoothed over his chest. Dear God, he was beautiful, she acknowledged as she caressed and felt the muscles of his chest and stomach, before sliding her hands around his neck.

When Conran began to ease her down to lie on her back, Evina clung to him with both hands and lips, and then gasped into his mouth as his hands began to move over her, caressing, tweaking and kneading her eager flesh. Her response became increasingly desperate as his hands moved lower. She felt one drift under the hem of her gown and then glide upward, pushing it and then the tunic too up over her hips. Evina sighed and shifted her legs restlessly, and then gasped and closed her legs when his hand drifted back down to slide between her legs.

Conran responded by breaking their kiss and trailing his mouth across her cheek and down her neck. But his hand continued to press between her legs, his palm moving back and forth against her core, until her legs unlocked and shifted restlessly before settling with her feet flat on the bed so that she could lift her hips into the caress. When his mouth found her breast again, her attention was divided between the two areas of pleasure he was causing, but then his mouth continued down. It drifted over her trembling stomach, and then farther, and in the next moment his hand had stopped pressing against her core and, instead, shifted to one thigh. Then his other hand pressed firmly against the other thigh, urging her legs wide open, Evina stiffened and held her breath and then released it on a soft cry when his mouth descended and he began to lash her damp, eager flesh.

Within moments Evina was a thrashing, frenzied wild thing in the bed, her breath coming in gasps and pants, her head twisting and body writhing under his ministration as she struggled toward the pleasure he offered. And then she stiffened, her body going as hard as a board, with just the faintest tremor before beginning to convulse and shudder as she found her release.

Chapter 13

*E*VINA'S HEART WAS STILL POUNDING A RAPID TATTOO, HER breathing still labored, when she opened her eyes and realized that Conran had shifted up next to her on the bed. She was now lying with her head on his chest, his arms around her and his hands moving soothingly over her back and side. She had absolutely no recollection of his moving, or of how she'd got where she was, and she just didn't care. Her body was still pulsing with the pleasure he'd given her, and Evina closed her eyes and decided she'd simply enjoy the afterglow while her body calmed.

That never really happened though. Just when Evina was starting to be able to breathe normally again, Conran's hand stopped its soothing movements and slid up to cup her breast. When he began to palm and caress again, she moaned and tilted her head up. He immediately claimed her mouth in a kiss that told her he wasn't done yet.

Evina stilled briefly, confusion sliding through her. The last two times he'd shown her pleasure, Conran had left her immediately afterward. This time he was stirring her passions again, his tongue thrusting and his hands beginning to move over her body, stoking the fires that had just been banked.

Groaning, Evina stretched against him, her body shifting and arching as it prepared itself for a second round. This time Conran never stopped kissing her. He continued to plunder her mouth even as his hands made quick work of removing the gown and tunic that had gathered around her waist, dragging both down over her hips and then off. Once he'd tossed them aside, his hands were free to slide over her body unhindered, and they did, seeming to find and caress every patch of skin they could before one delved between her legs so that his fingers could dance over her eager flesh. This time when Evina instinctively tried to close her legs, Conran shifted over her, one arm bracing his weight and keeping him from crushing her as his hips lowered to keep her legs from closing so that his fingers could continue their sweet torture unhindered.

Evina instinctively wrapped her legs around his hips, her heels pressing into his behind as she shifted her hips into his touch. When he began to press into her, she knew it wasn't his fingers. They were still dancing around the nub of her excitement and driving her crazy, but it felt so good she didn't protest. Instead, she shifted her hips, pressing up and egging him on until he filled her fully.

Conran stopped then, and started to break their kiss, but Evina caught her hands in his hair and refused to let him. She didn't want this to stop.

After a brief hesitation, Conran gave in to her demand and began to move again, withdrawing from her clinging body and then sliding into her again. Evina never noticed when his fingers stopped caressing, and it was instead his staff rubbing against her as he slid in and out. She was too caught up in chasing the pleasure just out of reach, and when she grew frustrated by how slow his strokes were, she unhooked her legs from around his hips, drew her knees up, pressed her feet to the bed and took over the motion, thrusting her hips up into him at the pace she wanted.

Much to Evina's relief, Conran didn't try to stop her or make her go at his pace. He held himself still, and continued to kiss her as she used him to get where she wanted to go. And then she was there. Pleasure crashed down over her and she was crying out into his mouth as her body began to shudder and shake, her muscles involuntarily clasping and squeezing him.

Evina was vaguely aware when Conran stiffened a moment later, his hips bucking so that he thrust into her hard and stayed there buried deep. She felt him twitch inside her and a spreading warmth as he spilled his seed, but she was still riding the waves she'd created, and merely clung to him. When he collapsed a moment later and rolled to the side, he took her with him, dragging her to her side so that they lay cuddled together, panting and trembling chest to chest, their injured sides up.

Evina was just starting to catch her breath again when Conran suddenly released her and rolled away to sit up on the side of the bed and then stand. Eyes opening, she peered at him with concern, wondering if she'd done something wrong as he crossed quickly to the table. Her worry eased though, and became curiosity instead, when she saw him pick up one of the clean scraps of linen Rory had left behind and dip it in the water pitcher there. When he then used it to clean himself up, Evina was suddenly aware of the cooling liquid seeping out between her legs.

She was just considering joining him at the table to clean up as well when he rinsed out the cloth, wrung it again and then started back toward the bed. Evina watched him approach, her eyes dropping over his body with appreciation. He was a gorgeous man, his body strong and hard, his muscles beautiful in movement. And then he was climbing back into bed next to her and kissing her.

Evina smiled against his mouth and then kissed him in return, only to gasp in surprise and pull back when he slid the cold damp cloth between her legs.

Conran grinned at her startled expression, but continued what he was doing and quickly and gently cleaned away the liquid gathered there.

"Are ye hungry?" he asked as he finished and dropped the used scrap of cloth on the floor next to the bed.

"Aye," Evina admitted, shifting to sit up next to him.

Conran's eyes slid down over her breasts as she did, drinking in the naked flesh on view. It was enough to almost make her pull the fur up to cover herself, but Evina resisted the urge. He was completely naked. Besides, he'd touched and licked nearly every patch of skin presently on display. It seemed silly to try to hide it now.

"Do ye want to eat here in bed, at the table or on the fur by the fireplace?" he asked, lifting his gaze back to her face.

"The fur," Evina decided at once. She didn't want to get crumbs in the bed, and eating at the table meant shifting everything that was presently on it. The fur would be comfortable and easy, she thought.

"The fur it is, then," Conran said lightly, and stood to find and don his shirt. Evina watched the material drop to cover all that male beauty, and then sighed and slid out of bed to look for her tunic as he collected the tray from the bedside table. Spotting the thin gown in a pile on the floor, she snatched it up and donned it as she followed him slowly to the furs.

"Are ye warm enough? Or should I make a fire?" Conran asked as they settled on the fur with the tray between them.

"I'm fine," she said a little breathlessly. "'Tis actually warm tonight."

"Aye," he murmured, and turned his attention to the food on the tray.

Evina glanced down at the offerings. There were cold capon pasties and crisps, and two trenchers filled with cold roasted chicken, and cheese. There were also a couple of peaches for after that looked ripe and sweet.

After all day without food and their activities, they were both hungry and ate in a comfortable silence, gobbling up every bite of food that had been provided. When she was left with just the peach, Evina picked it up, but then glanced toward the table and the tray that sat there. She knew the food Tildy had brought up earlier was probably no good after sitting out all day, but wondered if there was more fruit on that tray and got to her feet to go look.

Evina bit into her peach as she surveyed the missed meal the maid had brought up, and then stilled and glanced down. The peach was definitely ripe; its sweet juices had rushed out and run down her chin and neck to her chest the minute she bit into it. Chewing and swallowing the piece in her mouth, she reached toward the trail making its way down her chest between her breasts, only to glance up with surprise when Conran was suddenly there, catching her hand.

"Allow me," he murmured, and bent to catch the rolling liquid with his tongue just before it disappeared beneath the neckline of her tunic. He didn't stop there, however, but then licked his way back up the trail, cleaning her neck, her chin and then her lips before he gave her a quick, hard kiss.

"Sweet," Conran murmured, lifting his head and watching her through sleepy eyes as he clasped her hips and drew her forward to rest her lower body against his.

She could feel the effect his actions had on him when his hardness rubbed against her through her tunic and his shirt. Evina wasn't surprised. Having his tongue rasp its way across her skin to her lips had affected her as well. Her nipples were now tingling and hard, and a dampness was pooling low in her belly, and seeping lower to prepare her for the invasion it hoped was coming.

But Conran didn't do anything more at first. He merely stood still, watching her, their bodies pressed together, letting her know that he wanted her, but not doing anything to satisfy the need mounting between them. It was Evina who finally made the first move. She offered him her peach.

Conran blinked when she held it up to him, and then his eyebrows rose and he accepted it. The moment he raised it to his mouth to take a bite, Evina reached for the loose neckline of her tunic and tugged it down off first one shoulder and then the other and let it slide off her arms. It didn't fall to the floor, but caught just below her waist where their bodies touched, but it was enough. She was bare from the waist up and the sight made Conran's eyes widen and burn. It also made his erection harden further between them, she noted, and then was distracted when Conran lowered the peach and rubbed the juicy fruit over the nipple of her now-bare, uninjured breast.

She blinked in surprise at the suddenly wet nipple as cool juice gathered into a drop at the tip and dangled briefly. Just before it would have dropped, Conran caught Evina by the waist, lifted her to sit on the table and bent his head to catch the drop of sweet liquid before it fell.

Evina bit her lip and clasped his shoulders as he drew her nipple into his mouth and laved the rest of the juice away. When he straightened, and made as if to kiss her, she stopped him with a hand on his chest and then tugged his shirt up. Conran immediately set the half-eaten peach on the table beside her and helped, catching the hem of the shirt she'd lifted and tugging it up and off over his head.

By the time he finished, Evina had grabbed the peach. He grunted in surprise when she ran the cool fruit over one of his nipples, but didn't stop her as she then closed her mouth over his muscled chest and sucked the pebbling nipple between her lips.

Conran uttered another surprised grunt, and clasped her head with one hand as she did it, and Evina smiled and then nipped at his nipple, before releasing it and turning to apply the same treatment to his other one. When she finished and raised her head to meet his gaze, there was a somewhat bemused expression on his face.

"What?" she asked uncertainly. "Did ye no' like that?"

"Aye, much to me surprise I did," he admitted in a growl, and took the peach from her. "Take off yer tunic."

Evina raised her eyebrows at the demand, but caught the tunic where it had gathered around her waist, and lifted it off over her head. She then let it drop to the floor and lifted her chin to peer at him. Waiting to see what he did next.

What he did was offer her the peach back. Evina hesitated, half expecting him to move it away when she reached for it as she recalled his trick with the cherry in the clearing, but he didn't. He let her take it and murmured, "Ye should finish it. Ye need to rebuild yer strength."

Evina narrowed her eyes. There was something about his expression that made her suspicious, but after a moment, she raised the peach and took a bite. The moment she did, Conran lowered his head and began to nuzzle her ear. Closing her eyes, she chewed and swallowed and took another bite, her head tilting and a moan humming in her throat as he nipped her earlobe and kissed her neck. When she was down to the pit, he straightened and gestured toward the tray on the table behind her. Evina set the pit in the tray and then started to reach for one of the linens on the table, intending to wipe away the peach juice that had slid from the fruit and run over her hand, but Conran caught her by the wrist to stop her.

Blinking in surprise, Evina glanced to his face and then simply watched as he raised her hand to his mouth and began to lick away the juices, his tongue rasping over her palm. Her eyes widened slightly as the action caused a reaction in her body, but she began to squirm on the tabletop when his tongue ran between her fingers, sending butterflies fluttering in her stomach. That was unexpected, she thought, and when he closed his mouth over one finger and suckled as he drew it out, she couldn't resist reaching for him. Catching him by the hip, she tried to draw him closer, but he resisted and moved on to her second finger instead.

He was driving her crazy. Who could have imagined that licking her fingers could be so enervating? She'd licked her own fingers often enough and never felt this excited need that was building in her.

"Conran," she protested finally, pulling on her hand and his hip at the same time.

"Aye," he murmured, and gave up on her hand to kiss her lips instead.

Evina kissed him eagerly back, a combination of need and relief flowing through her as he moved closer and she was able to slide her arms around his waist. She wanted him again. Needed him even. She wanted to again experience that pleasure he'd shown her. She wanted her blood to sing, and her body to throb. She wanted him touching and licking and inside her, Evina thought, and tried to tell him that by reaching for the hardness between them and clasping it in hand, trying to draw him forward and into her.

When Conran caught her wrist and broke their kiss, she opened her eyes and scowled with frustration. For some reason, that made him smile, but he said, "Murine and Dougall arrived today and Niels is expected tomorrow."

Evina blinked, her mind slow to adjust to this new subject, but then she realized what he was saying. Niels and his wife were the last of his family coming. Once they arrived, her father would want to hold the wedding, she realized, and stared at him silently, her mind working. Evina's first instinct when her father had announced that she'd have to marry Conran had been refusal. She'd tried to talk him out of it and, failing that, had considered fleeing. But then Conran had started spending time with her in her room, talking and playing games to help pass the time.

It was the talking that had slowly begun to change her mind. Conran was a good man, a smart man, a patient man. Even when she'd got frustrated and testy at being stuck in her room, he'd remained good-humored and pleasant. And he'd promised never to hit her, she recalled. He'd even agreed to have it put in the wedding contract. And then there was the pleasure he gave her. That first time in the clearing had been just awful, but her experiences with him since then . . . There was no pain. It was all pleasure now, even when he'd joined with her again the last time. Her body had welcomed him . . . and it wanted him again. *She* wanted him again. The marriage bed was no longer something she feared but something Evina yearned for.

Still . . . She would be giving him power over her. She would lose the independence her father gave her, and Conran might not be as easygoing as him. He might expect her to actually follow the marriage vows and obey and—

"Evi?" Conran asked gently. "Will ye marry me?"

Evina stilled in surprise at the question. It was the first time she'd been asked. She'd been told she was marrying him by her father, but even he, who she knew loved her, hadn't made her feel like she had a choice, or that he cared whether she wanted to or not. Conran though was asking. She almost said yes for that reason alone, but then caught the word back and told him, "I won't promise to obey ye."

Conran nodded as if he'd expected as much and assured her, "That's fine. I wouldn't want ye to risk yer soul by lying before the priest and God anyway."

Evina smiled faintly, but still hesitated.

"But I'll add to me own vows and promise before the priest and God ne'er to hit ye," Conran said now. "I'll also have that put in the marriage contract as I said I would. I'll approach yer father about it first thing on the morrow."

The words made Evina relax completely. He hadn't forgotten his promise. With everything that had happened, she'd feared—

"Will ye marry me, lass?" he asked again, his voice solemn.

Swallowing, she met his gaze, and managed to get out the word, "Aye," in little more than a croak.

It was enough. Conran bent to kiss her again with a passion that startled her with its strength. He was like a conquering warrior claiming his treasure, his mouth and tongue devouring and demanding a response. Evina didn't hesitate more than a minute before giving it to him. She might have a few small qualms still in her mind, but her body knew what it wanted and was ready to celebrate this victory with him.

CONRAN WOKE UP ON HIS SIDE WITH EVINA CRADLED AGAINST him. Her bottom nestled against his groin and his arm wrapped around her waist and bent so that his hand could cup her breast. It was heaven, and he decided then that life would be a joy if he could wake up every morning just like this.

And he would, Conran reminded himself with a smile. As soon as Niels arrived they would have the ceremony and Evina would be his. At least, she would be if he got that marriage contract dealt with. Conran was surprised the Maclean hadn't already approached him about it, but it had to be taken care of before the wedding and that would be today if Niels arrived as expected.

Removing his arm from around Evina, he eased out of bed and then gently tucked the furs around her. The lass didn't even move. Conran wasn't terribly surprised. While they'd slept all day and evening the day before, they'd been up most of the night exploring each other's bodies. Evina was proving as bold and adventurous as he'd hoped when he'd thought her an experienced widow. The experience might be missing, but the enthusiasm was definitely present and they'd made love on the table, then the furs, and then she'd tried to pleasure him with her mouth and hand as he'd done for her. That had been more an exercise in frustration than anything, but she would improve with some tutelage, and he was pleased that she had been willing to try it. Besides, his frustration had given way to pleasure once he'd made her stop, rolled her onto her hands and knees and thrust into her from behind so that he could fondle her breasts and touch her as he drove them both to the edge of pleasure again and again until he'd relented and pushed them both over that edge.

Standing beside the bed, Conran stretched happily, and then moved to the ewer on the small table by the window and quickly washed himself down, his mind moving on to what he had to do today. Talk to her father about the contracts was first. Once that was out of the way, he intended to look into this business of her attacker. He'd finally convinced the lass to marry him. He wasn't going to risk losing her now to the man who had tried to drown her and then disappeared.

Conran frowned as his thoughts turned to that matter. Geordie had said Aulay and Laird Maclean had failed to catch up to the bastard. After the fact, he could see the mistakes they'd made. The delay in even entering the passage to begin with was a big one. But the man hadn't used that delay to make his escape. Instead, he'd somehow got around behind them and stabbed him. Why? What had he been doing while they were talking and then questioning Tildy again?

Shaking his head, Conran finished his cleanup and quickly pulled on his shirt, grimacing at the stench of it. It was the same shirt he'd had with him at the waterfall and that Gavin had brought back for him. It, and the now-bloody plaid, were the only clothes he had here. Unfortunately, not one of his brothers had thought to bring some of his clothes along to Maclean. And while Tildy had mentioned fetching him clothes twice now, she hadn't carried out the promise either time.

His gaze slid to the bloody plaid. It lay in a crumpled heap by the table. Crossing the room, he bent to pick it up and grimaced when it remained in the crumpled heap as he lifted it up. The blood had dried, turning it into a twisted statue. He definitely wasn't wearing that.

Dropping it with disgust, he walked to the door and opened it. Geordie and Alick were no longer asleep on the floor. In fact, neither of them were there now. Instead, Rory and Dougal stood outside the door, talking quietly, but that ended the moment he appeared.

Both brothers looked him up and down with interest, but it was Dougall who arched his brow and said, "I think ye may have forgotten something, Con. Ye might want to go back inside and try dressing again."

"Afraid Murine will see me and realize she married the wrong brother?" Conran taunted, mostly because he knew it would annoy him. It still bothered Dougall that he, Geordie and Alick had all been ready to marry the lass had he not claimed her. Although Conran only admitted it after the fact, he would have married the lass to save her from her brother too. He was glad now that had never been necessary. Evina was the woman for him.

"How is yer back?" Rory asked in an attempt to drag his attention away from Dougall.

Satisfied at the scowl now on Dougall's face, Conran turned his gaze to Rory and said, "Fine. 'Twas barely more than a scratch."

"Aye. A scratch," Rory muttered, rolling his eyes. "Turn around and let me look at it."

"Nay," Conran growled, waving him off. "'Tis fine. Ye can look at it later when I take me bath."

"Fine," Rory said with exasperation, and then arched his eyebrows. "So, why are ye standing about in naught but yer shirt?"

"Oh." Conran glanced down at his shirt. "Me plaid is unwearable. It dried bloody in a heap."

"Ah," Rory said with a grimace, not needing further explanation. They all knew what happened to any cloth when soaked in blood and left to dry. It grew hard and stiff. "I brought a spare plaid with me. I'll go fetch it."

"Thank ye," Conran murmured, and watched him hurry away down the hall to the room he now shared with both Geordie and Alick. Turning back to Dougall then, he commented, "Ye took over guarding the door for Geordie and Alick?"

"Aye. They went below to break their fast," Dougall said, and then added, "And Murine and I'll stay until the trouble here is resolved."

"Thank ye," Conran said with solemn sincerity.

Dougall shrugged. "Ye helped me keep me Murine safe when we had our troubles. The least I can do is return the favor and help ye keep yer lass safe."

"Land sakes, I've ne'er met a man who so much enjoyed strutting around naked or half-naked."

Conran glanced toward the stairs at that to see Tildy stepping onto the landing. Despite her disgusted words, he couldn't help noticing that she was perusing his naked legs with a rather lascivious interest. It wasn't the first time he'd caught her eyeing his nakedness like a dirty old woman. It was enough to make him think this was exactly why she kept "forgetting" to bring him a clean plaid. That thought in mind, he arched an eyebrow and said, "I'm no' naked. I'm wearing me smelly old shirt. The same smelly old shirt I've worn every day since arriving here. The only reason I'm no' also wearing me smelly old plaid too is because it was soaked in blood and left to dry in a pile and is now stuck in that shape. Rory's fetching me one of his plaids to borrow."

Tildy stopped and scowled at him with surprise. "Well, why the devil didn't ye just ask him to fetch back the clean shirt and plaid I set in yer room yester morn? No doubt it's still there since ye ne'er returned to collect it, but slept in me sweet innocent young lady's room as if ye had a right to."

"Now, now, Tildy," Dougall said mildly. "As everyone explained to ye last night, Evina's room was the best place for him. It made it easier to guard them both, and his presence would help deter another attack. Besides, Conran was stabbed yesterday and no doubt incapable of being a threat to yer lady's virtue."

"He was to sleep on a pallet, no' in her bed," Tildy snapped, and then eyeing Conran, she added dryly, "And he looks capable enough to me."

"Mayhap, but even so, me brother would ne'er *take advantage of an ailing lass in her sickbed*. Would ye, brother?" Dougall said dryly, reminding him of a certain fistfight that had started between them over Murine.

Much to Conran's relief, Rory saved him from replying by reappearing then, hurrying from his room with a fresh plaid.

"Ye can take that back, Lord Rory," Tildy said at once on seeing him. "I brought Lord Conran a plaid and shirt yester morn and left them on his bed. I'll just fetch them now."

"Isn't his bedchamber our bedchamber now?" Dougall asked with a frown and the maid stopped and glanced back with realization.

"Oh, aye. I forgot we put ye and yer wife in there," she said with surprise, and then added, "I'm sure ye moved the shirt and plaid. If ye'll tell me where to, 'twill save my searching."

"There was no plaid or shirt on the bed," Dougall said with a shake of the head.

"Oh." Tildy blinked, and then smiled faintly and said, "Well, no doubt yer lady wife saw it when she got there and moved it ere ye reached the room. I'll just—"

"Me wife and I went to the room together when we were shown to it," Dougall interrupted as she started to turn away again. "There was no plaid or shirt to move."

"Are ye sure?" she asked, looking flummoxed.

"Quite sure," Dougall assured the maid.

Tildy stood still for a moment, confusion and frustration flittering across her face until Rory said gently, "A lot happened yesterday, Tildy. Mayhap ye meant to take it up and put it on the bed, but ne'er got around to it."

Tildy hesitated, but then sighed and murmured, "Aye, mayhap. But I was sure I did." She shook her head and then turned to the stairs. "I'll find him another shirt and plaid."

"Ye look worried, Conny," Rory said solemnly once the woman had disappeared down the stairs.

Conran turned from watching the maid go and met his brother's expression briefly, but then shrugged. "Tildy hasn't appeared to be forgetful ere this. I mean, when she forgot to bring me a clean shirt and plaid as promised the first time, I assumed 'twas a deliberate forgetting because she was angry at me for compromising her lady. And that time she claimed she'd forgotten to fetch the items. This time she seems quite sure she did bring the items to me room though."

"There was no shirt or plaid there," Dougall assured him firmly. "No' on the bed or even on the floor around the bed."

"I believe ye," Conran assured him.

"But?" Rory prompted.

Conran shrugged. "Evina's attacker had to have hidden in one of the rooms to get behind us in the passages. What if 'twas me room?"

"And what if he took the plaid and shirt?" Rory finished when he left that unsaid.

Conran nodded grimly.

They were all silent for a moment, and then Dougall said, "Even if that is what happened to the plaid and shirt, it won't help him slip past the men at the gate and get into the keep. No' if he has the matted hair Tildy mentioned."

"Probably no'," Conran muttered, and then added, "But I think I'll just mention to the Maclean and Donnan the possibility that he might now have clean clothes so they can warn the men at the gate."

"A good idea," Dougall approved, but caught his arm to stop him when Conran headed for the stairs. When he turned his head to scowl at him for holding him up, Dougall added dryly, "*After* ye finish dressing."

Chapter 14

SMILING SLEEPILY, EVINA ROLLED ONTO HER BACK AND stretched, wincing when her back made a small complaint at the action. It was just a little twinge, nothing much. She'd barely noticed those twinges last night as Conran had infused her body with pleasure. Unfortunately, he wasn't infusing her with pleasure now, and the reminder of her wound's presence stole her smile and made her stop her stretch.

Grimacing, she turned on her side and peered at the space beside her, sighing when she saw it was empty. Every other time she'd woken during the night, Conran had been there, either sound asleep, in which case Evina had woken him with sweet kisses and caresses, or he had woken first and was already caressing and kissing her. But now it was morning, and sunshine was pouring through the open window shutters.

Time to get up, she supposed, and tossed the linen and furs aside to climb from her bed.

"The water in the ewer is clean. I took away the pitcher full of used water already."

Evina glanced around at that announcement to see Tildy stacking items on the tray on the table. That explained what had woken her, she supposed. Moving to the table by the window where fresh water, soap and a clean scrap of linen waited, she asked, "Where is Conran?"

"He's at the tables below with yer father and most of his brothers, discussing what to do about yer attacker," Tildy answered.

Evina scowled with irritation at this news. She would usually be in on such discussions. She trained the men here, and often ruled them too. Her father hadn't bothered much about things like that since her mother died. She'd have to explain that to Conran, Evina told herself solemnly. He didn't know how things worked here. But he would learn. While she was willing to share running Maclean with him, she wasn't willing to hand it over to him altogether.

Evina supposed that was something she should discuss with him before the wedding. She might want it put in the marriage contract too.

"Ye took yer wrappings off," Tildy said with dismay, hurrying to her side.

Evina glanced down at herself, but shook her head. "They were gone when—" She cut herself off, barely keeping herself from saying, "*When Conran had removed me tunic and gown last night.*" Instead, she said, "They must have unraveled while I was sleeping. I was probably thrashing about."

"Aye. Probably having nightmares of fighting off yer attacker," Tildy said grimly.

Evina shrugged. She didn't recall. If she'd had nightmares, Conran had managed to distract her from them on waking her. "They're probably in the bed somewhere."

"I'll look for them after I see ye dressed, but first I should apply more salve and wrap ye back up," Tildy said, poking at the entrance wound on her back before moving around to peer at the exit wound on her chest.

Evina grimaced at the thought and said, "Mayhap we should leave it unwrapped today. The wrappings are hot, and it might be good to let me wound dry out a bit."

Tildy considered the matter briefly and then said, "Mayhap. How are ye feeling otherwise?"

"Good," she answered easily, running the soapy linen over her body. "Fine."

"Is yer wound paining ye?"

"Less every day," Evina assured her.

"Then we'll leave the wrappings off for now," Tildy decided reluctantly. "But if it starts to pain ye, or the scab catches on yer gown and pulls, we'll have to put it back on."

"Aye," Evina agreed with relief as the woman walked away to grab a larger piece of linen from one of the chests against the wall. She could have just refused the wrappings instead of trying to convince Tildy, but the woman had ways of making her life miserable if she angered her. It was always best to humor the maid, she thought as she quickly rinsed off the soap on her skin, and then dried herself using the larger piece of linen Tildy handed her when she returned.

"Yer tunic was on the floor by the table," Tildy announced as she handed her a fresh one.

Evina stilled briefly, and then started to pull the tunic on over her head, avoiding the woman's eyes as she muttered, "'Twas hot last night."

"Aye, it was," she agreed, and asked with interest, "Was Lord Conran hot too?"

Evina sighed with irritation. "We are marrying today, Tildy."

"Is that what ye want?" Tildy asked softly.

"Aye," Evina breathed, and was surprised to realize that was true. She'd always planned to remain unmarried, rule Maclean and then pass it on to Gavin. But now the future unfolding before her was completely different. A husband to share the joys and burdens of life with, a whole passel of in-laws, some of which even came with nieces and nephews, and hopefully, someday, children of her own. Perhaps as soon as next spring, she thought, glancing down at her stomach.

"Do ye love him?"

Evina glanced around with surprise at that question. "Love?"

"Aye, lass. I ken ye always planned to avoid remarrying, and yet now ye seem fine with wedding yerself to Lord Conran. Do ye love him? Is that why?"

Evina considered the question with a frown. Love him? She liked him. She enjoyed talking to him, and hearing the tales of his childhood and his travels as an adult. She liked playing chess and Nine Men's Morris with him, and she most definitely appreciated the pleasure his body gave hers. But love? For some reason that word scared her. She didn't love him, did she?

Fortunately, a knock sounded at the door then, saving her from having to think about that further.

Leaving her to do up her tunic, Tildy moved to answer the door and Evina's eyebrows rose when she heard Saidh's voice, followed by the excited chatter of other women.

"Lady Saidh would like to ken if yer ready fer visitors?" Tildy asked, amusement ringing in her voice.

Since Tildy would have simply said no if there was a man in the group, Evina assumed it was women only and said, "Aye."

The moment she did, Tildy pulled the door wide and Saidh swept into the room with Jetta and two blond-haired women on her heels. Knowing from what Saidh had said that Murine and Edith were both blondes, Evina was just thinking that Niels must have arrived with his wife, Edith, when Saidh announced, "Evi, this is Dougall's wife, Murine, our sister-in-law and dear friend, and this is Jo Sinclair, a dear friend to all of us and sister of our hearts."

"Oh." Evina was a bit disappointed that the woman wasn't Edith, but she managed a smile. "'Tis a pleasure to meet ye."

"Thank ye. 'Tis a pleasure to meet ye as well," Jo assured her, and then added, "And I'm so sorry that we've just shown up like this. I fear we thought to surprise Saidh with a visit, and when we arrived at Mac-Donnell only to discover they were here, we thought to stop on the way home to at least say hello. But I promise we don't plan to stay and trouble ye with more guests."

"Oh, but ye must stay for Evina and Conran's wedding," Saidh protested, turning on her with a frown. "And then ye can come home with us to MacDonnell. Ye can hardly just turn and ride all the way home without visiting as planned."

"That would be lovely," Jo said, but then added with regret, "But I'm sure there isn't room here for us with the whole Buchanan clan already in attendance."

"Nonsense," Evina said at once. "We'll find room. Somewhere," she added with a frown as she realized they were fresh out of rooms. They were going to have to consider adding rooms above stairs now that she was marrying into such a large family, she thought.

"They can have the boys' room," Saidh announced, turning to Evina now. "Alick and Geordie probably won't be sleeping in there until yer attacker is found anyway, and Rory can sleep on a pallet in the hall with them, or go down to the barracks. If 'tis good enough for yer poor cousin Gavin, 'tis good enough for him."

"That would work best," Tildy murmured.

Evina nodded. It was probably the only solution.

"I'll go prepare the room after I have ye dressed," Tildy announced, and moved to the chests to fetch her a clean gown.

"I TOLD THE MEN AT THE GATE THAT THE BLACKGUARD THEY'RE looking for may have clean clothes now rather than dirty, ratty ones," Fearghas Maclean announced as he returned to the table, trailed by two huge deerhounds. "They're going to stop and check anyone who tries to enter."

Conran nodded as he watched the man reclaim his seat at the high table. Noting the caution with which he settled himself, Conran glanced to Rory. But his brother had noticed as well, and suggested, "Perhaps I should take another look at yer wound after we're done here, m'laird. Be sure infection has no' set in again, put some salve on and rebandage it."

The Maclean grimaced, but nodded on a sigh. "Aye, mayhap. I think 'tis just tender from me being overactive yesterday. But 'twould probably be good to be sure."

Conran relaxed a little, but then turned to glance along the table at his brothers, as well as Greer MacDonnell, and Cam Sinclair. "Is there anything else anyone can think of that we can do?"

When no one else spoke, Aulay commented, "All ye can do is put guards on Evina for now. Perhaps if we kenned more we could do more, but we have no idea of the who or why behind the attack."

"The why is usually coin or madness," Rory said, and when everyone turned to him, he pointed out, "Well, the woman who was trying to kill Jo was crazy."

"Aye," Cam Sinclair agreed grimly.

"As was yer aunt, Greer," Rory continued. When the man nodded, he added, "With Murine 'twas to take over Carmichael, or for coin."

"'Twas coin for Edith too, then, if ye count taking over Drummond as coin," Conran pointed out, and then frowned and added, "And madness."

"'Twas madness with Jetta too," Aulay put in.

Conran pursed his lips and then commented, "Do ye sometimes wonder what it means that so many of us have ended up with women who have mad people trying to kill them?"

Greer snorted at the question. "Forget that, what does it mean that so many of us have murderers in our life at all? Ye ken there are people out there who live their whole lives without ever encountering a killer, mad or otherwise? Yet this family constantly runs into them."

"Aye," Alick agreed. "'Tis like we're honey and the murderers are bees."

The Maclean guffawed at the claim and shook his head. "Bees make honey, lad. If murderers are bees, that would make ye lads flowers."

"No' us," Greer countered at once. "'Tis usually the women they're trying to kill."

"Aye," Dougall agreed at once. "Our women are the flowers that are attracting the killer bees."

"Just do no' mention that around Saidh or there'll be hell to pay," Greer said dryly.

"Aye, ye might no' want to mention it around Evina either," the Maclean murmured, but was smiling faintly.

They were all silent for a minute and then Alick commented, "On the bright side, we're quite good at handling them."

"We are?" Conran asked dubiously.

"Well, we're all alive, aren't we?" he pointed out. "And we learn from each one. For instance, ye thought to check under the clothes in the chests here because of what happened with—"

"There was nothing in the chests here," Conran interrupted him to point out.

"Still, ye checked. That's something," he assured him.

Conran just shook his head and then glanced to the Sinclair's young son, Bearnard, when the lad suddenly chuckled. Jo had left the boy with his father when she'd gone upstairs with the other women to meet Evina. The lad had dropped to sit on the rushes behind his father and both of the Maclean's huge deerhounds seemed to think this a fine game and had stood to approach and lick his face and head. They were giving him a fine bath and the four-and-a-half-year-old was laughing as they did.

Conran shook his head with amusement. Today was the first time he'd even seen the beasts. It seemed the men had been keeping them out of the way down at the barracks while the Maclean was on his deathbed. But now that he was much recovered and up and about, he'd sent for them. The affection between the man and his beasts was obvious. They hadn't let him out of their sight since he'd come below, following him from the keep and back and sitting by his position on the bench.

"Ah, dear lord, Bearnard," Cam Sinclair muttered, turning to grab his son by the arm and lift him to his feet. "What are ye trying to do? Get me in trouble with yer mother? Ye've got rushes all over yer plaid now, and she'd be fair froth if I let the Maclean's hounds eat ye."

"They wouldn't eat me, Da," Bearnard assured him on a laugh. "They like me."

"Are ye sure? It looked to me like they were tasting ye," he teased with a grin.

"Nay," Bearnard said seriously, and then cast an arm around the nearest dog and started talking to it instead.

Shaking his head, Cam glanced toward the stairs and then back to the men and said, "I think Jo is with child again."

"Congratulations," the group said pretty much as one.

"But what do ye mean, ye *think* she is? Don't ye ken for sure?" Rory asked.

"Nay. She's trying to hide it from me, but is showing all the signs she did each time she was with child," he said, and then muttered unhappily, "If she is, she most like won't tell me until she gives birth or loses it like she has the last two."

"She's just trying to save ye worry," Rory said quietly. "And many women lose a bairn or two between the ones that live. She'll give ye another healthy bairn, I'm sure."

"I don't care about another bairn. I mean, I do, but I'm more worried about Jo," Cam growled, and then added, "Which is why I suggested the surprise visit with Saidh and Greer. I knew at one point or another the women would insist on visits to Murine, Edith and Jetta."

"Aye," Dougall murmured. "Murine would be terrible upset if she found out Jo was in the south and had no' stopped to see her."

"Exactly," Cam said, and then turned to Rory and admitted, "I kenned we'd go to Buchanan at some point if we were in the south, and was hoping ye could take a look and be sure she is well."

Rory's eyebrows rose in surprise. "Jo and her aunt Annabel are fine healers, Cam. She no doubt has already—"

"Aye," Cam interrupted. "But ye're better, Rory. Ye've traveled far and wide to learn fancy tricks and such. I want the best care for me Jo."

Rory let his breath out on a sigh and nodded. "I'll speak to her while ye're here, and if she is with child and is willing, I will examine her to be sure all is well."

"Thank ye," Cam breathed, and then glanced around at his son again as he released another chuckle. The boy had an arm over the back of each hound and was hanging between the beasts, with his feet drawn up, letting them carry him. Cam smiled faintly and shook his head. "At least he's no' rolling around in the rushes."

"Afraid Jo would be froth?" Conran teased lightly.

"Damned right I am. That woman may look small and sweet, but when she gets her temper up, she kens how to turn the thumbscrew." He shook his head.

Conran smiled faintly, but knew the man was only half joking. From what he'd seen with his sister and brothers and their relationships, that was the problem when you loved someone. They knew you as well as you knew them, and knew how best to make you sorry if you angered them. Conran certainly wasn't looking forward to finding out how Evi would punish him if he made her angry now that she'd agreed to marry him. Not that he loved her, he added quickly with a frown. He liked the woman, thought her quick-witted, kind and brave. He'd even go so far as to say he loved lovin' her. But *love her*? Nay, he assured himself, and wondered why it sounded so much like he was trying to convince himself of it. It was a simple truth that needed no convincing. Wasn't it?

"THERE," TILDY ANNOUNCED, STEPPING BACK AFTER HELPING with her lacings. "Ye're all ready, m'lady. Now ye ladies go below and break yer fast and I'll prepare the room the lads were in for Lady Jo and Lord Sinclair and their son."

"Son?" Evina asked with interest as they headed for the door.

"Aye." Saidh grinned. "Bearnard. He's such a little cutie, and he's betrothed to the eldest of our triplets, Rhona."

"The eldest?" Evina queried with amusement. "They're triplets. They're all the same age."

"Aye, but Rhona came out first," Saidh explained. "She is the eldest by three hours."

"Three hours?" Evina asked with alarm. She hadn't really considered how triplets would be born, but would have thought they'd have come out one right after the other like plop, plop, plop.

"Aye," Saidh said with a grimace. "But Sorcha, the second oldest, dallies about doing everything. Once she was out though, little Ailsa followed almost on her heels."

"Oh," Evina said weakly as Tildy opened the door for them to exit.

"Ladies," Dougall greeted them as they filed out of the room. "Are we heading below stairs now?"

"Aye, husband," Murine said with a smile, and leaned up to kiss his cheek in passing.

"Good. I'm hungry," he commented, slipping an arm around her and holding her to his side.

"So am I," Murine admitted.

Dougall narrowed his eyes. "Ye did no' eat, did ye? I suspected ye had no' been down there long enough to break yer fast ere ye were rushing back up with Saidh, Jetta and Jo."

"Jo and I wanted to meet Evina. I will eat now, I promise," she said soothingly.

"Aye, ye will," he growled, and then narrowed his eyes. "Did ye take yer tincture this morn?"

Evina didn't know Murine well, but even she could tell from her expression that the answer to her husband's question was no. The guilt on the woman's face was priceless.

"Murine," he groaned. "Lass, ye have to take care of yerself. Beathan and I love ye to distraction. If ye faint and fall and hit yer head and die on us—"

"I'll get it right now," Murine said quickly, and then turned to smile apologetically at the other women. "Ye ladies go ahead below. I'll catch up in just a minute."

"Nonsense, we'll accompany ye," Saidh said at once, and then paused to glance to Evina. "Unless ye're weary and wish to head straight below? I ken ye're still healing."

"Nay. I'm fine," Evina said at once. She did hate being thought weak. Besides, she was doing okay at the moment. Of course, she knew that probably wouldn't last long. Still, she'd done all right last night with Conran. Although they hadn't really walked anywhere, and he'd done all the work, she supposed.

"Oh, good," Saidh said cheerfully. "Just tell us if ye weary and one o' the boys can carry ye."

Evina snorted at the suggestion. There was no way she'd ever be so weak that she'd willingly allow a man to carry her. Well, not unless it was Conran. He'd already carried her around a few places. But she wasn't going to look weak in front of his brothers unless she was gushing blood, or on death's door, she decided as they moved away from her door.

"How is me nephew doing, Murine?" Saidh asked suddenly as they started along the hall. Turning to Evina, she quickly explained, "Murine and Edith both have one child each. Both are little boys."

"Really?" Evina asked, glancing at Murine.

"Aye, we named our boy Beathan after me father," the woman murmured with a smile, and then glanced to Saidh and added, "And he's very well. Gaining weight every day."

"Did ye bring him with ye?" Evina asked with interest.

"Nay. He's only three months old. Far too young to travel. His nursemaid is watching him until we return. Fortunately, I have two cousins at Carmichael who gave birth around the same time as me, and they are taking turns feeding him with their own babies while I am gone."

Evina nodded. She knew a lot of nobles shunned suckling their bairns, seeing it as inconvenient. They usually had a woman in waiting who had recently given birth and could take over the chore, but Evina herself thought she'd rather feed her own child as well, so was glad these women seemed to agree with it.

"This is the first time I've been away from Beathan since he was born," Murine blurted suddenly, her tone fretful.

"He'll be fine," Jo said, patting her arm soothingly. "It's hard to leave them when they're so young. But 'tis better he's safe at home rather than traveling through rain and mud and perhaps growing ill from it."

"Aye." Murine managed a smile and then paused to open the door to the room she and Dougall shared.

"Do ye think Edith and Niels will bring young Ronny?" Jetta asked as all but the men followed Murine into the room.

The men took up a position on either side of the door in the hall, Evina noticed as she pushed the door closed. It seemed she had watchdogs.

"Oh, nay," Saidh said at once. "He's barely a month old."

"Ronny is Edith's son?" Evina asked with curiosity, moving to stand by the fireplace to make room for the other women who had clustered by the door.

"Aye," Jo agreed, moving farther into the room too. "I suspect that's why it's taken her and Niels so long to get here. Edith wouldn't trust just anyone with the baby after everything she went through with her aunt."

"Aye," Murine agreed solemnly, moving to a chest by the bed. "Fortunately, I wasn't betrayed by a Carmichael, so have no' issues with being able to trust them."

Here was another couple of stories she thought she might like to hear eventually, Evina thought as they waited for Murine to find her tincture.

"I thought ye had stopped needing the tincture to keep from fainting?" Jo said suddenly as Murine found what she was looking for.

"I did," she admitted with a wry smile. "Unfortunately, I was so sick while carrying Beathan I couldn't keep food down and started in fainting again. Dougall insisted I return to taking the tincture, and made me promise to take it for six months after the babe was born to ensure everything was all right before I stop again."

"Ah." Jo nodded, not seeming surprised.

Evina didn't have to ask what they were talking about. Saidh had told her a little bit about each of the women presently in the room and one of the tidbits she'd told her about Murine was that when they'd all first met her, the woman had a terrible habit of fainting at the drop of a cap. In the end, it seemed this had been a result of her not eating enough out of grief over the deaths of several family members one after the other. But it was a situation that had eventually cleared up when the Buchanan brothers had taken her under their care and made her eat more. Evina could understand how the morning sickness many women suffered while carrying their bairns could cause a return of the affliction for Murine.

"Evina, what's that on yer skirt?" Jo asked suddenly.

Eyebrows rising, Evina glanced at the pale blue skirt of the gown Tildy had chosen for her, but didn't, at first, see anything.

"Along the hem on the side," Jo explained, moving toward her.

Evina shifted her attention there and frowned when she saw some sort of black fluff clinging to the hem. Bending, she plucked several tufts of the black bits off her skirt and straightened to peer at them with a frown.

"There's some on the other side too," Jo announced, bending to flick it off for her, and then frowning, she added, "And some on the back too. What in heaven's name . . . It's all over the floor here. Caught in the rushes."

"It's getting caught on yer hem too, Jo," Saidh announced, taking a step toward them and then pausing and instead saying, "Come away from there, the two of ye."

They both moved away from the fireplace and closer to the other women, but Evina was staring at the black bits in her hand, her mind working.

"Is that hair?" Jetta asked with disbelief.

"Aye," Evina said.

"It's too dark to be Dougall's or Conran's," Murine commented, joining them to peer at the hair she held. "It's more yer cousin Gavin's hair color."

"Aye," Evina agreed. "But it's greasy and matted."

"Tildy said yer attacker's hair was greasy and matted," Jetta said with realization.

Evina nodded grimly.

They were all silent for a moment and then Saidh turned to Murine. "Muri, while I knocked on Evina's door when we first came up, I thought I heard Dougall ask ye if there was a shirt and plaid in here when the two o' ye first came to the room yesterday?"

"Aye. He said Tildy insisted she'd put a fresh plaid and shirt here for Conran, but Dougall had assured her there was no shirt and plaid. He thought he'd best ask me though, just to be sure there hadn't been, and he'd just missed my moving it."

"That's what I thought he'd said," Saidh admitted, and turned to meet Evina's gaze. "What do ye think he did with *his* clothes?"

"Who?" Murine asked with confusion.

"Me attacker," Evina answered quietly, not having any problem following Saidh's thoughts. Her own had been following the same line.

"Oh!" Jetta exclaimed with dismay. "Ye think he hid in here after trying to drown Evina, stole the clothes and shaved his head!"

"Oh, dear," Murine murmured.

"Ye're no' going to faint, are ye?" Evina asked with concern.

"Nay, I don't think so," Murine said with a frown, and then shook her head with more certainty. "Nay, I'm fine."

"Good," Evina breathed, and smiled at her with relief.

"Did he have enough time to shave his head though?" Jetta asked suddenly, her expression dubious.

Evina considered the question, trying to remember the timing of events the day before. It seemed to her that a goodly amount of time had passed between when she'd woken up after nearly being drowned and the men heading off into the passage. Tildy had explained what had happened: her father had ordered everyone out, but no one had moved quickly. There had been a lot of people and they'd all seemed reluctant to miss out on what was happening. And then, even once her father had opened the passage entrance, they hadn't headed in to search it. She and her father and Conran had talked a bit more, arguing over whether Gavin could be behind it before Conran had gone out to question Tildy . . .

"Aye," Saidh decided, even as Evina thought it. "He probably gave himself a cut or two in his rush, but he could have managed it."

Evina merely nodded and moved back to peer at the floor where she'd been standing. "It looks like he kicked the hair around a bit, trying to mix it in with the rushes to hide it."

"'Twould have worked too if ye hadn't chosen to stand there," Jo commented. "I didn't notice it until some caught on yer skirt, and with the weather this hot Dougall and Murine weren't likely to wish for a fire. There would be no other reason to come over here, really."

"True," Saidh murmured, looking around the room. "But where did he put his dirty clothes?"

"Does that matter?" Murine asked. "Ye've figured out how he managed to escape. He shaved his head, stole the clothes, changed into them and managed to blend in with the other men in the clearing the tunnel leads to because they were looking for someone with black matted hair and filthy clothes. They wouldn't have looked twice at a bald man in clean clothes."

Evina didn't respond. She wasn't quite sure that was true. Donnan had picked the men he took with him. If he'd seen her attacker, he would have recognized that he wasn't one of the men he'd picked, matted hair or bald. Besides, everyone at Maclean knew everyone else. A stranger in the area would have been noticed. Although there were several big bald men at Maclean, and if Donnan had chosen one among the men he took with him, the man might have got away. As long as he wasn't seen up close, or if he kept his face turned away, anyone who saw him might think he was the other fellow. He might have fooled them long enough to slip away, she thought, but it seemed a lot of ifs.

"The clothes can't be in here," Jetta said now. "The men searched the rooms."

"That's true," Saidh agreed with disappointment.

Evina nodded, but moved to kneel in front of the hearth and reached up into the fireplace, to feel around.

"What are ye doing?" Saidh asked with interest.

"There's a ledge built inside the fireplace in me room. A shelf of sorts," she murmured, lowering her head as she felt around. "If there's one here too, I thought mayhap—Aha!" Feeling cloth, she grabbed it and pulled and then backed up as she felt the material fall. They all stared at the filthy rags that tumbled out and lay in the empty hearth.

"His clothes," Saidh said with certainty.

Nodding, Evina stood up and glanced to the others. "Do ye suppose once they see this and ken the man has truly made his escape, Conran will stop having yer brothers follow me around for protection?"

The women all glanced at each other and then burst out laughing as one.

"I'll take that as a nay," Evina said dryly.

"Ye'll have to forgive us," Jetta said gently. "We're truly no' laughing at you."

"Oh, nay, we're no'," Murine said quickly, looking alarmed that she might think so.

"Nay," Saidh added. "We're laughing at the thought o' one o' me brothers no' being overprotective." Shaking her head, she added dryly, "'Tis what they do."

"Aye," Murine agreed, but she was smiling. Apparently pleased with that trait in the men. "Why, that is how Dougall and I ended up married. Me brother tried to sell me to Dougall and, when he refused, was going to offer me to our neighbor. Dougall, Conran, Geordie and Alick found me fleeing me brother on me bull and decided I needed their protection."

Jetta nodded, and added, "And Aulay found me floating on a mast in the ocean, pulled me in and, when I apparently said someone was trying to kill me, decided I needed to be kept safe while I healed from my injuries."

"And Jo's Cam, and me Greer, are the same caliber o' men," Saidh said with a grimace, obviously less pleased with this protective streak.

"Aye," Jo said. "Cam came across me struggling with a couple of bandits on my way to Scotland. He rescued me and got wounded doing it. Once he'd healed, he escorted me the rest of the way to me aunt and uncle's home."

"And Greer is forever fretting over me and trying to protect me," Saidh said solemnly, and then gave her a sympathetic look. "I struggle with it all the time, Evi. And trust me, I ken it can be a bother, but they do it because they care, and there are few enough men out there who care enough to bother."

The other women all nodded solemnly in agreement.

Sighing, Evina turned and headed for the door. It might not make a lick of difference when it came to her having guards, but she still had to tell the men. If for no other reason than that it would give her great pleasure to tell them she'd found something they'd missed. The thought made her grin as she opened the bedchamber door.

Chapter 15

"I CAN'T BELIEVE WE MISSED IT," CONRAN MUTTERED, staring at the bundle of filthy clothing lying on the hearth. The truth was though he couldn't believe the women had thought to look in the fireplace. That hadn't even occurred to him. But then they'd had the hair to make them look for the clothes. He'd never noticed it on the floor. He'd been looking for a man, not something that could be sprinkled among the rushes.

"Ye're no' wearing skirts that would have picked up the hair, which is what led them to look fer the clothes," Dougall pointed out with amusement. "'Tis no' like it's easy to see."

"Hmm." Laird Maclean kicked some of the rushes aside, revealing more hair. "This is how he slipped away, then. His head shaved and wearing a stolen plaid and shirt."

"'Twould seem so," Aulay muttered, but didn't sound convinced.

Conran couldn't blame him. He had his own doubts on the matter. The men in the clearing had been looking for someone who had attacked their mistress. Surely, they would have been hyperalert and would have noticed *anyone* in the area who didn't belong? After all, the attacker might not have been working on his own.

"Well, I suppose I'd best tell the men on the gate to watch for anyone coming and going that they do no' ken, but especially a bald man now," the Maclean said, and turned to head for the door. "I'll have Tildy send some women up to clear out the rushes in that corner and replace them too so ye needn't worry about lice or fleas and such."

Dougall grimaced at the words and Conran chuckled as he turned to follow his father-in-law.

"I think ye should continue to have a guard on Evina," Aulay commented as they left the room.

"I intended to," Conran assured him, and then added, "Although I plan to ask Donnan to supply a dozen trustworthy men to watch her in two shifts of six, rather than continue to depend on Geordie, Alick, Dougall and Rory."

"Ye don't trust us to keep her safe?" Dougall asked sharply.

"O' course I do," Conran said with irritation. "But ye did no' come here to play guard. Ye came as guests to attend me wedding. I'll no' trouble ye by making ye play guard while here."

"And that is yer problem," Aulay said with amusement.

"What?" Conran asked with confusion, pausing and turning to meet his gaze.

"That ye'd no' trouble us," Aulay said. When Conran just shook his head with bewilderment, he added, "Have ye ne'er noticed ye're forever helping out one of us, but ne'er ask fer help in return, Conny? And that's the way it has always been. Ye helped Dougall with his horses, and Niels with his sheep, Rory with his healing, and me with running Buchanan, yet ne'er asked fer our help in return."

Conran raised his eyebrows at the suggestion. "Because I don't need help."

"Everyone needs help some time, Conran," he said solemnly. "For instance, ye need it now with keeping Evina safe. Ye helped each o' us keep our women safe when 'twas needed, yet now will no' let us return the favor. Rather than 'burden' us, ye'd have strangers to guard the lass. And they're men ye obviously do no' trust with the task, else ye'd no ask for so many."

Conran frowned and shook his head. "I thought ye'd be pleased to be able to relax and enjoy a visit rather than have to stand guard and—"

"And help ye?" Aulay interrupted quietly. "Has it ne'er occurred to ye that as much as ye like to aid us, we might like to help ye in return too? That perhaps we feel we owe ye that help even, and so long as ye don't allow it, we're left owing ye?"

"I—" Conran blinked, and then said with dismay, "Nay. I ne'er considered ye owed me anything. I offered me help freely. There were no demands attached, no expectation that ye'd help me in return. And I ne'er even considered ye might feel that way."

"Good," Aulay said solemnly. "Because I'd have been sore disappointed if ye understood the unequal footing ye were forcing us all onto, and just enjoyed feeling superior to us with all yer helping." Smiling, he added, "But now that ye ken how helping us all the time without allowing us to aid ye in return affects us, I ken ye'll accept our help in guarding Evina and leave off having soldiers do it."

"O' course," Conran said at once.

"Good," Aulay said with satisfaction, and continued forward saying, "Then we'll take it in shifts, two brothers guarding Evina at a time."

"Ye can count me in on that," Cam announced, falling into step beside Aulay.

"Me too," Greer growled, following.

"Thank ye," Aulay said. "That means when Niels gets here we'll have eight men all told. Four shifts o' two men. Perfect."

"Perfect," Conran muttered, and shook his head as he followed the others. He had no idea how his brother had managed it, but he now felt guilty for trying to save them from having to guard Evina. He even felt guilty for helping out his brothers as he tended to do, as if his motives had been some underhand way to—How had Aulay put it? Set himself on a higher footing and make himself feel superior to them?

"Madness," he growled under his breath. He helped because they were his brothers and they needed help. As for why he didn't accept help, he usually didn't need it. It was that simple. Wasn't it?

"Conny!"

Conran glanced up at that shout from Aulay and hurried to the front of the group to reach his eldest brother's side at the top of the steps. "What?"

"The women are gone," he said grimly.

Conran turned to peer down over the great hall. It was busy, as usual, but it was also noticeably absent of every one of their women. From Evina to Aulay's Jetta, they were gone. Even Bearnard and the Maclean's dogs were no longer below.

"Don't set up such a fuss, Buchanan," the Maclean said with amusement, coming out of his room with a rolled-up plaid in hand.

Conran recalled Rory's advice to the man the day before about rolling up a plaid and setting it in a circle that surrounded and would protect his arse in the saddle, and could only assume the man intended to ride out to talk to the men at the gate. He wasn't surprised. While the Maclean was doing better, his injury pained him when he had to walk any distance.

"The women are all together and Gavin is with them," Fearghas Maclean continued as he joined them at the top of the stairs. Glancing down into the great hall, he added, "As are the dogs. No doubt the beasts needed to relieve themselves and Evina and the others accompanied them outside to get a breath o' fresh air."

Cursing, Conran started down the stairs at a run.

"What the devil!" he heard the Maclean say with surprise. "What's the matter with him? The lassies'll be safe enough outside with me nephew."

"So long as Evina's attacker isn't even now in the bailey, notching an arrow to a bow and aiming it at her."

It was almost like Aulay had read his mind, Conran thought as he heard his brother's words behind him. They were followed by several exclamations of dismay and the sudden thunder of all the men crashing down the stairs on his heels. Conran ignored it and merely hurried across the great hall. He burst out of the keep doors, fully expecting to find Evina and the others standing about at the foot of the stairs watching the Maclean's huge deerhounds lifting a leg, but they weren't there. Not on the steps, and not anywhere near them.

Fear clutching at him, Conran paused to scan the bailey from his elevated position at the top of the stairs, and was nearly sent tumbling down them when the keep doors opened behind him and someone crashed into his back.

"Sorry," Aulay muttered, catching Conran's shoulder, and saving him from the fall he'd nearly caused. Moving up beside him once sure Conran was steady on his feet again, he glanced around and asked, "Where are they?"

"That's what I was just wondering," Conran said grimly as the rest of the men moved out of the keep to take up position around them. "I don't see them anywhere."

"And me horse is gone," Fearghas Maclean growled with exasperation as he stepped up behind Conran and his brother.

"Well, I can't imagine Gavin agreeing to an outing outside the walls. Evina is too weak for that yet," Rory pointed out. "Mayhap there was somewhere within the bailey she wished to go and they used yer horse to get her there to save her exhausting herself with a long walk."

"Is there somewhere she'd want to go?" Aulay asked, turning to glance between Conran and the Maclean.

"Donnan told me she usually oversees the men at practice," Conran announced, starting down the stairs.

"Surely she wouldn't try to do that so newly from her sickbed though. Would she?" Rory asked with concern as he and the other men followed.

"Damned right she would," Conran and the Maclean said together, and then glanced at each other with surprise.

Grinning, the Maclean slapped him on the back and shook his head. "Ye'll make her a fine husband, lad. A fine husband indeed."

Conran smiled crookedly and shook his head. "If she lives that long."

"Nay, Cormag! Ye're holding it wrong," Evina called, frowning at the young man and moving through the battling men toward one with long, ginger hair and peach fuzz on his face. He was about Gavin's age, or a year younger, but hadn't developed as quickly. He was also a good distance from where she'd been standing with the women, and little Bearnard on the edges of the practice field with her father's horse and dogs. They had all been waiting at the tables in the great hall for the men to go take a look at the dirty clothes and shorn hair they'd found. Evina had wanted to go with them and be in on any discussion that followed. However, she had been ordered to stay behind by both her father and Conran, who had said it at the same time as if they shared a mind. The order had frustrated and angered her, and normally Evina would have ignored it and followed them up anyway.

Unfortunately, the trip down the stairs had been exhausting. So much so that she'd had to stop to rest halfway down, holding up the other women as well as Dougall and Rory, who had followed them. She had just finished gasping out a refusal to Dougall's offer to carry her the rest of the way, insisting she just needed a moment's rest and could manage on her own, when Conran had spotted them on the stairs. He'd immediately rushed up to scoop her into his arms and carry her down the rest of the steps. The man had berated her the whole way to the table for wearing herself out so while still healing. She should still be abed, he'd growled as he'd set her down on the bench and taken a seat beside her.

Of course Evina had still been out of breath from her trek and unable to tell him to bugger off, or explain what they'd found in the bedchamber Dougall and Murine now shared. That had been left to the other women. She'd got to watch the shock and uproar that caused though, and then the men had rushed above stairs, barking at the women to remain at the table with Gavin to guard them.

Evina had never been good at obeying orders. The moment she'd drank the mead that was set before her, and regained her breath, she'd commented that the dogs were pacing and no doubt in need of a walk-about outside. When Gavin had then stood to take them out, she'd pointed out that he was supposed to guard them and shouldn't go without them. While he'd stood, frowning over the matter, she'd stood as well and commented that some fresh air would be nice after being stuck in her room so long. She'd then slid her arm through his and urged him toward the keep doors, calling the dogs to come with them even as the women had all jumped up to follow.

When they'd gotten outside and she'd spotted her father's horse at the foot of the stairs, Evina had announced she'd like to just go check on how Donnan was getting along training the men in her absence. While the big man was brilliant at training the more seasoned soldiers, the younger ones found his size a bit intimidating and couldn't retain a thing he said. It was why Donnan had set her to training the younger lads when she was just a girl. He'd been training her at that point. He knew she knew her business, so he'd suggested she teach some of the younger lads, leaving him free to concentrate on training the older ones. As Evina had aged, the ages of the men she'd trained had grown with her.

"I'm going to get in trouble for this, am I no'?" Gavin had said with disgust as he'd helped her up onto her father's mount.

Smiling at her cousin sweetly, Evina had murmured, "Mayhap. But I think ye owe me after skulking around spying on Conran and me for Da, and then reporting to him what ye saw. Don't you?"

Gavin had grimaced. "Sorry, Evina. But he's me laird as well as me uncle, and he gave me an order."

"Well, before going above with the men, he did no' order ye no' to let me ride across the bailey to see how the men are doing in the practice field. Besides," she'd added, "if we're quick, we'll be back before they come below."

Of course, that had presumed she wouldn't see she was needed and decide to help some of the younger men, Evina acknowledged as she reached young Cormag Maclean, a cousin three times removed or something.

"M'lady?" Cormag turned to her, looking uncertain. "But I'm grasping it like ye told Laichaidh to. I heard ye tell him, '*Grip it firmly with the right hand below the guard, and grab the pommel with the left,*' and 'tis what I am doing."

"Aye, but he's right-handed," Evina explained as she paused beside him. She then scowled at the breathy sound to her voice after such a short walk. It was truly pathetic. Shaking her head, she took a deep breath to try to settle herself and then continued. "Ye favor yer left hand. That means yer left arm is stronger. Ye'll want to do the opposite o' Laichaidh and grasp it below the guard with yer left, and grab the pommel with yer right."

"Oh," he said with understanding. Smiling, he changed his handhold. "Like this?"

"Good." Evina nodded. "Now, hold it so the pommel is just above here," she said, patting him where she thought his belly button probably was. "But ne'er rest it against yer stomach. And keep it at an angle that places the tip between yer opponent's heart and throat."

Nodding, Cormag adjusted his hold.

"Good, now place yer right foot behind yer left and stand on the meat at the front o' yer right foot," she instructed. "'Twill help ye keep yer balance as ye lunge forward during the blow."

"Evi!" Jetta called.

"Just a minute," Evina called back, busy with her instruction. She heard her call to Saidh next, but ignored them. "Now, when ye go to strike, bring yer sword up until yer right hand is up higher than yer eyes, and then bring it down using yer left hand to direct the blade. Yer right is to provide the force o' the blow."

"Evi! Saidh!"

Ignoring the shouts for now, Evina started to step back out of the way as the lad lifted the sword up, but then quickly stepped forward again and caught his arm to stop him. "Nay, nay! Keep yer left arm straight, but do no' lock it like that, else ye could break it when ye—"

"Evi! Saidh!"

Breaking off, Evina turned with exasperation to the women standing on the sidelines by her father's horse and deerhounds. Jetta, Murine and Jo were all looking a bit alarmed, but she had no idea why. Frowning, she asked, "What is it?"

"I think they've been trying to tell us that our men are coming," Saidh commented with amusement, breaking off the practice battle she'd been having with Gavin and moving to her side.

Evina followed her gaze toward the large group of men hurrying across the bailey toward them and sighed. "O' course they are."

"O' course," Saidh agreed good-naturedly. "Goodness, my Greer and yer Conran look ready to choke someone."

Evina considered the men and had to agree. They certainly did look upset. Glancing to Saidh with curiosity, she said, "Ye do no' seem worried."

Saidh shrugged with unconcern. "Greer would ne'er hurt me, and Conran wouldn't hurt ye either. They'll sputter and growl about yer safety, and me playing at swords while with child, and no doubt drag us back to the keep berating us the whole way. O' course," she added, "ye and I will act annoyed and refuse to speak to them and they will take us to our rooms to apologize and end up pleasuring us in the end." Grinning, she glanced to Evina and assured her, "Ye'll find there is nothing sweeter than a joining to make up after a fight. They are most eager to please then."

Evina's eyebrows rose at this news. She found it hard to imagine that Conran could do more to please her in the bedchamber than he already had. But she was willing to find out if there was. She also appreciated Saidh's blunt speech. She was really beginning to like the woman a good deal and thought they could be grand friends. She liked the other women too, and was starting to think she was lucky to be marrying into this large family.

"Evina!"

"Saidh!"

"Here we go," Saidh murmured as the men reached the practice field and Conran and Greer broke off from the group to start through the battling warriors toward them. She then said under her breath, "Remember, ye must act very annoyed and use words like *high-handed* and phrases about his *ordering ye about like a child* and such."

Evina merely smiled with amusement and shook her head. She wouldn't use those words unless Conran actually acted high-handed and ordered her about like a child. Of course, judging by the expressions on the faces of the two men as they approached, she suspected both of them would.

Conran was the first to reach them. He grabbed her hand and tugged her toward him, his mouth opening to begin his berating when a grunt of pain from behind her made Evina turn toward Cormag. She expected to find he'd dropped his sword on his foot, or given his battle partner a blow that had left his arms vibrating. Instead, she found herself staring blankly at the arrow sticking out of his back. She'd barely registered with bewilderment that that was what it was when the lad started to fall and someone—Conran, she presumed—tackled her from behind and dragged her to the ground.

Evina hit the hard-packed earth with a pained grunt of her own, and then promptly tried to crawl out from under Conran to get to Cormag. The lad had fallen just a foot away from her, and she wanted to check him, but Conran caught her around the legs and repositioned himself over her until his body shielded all of hers.

"Stay put," he growled.

Evina was surprised she actually heard him over the hue and cry that was taking place around them as the Maclean warriors took note of what had happened and began to spread out in search of the culprit behind the arrow. A glance around showed that Jetta, Murine and Jo were now being covered by their husbands. Jo held little Bearnard tight to her chest, and her husband had his arms around both of them. Meanwhile Geordie, Rory and Alick were making their way toward them through the shifting bodies of the shouting Maclean warriors.

"Are ye all right, Evina? Ye were no' hit, were ye?"

Evina turned her head to see that Gavin had rushed over to kneel next to them. Beyond him, she could see Saidh on the ground with Greer shielding her with his body as Conran was doing with her.

"Nay. I'm fine," she said a little breathlessly. It was hard to breathe with Conran on her back. Her gaze slid to Cormag then and she asked with concern, "Is he alive?"

Gavin shifted to lean over the lad. Cormag had landed on his stomach, but her cousin now turned him onto his side and after a moment announced, "He's breathing."

Evina closed her eyes with relief, and then opened them again to glance around and see how close Rory was. Cormag needed him. She would never forgive herself if the boy died. This was all her fault. The arrow had no doubt been meant for her, and probably would have hit her had Conran not grabbed her hand and tugged her toward him when he had. Her attacker was still here and out to get her, and she'd brought him down on the men by coming here herself. Cormag's getting hit with the arrow was all her fault.

"Is she all right?"

Recognizing Rory's voice, Evina glanced around at that question, and nodded abruptly. "Aye. I'm fine. But Cormag needs ye."

"We need to get Evina and the other women back to the keep," Conran said as soon as Rory moved to kneel next to Gavin.

Geordie nodded. "Aulay and the others have already started back with the other women. 'Tis just Evina left. We'll accompany ye and watch yer back."

Evina's eyes widened at those words and she glanced to where Saidh had been just a moment ago, surprised to see that the woman was gone. A glance in the direction of the keep showed Greer carrying her away at a run. The other men were ahead of them, each man carrying their own wives like precious children as they raced toward the keep.

It seemed the Buchanan men and their friends MacDonnell and Sinclair had a fondness for carrying their wives, she thought wryly, and then gasped in surprise when Conran was suddenly off of her and scooping her up too. He broke into a run the minute he had her in his arms, and Alick and Geordie fell in behind them, literally guarding his back.

Frowning, Evina glanced past them and yelled, "Donnan, bring Cormag up to the keep for Rory. He needs to tend him!"

Much to her relief, the man heard her. He continued barking orders at the men around him, sending them to search the bailey from top to bottom, but he also glanced her way and nodded to let her know he'd heard. Then he moved to where Rory and Gavin still knelt by Cormag. Alick and Geordie moved closer together then, blocking her view, and she settled into Conran's arms with a sigh as he carried her to the keep.

He didn't berate her the whole way back as Saidh had predicted. But then the situation had changed somewhat and Conran probably didn't have the breath to berate her as he ran, Evina thought as he charged up the stairs to the keep, bouncing her around in his arms. He didn't slow once in the keep as she'd expected; instead, he charged across the great hall, hurrying past the group made up of his family and the Sinclairs, and started up the stairs.

"Conran, we have to discuss what to do about—" Aulay began with concern.

"I'll be right back," he growled, not slowing.

Evina eyed him warily as he reached the top of the stairs and carried her to her door. Geordie and Alick were still following and Geordie rushed around to open the door for him.

Conran grunted a "Thank ye," carried Evina inside and kicked the door closed. He then let her legs drop to the floor, turned her to face him and kissed her. It was so not what she'd expected, and Evina was slow to respond. By the time she gathered herself enough to do so, he was lifting his head. That is when the berating began.

"What on earth were ye thinking? Ye ken someone is out to kill ye and yet ye took yerself off to the bailey as if ye've no' a care in the world. Ye put yerself and everyone else in jeopardy with yer thoughtless . . ."

That's when Evina stopped listening, and lowered her head. She simply couldn't listen anymore. Her own mind was already saying much the same things. This *was* her fault. Cormag might die because she'd just *had* to rebel and disobey the order to stay put with Gavin at the table. The boy had seen barely sixteen years, but might not see another thanks to her. She knew that. Conran didn't have to tell her.

Aware of a sudden silence, Evina lifted her head and peered at Conran in question. He was standing perfectly still, his eyes closed, she saw, and then he breathed out a sigh and opened his eyes. "I'm sorry, love. I ken ye just had a scare, and berating ye is no helping. I just—"

He paused with surprise when Evina covered his lips with a finger.

"Nay," she said solemnly. "Ye're right. If Cormag dies 'twill be all me fault fer going to the practice field. I was no' thinking o' anyone but meself and me wants when I went there. I should ha'e done as ye and Father ordered and stayed at the table until ye returned below."

Conran frowned at her guilt-ridden voice and shook his head. "Nay, Evi. This isn't yer fault. Ye're no' the one who shot the arrow. But 'twas pure luck that ye were no' hit by it."

"No' lucky fer Cormag though," she said unhappily.

"Evi," he began, and then sighed and shook his head. "We will have to talk about this later. The others are waiting below. But 'tis no' yer fault," he repeated firmly, and then turned to head for the door. He opened it, and stepped to the side, then frowned and glanced around when he realized she hadn't followed him. "Are ye no' coming?"

"Nay. I'm tired," she said quietly, but the truth was she was ashamed of herself and didn't want to face the accusing eyes of the others. For surely they must blame her for the danger she'd put everyone into with her little jaunt.

Conran hesitated, but then nodded solemnly. "I'll send word about Cormag as soon as there is some, and return as soon as I can. In the meantime, why do ye no' try to rest?"

Evina nodded and walked over to lie down on the bed on her side.

Conran hesitated another moment, but then turned toward the door. "Geordie and Alick are standing guard outside the door. Shout if ye need anything."

Evina merely watched the door close behind him and then turned her head back to stare at the drapes overhead with a sigh. She felt a complete ass, a selfish monster. And she kept seeing Cormag's eager face as she'd explained how he should hold the broadsword, and then his crumpled form and the arrow sticking out of his back afterward

Closing her eyes, she tried to block those images from her mind, and sleep, but sleep wouldn't come and she laid there for a long time with those images replaying through her thoughts until she thought she would go mad.

Evina was finally able to push them from her mind by turning to thoughts of how to catch her attacker. That was the only way to ensure no one else was hurt by the man—capturing him and eliminating him as a threat. Evina knew the men were probably looking for him even now, but he had proven elusive before and she had no doubt would again. It seemed to her that luring him into a trap was the only answer, and she was pondering just how to do that when a knock sounded at the door. Sitting up abruptly, she glanced toward the door, and called, "Enter." She then got to her feet as it opened, and she saw that it was her cousin Gavin.

Moving toward him, she asked, "What news?"

"Conran asked Rory to let ye ken how Cormag was," he explained as he closed the door.

"And?" Evina prompted anxiously, taking his hands in hers.

"And Cormag's going to be fine, cousin," Gavin assured her, squeezing her hands. "Rory is still sewing Cormag's wound, but didn't want ye fretting any longer than necessary. He said 'tis just a flesh wound. It missed bone and everything else. He'll be up and back in the practice field within two or three days."

"Thank goodness," Evina breathed, and bowed her head with relief.

"'Twas no' yer fault, cousin," Gavin said quietly, slipping a supporting arm around her back and patting her awkwardly. "Ye did no' shoot the arrow at him. 'Twas just good luck it missed ye and hit him instead."

Evina pulled back to peer at him with eyebrows raised. "Good luck?"

"Well, I consider it good luck," he admitted with an apologetic smile. "I ken I probably should no' and Cormag may no' agree, but I'm glad ye were no' killed."

Smiling crookedly, Evina hugged him tightly and then stepped back to ask, "Did I get ye in trouble fer letting me go down to the practice field?"

"Nay. No one's said aught about it. Yet," he added dryly. "They're all busy at present."

"Doing what?" she asked. "Trying to sort out what to do about me would-be killer?"

"Nay. There's little enough to say about that. No one can figure out the who or why of it, other than that 'tis most likely that bandit I let escape from the clearing," he added, his mouth tightening unhappily. "I should have chased the bastard down and run him through at the time. I was just so worried about yer wound and getting ye back to the keep and help, I—"

"Ye did right," she interrupted to assure him solemnly. "I might ha'e died had ye and Conran no' got me back to the keep and tended me wound so quickly."

"And ye might still do so do we no' catch the bastard," Gavin growled.

Evina patted his shoulder soothingly, and urged him toward the door. "Why do we no' go below and see if Cook has anything to feed us? I'm hungry now that I ken Cormag will be all right."

"I doubt he will," Gavin said. "He and his helpers were forced into the great hall along with everyone else during the search."

"What search?" Evina asked with surprise as he reached for the door to open it for her. But she forgot the question and gaped in amazement as she saw the soldiers marching past in the hall.

"That search," Gavin said dryly. "Conran and the others are searching the bailey, the practice field and everywhere else within the wall with Donnan and most of the soldiers, and Uncle Fearghas has the rest of the soldiers searching inside the keep itself for yer attacker. They're determined to find him this time."

"Oh," Evina breathed, and then gave her head a shake and straightened her shoulders. "Well, if they are up here, they must be done below, which means Cook might be able to scratch up something for us."

Stepping out into the hall, she offered a smile to Geordie and Alick when they immediately straightened and moved closer. Evina slipped her arm through her cousin's, and urged him around the soldiers moving past and toward the stairs.

"Will ye be able to manage the stairs?" Gavin asked with concern, drawing her to a halt at the top. "I can carry ye, if ye like."

Evina wrinkled her nose at the suggestion, and raised her shoulders determinedly. "I can manage. We'll just go slow."

Ignoring his dubious expression, Evina tightened her hold on his arm and reached for the rail with her other. She started down at an extremely slow pace that she knew chafed the men's patience, but she had to regain her strength and wasn't likely to do so if she wasn't allowed to use her muscles. Still, Evina was regretting her decision by the time she stepped off the last stair tread. By then her legs were shaking, and she was panting as if she'd just finished a run across the bailey.

"Let me carry ye the rest o' the way, cousin," Gavin insisted, turning to face her.

With a hand pressed to her breast as she tried to regain her breath, Evina glanced to the trestle tables and almost moaned at how far away they looked to be. But she shook her head. "I needs must—Oomph!" she gasped as Geordie suddenly scooped her up off her feet to stride toward the tables.

Evina took another moment to regain her breath and merely scowled at the man as she did. They were nearly to the table before she had enough breath to mutter, "I notice ye Buchanan men have a terrible habit o' carrying women around whether they like it or no'."

"And I notice ye're as stubborn as our Saidh," Geordie responded dryly, and then shrugged. "There is no arguing with stubborn, and I'm too thirsty to wait another half hour fer ye to get across the hall so I can have a drink."

Evina merely shook her head and then forced a smile for Saidh and the other women as Geordie set her on the bench next to them.

"How are ye?" Saidh asked at once. "Ye were no' hurt, were ye?"

"Nay. I'm fine," Evina assured her.

"I thought so, but when Conran carried ye straight above stairs I feared he'd knocked the wind out o' ye or bruised ye up when he tackled ye to the ground," she said with a grimace.

Evina shook her head, and then reluctantly admitted, "I was upset that Cormag got hurt in me place."

"Aye. I can imagine. I'd feel the same way and no amount o' being assured 'twas no' me fault would help," Saidh murmured with under-standing, and then said firmly, "We must do something about yer attacker."

"Do no' fret about it," Geordie said, bending to lean between them to grab a mug and pitcher of ale off the table in front of them. Straightening, he began to pour himself a drink and added, "The men are no' just searching the keep. They'll be searching everywhere inside the outer wall of Maclean. They'll find the bastard."

Evina glanced to Saidh, unsurprised to see the doubt on her face as well, and when the woman turned that expression to her, she said, "I have thought of a way to trap the man if they don't find him in the search."

Saidh straightened and grinned. "Do tell."

"Ah, hell," Alick muttered behind them. "The women are thinking. Ye ken there's always trouble when the women start in thinking."

Ignoring him, Evina leaned toward Saidh and began to tell her what she'd come up with in her room.

Chapter 16

"**W**ELL?"

Conran glanced up at that barked question from the Maclean as he led his brothers and Donnan to the stairs of the keep. He spotted Evina's father halfway up the steps, but before he could respond to the man's question, a soldier shouted Donnan's name. Conran glanced around just in time to see the big man break off from the group to head back across the bailey. He watched him head for the gates and then turned back to the old man he was approaching. Noting his questioning expression, Conran shook his head wearily and said, "We coordinated with Donnan and the soldiers and searched every square inch within the walls. We also questioned everyone we encountered and—" his mouth tightened with frustration "—nothing." Pausing on the steps next to the Maclean, he asked, "Did ye have yer men search the keep?"

"Aye." Fearghas sighed the word, as weary and disappointed as him. Conran wasn't surprised when he said, "And they found nothing either."

Nodding, Conran continued up the stairs, saying, "Then he must have a hidey-hole somewhere here. We'll have to keep Evina guarded and come up with a trap to catch the bastard."

"Aye," the Maclean muttered, hobbling up the steps on his heels.

Conran had just reached the door to the keep when he heard shouting from the gate. Pausing, he turned to peer back to see what the ruckus was. His eyebrows rose when he saw that the gates were opening and the drawbridge being lowered. He'd ordered the gates closed and draw-bridge drawn up when they'd started the search. He hadn't wanted the confusion of people coming and going while they were conducting their search, and he'd forgotten to tell the men they could open both again. They were doing so now though, and he could see Donnan striding back across the bailey from that direction. Obviously, the men on the gate were who had called out to him, and Donnan had given them permission to open Maclean again to the outside world.

"Ah," Aulay said as a good-sized retinue of riders rode into the bailey bearing the Drummond flag. "Niels is here."

When the Maclean turned to him, a question in his eyes, Conran nodded firmly. "Send someone to fetch yer priest, m'laird, and we'll hold the wedding. We might yet succeed at something today at least."

Conran turned to grab the door handle again and added, "I'd best let Evina ken," as he pulled the door open and rushed inside.

He expected her to still be up in her room, so had automatically headed to the stairs, but was only halfway to them when a burst of female laughter caught his ear. It was full, honest and uninhibited rather than the more subdued feminine chuckles most ladies allowed themselves. There were only two women Conran knew who laughed like that: Saidh and Evina. But Evina's voice was a touch huskier than Saidh's, and that was whose laughter he'd heard. Turning toward the table, he spotted her at once. All the women were there, enjoying a beverage and a laugh, but Evina sat with Saidh on one side of her, and her cousin Gavin on the other. Geordie and Alick stood behind her, chuckling too at whatever had amused everyone so, but their gazes were shifting around the great hall, aware and alert.

Conran paused a moment just to peer at Evina and enjoy the knowledge that she would soon be his wife—very soon. The idea was oddly startling. He'd known it was coming, had been working toward it and had gained her agreement just last night, yet some part of him must have doubted it would ever really come to pass, because he presently found himself almost staggered by the realization that it would indeed happen now that Niels had arrived. He would marry Evina, be her husband, claim her to wife. He would spend the rest of his life with this woman— making love, running Maclean with her, arguing, making up, having children and hopefully even, one day, grandchildren with Evina Maclean MacPherson, soon to be Buchanan.

And she'd agreed to it.

He stared at her silently as she laughed again and an odd ache began in his chest.

"Heartburn?"

Lowering the hand he'd been unconsciously rubbing his chest with, Conran glanced around at that question and smiled wryly when he saw that Donnan had entered the keep and joined him. "The others stayed to greet Niels and Edith, I presume?"

Donnan nodded solemnly. "They should be in shortly."

Nodding, Conran glanced back to Evina as another burst of laughter filled the air.

"The Maclean hailed one of the lads and sent him to fetch the priest back to hold the ceremony just ere I entered," Donnan announced as they watched the people at the table.

"Then I'd best warn her that Niels and Edith are here and the wedding will be held directly," Conran murmured, but didn't move. Instead, he stared at Evina's laughing face and felt the ache in his chest begin again.

"Heartburn?" Donnan repeated, drawing his attention to the fact that he was rubbing his chest once more.

"Aye, heartburn," he muttered, letting his hand drop, but knew that wasn't his ailment. Somehow, he'd fallen in love with the wench. That was the only explanation for the panic he'd felt when he hadn't found her at the table earlier, and had realized she was out and about with a killer after her. Never mind the way his heart had stopped when he'd seen the arrow narrowly miss her and hit the lad behind her. He'd wanted to cut his chest open and take her inside himself to keep her safe. And every time he looked at her, he was filled with longing and an ache that he knew would probably never go away. He loved the stubborn, reckless, beautiful woman, and nothing in his life had scared him more than that realization. It made him vulnerable. If he didn't catch the man targeting Evina and the bastard succeeded in killing her . . . Conran didn't think he could bear that. They *had* to catch him, he thought as he started for the head table and the women seated there.

"He didn't?" Evina gasped the words with disbelief as he approached, stirring his curiosity.

"Aye. He did," Saidh assured her, and then suddenly glanced around as if she'd noticed his approach out of the corner of her eye. Smiling when she saw him, she said, "And here he is now."

Evina turned then, and saw him as well. He watched the smile of greeting that bloomed on her face and marveled again that she would soon be his wife. It made Conran wonder how he had got so damned lucky, and then he smiled wryly as the answer popped up in his mind that it had been purely by accident. Evina had set out to fetch Rory Buchanan, a Highlander known for his healing, and ended up kidnapping and dragging him home instead. It made him the luckiest bastard in Scotland, if not the world.

"Yer mood seems much improved," Conran commented as he paused behind and to the side of her.

"Aye," she said, her smile sobering a touch. "Well, 'twas a relief to learn Cormag will be well, and to see him up and about."

"Oh?" He glanced around. "Where is he?"

"He had a drink with us and then went to lie down," she explained. "While he sustained only a flesh wound, it doesn't make it pain less and that can take a lot out o' ye too," she pointed out.

"Aye," Conran agreed, his gaze settling on her again. He stared at her for one moment, and then announced abruptly, "Niels and Edith have arrived."

"Oh!" Saidh beamed at the news and turned to Evina. "Edith is a dear. Ye shall like her too."

The other women agreed enthusiastically with her words, and then Saidh added, "And this means we can have the wedding tonight."

"'Twill be sooner than tonight," Conran assured them. "The priest is being fetched as we speak."

"What?" Evina looked alarmed at this news. "But—"

"Nonsense," Saidh said, interrupting her, and then patting Evina's hand, she added, "It can no' possibly be held until we've bathed and readied Evina. And ye must bathe too."

"Bathe?" he echoed with surprise. "There is no need for us to bathe. We—"

"O' course ye must bathe," Saidh said firmly. "'Tis yer wedding day. Ye should both be bathed and pampered and made pretty for the bedding ceremony. We could probably manage all that just ere the sup if we get started quickly," she said firmly, and then glanced around. "Where did yer lovely Tildy get to, Evi? We should have her order the water to be prepared fer ye both."

"We only have the one tub," Evina said with a frown.

"Nay," Gavin corrected her. "There are two tubs. One is kept for the servants to use in the kitchen as they wish, but we could cart both up for the two o' ye to use."

"To use where?" Evina asked with a frown. "I can have mine in me chamber, but Conran gave up his room to Dougall and Murine."

"He can bathe in yer father's room," Tildy suggested, appearing next to Conran. He had no idea where she'd come from, but she'd obviously heard at least part of the conversation.

"Aye," Evina breathed, relaxing. "Father'll no' mind."

"Hopefully, he'll no' mind joining Gavin and the others in the barracks to sleep this night too," Tildy said now with a frown. "Otherwise I've no idea where I'll put Laird and Lady Drummond."

"Oh." Evina smiled suddenly at Saidh, and then turned to the maid and said, "There's no need to put Da out like that, Tildy. Edith and Niels may have me room."

"What?" Conran gasped with shock. "Where are we to sleep, then?"

"Aye," Tildy said with some concern of her own. "If they're in yer room, where will ye and Lord Conran spend yer first night as husband and wife?"

"Ne'er fear," Evina said, smiling mysteriously. "The ladies and I have come up with a plan."

"Aye, they have," Alick told him, and then warned, "They got to thinking while the rest o' ye were busy with yer hunt."

"What is this plan?" Conran asked with concern, but before anyone could answer, the keep doors opened and the women all jumped up squealing and rushed away to greet Edith as she entered. Conran stared after them, narrow-eyed, knowing that while they were happy to see Edith, they were also taking advantage of her arrival to avoid answering his question. At least Evina was. She didn't even know the women but was rushing away from the table too, at least as fast as she could rush. Scowling, Conran turned to his brothers and ordered, "Tell me."

"There." Tildy finished fiddling with her hair and stepped back to survey her handiwork with a smile that turned into a frown as her gaze dropped over the gown Evina was wearing. Shaking her head, she sighed with regret. "I'm so sorry, m'lady. We kenned this was coming and should have made ye a fine new gown for the occasion. Most o' yers are frayed and old, and this is the best o' the lot left that does no' have an arrow hole in it, or is filthy from rolling in the dirt today."

Evina glanced down at the pale yellow gown she wore, and plucked at the frayed cloth a bit fretfully. She'd never been much concerned with what she wore. So long as it covered her decently, 'twas good enough to her mind. Until now. She would have liked a beautiful gown to marry in. Something that would have made Conran proud to claim her to wife. Forcing a smile, she shrugged. "Well, if this is the best o' the lot, then 'twill have to do. 'Tis fine," she added the lie bravely. "I'm sure Conran'll no' even notice what I'm wearing."

Tildy was peering at her pityingly for the obvious lie when a knock sounded at the door. It opened without the caller waiting to be invited.

Evina watched wide-eyed as Saidh, Murine, Edith, Jo and Jetta rushed in in an excited cluster, all of them chattering at once.

"'Tis done!" Saidh announced triumphantly as Geordie pulled the door closed behind them.

"Aye, and 'tis beautiful," Jo told her happily.

"It is," Murine assured her. "I did no' think it could be, but it truly is."

"Aye," Jetta agreed with a grin. "We pilfered furs and pillows and bolsters from every room in the keep, and filled it with candles and torches, and even a table fer the two o' ye to sit at."

"And the chests, o' course," Edith said meaningfully.

"It sounds wonderful," Evina said, her face relaxing into a true smile. "I can no' wait to see it."

"Ye'll be pleased," Saidh assured her, and then added solemnly, "Now we just have to hope the trap works."

Silence fell briefly in the room as the women all nodded solemnly, and then Murine moved forward, her smile returning. "Ye look lovely, Evina. Tildy, ye've done wonders with her hair."

"Aye," Edith agreed, moving closer as well to get a look at the braid Tildy had woven around her head and set flowers in. "She looks like a fairy princess with the flowers woven through her braid like that."

Tildy beamed at the compliments, until the women turned their attention to Evina's gown. Sighing then, she said, "I should have made something special for the day, but with all the company, I didn't think on it and this is the only gown that is clean and without holes or terribly frayed to an indecent degree. I fear m'lady has ne'er troubled herself over much about such things as fashion."

"'Tis fine," Evina repeated, forcing another smile. "Tildy did such wonders with me hair, no one will even notice me gown."

"Hmm." Jo moved up to stand beside her and glanced from Evina to herself and then asked the others, "She is about my size, is she no'?"

"Aye, she is," Murine said, a smile beginning to curve her lips. "Pray, tell us ye have something she might wear for the wedding."

"I believe I do," Jo said with a nod, and headed for the door. "I shall be right back."

"Whatever she brings back'll be wondrous," Murine promised with a grin as the door closed behind Jo.

"Whether it is or no', 'tis kind o' her to trouble herself so," Evina said quietly. "She seems a very nice woman. 'Tis hard to believe she's English."

"Only half-English," Saidh corrected her firmly. "Her father was a Scot. Most like that's why she ended up kind and good. By all accounts her mother was a right English bitch."

"Saidh!" Jetta said with dismay. "Ye might hurt Jo's feelings did she hear ye say that."

"But she did no' hear, did she?" Saidh said with a shrug, and then added, "Besides, she'd tell ye that herself. She's no love for her birth mother. Ne'er even kenned her and was as horrified as everyone else to hear how the woman had tried to kill her own sister, Lady Mackay."

"Wait," Evina said with a frown. "Jo's mother tried to kill her own sister?"

"Aye," Edith said, but glanced toward the door when it opened again and fell silent as Jo entered with a royal blue gown across her arms.

"I'll tell ye the story another time," Saidh murmured as they watched the other woman approach, and then added, "If she does no' tell ye herself."

Evina merely nodded and greedily eyed the gown Jo was holding. It was beautiful. Much nicer than the gown she presently wore. Eyeing the bits of detailing she could see, she began to pray it would fit.

"Well, let's get this gown off ye so ye can try that one," Tildy said, all business. The other women immediately gathered around to help and, within moments, Evina's prayers were answered and she was wearing the blue gown. It fit like a glove. She peered down at herself as the women stepped back and could have wept. Evina had no idea how it looked on her, but it was stunning to look down at, and she felt pretty in it.

"It's perfect," Murine whispered.

Evina glanced up hopefully at the words and saw admiration on the expressions of the other women.

"Aye. 'Tis perfect on you," Jo said solemnly. "It is new. I've ne'er worn it and now I ne'er could. 'Twould ne'er look that good on me. I think ye must keep it."

"Oh!" Evina's eyes widened with shock. "Nay. I could no' keep it."

"Aye, ye can," Jo assured her. "Consider it a wedding gift."

Evina opened her mouth, and then closed it again and, embarrassed to feel her eyes glaze with tears at the kindness, peered down at the beautiful gown again. "Thank ye," she managed after a moment, and stiffened slightly when Jo suddenly stepped forward to embrace her.

"'Tis my pleasure," Jo assured her, hugging her tightly. "And ye look ravishing in it."

After a hesitation, Evina slid her own arms cautiously about the woman and hugged her back. But she felt strange doing it. No one but Conran had hugged her since her mother's death, and this was different than the hugs Conran had given her so far. His hugs had been during or after fornicating, and to comfort her after she'd nearly been drowned. This was a hug of pure affection. She was unused to the feelings it brought welling up within her, but suspected she'd best get used to it when the other women all crowded around to hug the pair of them.

"Oh!" Murine gasped suddenly, pulling back from the group hug. "We'll wrinkle her gown!"

Evina suddenly found herself released as the women all backed away to examine her and be sure they hadn't done the gown damage.

"'Tis fine," Edith said with relief, and then smiled wryly. "But I'd best go clean up and prepare meself fer the wedding too. Me gown is dusty from the journey and I'll look the poor cousin next to Evina do I no' change."

"Ye can change in the chamber Dougall and I are using while here," Murine offered.

"Wait," Evina protested. "She is to stay in me chamber anyway. I'll leave and let her change here."

"Ye can't," Saidh said at once. "Conran might see ye. Ye have to wait here until he is at the chapel steps and then yer father will come fetch ye to take ye to the steps to meet him before the priest."

"Oh," Evina said nonplussed. She'd had no idea there were rules about this kind of thing.

"'Tis fine," Edith assured her with a smile. "I'll use Murine and Dougall's room. Me chests are out in the hall still at the moment anyway."

"We should all get moving," Jetta said now. "We're all supposed to be waiting at the chapel when she comes, and I need to change as well. I got a might sweaty and dusty working on the tent."

"So did I," Saidh admitted, brushing at the dust on her skirts with irritation. "I guess I'd best change too."

Murmuring agreement, the other women all began to move. They left the room in almost the same cluster as they'd entered, taking all the noise and laughter with them. Evina stood in the center of the room and watched them go, feeling a little lost and alone.

Rustling drew her attention to Tildy then, and she turned to see that she was dragging the furs off the bed. Taking a steadying breath, she forced a smile and said, "There's no need to do that now, Tildy."

"Aye. There is," she responded at once, and pointed out, "I have to prepare the room fer Laird and Lady Drummond to use this night."

"Oh, aye," Evina murmured, and moved to the bed to help when the maid started to strip linens from the bed.

"Ger off with ye," Tildy said at once. "Ye'll wrinkle yer gown or muss yer hair. Just go settle yerself at the table and wait."

Evina frowned, but did as she was told and moved to sit cautiously at the table by the fire. But she felt less than useless just sitting there watching the maid work.

"They're a nice lot o' women," Tildy commented solemnly, carrying the dirty linens to the door and dropping them in a heap next to it.

"Aye," Evina agreed as she watched her collect clean linens from one of the chests and start to remake the bed.

"And they've already accepted ye as one o' their own," Tildy added as she worked. "'Twill be nice fer ye to have female family again."

Evina's eyes widened slightly at the comment and then she frowned as she tried to sort out the tone in Tildy's voice. It wasn't resentful, so much as regretful, which she didn't understand. The old woman was obviously upset somehow, but since she didn't know why or what about, she wasn't sure how to comfort her. Evina stood, and moved toward the bed, trying to get a better look at the woman's face, but suspected Tildy was deliberately keeping it turned away from her. In the end, she simply went with her last words and said, "Ye're female and family, Tildy."

"Nay, lass," Tildy said, that quiet regret deepening in her voice, and then she straightened and met her gaze as she admitted, "I've always thought o' meself as family to ye, and I've been with ye yer whole life, it's true, but as I watched them all embrace ye just now, I realized I ne'er once offered ye that kind o' comfort meself. No even the day yer mother died, and ye were just a wee lass, sobbing fit to burst."

Evina turned slowly as she watched her move about the room straightening this and dusting down that. She was remembering the day in question, and what Tildy said was true. And it wasn't. Clearing her throat, she pointed out, "That's as may be, Tildy, but as I recall, ye mopped up me tears when I finished weeping, set me in the wagon and sat beside me fer the rest o' the journey home, offering me silent comfort."

When Tildy merely frowned slightly at the words and continued puttering around gathering the yellow gown she'd originally planned to wear, and her dirty tunic, Evina added, "And ye were always there to tend me injuries and wounds when I fell or hurt meself too . . . and to nag at me to eat before I ran off to order the men about, or give me the stink-eye when I was misbehaving. Ye *are* family, Tildy," she assured her gently. "Hugging is just no' yer way."

"Aye, well . . ." Tildy shifted, looking uncomfortable, and then shook her head. "But I should ha'e made it me way. Ye were just a child, lass, and I let ye down as badly as yer father did. He left ye to fend fer yerself tending to Gavin and running the keep, and I did no' give ye the affection every child needs. Between the two o' us, 'tis no wonder ye did no' want to marry and depend on someone else who might let ye down, and I'm sorry fer that," she said with agitation.

Evina shook her head at once. "That is no' why I didn't want to marry. I didn't wish to risk a husband like the MacPherson brat, or one who might beat me like Uncle Garrick did Aunt Glenna."

"Oh, lass," Tildy said, straightening to eye her with exasperation. "Ye can tell yer da that to spare his feelings do ye wish it, and ye can even tell yerself that so ye needn't think on it, but ye can no' fool me. Were a man foolish enough to hit ye, ye'd hit him right back, and no doubt knock him on his sorry arse. I've seen ye do it often enough to the soldiers when they were in their cups and got lippy," she pointed out. "I suspect that's half the reason ye trained so hard in battle with Donnan."

"I—" Evina shook her head weakly.

"And if any man who married ye was stupid enough to try to beat ye, it'd be the last beating he gave anyone. Once ye healed, ye'd no doubt sew him up in his bed linens, beat him to within an inch o' his life and dump him in the woods to live or die as God saw fit to have it, and then ye'd lock up the gates and refuse to let him back in if he did survive. Nay," she added firmly. "Ye're no' afraid o' a man hurting ye physically. I'd wager me life on it. 'Tis their letting ye down that ye're afraid o'. Ye can build yer muscle and skill all ye like, but it'll no' stop yer heart being broken when a man abandons ye to fend fer yerself like yer da did when yer mother died."

Sighing, she peered at her solemnly for a moment, and then added, "Thank God the Buchanan came and rescued ye from us, is all I can say. He'll ne'er let ye down like we did. From what I've overheard, he's all about family and responsibility. Forever helping one or the other of them brothers and brother-by-marriage with something. Rory with his healing, Dougall with his horses, Niels with his sheep." Nodding firmly, she added, "And if he gets injured, or—Lord help us—dies, his brothers and sister will step in to help and there's no doubt in me mind on that," she said firmly. "They're all about family, those Buchanans. They'll no' just show up fer any battle Maclean might face, they'll show up fer everything. Births. Deaths. Weddings. Holidays. Celebrations, and hell, just to visit. Which reminds me," Tildy said suddenly with a frown. "We need to add more bedchambers to accommodate them all."

She didn't wait for a response, but headed for the door, muttering, "I'm done here. Why do ye no' rest a bit while ye wait? I'll go see how long 'twill be ere yer father comes to fetch ye."

Tildy dropped the dirty clothes she'd collected onto the pile of dirty linens, opened the bedchamber door and then gathered up the whole heap to carry them out of the room.

Geordie was again the one to pull the door closed. He reached in to grab the handle, and then stilled, his eyes widening slightly when he spotted her standing there in the center of the room. He stared at her wide-eyed for a moment, and then smiled and told her, "The day ye mistook Conran fer Rory was the luckiest day o' his life, m'lady. Ye're absolutely stunning."

"What?" Alick asked from the hall, and then the younger brother appeared beside Geordie and looked into the room. She saw his eyes widen and heard his awed, "Gor!" as Geordie pulled the door closed.

Evina stayed right where she was even after the door closed. She couldn't have moved if she'd wanted to. Tildy's little speech had left her shocked and frozen as the words replayed in her head.

"Ye're no' afraid o' a man hurting ye physically. I'd wager me life on it. 'Tis their letting ye down that ye're afraid o'. Ye can build yer muscle and skill all ye like, but it'll no' stop yer heart being broken when a man abandons ye to fend fer yerself like yer da did when yer mother died."

Evina sank weakly to sit on the side of the bed.

Was that really why she'd avoided marriage? Evina wanted to deny it, but everything Tildy had said was true. She *would* punch any man foolish enough to hit her. And were he enough of an idiot to perform the supremely stupid act of beating her, he'd best hope he beat her to death the first time, because he'd not get a second opportunity to do it.

"Dear God," Evina breathed, rubbing her hands over her face. She'd been lying to herself for years. Why the devil would she lie to herself?

The answer was easy. As Tildy had said, so she wouldn't have to think on it. She wouldn't have to face the fact that her father hadn't cared enough about her to be there for her. To continue to live. To run Maclean and be the father she'd needed. In a way, he'd died that day at the river as surely as her mother, her husband and Lachlan had. Evina had been as good as an orphan, left to raise herself. Her father was the man she'd most depended on, and he'd let her down. After her mother's death, he had not been there for her. He'd not been there for anyone. Maclean would have gone to rot and ruin if she hadn't stepped up and done her best to keep it running. As for Gavin, despite Aunt Glenna's hopes, her father hadn't been there for him either. and Evina had been left the chore of raising her cousin as well.

Evina knew she'd done a terrible job of both tasks at first. Fortunately, Donnan, Tildy and the other soldiers and servants had done their best to aid her where they could. They'd left the final decisions up to her, but had tried to steer her in the right direction. Evina had grown up quickly, taking care of her cousin and all of Maclean in her father's stead. She'd even taken care of her father, insisting he eat when he wanted to skip his meals, taking away the liquor when he began to depend on it too heavily. And even when the first mourning and depression passed after her mother's death, he didn't bounce back and take up the reins of his responsibilities again. He'd decided she was doing a fine job, named Donnan as his first, replacing the man who had died trying to save her mother and husband, and announced that she'd inherit the title of clan chief when he died. He'd then gone hunting, and fishing, and visiting old friends.

Dear God, she hated him for it, Evina admitted to herself.

And she loved him, she acknowledged grimly.

And that was why she'd lied to herself. Evina loved him for the father he'd been before her mother's death, and hated him for the weak, helpless man he'd become when her mother had died, and the burdens that had placed on her young shoulders. It shouldn't have been like that. Conran certainly wouldn't have fallen apart as her father had. He'd have dragged himself from his bed and done what needed doing. She was sure of it. And if he hadn't, his brothers and Saidh would have descended on him and dragged him from his bed and made him do it, helping him fight his way through his grief until he could manage on his own.

Her father hadn't had brothers and sisters like the Buchanans though, Evina acknowledged. Instead, he'd had one sister who had arrived on his doorstep a few short months later, dying. Another sorrow to pile on top of his grief. And then she'd left Gavin in his care, adding another burden to Evina's shoulders. Not that she minded. Gavin had been the only bright spot in her life at that point. He might even have been her saving grace. She'd had to continue for him.

And that was the hell of it, Evina thought unhappily. She'd often wanted to give up and spend her days moping and weeping over what she'd lost as her father did, but hadn't been able to because of Gavin, and the people of Maclean. She'd had to be strong for them. Her father, however, hadn't done that. Not for them, and not for his own daughter.

"Bloody hell," Evina muttered, giving her head a shake. This was her wedding day. It was no time for soul searching and dealing with issues that couldn't be resolved. There was nothing that could be done to change the past. It was over. Now was the time to look to the future, and her future was the man she was going to marry. Conran.

Evina breathed out slowly, just the thought of him calming her somewhat. Aye, Conran was nothing like her father. He would not let her down. And if he did, Saidh would help her kick his arse, she thought, and smiled.

Tildy was right. She was marrying into a large family who put their family first. They would be there, not just for Conran, but for her now too. As well as for any children they had, she thought, and decided then that Conran had the right of it. They should have a lot of children, seven or eight like Conran's parents had had. That way, if she and Conran died, they would all have each other to depend on.

Smiling faintly, she peered down at the skirts of the lovely gown she wore, recalling Geordie's and Alick's reactions to seeing her in it.

The day ye mistook Conran fer Rory was the luckiest day o' his life, m'lady. Ye're absolutely stunning, Geordie had said, and Evina wondered if Conran would agree. Was he glad they were going to wed? Her father had pretty much tricked and trapped him into this marriage.

Evina smiled wryly at the thought. After years of leaving her to fend for herself, Fearghas Maclean had suddenly recalled he was her father and tried to see to her future. She may have fought him on it, but would have to give him credit for that. He'd chosen a fine time to do it, and a fine man to see her married to. Because she certainly felt lucky that she'd brought the wrong Highlander home and was going to marry him. Had she brought Rory home that day, as intended . . . well, he was nice enough, and no doubt family was as important to him as the rest of the Buchanans, but Evina really didn't think the healer's temperament would suit hers. Not that she'd set out to bring back the Buchanan healer with marriage in mind. In fact, that had been the furthest thing from her thoughts at the time. But she was glad now that she was marrying Conran. He was a man she knew she could depend on.

He also made the bedding a pleasure she couldn't imagine experiencing with anyone else. All the man had to do was look at her with that hungry expression he got, and she began to tingle in places that had never tingled before. And once he kissed or touched her? Forget everything else. She was lost. Evina became nothing more than a mass of trembling need and desire, ready to lie down and spread her legs for him.

Aye, she'd got the right Highlander in the end. She liked him, respected him, found pleasure with him and . . . She might even love him, Evina admitted solemnly to herself. Certainly, if she didn't already, she was headed that way. She was beginning to find it hard to imagine life without him, and certainly couldn't begin to envision sharing her life and body with anyone else.

Aye, she probably loved him, Evina acknowledged, and then grimaced at herself for her cowardice, and admitted that aye, she did love Conran Buchanan. He was a good man, a strong man, a brave man, and intelligent. But he was also gentle, and patient and kind. She loved him and wanted him, and was eagerly looking forward to being his wife, she acknowledged, and then stilled when she heard a shuffling sound behind her. It was much like the sound she'd heard just before someone had tried to drown her in her bath.

But the passage entrances were all locked now, Evina reminded herself. It must be mice this time, she reassured herself. Still, she started to turn to see what was causing the sound . . . and then paused halfway, jerked back around to face the door when a knock sounded.

Shaking her head at how jumpy she was, Evina called out, "Enter," and stood up to brush her skirts down as the door opened.

Evina half expected it to be her father come to collect her. But since her feelings about that man were presently somewhat muddled, she was relieved when Gavin stepped inside.

"Ye look beautiful, cousin," he said with a combination of awe and pride as he closed the door and looked her over.

"Thank ye," Evina murmured, shifting uncomfortably under the praise, and then to change the subject, she asked, "Is everything all right? I was waiting for Da to come get me."

"Aye. Uncle Fearghas sent me to fetch ye down. He's a bit tender at the moment and didn't think he could manage the stairs," Gavin explained.

Some voice in Evina's mind pointed out that he was failing her again, but she pushed it away. The past was the past, she reminded herself firmly.

"Ye were no' planning to run away, were ye?" Gavin asked suddenly.

Evina dragged herself from her thoughts to peer at him with confusion. Her bewilderment showed in her voice when she asked, "What?"

When Gavin raised his eyebrows and gestured behind her, Evina turned and saw that the entrance to the passage was open. She stared at it with shock. It hadn't been open when the women were here, or while Tildy was cleaning. They would have noticed. And it shouldn't be open now. Her father had locked down the passages from the inside. No one should have been able to open it from the passage.

"I thought ye wanted to marry Conran?" Gavin said behind her, and she could hear the frown in his voice.

"Aye," Evina breathed, and then moved quickly toward the opening, intending to close and lock it. She'd then have Gavin fetch Conran and the others to search the passages again. The attacker was obviously in there. At least, that was her thinking. But she never made it to the entrance. Evina had barely taken a step past the bed when movement out of the corner of her eye caught her attention. She started to turn, but was too slow. Even as she spotted the tall, balding man in a semiclean plaid raising up from his crouched position on this side of the bed, he was grabbing her arm and dragging her up against his chest.

"Gav—!" she managed to shout before he covered her mouth with one hand, and pressed a knife to her throat with the other.

"Whist, lass, ye'll be drawing company we do no' want," he growled, pressing the knife sharply against her neck.

"Let her go," Gavin demanded, drawing his sword from his belt and raising it threateningly.

"Lower the sword, lad," her captor hissed. "And do no' even think o' callin' out fer help, else I'll slit her throat right now."

Gavin hesitated, his hand tightening on his sword, but then he firmed his chin and shook his head.

Her captor released a low chuckle. "Hold on to it, then. But that broadsword looks heavy. Ye'll tire eventually . . . and I can outwait ye. I hold all the cards."

They all stood at a stalemate for what seemed an interminable amount of time, and then a knock sounded at the door.

Chapter 17

"THERE," AULAY SAID, TUGGING AT A PLEAT HERE AND THERE. "Ye look fine."

"Thank ye," Conran muttered, sliding his sword into his belt. "And thank ye for the loan o' the clean shirt and plaid. 'Tis most annoying no' having any o' me own plaids and shirts here."

"I can imagine," Aulay murmured, stepping back to peer at him before admitting, "'Twas a gift from Niels. Made from his own sheep."

Conran raised his eyebrows at this news. "Then why did he no' bring it to me?"

"He wanted to, but I said I would," Aulay admitted. "I wanted to talk to ye."

Conran sighed and shook his head. "I am marrying her, brother. There's no need for threats, or beatings. I—"

"I ken that," Aulay interrupted dryly. "Any fool could see ye're in love with the lass and happy to marry her."

Conran stiffened at the words and then grimaced slightly. "That obvious, is it?"

"Aye," he said with amusement. "But that's no' what I came to talk about."

"What did ye come to talk about, then?" Conran asked, his eyebrows rising.

"The plan the ladies cooked up," Aulay said. "The tent."

"Oh. Aye. The Sinclairs' traveling tent," he said heavily, recalling the plan the women had hatched up. He and Evina were to sleep in the tent tonight, their first night as husband and wife. It was supposed to be because with so many guests there was no room in the keep itself. But the truth was, the women were hoping that the bastard who kept trying to kill Evina would see their sleeping in the tent as a perfect opportunity and make one last attempt.

"Ye do no' like the plan?" Aulay asked, not seeming surprised. "I thought it a good one."

"Well, 'tis no' yer Jetta who will be in the tent in peril if the bastard does make another attempt to kill her," Conran pointed out shortly.

"Nay," Aulay agreed. "'Twill be Evina."

"Aye," Conran growled.

"He may no' attack," Aulay pointed out soothingly. "We will have men stationed at the entrance and at each corner o' the tent to make it seem like ye're well-guarded."

"Until the two at the back move forward to talk to the men at the front corners, leaving the back unguarded," Conran said grimly, recalling what Alick and Geordie had told him when he'd pressed for an explanation. "And then he's likely to slice through the back o' the tent to enter and try to kill us while he thinks we're sleeping. And *hopefully*, Geordie and Alick will be able to get out o' the chests they're hiding in quickly enough to stop him from harming Evina."

"Dougall and Niels and I will be watching from the passage too," Aulay reminded him. "'Tis why they had the tent set up amid the apple trees behind the kitchens. Besides, ye and Evina will have yer weapons too, and I doubt ye'll be sleeping for worry that a murderer might be creeping up on the tent. Then too, just seeing how well-guarded the tent is at first might scare him off before the men move forward," Aulay pointed out. "It may no' work."

Conran merely nodded, but he was torn between hoping the plan did, and didn't, work. He wanted to catch the bastard, but would prefer a trap that didn't put Evina in peril. Unfortunately, he hadn't come up with one yet, and as much as he hated to admit it, Evina's plan was a good one. She really was a clever wench.

"Anyway," Aulay said now, "I just wanted to be sure ye kenned the plan."

"Aye, I ken it," Conran muttered with a sigh.

"Good. Then let's go see ye married, brother," Aulay said, heading for the door.

Grunting, Conran followed him to the door, and led the way out when Aulay opened it for him. He paused in the hall though when he saw Geordie and Alick crouching in front of Evina's door, alternately pressing their ears to it, and then apparently trying to see through the wooden slats.

Conran was just opening his mouth to ask what the devil they thought they were doing when Geordie turned his head and spotted him and Aulay. Putting a silencing finger to his mouth, the man stood abruptly and hurried to stop them before they moved too close to the door to risk speech.

"What are ye doing?" Conran asked in a quiet hiss.

"Gavin just went in a minute ago," Geordie explained.

"So?" Conran asked. "He is her cousin. He is probably fetching her for Laird Maclean. He was hobbling pretty good earlier. His wound is most likely troubling him. Between that and Evina's still being weak, I suspect the two o' them will have to take horses to the chapel."

"Aye," Geordie agreed.

"Did ye tell them?" Alick asked anxiously, joining them then.

"I was just about to," Geordie said with irritation.

"Tell us what?" Aulay asked.

"We think someone is in there with them," Alick said, his expression a cross between worry and excitement.

"Who?" Conran asked at once.

"We do no' ken," Geordie admitted. "The women went in and came out, and then Tildy came out and Gavin went in. Gavin and Evina should be the only ones in there."

"What makes ye think they're no' alone, then?" Conran asked with a frown.

"Because shortly after Gavin went in, Evina started to shout his name, and then it sounded like two men were talking. At least, we heard Gavin speak and then someone answered in a voice almost too quiet to hear."

"Mayhap 'tis Evina," Aulay suggested.

The two younger brothers shook their heads at once, and then Geordie said, "'The voice sounds too deep and raspy. 'Tis a man, I'm sure."

"And ye did no' go in to see what is about?" Conran asked with disbelief.

"It just happened, and we were trying to listen to see what was being said and decide what to do. If there *is* a man in there, our entering unexpectedly could put Evina and her cousin in peril," Geordie pointed out. "Besides, we checked the room ere we let Evina in, and no one went past us, and the passages are all locked from the inside. There should be no one in there."

Conran frowned and then said, "Ye'll have to knock at the door. We need to ken if something is amiss or no'."

"What do I say when one o' them opens the door?" Geordie asked with a frown.

"If 'tis Gavin and ye can see into the room, just say ye were checking that all was well. But if ye can no' see into the room, or he looks like something may be amiss, say ye just thought to let Evina ken that Aulay and I just headed down to the church so they may want to wait a few minutes before heading down themselves."

"Why?" Geordie asked with confusion.

"Because he shall see me standing beside ye and ken we suspect something is amiss," he pointed out patiently. "He may be able to give us a hint o' what is happening."

When Geordie said, "Right," and nodded with understanding, Conran urged him back to Evina's door and then stepped to the side, saw that Aulay was out of sight on the other side of the door and nodded at Geordie to go ahead.

His younger brother took a deep breath and then knocked at the door.

They all stood waiting for it to be answered, and it definitely took longer to be answered than it should have, Conran decided as they waited. Geordie was just raising his hand to knock again when the door was cracked open and Gavin peered out. The young man's eyes slid over the four of them and then returned to Geordie.

"I was just . . . er . . ." Geordie glanced to Conran, and then tried again. "I just thought to let ye ken that Conran and Aulay have headed down to the chapel. Evina may want to wait a moment as she does no' want him to see how lovely she looks in her dress yet."

Gavin's gaze sharpened, and he glanced to Conran, relief clear on his face. He obviously understood they suspected something. There was someone in there with them. Conran was sure of it, and was just trying to think of a question he could whisper to Geordie for him to ask that might gain them more information when Gavin—clever as his cousin—said, "I am glad to hear it. I feared he might try to escape marrying Evi by slipping away through the passages."

Conran got the message loud and clear. Approach from the passage. Leaving Geordie to respond, he turned away at once, and slid along the hall back to Laird Maclean's door.

"The Maclean locked the passages."

Conran nearly jumped out of his skin at that whisper behind him, but then glanced over his shoulder to see that Aulay had followed and shook his head. "Obviously, someone unlocked them. Or at least the one to Evina's room and whichever one they entered through to get to it."

"Do ye ken how to unlock the Maclean's passage?" Aulay asked as they slipped into the old man's room.

"Aye," he assured him, and slid his sword out as he strode across to the fireplace. Conran quickly turned the rock he'd seen the Maclean use to lock the entrance, and then turned the torch holder to open the passage. He held his breath as it slid open, and then moved to peer cautiously into the dark space. It looked empty, but there was a square of light pouring from the entrance to Evina's room next door. The entrance in her room was open. Raising his sword, Conran entered the dark passage and began to creep silently toward that square of light.

"NAY, NAY. CONRAN WANTS TO MARRY YER COUSIN, AND WE ALL want him to as well," Evina heard Geordie say from the other side of the door. "We'll be happy to welcome her to the family."

There was silence for a minute, and then Gavin said, "I'll tell Evina that we should wait a few minutes, then."

"Aye, ye do that," Geordie muttered, and then as her cousin started to close the door, he added, "We'll be right here. Waiting."

Gavin finished closing the door and then turned to face Evina and her captor with a tight expression. She suspected he'd passed a message to the men in the hall with that comment about Conran escaping through the passages, but wasn't sure if they'd got the message. And her cousin seemed to her to be trying to avoid looking at her. Evina didn't know what that meant. And she didn't like how still and quiet the man holding her was either. She feared he too suspected Gavin had tried to give the men a message with that comment. Trying to distract him, she asked, "The passages were locked. How did ye get in?"

"I unlocked them, did no' I?" he said dryly, but his voice sounded distracted to her.

"How did ye even ken about the passages?" she asked, thinking that keeping him talking had to be good. It meant he couldn't think. Hopefully. And if Gavin's message had been understood and someone was even now coming up the passage from one of the other rooms to help them, she needed to give them time to get there. The problem was, Geordie and Alick didn't know how to open the passages, or even exactly where they were. They'd need to fetch her father. They needed time.

"Me wife," the man muttered, and Evina started to glance around in surprise, but stilled when the knife dug in deeper at her throat.

"Yer wife?" Gavin asked at once, drawing his attention again. "Who is yer wife? Is she a servant here?"

Much to her relief, the knife at her throat eased again as the man said with disgust, "Nay. Do I look like peasant stock to you? Me wife was Glenna MacLeod. Glenna *Maclean* MacLeod."

Evina blinked at that announcement and met Gavin's gaze, sure her expression was as bewildered as his by the claim. The man was obviously mad if he thought they'd believe Glenna had been married to a bandit ere marrying the MacLeod. Apparently, Gavin thought so too, because he raised his sword and eased a step closer.

"Nay," her captor hissed at once, drawing Evina back a step toward the passage entrance. "Just stay still, and stay calm, son. Everything is fine. In fact, just stay out o' this. I'm no' here fer you."

"That's as may be," Gavin growled, moving another step closer. "But if ye threaten me cousin, ye'll be dealing with me as well. And if ye do no' unhand her at once, I'll call out to the men in the hall and ye'll have a hell o' a lot more than me to deal with."

"Open yer mouth and I'll slit her throat at once, son," the man threatened.

"Stop calling me 'son,'" Gavin snapped. "I'm no relation to you."

"Aye, ye are," the man growled, and then shook his head and said with exasperation, "I do no' ken why ye're making this difficult. I'm doing this fer yer benefit."

"Me?" Gavin gasped the word with disbelief.

"Aye." The man holding her sighed his foul breath across the side of her face, and then said, "I am yer da, boyo. I'm Garrick MacLeod. Yer father."

Evina stiffened, and jerked her head around, getting a quick glimpse of his face before the knife digging into her throat made her turn forward again. It was enough. She suddenly realized why he had looked familiar to Tildy. The man had Gavin's face, just older, rougher and with less of the intelligence evident on Gavin's. That was enough to make her believe he was who he claimed to be, and that Garrick MacLeod hadn't died as his brother had claimed.

Gavin obviously didn't believe it though. He snorted at the claim and said coldly, "Me father is dead. He broke his own fool neck falling off his horse while riding drunk." Mouth tightening, he added, "And none o' this is for me. I have no desire to see me cousin dead. Besides, ye tried to kill me in the clearing. Was that fer me benefit too?"

"I didn't ken 'twas you, did I?" Garrick MacLeod hissed defensively. "But as soon as the wench called ye Gavin, I realized ye were me boy and gave off and fled," he pointed out, and then added, "Trust me, laddie, had I wanted ye dead, ye would be. Ye're no' bad with a sword, but I'm still the best who ever lived."

Evina rolled her eyes at the bragging. Her father had once said Garrick MacLeod had been a braggart and liar in life who took what he wanted when he wanted it. Her father had also told her that he'd tried to convince his father not to make his sister, Glenna, marry the man, but his father wouldn't listen. If the fact that the man had beaten his wife to death hadn't already convinced her that her father was right about him, this would. The MacLeod wasn't dead, and he may have fallen on hard times, but he obviously still retained his bloated belief in his esteem and that he was entitled to anything he wished.

"Look boy," the man said now, "I *am* yer da."

"Ye're lying," Gavin said baldly, and glanced to Evina. "Isna he?"

She knew he expected her to agree at once, but she hesitated and then admitted, "I think he might be telling the truth, Gavin. I think he might be yer father." It made more sense than that someone else not only knew about the passages, but how to unlock them. She could imagine her aunt being young and foolish enough to tell him about them when she was first married and didn't realize the kind of man she'd been wedded to.

Gavin blinked at the suggestion and then frowned and asked accusingly, "Then why did ye and Uncle Fearghas say he was dead?"

"Because we thought he was," she assured him quickly. "I was there when Da was told he'd died. Yer uncle Tearlach is the one who told him that. Garrick MacLeod's brother. We had no reason not to believe him."

"Tearlach." Garrick spat the name with loathing. "That bastard stole everything from me."

"No' quite everything," Evina argued quietly, thinking of the wife he'd beaten to death. Her aunt Glenna.

"Everything," Garrick insisted. "He stole MacLeod right out from under me. And I'll no' let this wench do the same to you," he growled, pressing the knife tighter to her throat.

"Nay!" Gavin took another step closer, alarm filling his face. "Do ye harm her I'll kill ye."

"Don't be foolish, son. I'm looking out fer yer best interests here. And while I'm sure ye care for the wench, ye need to think on yer future now. The Maclean is old and like to die soon. He already very nearly did before the Buchanan came and healed him," he added with irritation, and then continued, "Right now, the lass'd be the only thing standing between ye and inheriting Maclean when the old bastard kicks off. But does she marry the Buchanan and have children with the bastard . . ." He shook his head. "Ye'll ne'er gain the title then."

"I don't care," Gavin growled. "I'll no' let ye hurt Evina."

"Ye do as I say and ye can have no' just Maclean, but MacLeod as well," he argued with frustration. "And it's yer birthright."

"What?" Gavin asked with disbelief. "Ye left MacLeod to me uncle. I'll ne'er rule there."

"Nay. I didna," he assured him. "Tearlach tried to force me to. He came to me after Donnan left with ye and yer mother, and said that if Glenna died, I'd hang for it, but he could protect me. I thought the bastard was finally going to be the supportive brother I needed, but wrangling MacLeod out o' me was what he was about. He said he'd claim me dead, and save my neck from the noose, but I'd have to sign a new will and make him me heir."

"And ye did," Gavin pointed out with disgust.

"I didn't have a choice, did I?" the MacLeod snapped. "Events were conspiring against me. First Donnan betrayed me by sneaking away with me boy and wife, and then there was yer mother running off and killing herself, and then me brother—"

"Mother did no' kill herself," Gavin snapped. "Ye beat her to death."

"She'd have lived had she stayed at MacLeod," the man hissed furiously, sending spittle flying past Evina's face. "Old Betty would have seen her well. She'd seen her back from worse beatings than that one. 'Twas her running off to Maclean with Donnan while sore injured that killed her."

Evina shook her head slightly with disgust even as Gavin did it fully.

"Anyway," Garrick added on a sigh. "I did no' sign away MacLeod on ye. I saved it for ye so ye could return and claim it when ye were old enough to keep yerself safe from me brother."

"Ye signed it away," Gavin said heavily. "There was a will naming him as heir."

"Aye," Garrick admitted, and then grinned and added, "But I did no' sign my name, I signed yers."

"What?" Evina gasped even as Gavin did.

"I signed Gavin MacLeod rather than Garrick MacLeod," he said patiently. "And Tearlach did no' even notice. He was too busy pouring himself a drink to celebrate his forcing me to take everything from me boy and giving it to him. I signed yer name, he gave it a cursory glance, no doubt noticed naught but the big *G* and *MacLeod* and rolled it up and tucked it away in his chest of important papers where it's no doubt now buried under every other important paper he's ever collected since."

"He's probably got rid of it by now," Gavin said with a frown.

"Nay. He throws nothing away. *Nothing*," Garrick emphasized. "The bastard hoards everything he lays his hands on." He paused briefly, and then said with satisfaction, "So ye see, lad, all we have to do is kill yer cousin here, and that old bastard Maclean, and ye'll have two castles. Ye'll be a fine rich laird, all thanks to me."

"Well, if what ye say is true and I need only go claim MacLeod, why kill Evi and Uncle Fearghas?" Gavin asked with a frown. "What do I need with Maclean if I can claim MacLeod?"

"Because yer uncle Tearlach is a useless fool who gambled away and lost most everything at MacLeod except the land," he growled, sounding furious. "Ye'll need the wealth o' Maclean to help ye bring MacLeod back to the state 'twas when I ruled it. And I'll help ye with that. We just need to kill the girl here, and her father," he insisted, digging the knife in a little deeper.

"And, o' course, ye want nothing for this service," Evina mocked dryly.

"Shut up," Garrick growled, pressing the knife tighter again.

He was slicing her throat each time, Evina knew. She could feel the blood dripping down her throat. But she didn't think he was cutting too deep. At least, she hoped not. But noting the anxious way Gavin was eyeing her neck, she began to wonder. Mayhap he *was* cutting deep. Mayhap there was more blood than she realized, and it just didn't hurt much because of the situation. Mayhap she was dying as she stood there.

The thought was an alarming one. Evina didn't want to die. Especially not now. Not when things were just starting to get good. She was about to marry Conran, a man she was quite sure she probably loved . . . maybe. Coward, she thought, and then admitted that aye, she did love the man.

And was not that just her luck? Evina thought. To find a man she liked, respected and loved, and then die before she could enjoy it and have a life and children with him?

Well, she'd enjoyed it a bit, Evina supposed. Certainly, she'd at least experienced the pleasure he gave her with his mouth and hands, and yes, even his cock. While that first time in the clearing she had definitely not been a fan of what his manhood could do, she had since learned it was really quite wonderful. It was also apparently quite sizable, she'd learned while talking with the other women at the table this afternoon before Conran had returned. And had that not been an amusing discussion?

Aye, she definitely must be dying, Evina decided. There was no other explanation for why she was standing there rhapsodizing over Conran's cock when she had a murderous villain at her back, and a knife to her throat.

"Do ye want something fer it?" Gavin asked suddenly, rushing the words out and moving another step closer. She suspected by his anxious expression that it was an effort to get his father to stop sawing through her neck.

"Nay, o' course no'. 'Tis all fer you," the MacLeod said at once, but then added in a wheedling tone, "O' course, with ye having two fine keeps, surely ye can find a little room in one of them fer me, eh? A room o' me own to live out me dying days in warmth and comfort, with whiskey to warm me belly and a young maid in me bed. That'd be grand after so many years sleeping in the cold and going without. And it seems a fair enough payment fer giving ye so much."

Evina had been watching Gavin as the man spoke, and twice he'd glanced slowly down to her side and back. The third time he did it was as the MacLeod fell silent and awaited his response. That was when she finally realized he was trying to send her a message. She couldn't see what her cousin was looking at, but her hands were free. Reaching cautiously down with her left hand, she moved it around and then blinked in surprise when her fingers brushed up against cold metal. The MacLeod had stepped back and to the side each time Gavin had moved forward, and he'd dragged her with him. It seemed they were now standing right next to the fireplace, because Evina was quite sure what her hand had encountered was the poker that hung from a hook to the side of the fireplace.

Moving cautiously, she slipped it off the hook and grasped it firmly and then tried to decide the best way to use it. Jab it into his leg? Swing it over her head and hopefully hit his? Bend her arm, and jam it back into his stomach? She really wasn't quite sure which was least likely to get her throat slit. All of them seemed rather risky. On the other hand, not doing anything would definitely see her throat slit. There was no way Gavin could prevent it, and sooner or later the MacLeod was just going to do it.

"Well?" the MacLeod snapped impatiently, and took the knife away from her throat to point it at Gavin angrily. "Ye're a damned fool if ye do no' listen to me. Now answer me, dammit!" he barked, and started to bring the knife back, only to howl in pain when Evina quickly shifted her hold on the poker, bent her arm and jammed the pointed tip back into his stomach.

The MacLeod released her at once to grab his stomach, and Evina leapt away toward her cousin, who promptly pulled her behind him and faced his father. Hurrying to her chest, Evina grabbed her sword and then whirled to rush back to Gavin, noting that there was blood slipping from between the MacLeod's fingers. She'd used more force than she'd realized, and actually done some damage with the poker, it seemed. Good.

"Nay." That word from Gavin made both of them glance toward him with surprise as he continued. "I'll give ye nothing. Ye killed me mother. I'll no' let ye kill me uncle, and the woman who was both mother and sister to me all me days. And I'll be damned if I ever let ye live in the same castle as me. Unless ye're in the dungeon."

The MacLeod's mouth dropped open briefly at the words, and then snapped shut and he straightened grimly and raised his sword. "Why ye ungrateful, sniveling little bastard. After all the trouble I've gone to, ye think to treat me like this? I'll teach ye to mind yer betters, ye—" His words died abruptly when Conran slid from the dark passage behind him and pressed his sword into his back.

"Ye'll be teaching him naught," Conran said coldly as Aulay slipped out of the passage behind him. "Evina's already taught Gavin all he needs to ken."

"Aye, she has," Gavin said with a smile, his stance relaxing.

Conran smiled at him, and then raised his eyebrows and asked, "What do ye want to do with him?"

"Do?" Gavin asked, looking suddenly uncertain.

"Well, we have to lock him in the dungeon for now so we can hold the wedding," Conran pointed out. "But what we do with him after the ceremony is up to you. We can deliver him to the king to have him strung up for murder, or just keep him locked up in the dungeon for the rest o' his days."

"Neither," Garrick said at once. "Let me go, son. I'm yer father. And ye need me to get MacLeod back, I can tell everyone that Tearlach forced me to sign the will."

"Or we could ride to MacLeod, ask to see the will and point out that the name on it is Gavin MacLeod, no' Garrick as Tearlach claimed it to be," Conran pointed out as Aulay moved around the two men and walked to the door to open it and let Geordie and Alick in. "'Twould either be deemed a fake, or a will ye had drafted and signed for Gavin as a boy. Either way, Gavin would get MacLeod back without needing to suffer yer presence further."

"Aye," Gavin breathed, and glanced to Evina to grin. "Ye'll help me settle in at MacLeod will ye no'?"

"O' course," she agreed with a smile, squeezing his arm.

"Well?" Conran asked gently, and then grimaced and added, "The priest is waiting on us, Gavin."

"Oh, aye, sorry," he muttered, and then frowned at the MacLeod and shook his head. "I ken I said that about the dungeon, but I don't really want him here. The truth is, I don't even want to think on him again. I suppose we should let the king deal with him."

"Good enough," Conran said as the MacLeod sagged in defeat. "We'll put him in the dungeon for now, and then have Donnan arrange to see he's transported to the king."

"We'll take him down to the dungeon fer ye," Geordie offered, moving from his position by the door to stand next to Conran. "And then join ye at the church."

"Thank ye," Conran murmured, taking the MacLeod's knife and sword and stepping back as Geordie and Alick stepped up. "Make sure ye check to be sure he does no' have other weapons."

As Geordie nodded and started to search the man, Conran moved around them to set the weapons on the table next to Evina and then turned toward her. He was just reaching for her when a grunt made her glance around. She was just in time to see Geordie falling backward, clutching his arm, and then the MacLeod was rushing toward her.

Before either Evina or Conran could move, Gavin had stepped in front of them, his broadsword pointed at a spot between his father's throat and chest. He didn't raise and bring it down. There wasn't time. Gavin merely lowered the tip slightly and lunged forward, stabbing him through the heart.

The MacLeod looked surprised, and then the light went out of his eyes. Gavin stepped back, withdrawing his sword, and they all watched his father drop to the ground.

Evina let her breath out slowly, and started to move toward Gavin, but paused and glanced down with surprise when she couldn't. She stared at the arms around her with surprise then. She hadn't even realized Conran had grabbed her. Even as she looked down, he released her though, and moved to his brother's side.

"Are ye all right, Geordie?" he asked with concern, helping him up.

"Aye. He caught me by surprise, but 'tis just a scratch, I think," Geordie muttered as he stood up. He lifted the hand covering his arm, revealing a slice across the forearm.

It was bleeding freely, but would heal quickly with a couple of stitches, Evina was sure as she watched Alick and Aulay usher the injured man out. She glanced around with a start though when Conran clasped her chin and lifted it.

"Ye took a couple o' nasty cuts too," he said with concern as he examined her throat.

"I'm fine, 'tis fine," Evina murmured, trying to tug her chin free. But he was having none of that and urged her to the pitcher and ewer on the table by the window. Grabbing the clean linen Tildy had set there, he dampened it in the water in the pitcher, and gently ran it over her neck.

"'Tis still bleeding," he said with a frown. "Ye may need stitches."

"I do no' need stitches," she said at once, and took the cloth from him to press firmly against the injured area. "'Twill stop. 'Tis fine," she assured him, and then turned to peer at her cousin. He hadn't moved, and was still staring at his father's corpse. Frowning, Evina handed Conran the bloody cloth and moved to her cousin's side. When he didn't seem to notice her presence, she clasped his arm gently, drawing his fixed gaze away from the MacLeod's body.

"Are ye all right?" she asked, concerned about how he was handling having just killed his own father. It had been in self-defense, and the man had been horrible, but he was still Gavin's father.

"Aye," he muttered, patting her hand and turning his eyes back to the MacLeod. "'Tis fine. I'm fine."

Evina eyed him dubiously. "I do no' think ye are, Gavin. He—"

"I am," he said, finally meeting her gaze. "In truth, I'm glad he made me kill him. He killed me mother, and tried to kill ye. He got what he deserved, and I've avenged both of ye," he said solemnly, and then smiled crookedly. "I really am fine."

Evina relaxed a little, but then gave a sniff and shook her head woefully. "I think ye've spent too much time around Conran. He had blood pouring down his back and still claimed he was fine too."

"Me?" Conran asked with disbelief, crossing the room to join them as Gavin smiled faintly and murmured something about removing the body. "Ye do the same thing. Ye did it just now about yer neck," he pointed out. "And 'tis ye he grew up around and learned it from."

"Oh, aye," Evina murmured the admission, and then smiled and shrugged. "Well, I guess 'tis fine, then."

Conran chuckled at the words and kissed her quickly. He then lifted her chin and peered at her neck again. "The bleeding has stopped."

"I told ye 'twould," Evina responded at once, but was secretly relieved. She hadn't at all been sure it would stop bleeding. She just hated stitches.

"Aye, ye did," Conran agreed, and then raised his eyebrows and asked, "Now, will ye please accompany me to the church so I can marry ye before something else happens to delay it?"

"Aye," she said with a smile. However, she immediately dug in her heels when he tried to usher her away and said, "But . . ."

Pausing, he turned to look at her in question. "But?"

Evina glanced around, and then waited until Gavin had dragged the MacLeod's body out of the room before turning back. Taking his hands then, she glanced down at them solemnly for a moment, before raising her gaze to his face to say, "Do no' laugh, m'lord. But I think I love ye."

Conran blinked at her words. "Ye think . . . ?"

"Aye." She nodded. "'Tis ridiculous I ken after the fuss I made about no' wanting to marry ye, but I was thinking on it while waiting for Da to collect me, and again while waiting for Garrick to kill me, and I decided I must love ye. That or I'm mad, because while I love me father and Gavin, and even Tildy, 'twas ye I fretted most over about leaving. Ye and all the things I would miss."

"What would ye miss?" Conran asked, his voice husky and a soft smile curving his lips.

Evina shrugged helplessly. "The life I could have had with ye. The bairns we would have had. The talking and laughing. Having ye to share me burden with. Yer smile, yer laugh, yer cock, yer—"

"Me cock?" Conran choked out with amazement.

Evina frowned at him for the interruption, but admitted, "Aye. I quite like it."

"Oh—I—That's . . . good?" he finished lamely.

"Aye, well, I realize that may be surprising," she admitted. "I mean, I didn't at first as ye ken." When he nodded weakly, she assured him, "But, as I told Saidh, I've become quite fond of it o' late."

"Ye told Saidh that?" he asked with alarm.

"Well, aye. We were discussing how painful the first time was fer me, and I had to assure her that we had got past that," she explained.

"Ah, I see," he said, and then cleared his throat. "Well, I'm flattered, o' course. But mayhap ye might refrain from mentioning that to any o' the other women."

Evina raised her eyebrows. "So ye don't want me to tell anyone how ye've a big cock and it gives me much pleasure?"

Conran opened his mouth, closed it again briefly to consider and then began to smile and said, "Well . . . I suppose ye can mention it to— Nay," he cut himself off suddenly, shaking his head firmly. "As much as I would enjoy such rumors spreading around about my . . . er . . . virility, ye probably, definitely, shouldn't say it to the other ladies," he decided.

Evina nodded, but said, "Too late."

"What?" he asked, aghast.

Evina scowled at his dismay. "Well, what the devil do ye think we women talk about when ye men aren't around? The weather?"

Horror began to dawn on his face. "Surely, ye don't talk about . . ."

"Aye," she said when he couldn't finish.

"Oh." He stared at her blankly for a minute, and then seeming to realize she was waiting for him to say something, he cleared his throat and got out, "Well . . . I'm quite fond of yer . . . lady parts too."

"Really?" Evina asked dryly. "I can say cock, but ye can't bring yerself to say—"

Conran covered her mouth quickly and glanced around as if expecting someone to appear in the empty room. Reassured that they were alone, he turned back and half whispered, "Wife, I'm a Highlander. And Highlanders don't use that word in front of ladies. Me mother drummed that into me at a young age. We could say any other curse we wished, but no' *that* one."

"A Highlander," Evina murmured with a small smile. "My Highlander." Shaking her head then, she asked, "Is it no' funny?"

"What?" he asked uncertainly.

"If I hadn't kidnapped the wrong Highlander that day, we may ne'er ha'e met," she pointed out.

Conran relaxed, no doubt relieved at the change of subject. But then he asked, "Are ye sorry?"

"That I kidnapped ye and no' Rory?" she asked.

"Aye. But 'twas no' kidnapping," he reminded her. "At least, we'll ne'er admit 'twas to our children."

"Really? We can no' tell them the truth o' how we met?" she asked with surprise.

"Definitely no'. Especially if they are lasses," he added grimly, and then said, "Now tell me. Are ye sorry ye kidnapped me and no' Rory?"

"Nay," she assured him. "I may have kidnapped the wrong Highlander, but ye were the right man fer me."

"Oh, lass," Conran sighed, pulling her into his arms. "I fear I love ye too."

"And why do ye fear that?" she asked uncertainly as he began to press kisses along her throat.

"Because now I want to show ye just how much," he murmured, his hands sliding down to cup her bottom and lift her against him until his hardness pressed between her legs.

"Aye, well, Lord Pleasure-Cock, ye'll have to wait until after the wedding for that," Aulay growled impatiently from the door. "The entire population o' Maclean, plus yer brothers, sister and their mates, as well as the Sinclairs, are all waiting at the damned church fer ye and have been fer quite a while now. Get a move on, ye two."

Sighing, Conran eased her back to the ground. "We'll have to continue this later."

Nodding, Evina let him take her arm and urge her toward the door.

"Did I mention how lovely ye look yet?" Conran asked as they stepped out into the hall.

"Nay," she answered at once.

"Well, ye do. Ye quite take me breath away every time I look at ye, ye're so lovely," he assured her.

"Thank ye," she murmured, and then eyed his face curiously, and asked, "Why are ye smiling so?"

"Aulay called me Lord Pleasure-Cock," he reminded her, his grin widening.

"And?" she asked uncertainly.

"He's ne'er going to let me live that down," he explained.

"Ye do no' seem upset," she pointed out.

"Hell, no," he said on a laugh. "They are all calling Greer Fretting Fiona since hearing Saidh say that about him. But I get Lord Pleasure-Cock. As brotherly torments go, 'tis a damned fine one. Do no' tell him though. He might stop."

"As ye wish," she said with amusement.

"Ah, Evina," he sighed, scooping her up in his arms to carry her down the stairs, "I kenned the minute I saw yer sword hilt swinging toward me head that ye were the woman fer me."

"No, ye didn't," she protested as they reached the main floor and he headed for the keep doors.

"Aye, I did," he assured her.

Evina chuckled and shook her head "Ye're a strange man, Conran Buchanan."

"Aye, but I'm *yer* strange man, Evina soon-to-be Buchanan," he assured her.

"Aye, ye are," she agreed softly as he carried her out of the keep, heading for the chapel where the priest waited to marry them.

Keep reading for a sneak

peek of Lynsay Sands'

latest paranormal romance

THE TROUBLE
WITH VAMPIRES

Coming May 2019

from Avon Books

"You SHOT ME!"

"Yeahhh," Pet drew out the word on a wince. "Sorry about that, kiddo. It was an accident. I was shooting at the mutants and your big butt got in my way."

"Yeah? Well this is an accident too," Parker snapped, turning his gun on her character.

"Oh, come on!" Pet squawked, quickly moving her character behind the cover of some trees to avoid the rapid-fire spray of bullets. "It was an *accident*," she protested. "Gees. I thought we were on the same side."

"You shot me first," Parker pointed out, making his character rush after hers.

"Friendly fire. You'll never make it out of the next level without me, Parker. Just—" A shriek from downstairs caught her ear, and Pet lowered her game controller and glanced toward the bedroom door.

"Is Oksana watching TV or some—?" she began, but stopped when the shriek ended and the housekeeper began shouting, "Home invasion! Home Invasion!"

"Crap!" Dropping her game controller, Pet jumped up from the floor and rushed to the door. Once there, she hesitated though, and then cracked it open to listen. A frown claimed her lips when she heard the deep rumble of an unfamiliar male voice below and then silence.

Reaching for her cell phone, Pet glanced around for Parker and scowled when she saw that her nephew hadn't moved. The eight-year-old was busily shooting her video game character while she was distracted.

"Parker!" she hissed punching in 911. "Stop that! We have a situation here. Didn't you hear Oksana yelling home invasion?"

"She always yells home invasion," Parker said with a shrug. "Oksana forgets to close the front door after checking the mail, grabbing the newspaper, or sweeping the front porch. Everyone from neighbors to delivery guys have come in afraid something was wrong 'cause the door is open. When they do, she shrieks home invasion every time. She even yelled home invasion when Mr. Purdy's cat came in yesterday. It's her thing."

"Oh," Pet breathed, relaxing a little. She didn't hit the call button on her phone, but she didn't delete the numbers she'd entered on the keypad either. Oksana still hadn't spoken again. Pet was debating whether she should call out and ask if everything was okay, or keep their presence in the house a secret and tiptoe to the end of the hall to get a look at who was in the entry, when she heard a soft whisper and then a deep male voice boomed, "Hello? Neighbor!"

"That's not a neighbor."

Pet jumped a good foot in the air when Parker spoke those solemn words right next to her. Clutching her chest, she briefly closed her eyes before letting out a slow breath and asking, "How do you know?"

"Because no one in the neighborhood has an accent like that. At least I don't think anyone does," he added with a frown.

Pet hadn't noticed an accent. It had only been two words for heaven's sake. How had he picked up an accent in two words? She gave her head a slight shake. The kid was just . . . different. Super smart and different. Letting her hand drop from her chest she said, "Well, could it be a *new* neighbor then?"

"I guess," Parker agreed dubiously.

"But," Pet added, debating the matter aloud, "it's hard to imagine Oksana mistaking a neighbor for someone committing a home invasion."

Parker arched his eyebrows. "You heard the part about Mr. Purdy's cat, right?"

Pet merely scowled and shifted her feet as she listened anxiously for Oksana to say something. When there was nothing but silence, she glanced to her phone and then hesitated. She didn't want to call the police only to find out that it really was a new neighbor just checking on them. Sighing, she asked, "Do you have a phone in here?"

"Yeah. I got a cell phone for Christmas."

"A cell phone?" she squawked. "You're like *eight*. Who the hell buys an eight-year-old a cell phone?"

"Mom and Dad," he said with a grin.

"Right," she said with disgust, and then added, "Fine. Then grab your cell phone and stay here. I'm going to go downstairs and see what's happening. But if I say 'Spidey, come on down,' lock your door, hide, and call 911. Okay?"

"Spidey?" he asked, wincing slightly. "Seriously?"

Pet rolled her eyes at the complaint. "If they know your name is Parker Peters they'll just think it's a nickname. Get it? Parker Peters? Peter Parker? Spiderman?"

"I got it before you explained it," he said with derision. "But it's just so juvenile and lame."

"Are you calling me lame?" she asked with amazement, and then realizing this wasn't the moment for this discussion, muttered, "Whatever. Look, sweetie, this is serious. Just call 911 if I call you Peter then, okay?" She waited for him to nod, and then turned and eased the door open, pausing only to hiss "stay here" before sliding out of the room.

The hallway was surprisingly dim for seven o'clock in early June when the sun stayed up until nine or so, but it was light enough to see still. Pet had crept about halfway to the stairs at the opposite end of the hall when a voice called out, "Hello?"

The voice this time was female . . . but not Oksana's. Pet paused to snatch up a crystal vase from a side table, hid it behind her back and moved to the railing that overlooked the front door entry.

Her eyes widened slightly when she saw the group of people crowding the large entry. Four men and a woman surrounded Oksana, and every one of them was dwarfing the housekeeper, who was a few inches taller than Pet's own five foot two. They were also all staring up at her, she noted and then her gaze settled on the couple next to Oksana.

Pet felt her shoulders relax as she recognized the pair; Marguerite and Julius Notte. They'd been on the front porch talking to her sister, Quinn, when she'd arrived that afternoon, and had stuck around long enough for introductions before heading back to the Caprellis where they were staying for a couple of weeks. They were house-sitting while the older couple visited their daughter in Texas.

Her gaze slid to the other three men now, and her eyebrows rose slightly. All of them were big, but while two were just tall and muscular, the third was a complete behemoth, taking up twice as much space as anyone else in the entry. He was the biggest man Pet had ever seen, and that was saying something. She dealt with a lot of jocks in her work, but not one of them could have measured up to this guy. The shoulders on him! Good Lord! She'd heard black was supposed to be slimming, but the black T-shirt he wore just seemed to emphasize the width and muscle it was stretching to cover. His black jeans, on the other hand, were making his hips look tiny, or maybe they just *were* tiny in comparison to his shoulders. She followed the line of the jeans down to the black Doc Martens he wore and then slid her gaze back up again, taking in his shaved head and the fact that he wore rings on every one of his fingers. They could have been mistaken for brass knuckles except that they were silver. All told, the guy definitely didn't look too safe to be around.

"Hello, Petronella. How nice to see you again."

Pet forced her gaze back to Marguerite and almost sighed aloud with depression. Honestly, the woman was everything she wasn't but had always longed to be—tall, curvaceous and beautiful with long, wavy auburn hair, and perfect pale skin. Marguerite was wearing a pretty summer dress and sandals that just emphasized her femininity and made Pet feel like a slob in her T-shirt and shorts.

Realizing they were all waiting for her response, Pet forced a smile and murmured, "Hello, again."

"We just came by to introduce you to our nephews and their friend. The boys stopped by on their way back from the east coast and have decided to stay awhile. We didn't want you to be concerned if you saw them coming and going," she explained and then smiled wryly and added, "But we got here to find the front door wide open. When we didn't see anyone around, we thought we'd better make sure everything was all right. I fear we startled your sister's poor housekeeper."

"Oh," Pet breathed, her gaze sliding back to Oksana. A frown curved her lips downward when she noted that the woman was just standing there, staring straight ahead at nothing. Although, she could be watching out the side window for her husband, Pet supposed. Oksana's husband was supposed to pick her up at seven. Pet shifted her attention back to Marguerite, stilling slightly as she noted her eyes. Marguerite and Julius had both been wearing sunglasses when she'd met them that afternoon. They weren't wearing them now, though, and she could see that Marguerite's eyes were blue while Julius's were black, but both had silver flecks in them. It was as if someone had blown glowing silver glitter into—

"You know these people?"

Pet turned in surprise to see Parker at her side. The boy was frowning down at the people in the entry with Oksana. Taking her nephew by the arm, she gave him a push, trying to send him back the way he'd come. "You were supposed to wait in your room."

Ignoring her urging, Parker held his ground and said, "They don't live on this street."

"Your mother introduced me to them when I got here. They're house-sitting for the Cabellies," she explained, still trying to urge him back toward his room.

"Caprellis," he corrected even as Marguerite did.

"Jinx," the woman said lightly, her smile widening. "It's a pleasure to meet you, Parker. Your mother and aunt were bragging about you this afternoon. Were your ears ringing?"

Parker shook his head, and then asked, "Who are you?"

"Marguerite Argeneau Notte," she introduced herself solemnly, and then began introducing the others. "And this is my nephew Zanipolo Notte," she gestured to the man on her right who was tall, and slender with lean muscle and long black hair pulled back into a ponytail. Gesturing to the man just past Zanipolo, she continued, "And a family friend, Justin Bricker."

Pet noted his short dark brown hair, handsome face, and laughing green eyes . . . again with silver flecks.

"Our nephew Santo Notte," Marguerite added, gesturing to the bald behemoth.

Pet slid her gaze over the taller man's eyes. They were as black as Julius Notte's, but there was much more silver in his eyes, and the lighter color seemed to be growing, she noted grimly.

"And, of course, my husband, Julius." She turned and placed a hand on the arm of the man on her left. He was the only man here not wearing black. The other three men were decked out in black jeans, black T-shirts, and black Doc Martens. It was almost as if it were some sort of uniform. Julius, however, wore the same blue jeans and white T-shirt he'd had on when she'd met him earlier.

Every one of the men were over six feet tall, but Justin Bricker and Zanipolo were closer to six feet, while Santo and Julius were at least six-foot-six or better. The two shorter men were also lacking a lot of the muscle Santo had. They were still muscular, but with a leanness to them rather than the solid bulk he had. Julius was somewhere in the middle.

"Where are the Caprellis?" Parker asked suddenly, sounding suspicious.

"Texas." The answer was a rumble of sound from the behemoth Marguerite had introduced as Santo. Pet had always gravitated toward deeper voices, and his seemed to vibrate right through her.

"They wished to visit their daughter," Marguerite added now, drawing Pet's reluctant gaze away from the big man. "I gather she moved there last year and they've been missing her and their grandbabies, so they put their house up on the House Swap exchange. We saw it and applied for a trade."

Parker immediately relaxed and began to grin. "I signed them up on the House Swap site," he announced gleefully, and was suddenly racing eagerly down the stairs.

Cursing under her breath, Pet immediately gave chase. She caught up with Parker as he reached the group in the entry, and started to reach for him, only to realize she still held the vase. Flushing guiltily, she set it quickly on the hall table and then caught Parker by the shoulders and dragged him back until his back bumped against her front.

Hardly seeming to notice the protective maneuver, her nephew exclaimed, "I didn't think it would work this quick, though. So you guys are from Texas?"

"Italy," Santo said, and Pet couldn't keep from looking at him again. He really was beautiful, with high, carved cheekbones, and full sensual lips. She avoided looking at his eyes and glanced down at her nephew as he asked, "Italy?"

She noted the suspicion returning to his face, and unconsciously tightened her hands on his shoulders, drawing him more firmly back against her.

"There was a couple in Texas who wanted to see Italy," Marguerite explained with a shrug. "And we wanted to come to New York, so we did a three-way swap. The Caprellis went to Texas, the couple from Texas went to our home in Italy, and we came here."

"Oh," Parker breathed, his eyes wide. "I didn't know you could do three-way swaps, but that's cool."

"Yes," she agreed. "But I understand and appreciate your concern for the Caprellis. They were waiting to give us the house keys when we arrived, and they seem like a very nice couple."

"Yeah, they are," he agreed.

"Are all your neighbors as nice?" Marguerite asked.

Parker nodded. "Yeah. But the Caprellis and Mr. Purdy are the best."

"Mr. Purdy?" Marguerite queried with interest. "Where does he live?"

"He's our neighbor on the other side," Parker explained, but his voice was quiet now, almost fretful, Pet noted with concern. She peered at him for a moment, and then glanced to Marguerite, whose expression was oddly concentrated as she looked at Parker. So were the men's, Pet realized, and had to fight a sudden urge to drag her nephew upstairs and away from these people.

"Ach," Oksana said suddenly. "There is husband. Time to go."

Pet blinked at that announcement from the housekeeper and turned to see her gathering her purse from the hall table.

"We should probably go too now that we've introduced the boys," Marguerite announced as Santo opened the door for the housekeeper to leave. "As I said, we just wanted you to know who the boys were if you saw them coming and going."

Pet shifted her gaze from the old Ford truck that had pulled into the driveway, and to the others as they now followed Oksana out of the house.

"Make sure you lock up," Marguerite suggested as she led the men across the porch. "This is a nice neighborhood, but leaving the door wide open is a bit risky."

"Yes. Good night," Pet murmured as she watched them leave, but doubted if they'd even heard her. There hadn't been much power behind the words. She watched Oksana hop up into the truck, and that pull away, and then followed Marguerite and the men with her eyes until they disappeared around the hedges that lined the driveway between her sister's house and the Caprellis'.

"Come on," Parker said, heading back upstairs as she closed and locked the door. "I left the game running and we're both probably dead by now. We'll have to start from the last save."

"Are you sure you want to play with me? I mean, if I'm so lame . . ." Pet drawled dryly, still smarting from the earlier comment.

"Well, it's not like there's anyone else here to play with," he said, pausing on the steps to grin back at her.

"You hugged me when I got here and said I was your favorite aunt," she reminded him with exasperation. "Now I'm lame?"

"You're my *only* aunt," he pointed out, rolling his eyes. "That makes you my favorite, lame or not. Duh."

Pet's gaze narrowed. "When did you become such a little smart asaleck?" she ended, catching herself before she finished the cuss.

But not quick enough. She could tell by Parker's knowing look before he shrugged and said, "I don't know."

Scowling at him, she started up the stairs.

"But Dad blames you for it," he added.

Pet stopped, her head snapping up with shock. "What?"

Parker nodded. "He thinks I spend too much time under your 'undo influence' and it has led to a bad attitude." Shrugging, he added, "His words."

Pet ground her teeth with irritation. Her sister was married to an arrogant asshat. Pet had never liked him and had no idea why Quinn had married the man.

On the other hand, if she hadn't, there would be no Parker, and Pet did love the little smart ass dearly, so . . . Giving him a push to get him moving up the stairs again, she growled, "I'm so gonna shoot you in the butt. On purpose this time."

"You can try," Parker taunted, rushing eagerly up the rest of the stairs.

Pet followed more slowly, her smile fading and gaze sliding back to the front door as her troubled thoughts returned to her sister's temporary new neighbors . . . and their glowing eyes.